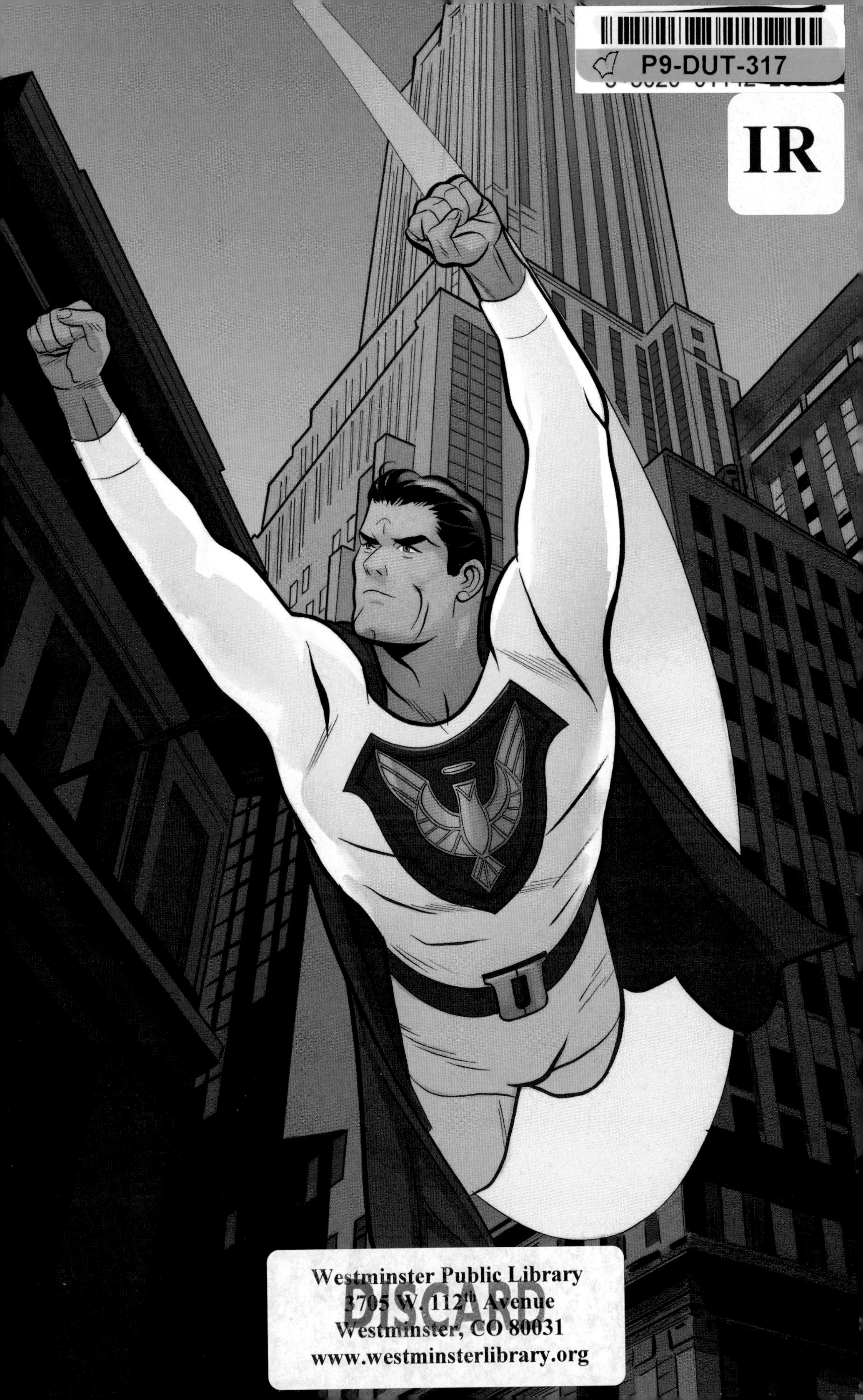

JUPITER'S LEGACY

VOLUME 2

MARK MILLAR
WRITER

WILFREDO TORRES
ARTIST (CHAPTER 1, 2-PAGES 10, 12-14, 18-23, 6)

CHRIS SPROUSE
Pencils (CHAPTER 3-PAGES 1-5)
Breakdowns (CHAPTER 3- PAGES 6-20,
4, 5-PAGES 1-15)

WALDEN WONG
Finishes (CHAPTER 3-PAGES 6-20,
4, 5-PAGES 1-15)

DAVIDE GIANFELICE
Artist (CHAPTER 2-PAGES 1-4, 15-17)

RICK BURCHETT
Artist (CHAPTER 2-PAGES 5-9, 11)

KARL STORY
Inks (CHAPTER 3-PAGES 1-5)

TY TEMPLETON
Artist (CHAPTER 5-PAGES 16-24)

IVE SVORCINA
Colors

MIROSLAV MRVA
Colors (CHAPTER 6-PAGES 1-13)

PETER DOHERTY
Letters and Design

FRANK QUITELY
Cover Illustration

BILL SIENKIEWICZ
Chapter Illustrations

NICOLE BOOSE
Editor

RACHAEL FULTON
Associate Editor

PETER DOHERTY & DREW GILL
Production

MELINA MIKULIC
2020 Collection Cover Design

LUCY MILLAR
CEO

IMAGE COMICS, INC. · Robert Kirkman: Chief Operating Officer · Erik Larsen: Chief Financial Officer · Todd McFarlane: President · Marc Silvestri: Chief Executive Officer · Jim Valentino: Vice President · Eric Stephenson: Publisher / Chief Creative Officer · Jeff Boison: Director of Sales & Publishing Planning · Jeff Stang: Director of Direct Market Sales · Kat Salazar: Director of PR & Marketing · Drew Gill: Cover Editor · Heather Doornink: Production Director · Nicole Lapalme: Controller · IMAGECOMICS.COM

JUPITER'S LEGACY, VOL. 2 TP (NETFLIX EDITION). First printing. October 2020. Published by Image Comics. Inc. Office of publication: 2701 NW Vaughn St., Ste. 780, Portland, OR 97210. Copyright © 2020 Netflix Entertainment, LLC. All rights reserved. Originally published in single-magazine form as JUPITER'S CIRCLE 2 #1-6. "Jupiter's Legacy" the Jupiter's Legacy logo, and all characters and institutions herein and the likenesses and/or logos thereof are trademarks of Netflix Entertainment, LLC unless otherwise noted. "Image" and the Image Comics logos are registered trademarks of Image Comics, Inc. No part of this publication may be reproduced or transmitted. in any form or by any means (except for short excerpts for journalistic or review purposes) without the express written permission of Netflix Entertainment, LLC. All names, characters, events, and places in this publication are entirely fictional. Any resemblance to actual persons (living or dead), events, or places, without satiric intent, is coincidental. Printed in the USA. For international rights, contact: lucy@netflixmw.com. ISBN: 978-1-5343-1811-3.

CHAPTER 1

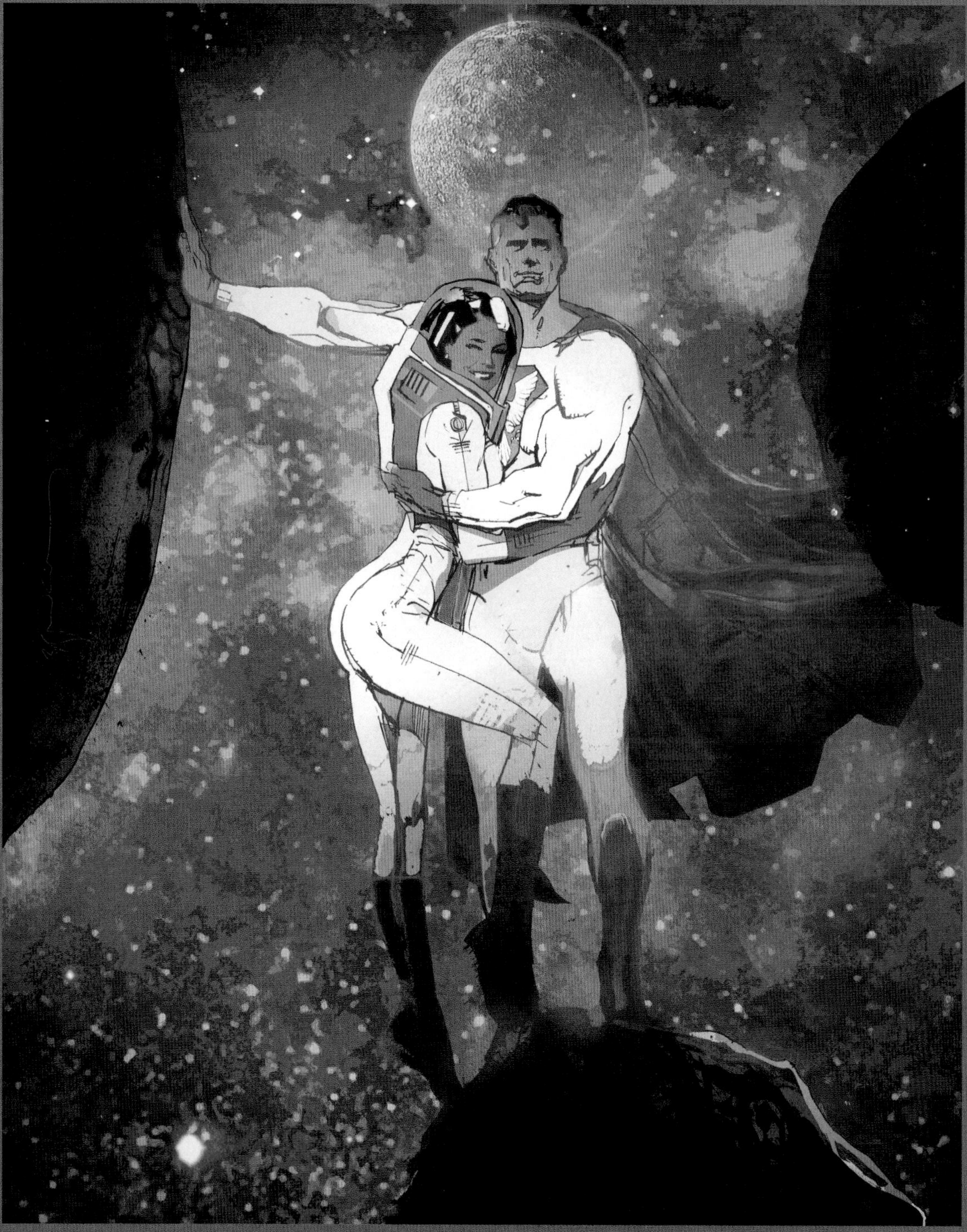

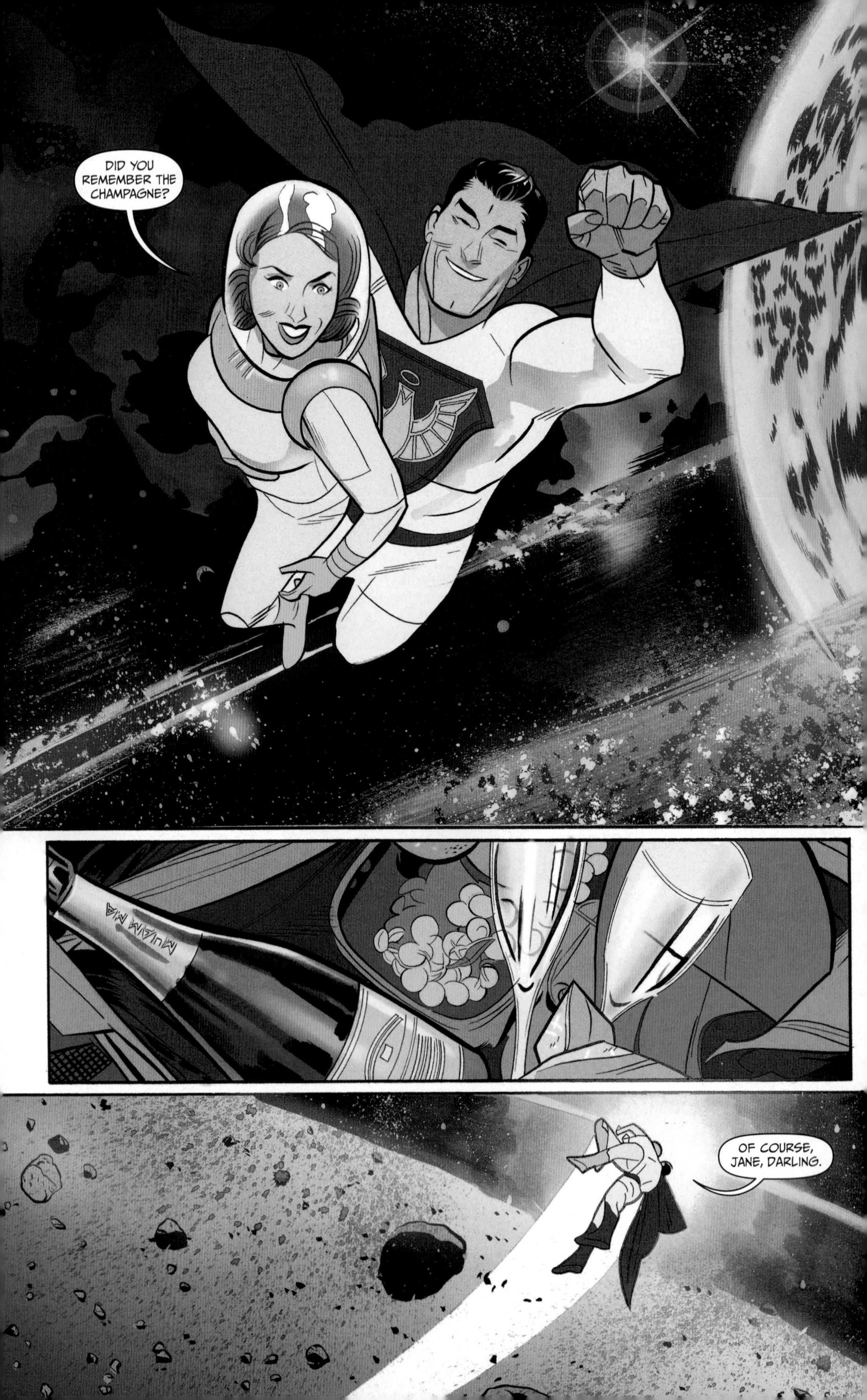
DID YOU REMEMBER THE CHAMPAGNE?
OF COURSE, JANE, DARLING.

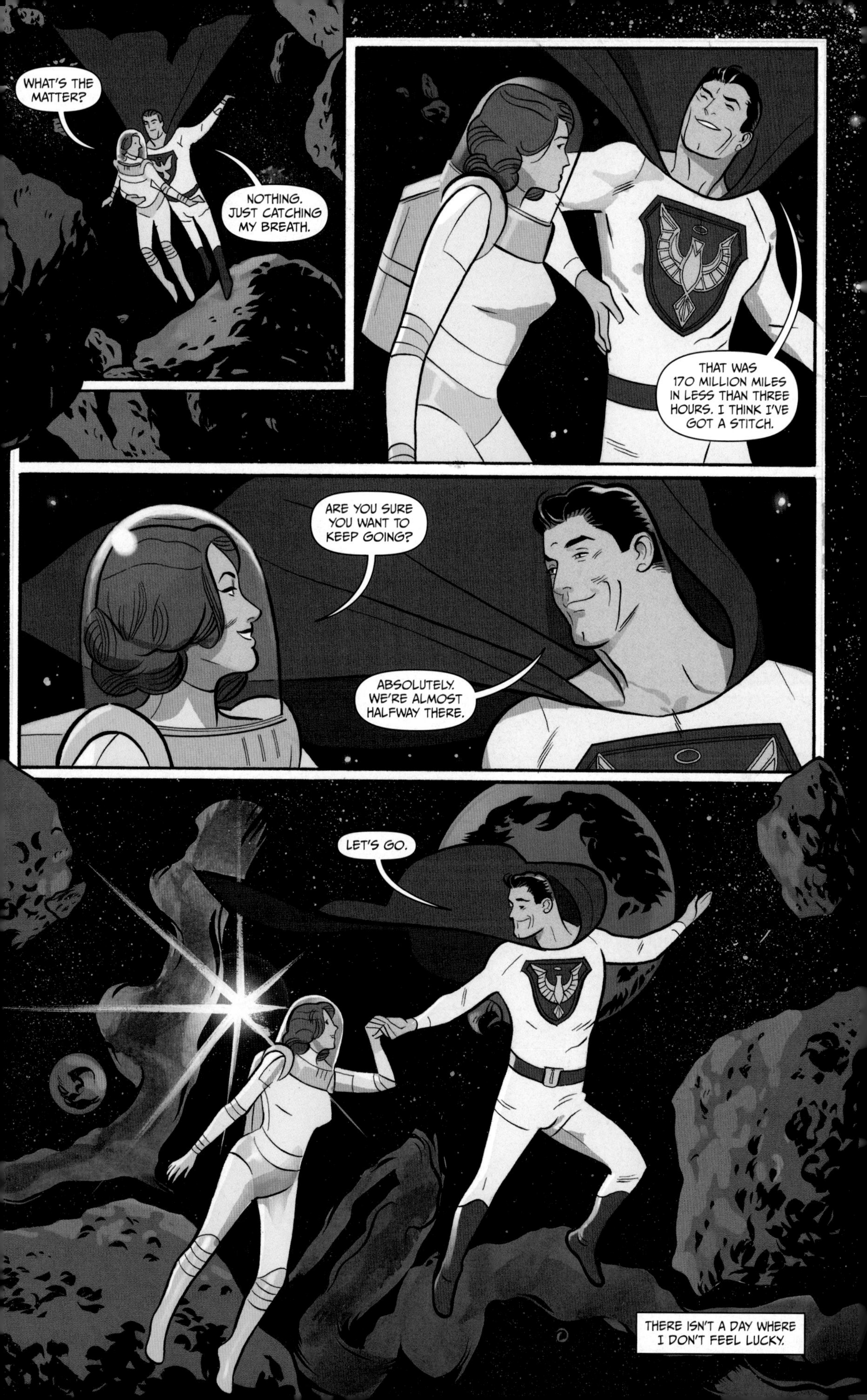
WHAT'S THE MATTER?
NOTHING. JUST CATCHING MY BREATH.
THAT WAS 170 MILLION MILES IN LESS THAN THREE HOURS. I THINK I'VE GOT A STITCH.
ARE YOU SURE YOU WANT TO KEEP GOING?
ABSOLUTELY. WE'RE ALMOST HALFWAY THERE.
LET'S GO.
THERE ISN'T A DAY WHERE I DON'T FEEL LUCKY.

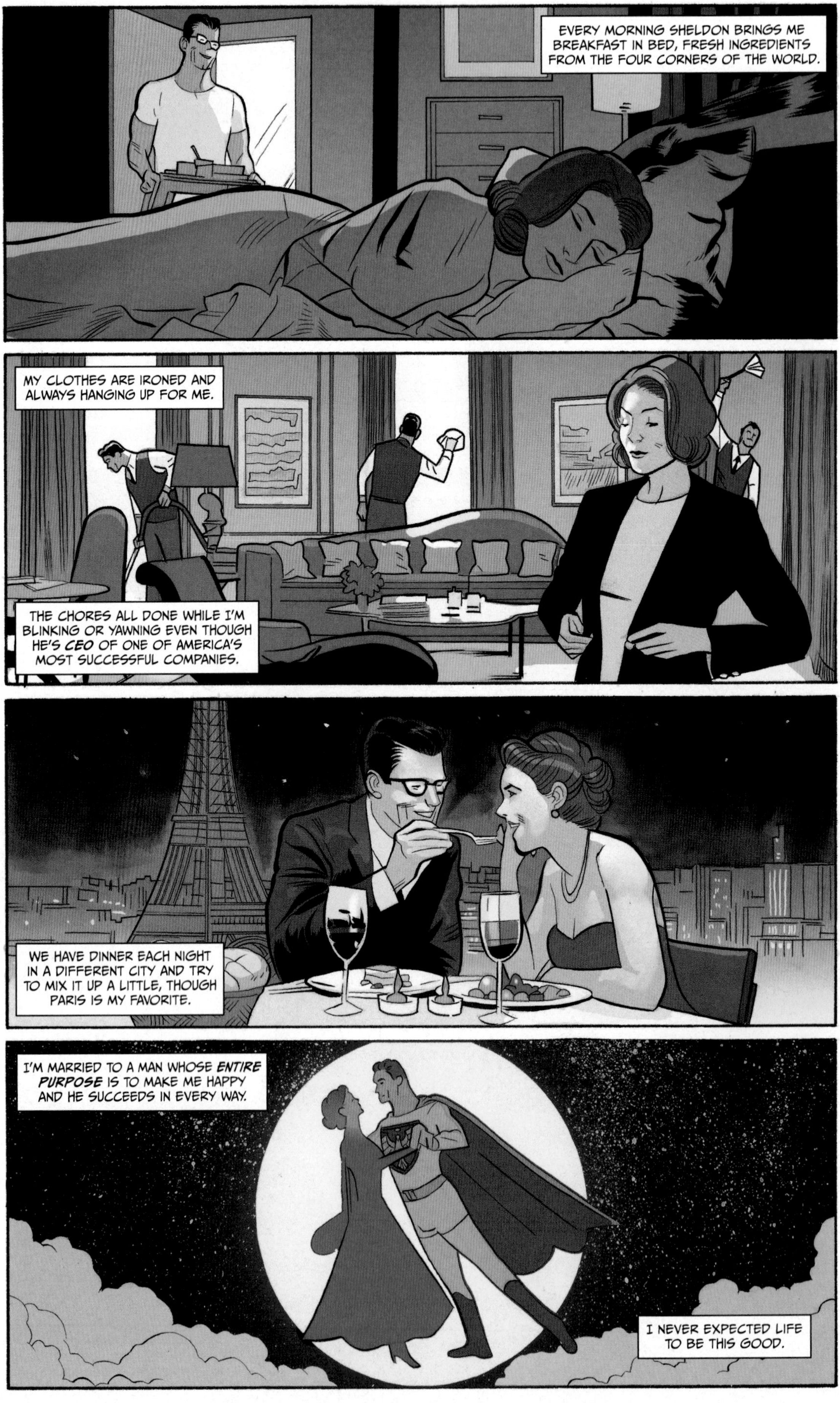
EVERY MORNING SHELDON BRINGS ME BREAKFAST IN BED, FRESH INGREDIENTS FROM THE FOUR CORNERS OF THE WORLD.
MY CLOTHES ARE IRONED AND ALWAYS HANGING UP FOR ME.
THE CHORES ALL DONE WHILE I'M BLINKING OR YAWNING EVEN THOUGH HE'S *CEO* OF ONE OF AMERICA'S MOST SUCCESSFUL COMPANIES.
WE HAVE DINNER EACH NIGHT IN A DIFFERENT CITY AND TRY TO MIX IT UP A LITTLE, THOUGH PARIS IS MY FAVORITE.
I'M MARRIED TO A MAN WHOSE *ENTIRE PURPOSE* IS TO MAKE ME HAPPY AND HE SUCCEEDS IN EVERY WAY.
I NEVER EXPECTED LIFE TO BE THIS GOOD.

To: Herald Tribune Lonely Hearts Page

Attractive, single lawyer would like to meet professional man.

Looks not important.

Seeking someone kind.

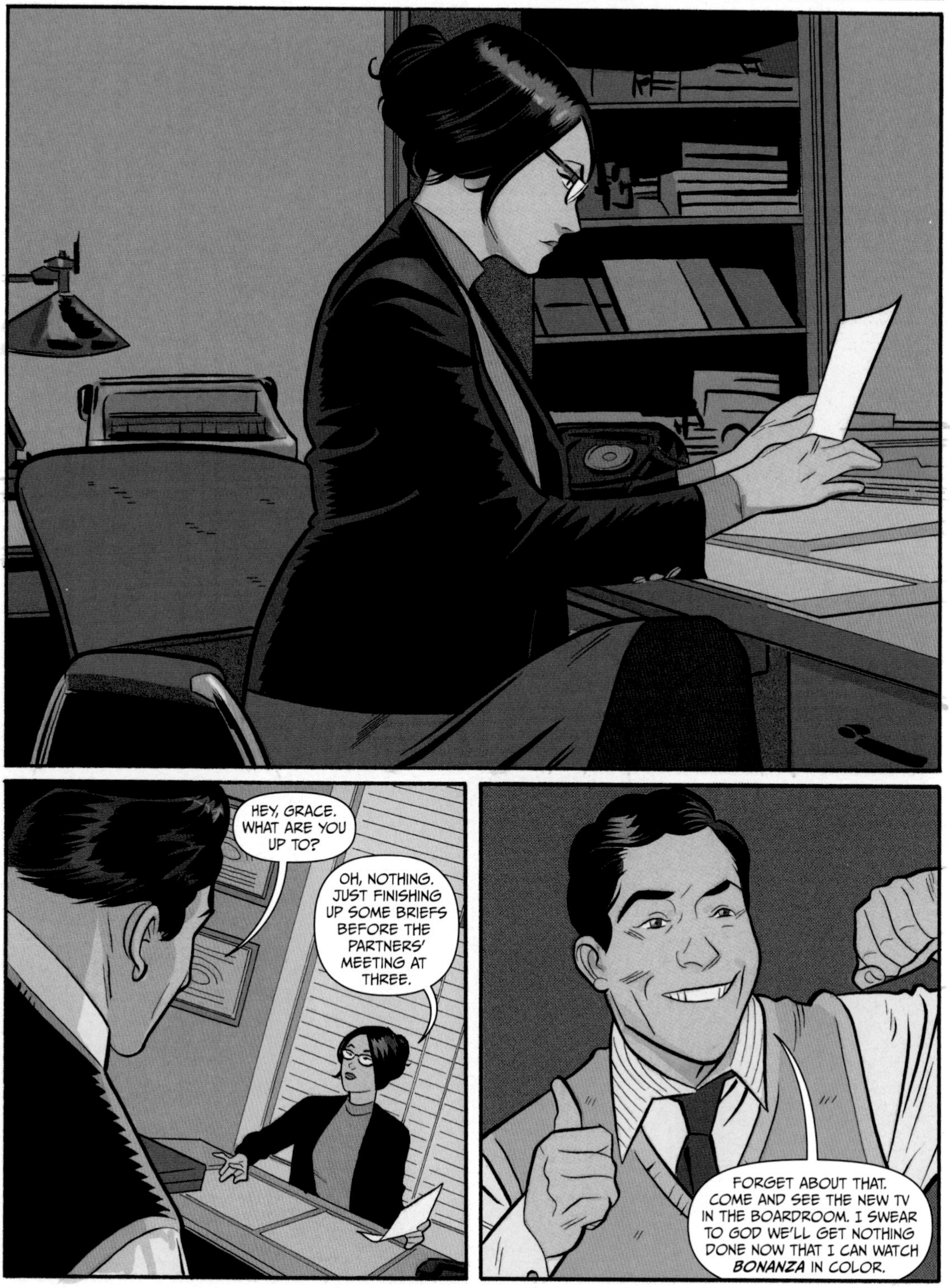
HEY, GRACE. WHAT ARE YOU UP TO?
OH, NOTHING. JUST FINISHING UP SOME BRIEFS BEFORE THE PARTNERS' MEETING AT THREE.
FORGET ABOUT THAT. COME AND SEE THE NEW TV IN THE BOARDROOM. I SWEAR TO GOD WE'LL GET NOTHING DONE NOW THAT I CAN WATCH *BONANZA* IN COLOR.

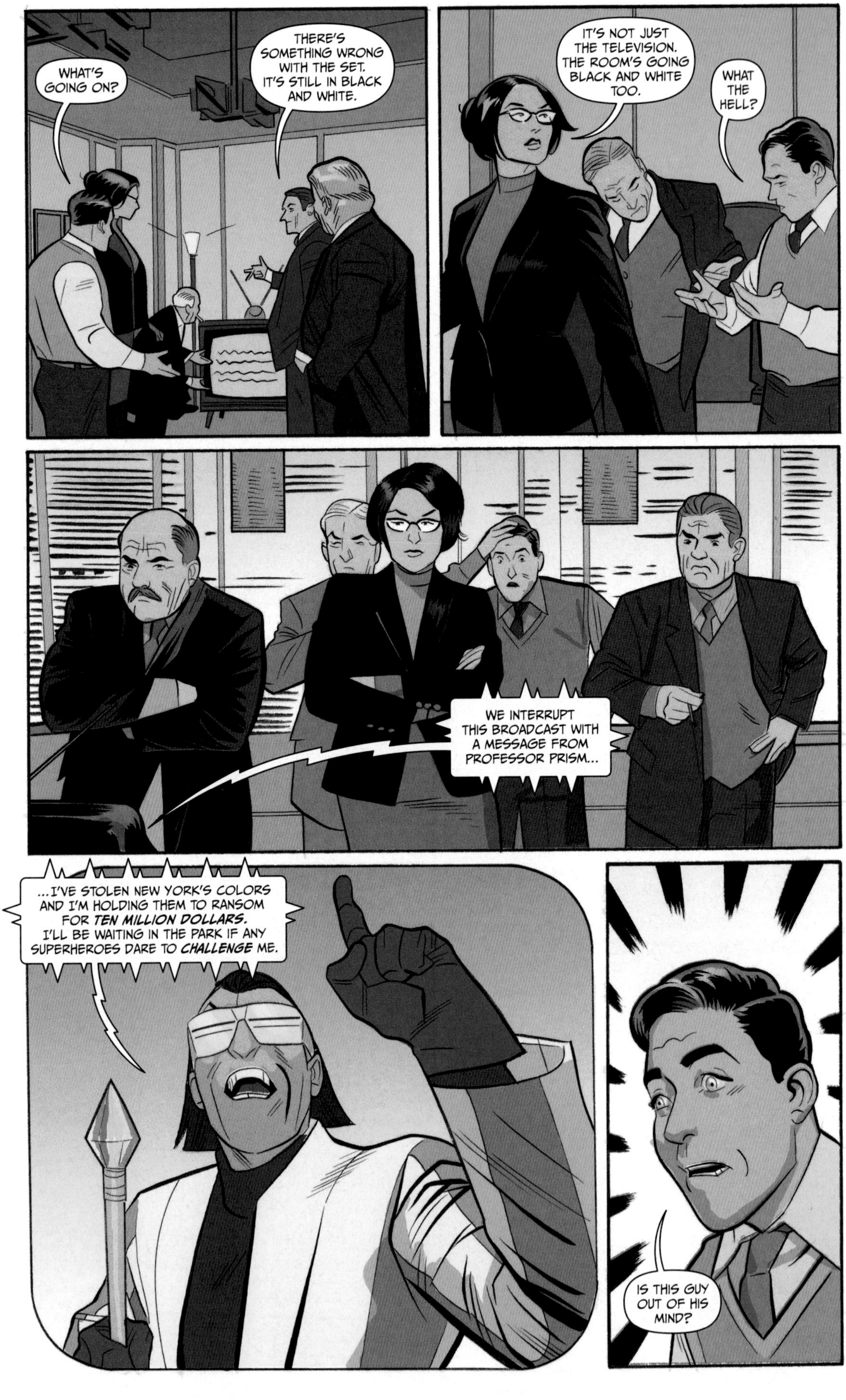
WHAT'S GOING ON?
THERE'S SOMETHING WRONG WITH THE SET. IT'S STILL IN BLACK AND WHITE.
IT'S NOT JUST THE TELEVISION. THE ROOM'S GOING BLACK AND WHITE TOO.
WHAT THE HELL?
WE INTERRUPT THIS BROADCAST WITH A MESSAGE FROM PROFESSOR PRISM...
...I'VE STOLEN NEW YORK'S COLORS AND I'M HOLDING THEM TO RANSOM FOR *TEN MILLION DOLLARS.* I'LL BE WAITING IN THE PARK IF ANY SUPERHEROES DARE TO *CHALLENGE* ME.
IS THIS GUY OUT OF HIS MIND?

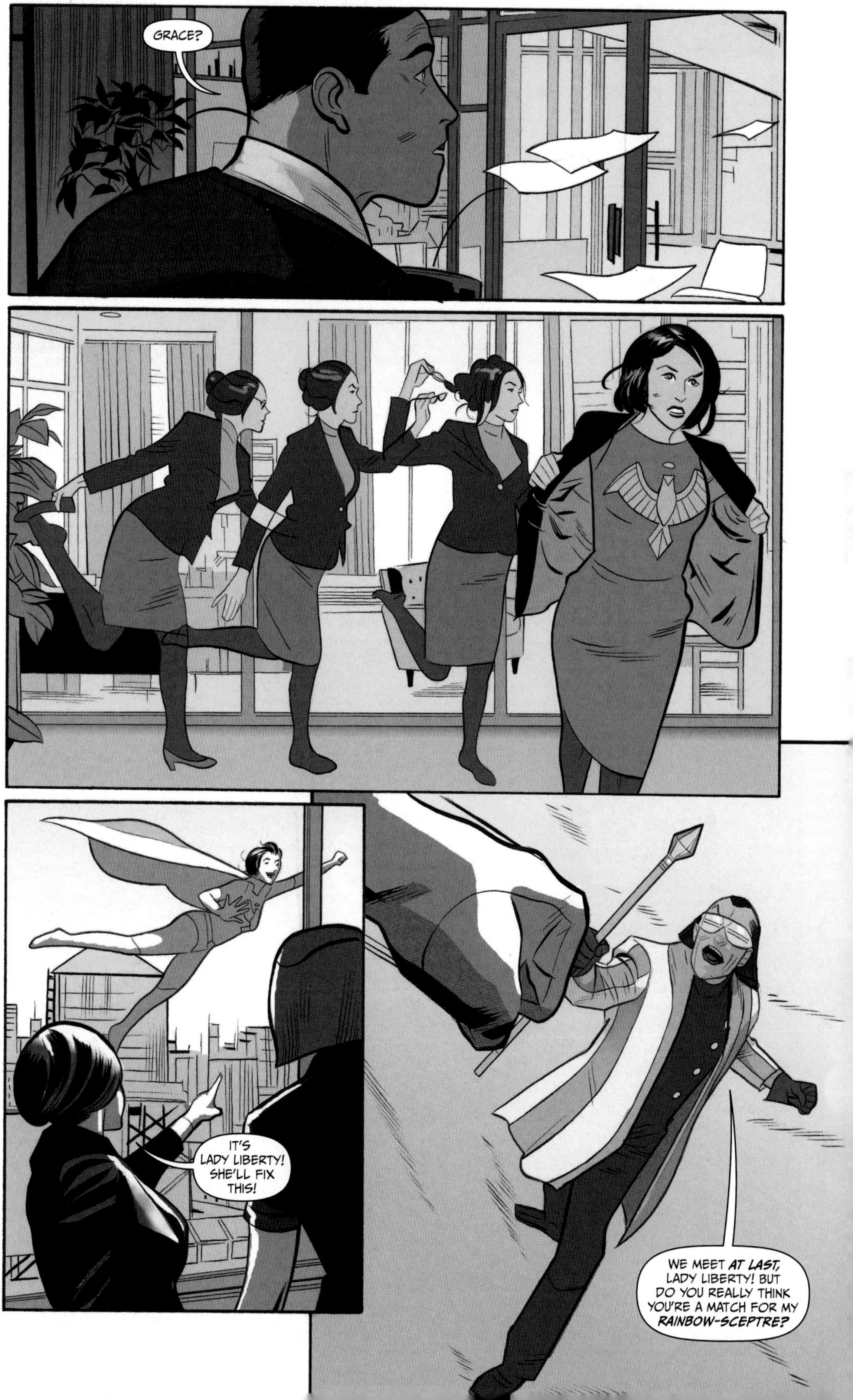
GRACE?
IT'S LADY LIBERTY! SHE'LL FIX THIS!
WE MEET AT LAST, LADY LIBERTY! BUT DO YOU REALLY THINK YOU'RE A MATCH FOR MY RAINBOW-SCEPTRE?

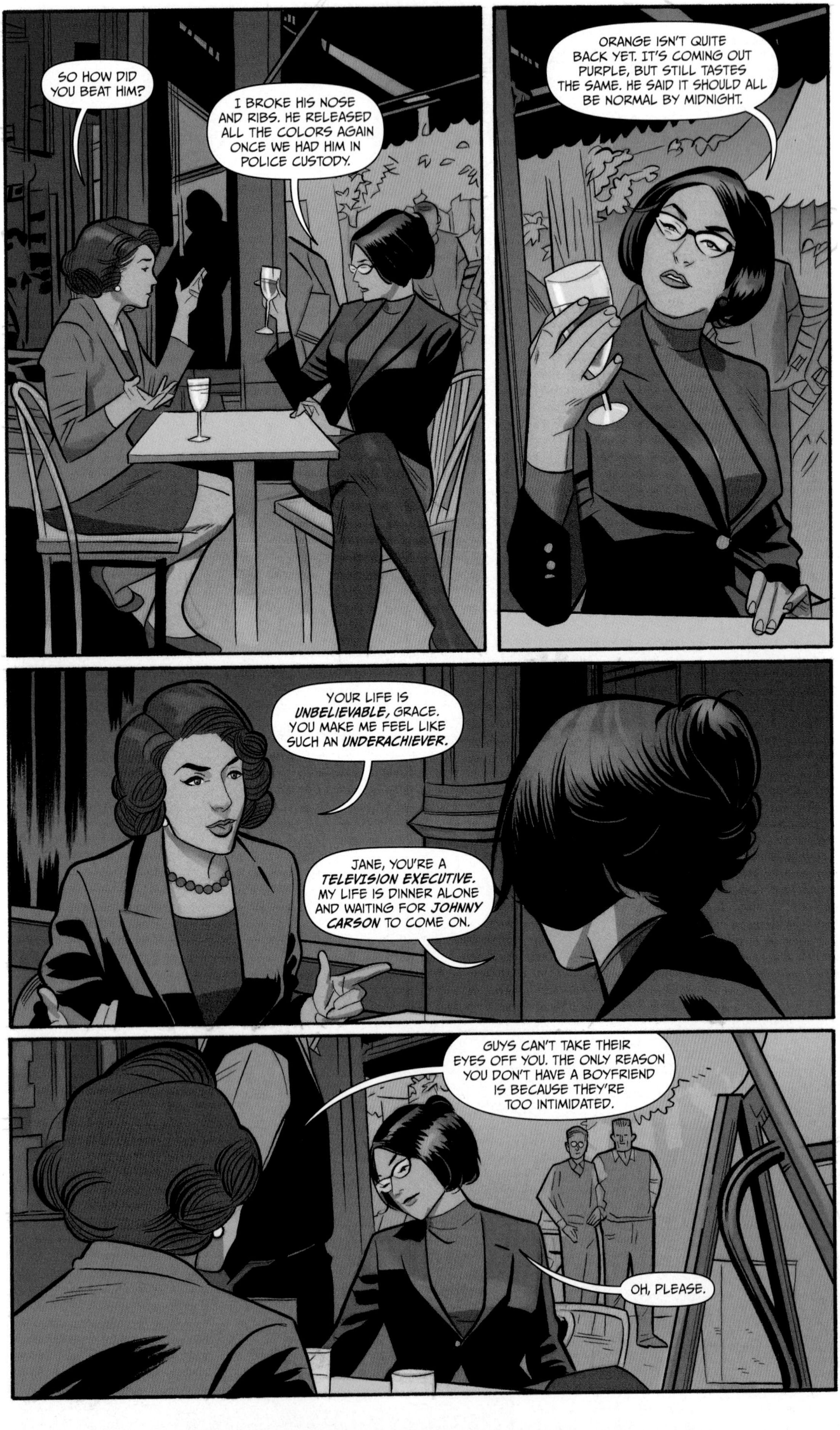
SO HOW DID YOU BEAT HIM?
I BROKE HIS NOSE AND RIBS. HE RELEASED ALL THE COLORS AGAIN ONCE WE HAD HIM IN POLICE CUSTODY.
ORANGE ISN'T QUITE BACK YET. IT'S COMING OUT PURPLE, BUT STILL TASTES THE SAME. HE SAID IT SHOULD ALL BE NORMAL BY MIDNIGHT.
YOUR LIFE IS UNBELIEVABLE, GRACE. YOU MAKE ME FEEL LIKE SUCH AN UNDERACHIEVER.
JANE, YOU'RE A TELEVISION EXECUTIVE. MY LIFE IS DINNER ALONE AND WAITING FOR JOHNNY CARSON TO COME ON.
GUYS CAN'T TAKE THEIR EYES OFF YOU. THE ONLY REASON YOU DON'T HAVE A BOYFRIEND IS BECAUSE THEY'RE TOO INTIMIDATED.
OH, PLEASE.

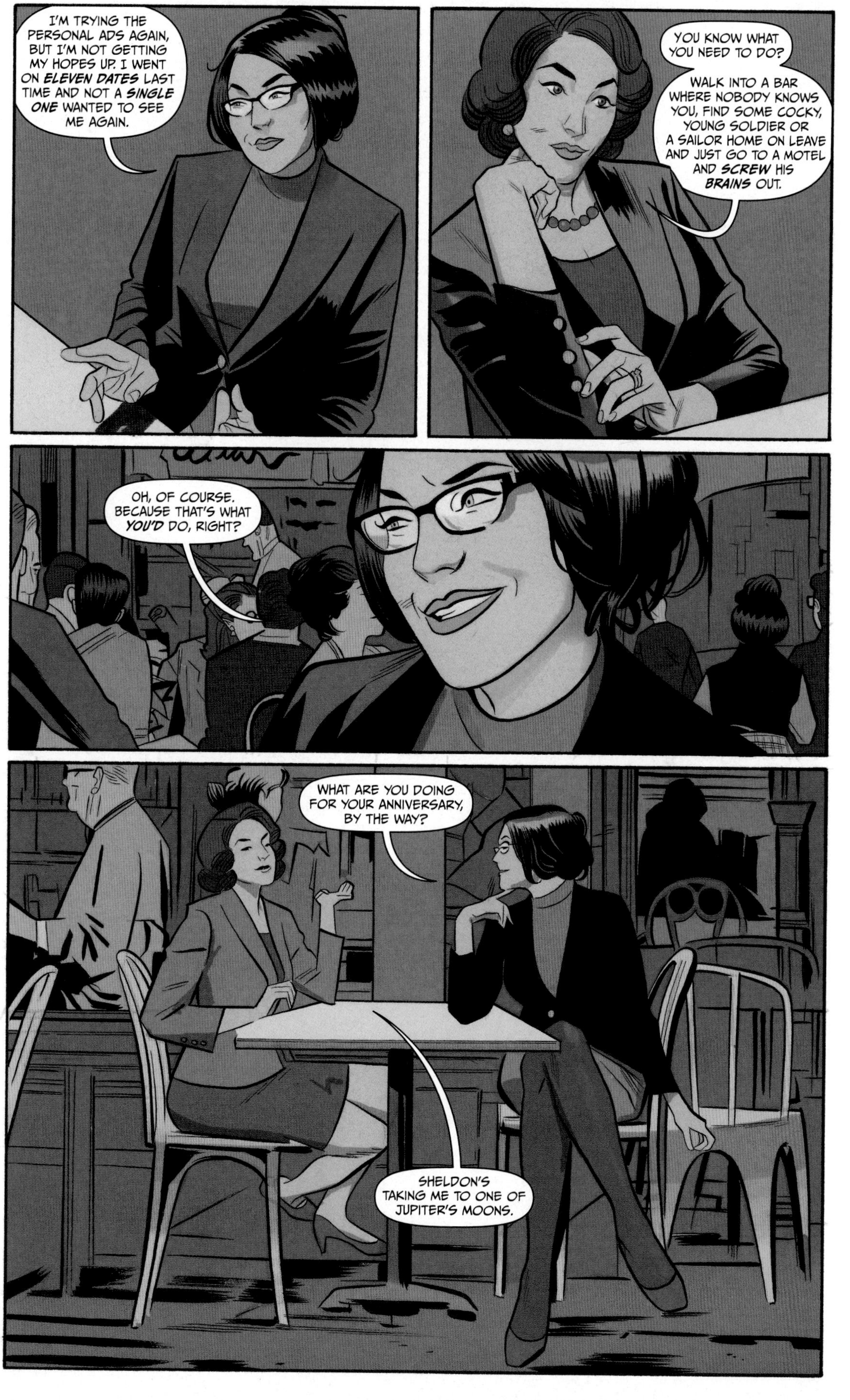
I'M TRYING THE PERSONAL ADS AGAIN, BUT I'M NOT GETTING MY HOPES UP. I WENT ON ELEVEN DATES LAST TIME AND NOT A SINGLE ONE WANTED TO SEE ME AGAIN.
YOU KNOW WHAT YOU NEED TO DO?
WALK INTO A BAR WHERE NOBODY KNOWS YOU, FIND SOME COCKY, YOUNG SOLDIER OR A SAILOR HOME ON LEAVE AND JUST GO TO A MOTEL AND SCREW HIS BRAINS OUT.
OH, OF COURSE. BECAUSE THAT'S WHAT YOU'D DO, RIGHT?
WHAT ARE YOU DOING FOR YOUR ANNIVERSARY, BY THE WAY?
SHELDON'S TAKING ME TO ONE OF JUPITER'S MOONS.

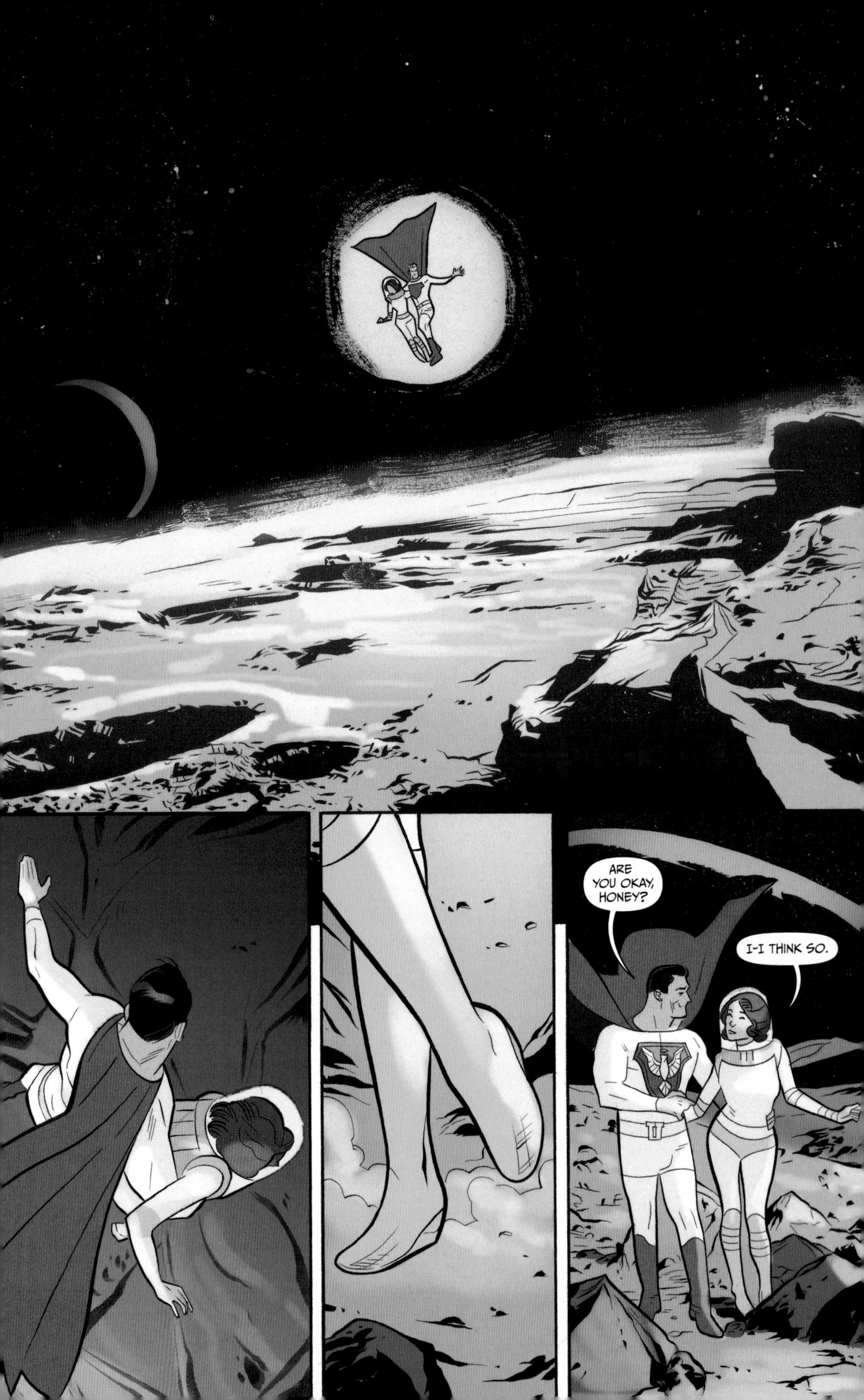
ARE YOU OKAY, HONEY?
I-I THINK SO.

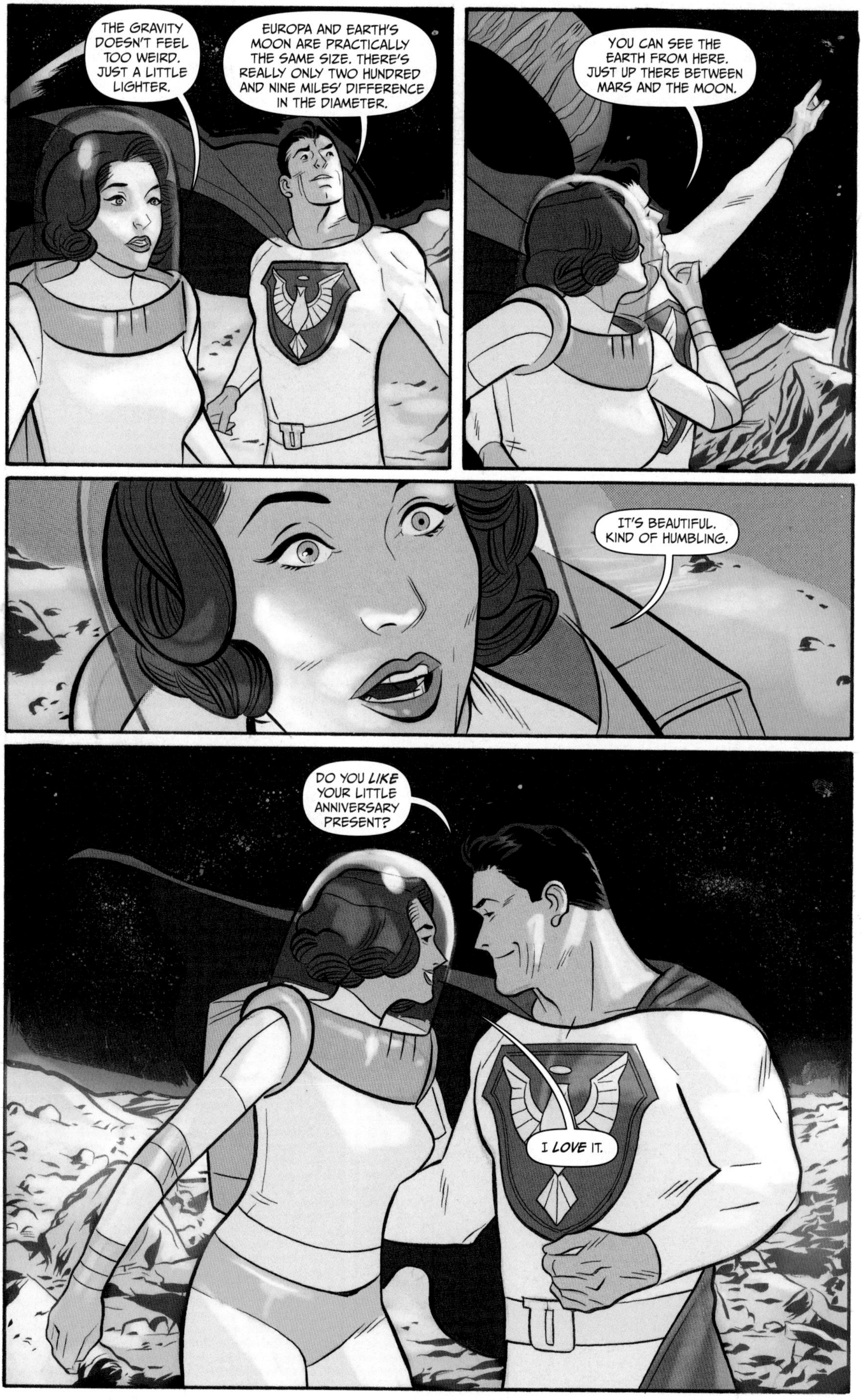
THE GRAVITY DOESN'T FEEL TOO WEIRD. JUST A LITTLE LIGHTER.
EUROPA AND EARTH'S MOON ARE PRACTICALLY THE SAME SIZE. THERE'S REALLY ONLY TWO HUNDRED AND NINE MILES' DIFFERENCE IN THE DIAMETER.
YOU CAN SEE THE EARTH FROM HERE. JUST UP THERE BETWEEN MARS AND THE MOON.
IT'S BEAUTIFUL. KIND OF HUMBLING.
DO YOU *LIKE* YOUR LITTLE ANNIVERSARY PRESENT?
I *LOVE* IT.

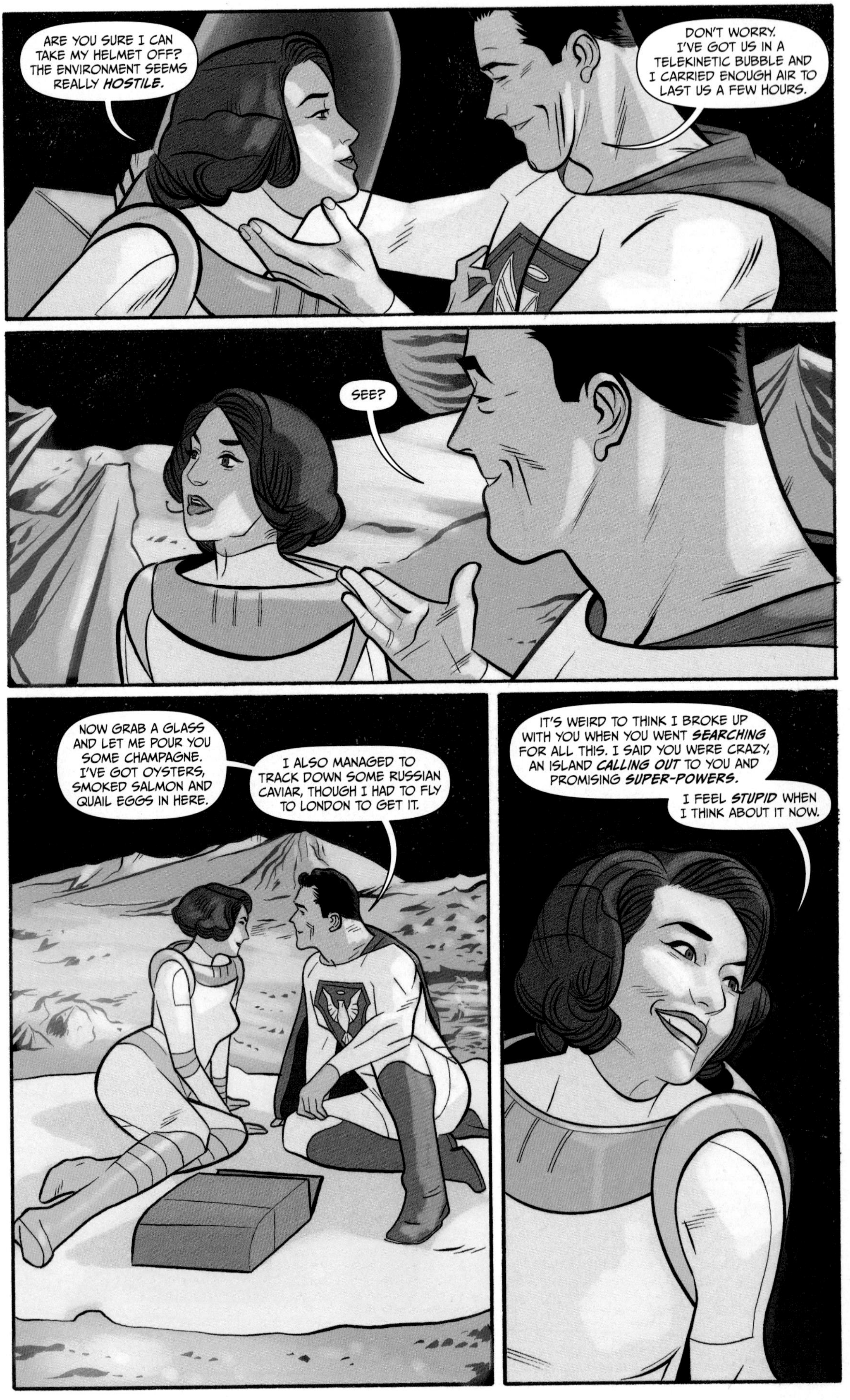
ARE YOU SURE I CAN TAKE MY HELMET OFF? THE ENVIRONMENT SEEMS REALLY *HOSTILE.*
DON'T WORRY. I'VE GOT US IN A TELEKINETIC BUBBLE AND I CARRIED ENOUGH AIR TO LAST US A FEW HOURS.
SEE?
NOW GRAB A GLASS AND LET ME POUR YOU SOME CHAMPAGNE. I'VE GOT OYSTERS, SMOKED SALMON AND QUAIL EGGS IN HERE.
I ALSO MANAGED TO TRACK DOWN SOME RUSSIAN CAVIAR, THOUGH I HAD TO FLY TO LONDON TO GET IT.
IT'S WEIRD TO THINK I BROKE UP WITH YOU WHEN YOU WENT *SEARCHING* FOR ALL THIS. I SAID YOU WERE CRAZY, AN ISLAND *CALLING OUT* TO YOU AND PROMISING *SUPER-POWERS.*
I FEEL *STUPID* WHEN I THINK ABOUT IT NOW.

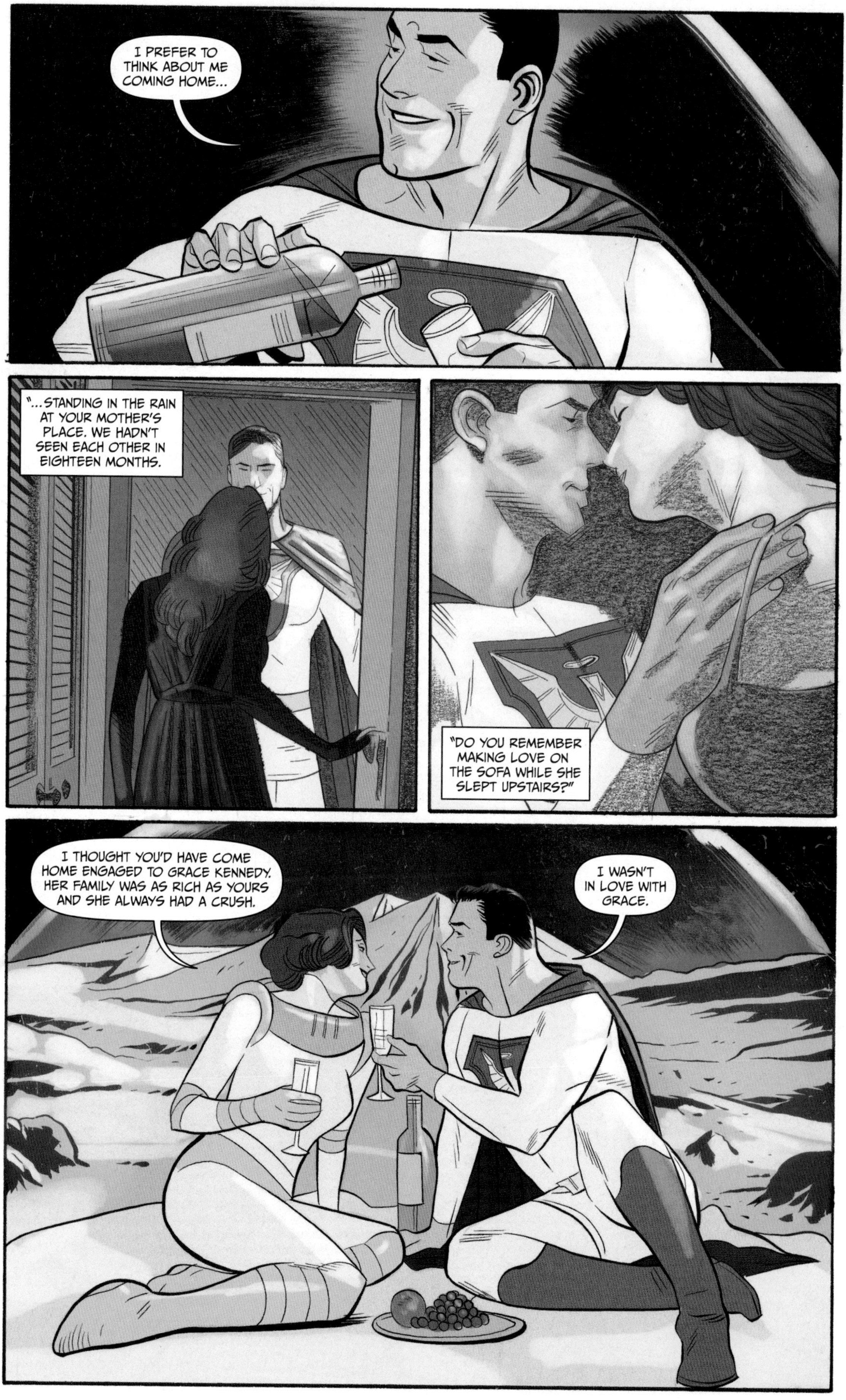
I PREFER TO THINK ABOUT ME COMING HOME...
"...STANDING IN THE RAIN AT YOUR MOTHER'S PLACE. WE HADN'T SEEN EACH OTHER IN EIGHTEEN MONTHS.
"DO YOU REMEMBER MAKING LOVE ON THE SOFA WHILE SHE SLEPT UPSTAIRS?"
I THOUGHT YOU'D HAVE COME HOME ENGAGED TO GRACE KENNEDY. HER FAMILY WAS AS RICH AS YOURS AND SHE ALWAYS HAD A CRUSH.
I WASN'T IN LOVE WITH GRACE.

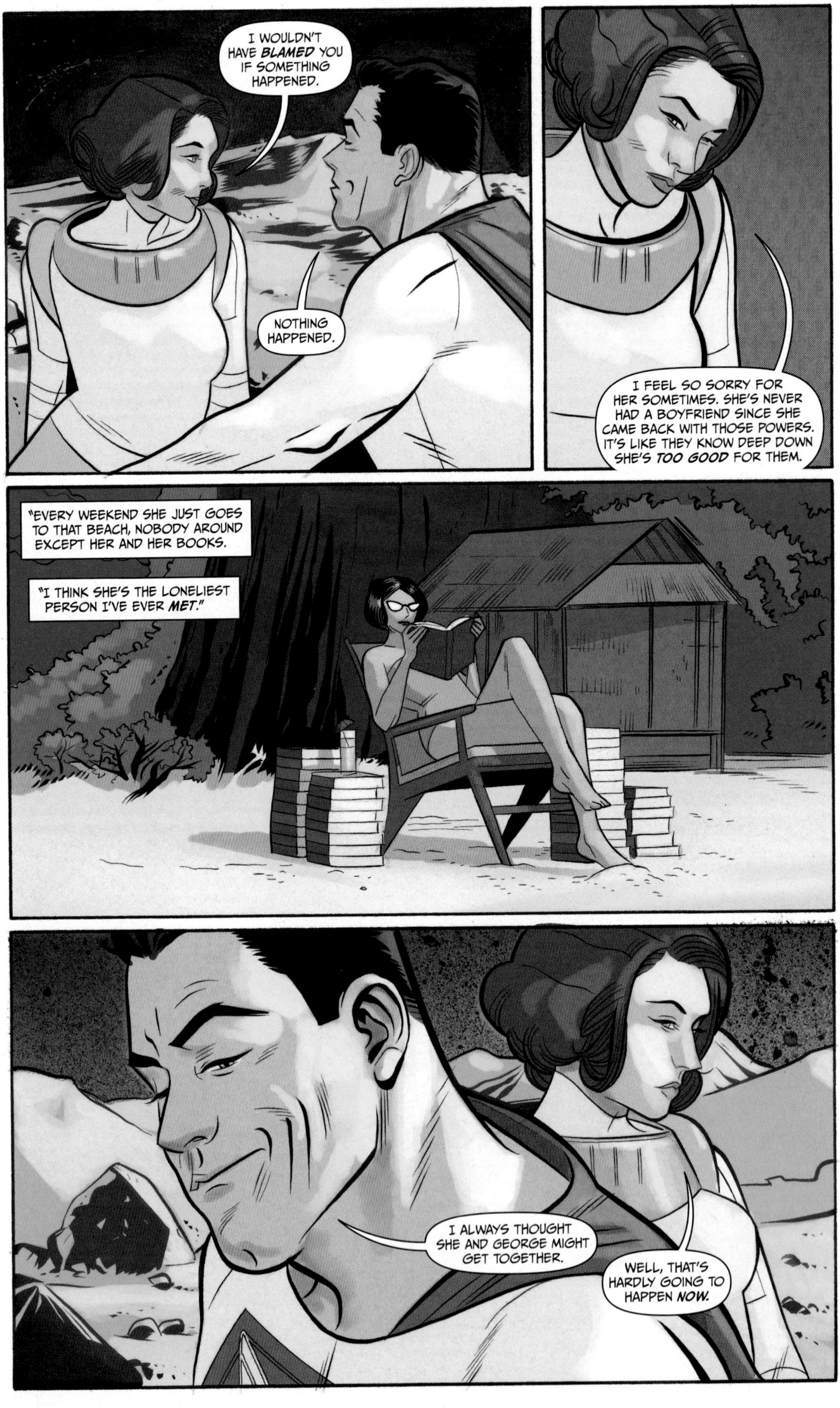

I WOULDN'T HAVE *BLAMED* YOU IF SOMETHING HAPPENED.
NOTHING HAPPENED.
I FEEL SO SORRY FOR HER SOMETIMES. SHE'S NEVER HAD A BOYFRIEND SINCE SHE CAME BACK WITH THOSE POWERS. IT'S LIKE THEY KNOW DEEP DOWN SHE'S *TOO GOOD* FOR THEM.
"EVERY WEEKEND SHE JUST GOES TO THAT BEACH, NOBODY AROUND EXCEPT HER AND HER BOOKS.
"I THINK SHE'S THE LONELIEST PERSON I'VE EVER *MET*."
I ALWAYS THOUGHT SHE AND GEORGE MIGHT GET TOGETHER.
WELL, THAT'S HARDLY GOING TO HAPPEN *NOW*.

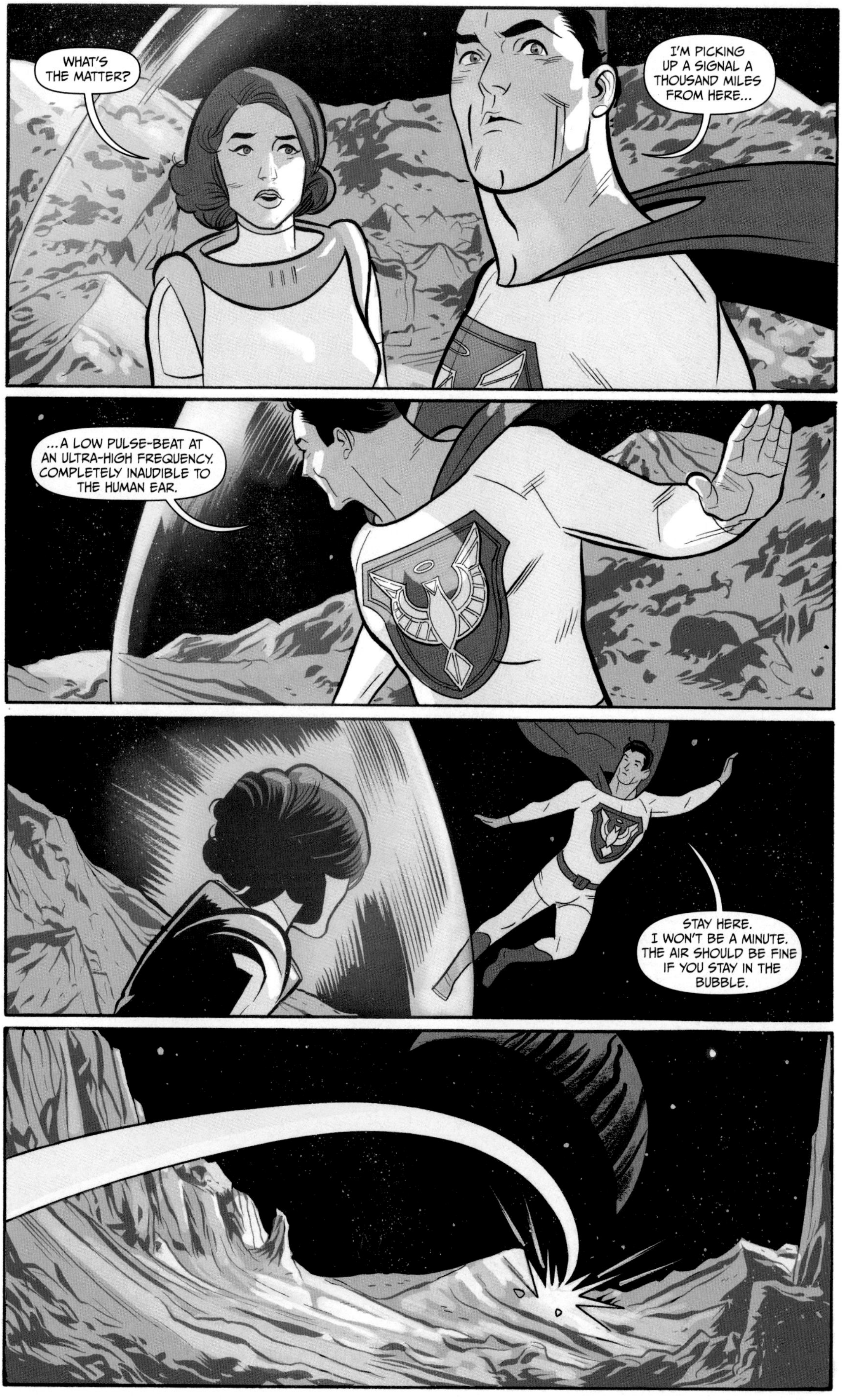
WHAT'S THE MATTER?
I'M PICKING UP A SIGNAL A THOUSAND MILES FROM HERE...
...A LOW PULSE-BEAT AT AN ULTRA-HIGH FREQUENCY. COMPLETELY INAUDIBLE TO THE HUMAN EAR.
STAY HERE. I WON'T BE A MINUTE. THE AIR SHOULD BE FINE IF YOU STAY IN THE BUBBLE.

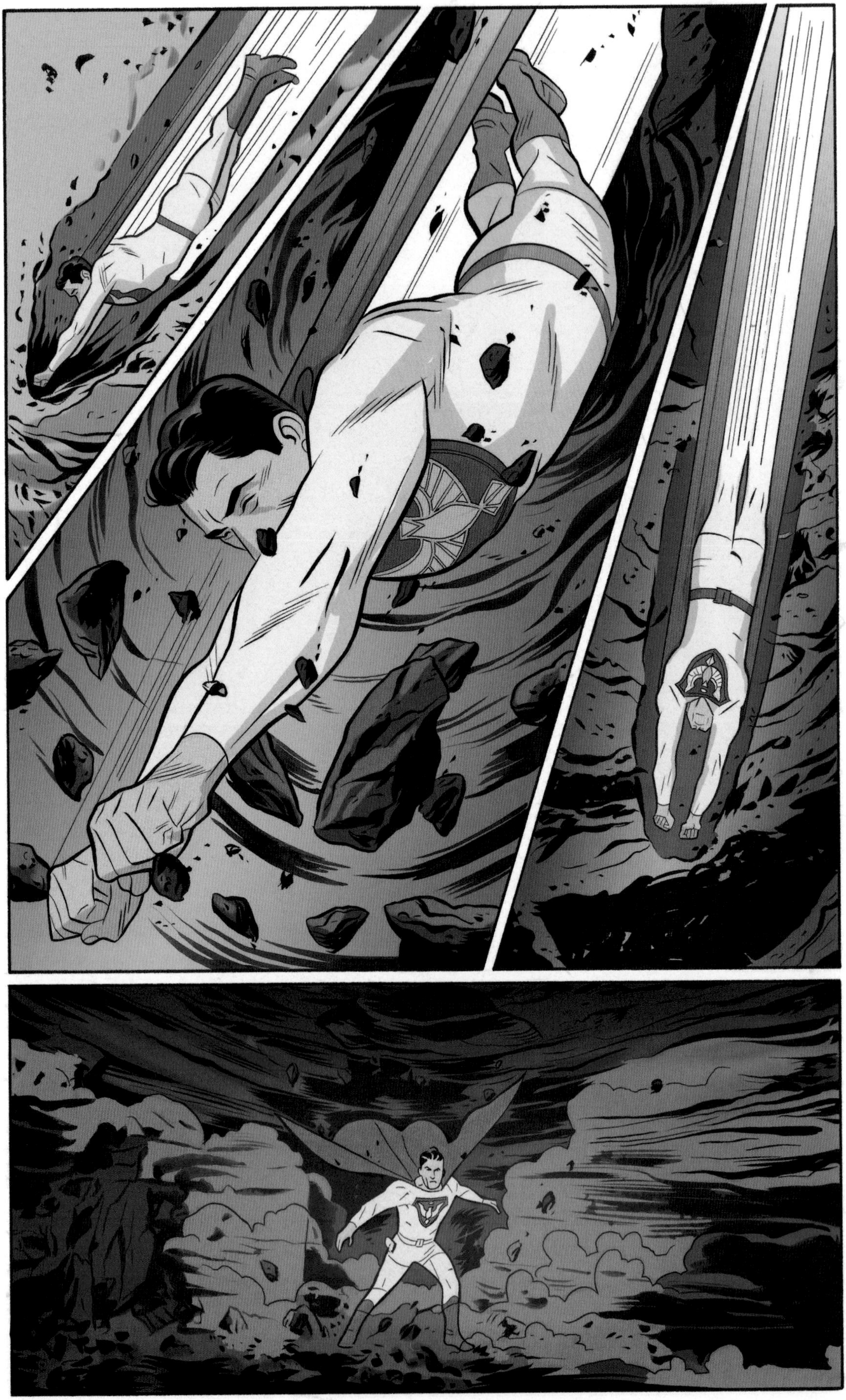

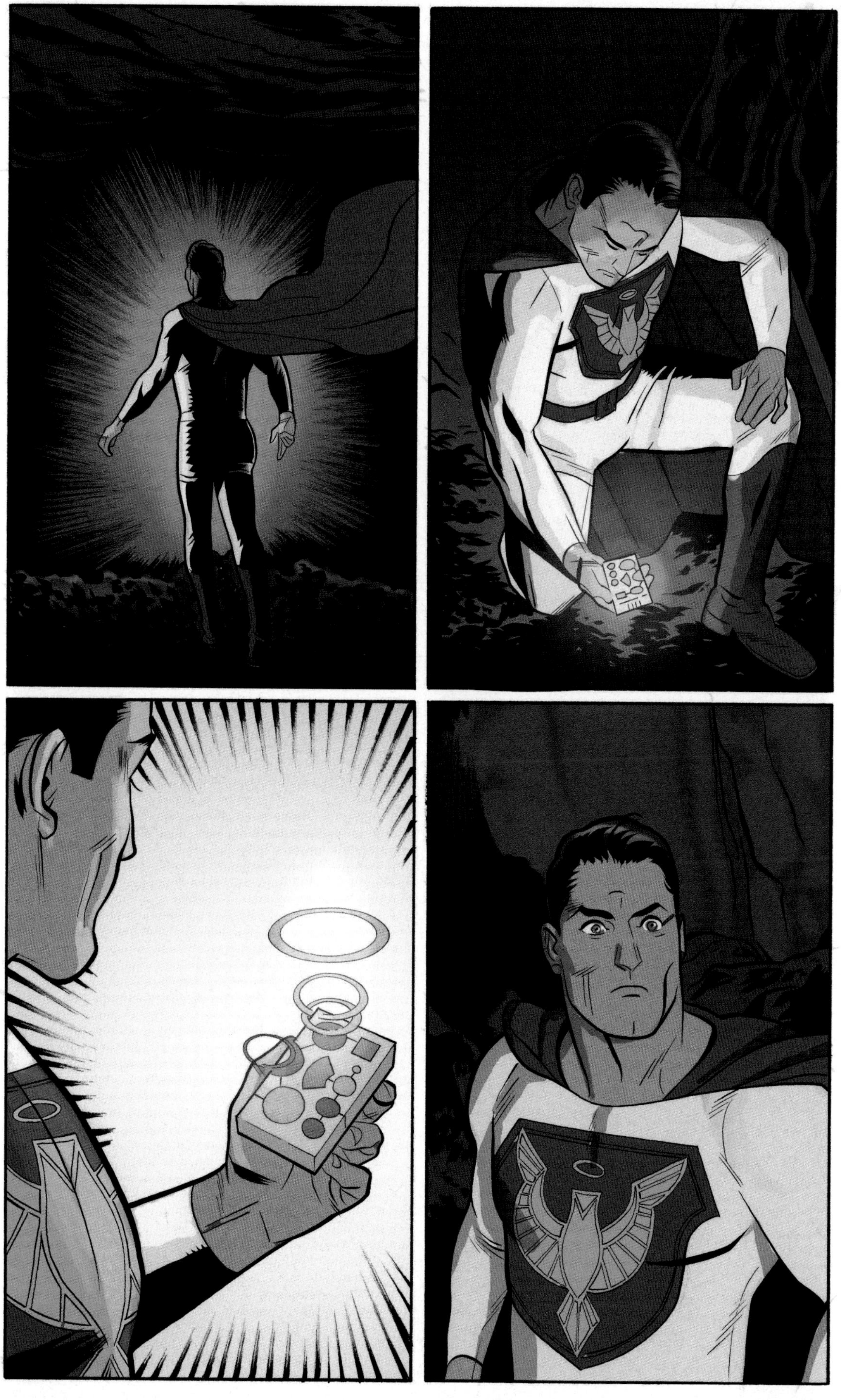

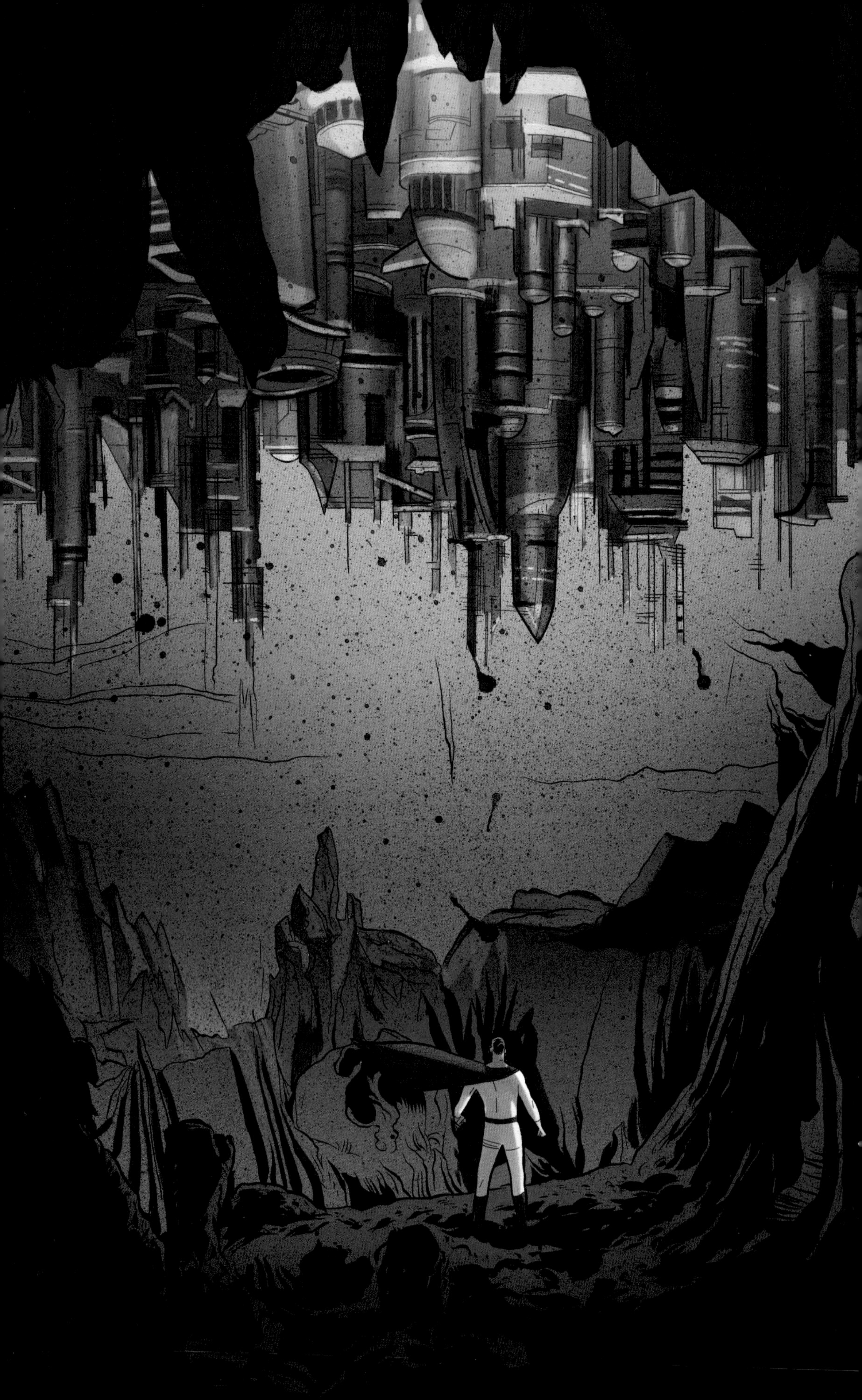

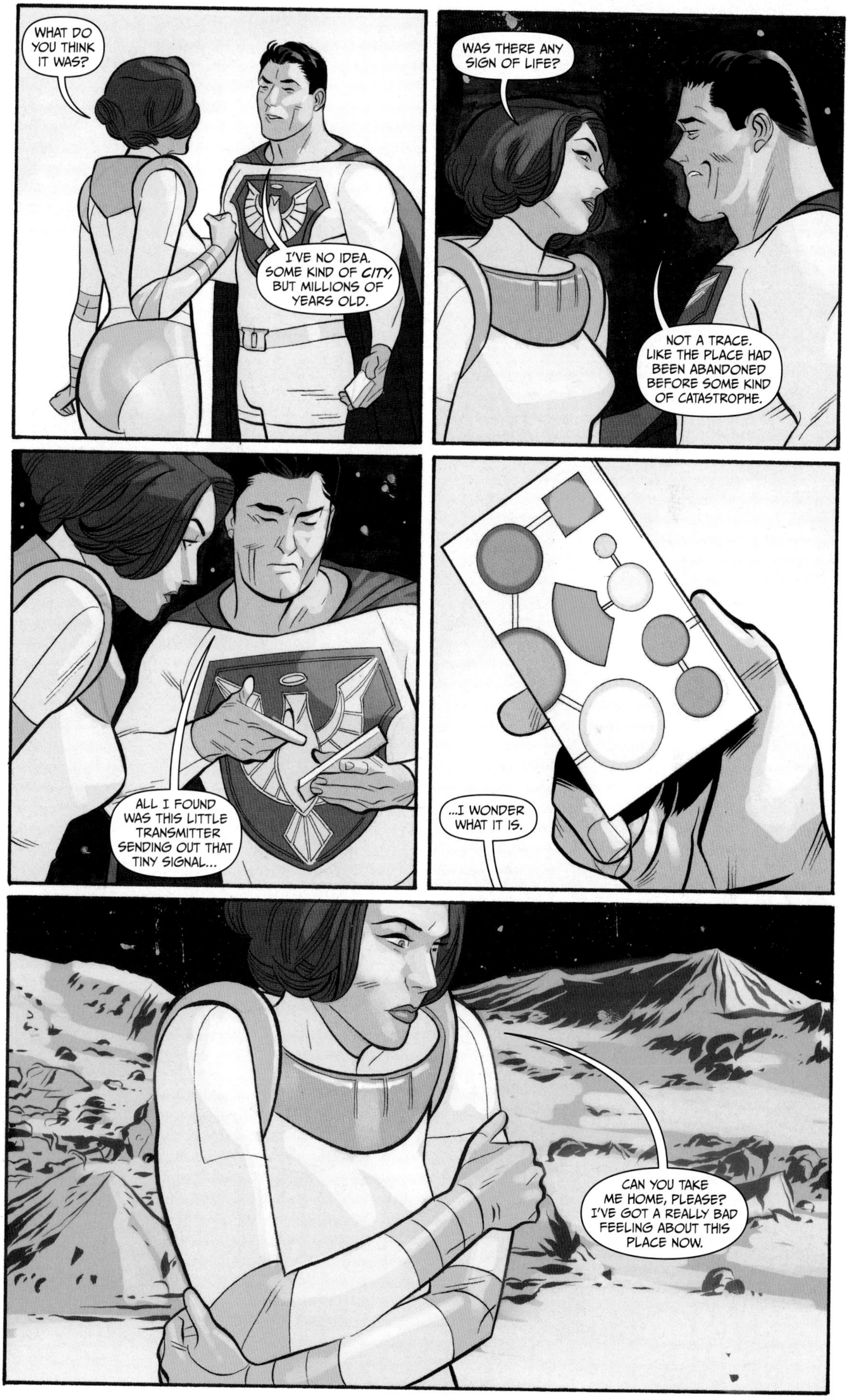
WHAT DO YOU THINK IT WAS?
I'VE NO IDEA. SOME KIND OF *CITY,* BUT MILLIONS OF YEARS OLD.
WAS THERE ANY SIGN OF LIFE?
NOT A TRACE. LIKE THE PLACE HAD BEEN ABANDONED BEFORE SOME KIND OF CATASTROPHE.
ALL I FOUND WAS THIS LITTLE TRANSMITTER SENDING OUT THAT TINY SIGNAL...
...I WONDER WHAT IT IS.
CAN YOU TAKE ME HOME, PLEASE? I'VE GOT A REALLY BAD FEELING ABOUT THIS PLACE NOW.

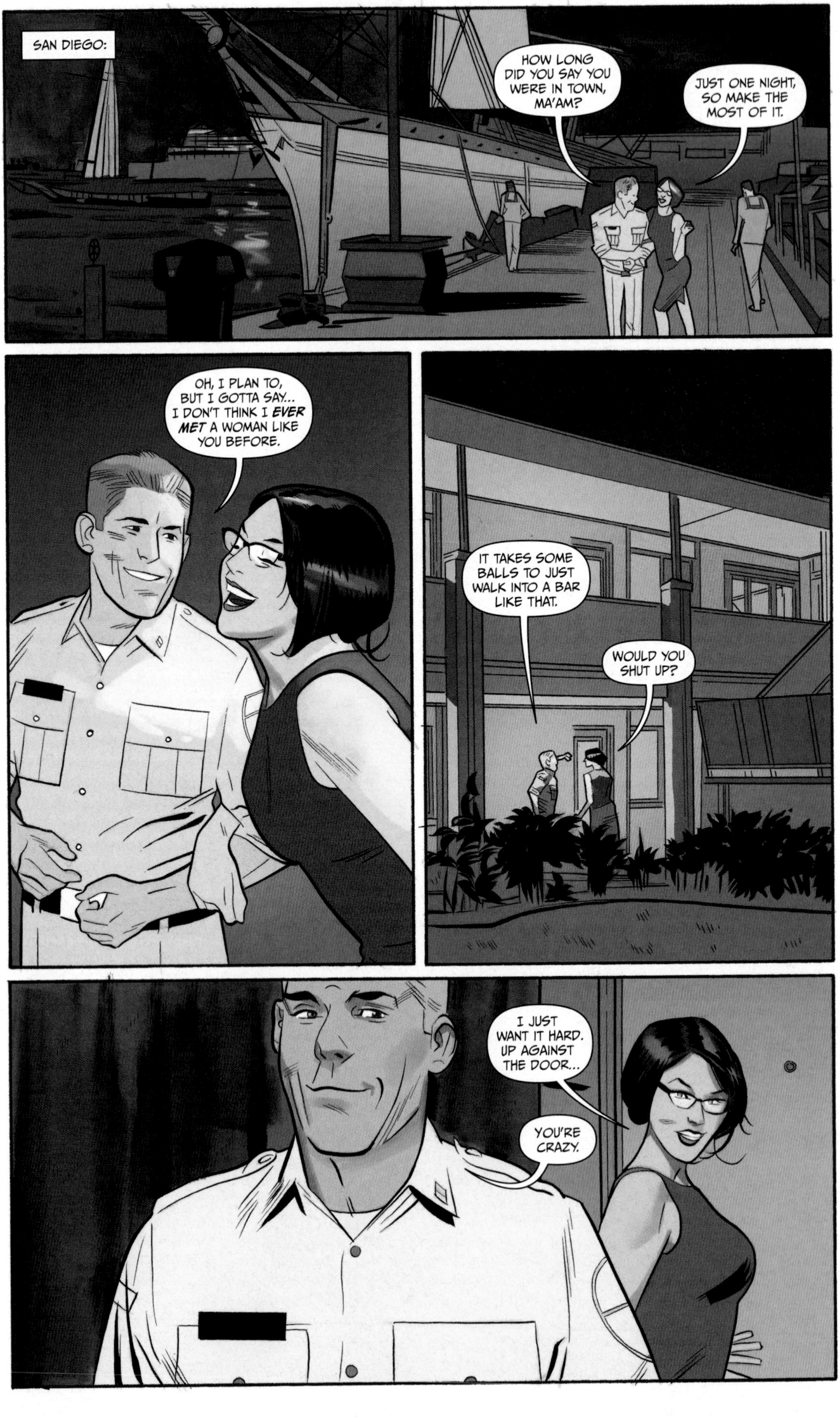
SAN DIEGO:
HOW LONG DID YOU SAY YOU WERE IN TOWN, MA'AM?
JUST ONE NIGHT, SO MAKE THE MOST OF IT.
OH, I PLAN TO, BUT I GOTTA SAY... I DON'T THINK I **EVER MET** A WOMAN LIKE YOU BEFORE.
IT TAKES SOME BALLS TO JUST WALK INTO A BAR LIKE THAT.
WOULD YOU SHUT UP?
I JUST WANT IT HARD. UP AGAINST THE DOOR...
YOU'RE CRAZY.

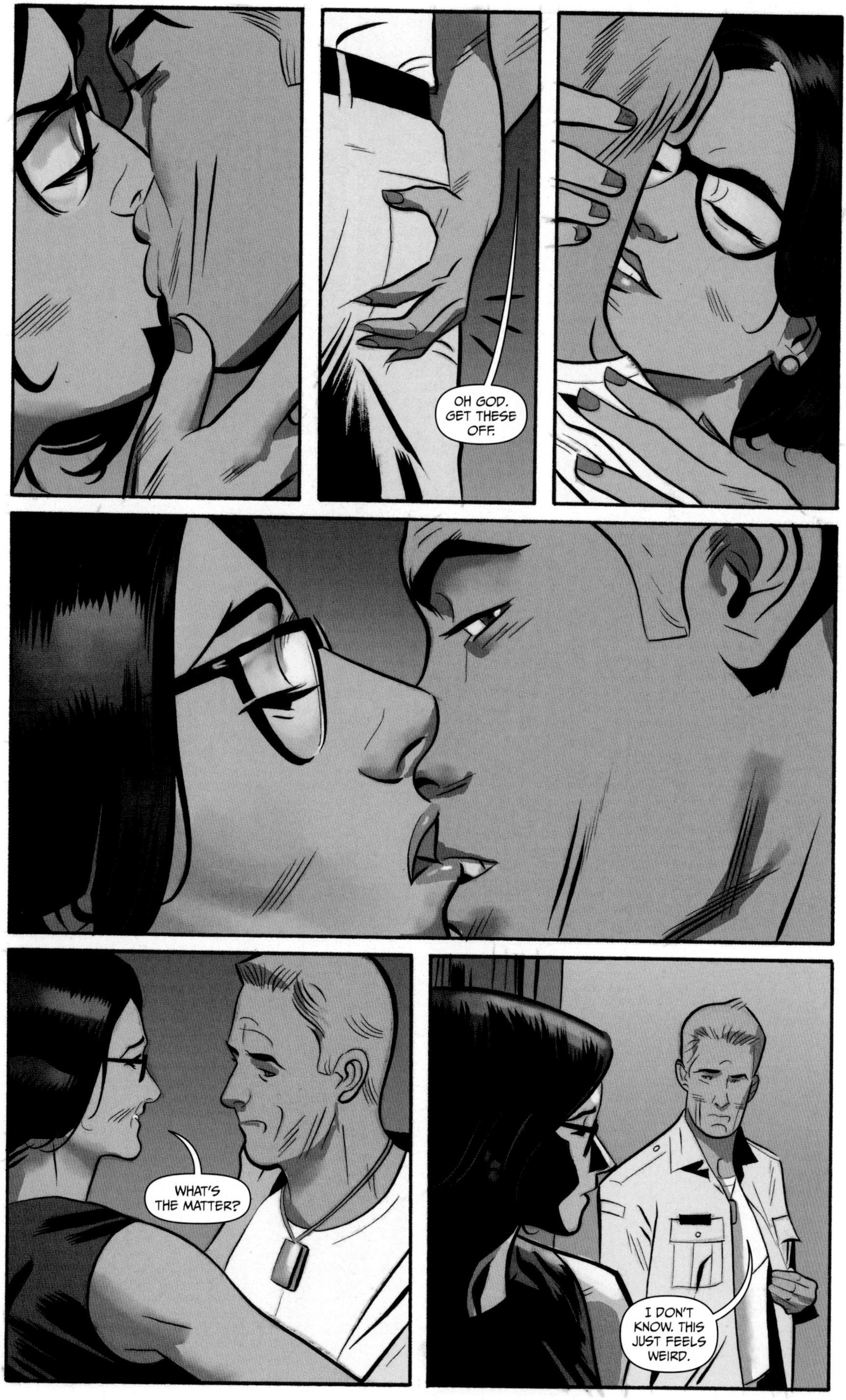
OH GOD. GET THESE OFF.
WHAT'S THE MATTER?
I DON'T KNOW. THIS JUST FEELS WEIRD.

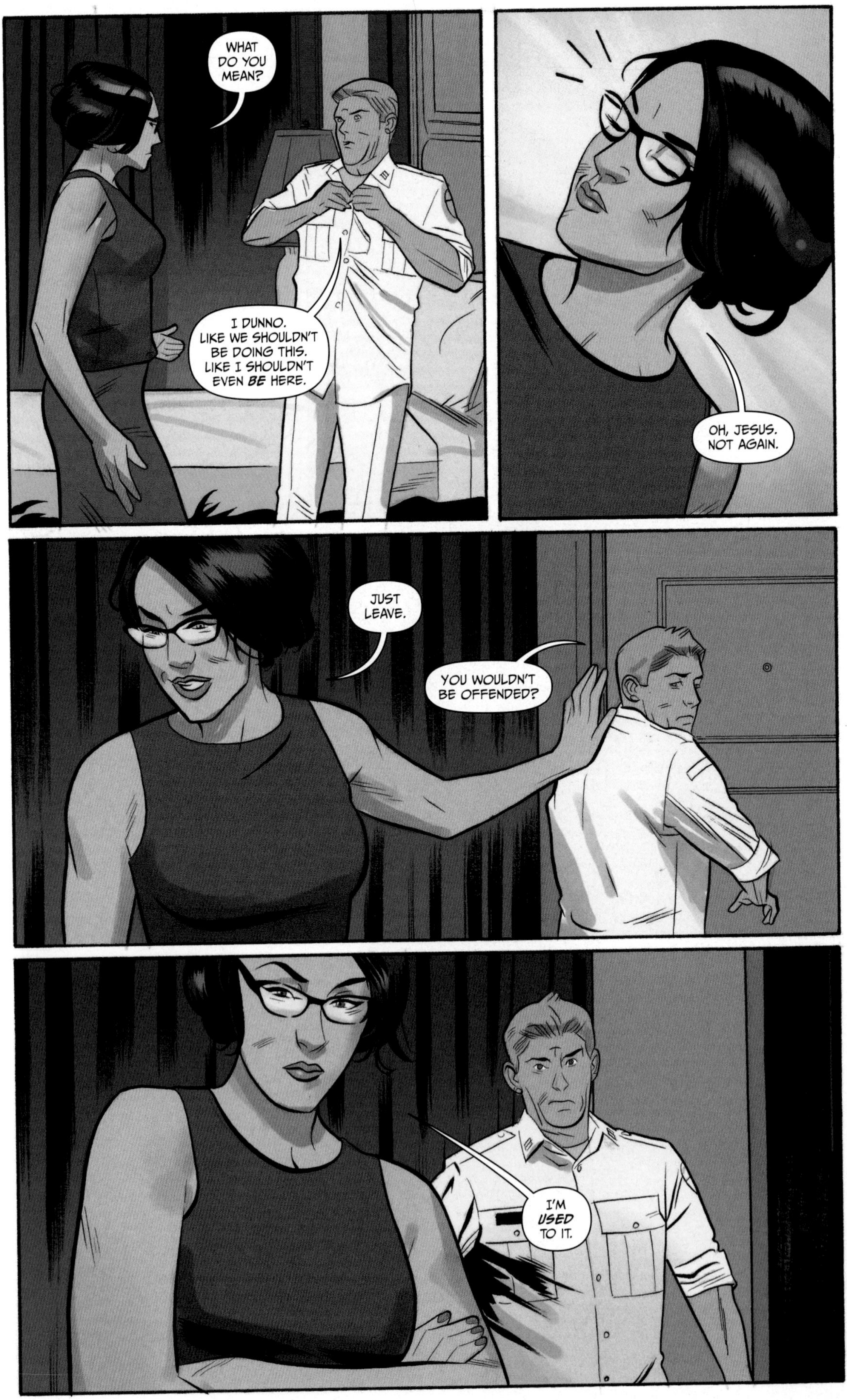
WHAT DO YOU MEAN?
I DUNNO. LIKE WE SHOULDN'T BE DOING THIS. LIKE I SHOULDN'T EVEN *BE* HERE.
OH, JESUS. NOT AGAIN.
JUST LEAVE.
YOU WOULDN'T BE OFFENDED?
I'M *USED* TO IT.

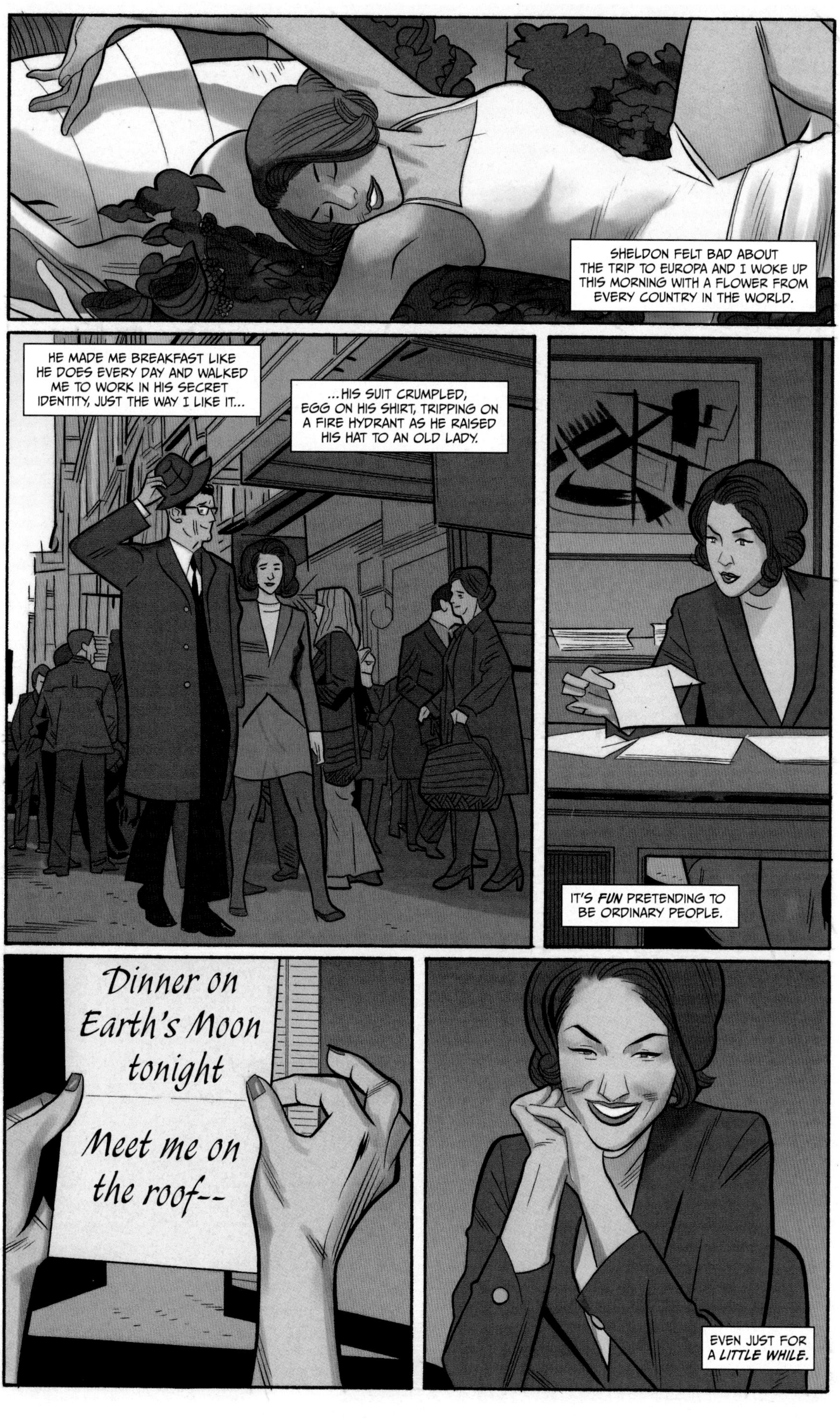
SHELDON FELT BAD ABOUT THE TRIP TO EUROPA AND I WOKE UP THIS MORNING WITH A FLOWER FROM EVERY COUNTRY IN THE WORLD.
HE MADE ME BREAKFAST LIKE HE DOES EVERY DAY AND WALKED ME TO WORK IN HIS SECRET IDENTITY, JUST THE WAY I LIKE IT...
...HIS SUIT CRUMPLED, EGG ON HIS SHIRT, TRIPPING ON A FIRE HYDRANT AS HE RAISED HIS HAT TO AN OLD LADY.
IT'S FUN PRETENDING TO BE ORDINARY PEOPLE.
Dinner on Earth's Moon tonight
Meet me on the roof--
EVEN JUST FOR A LITTLE WHILE.

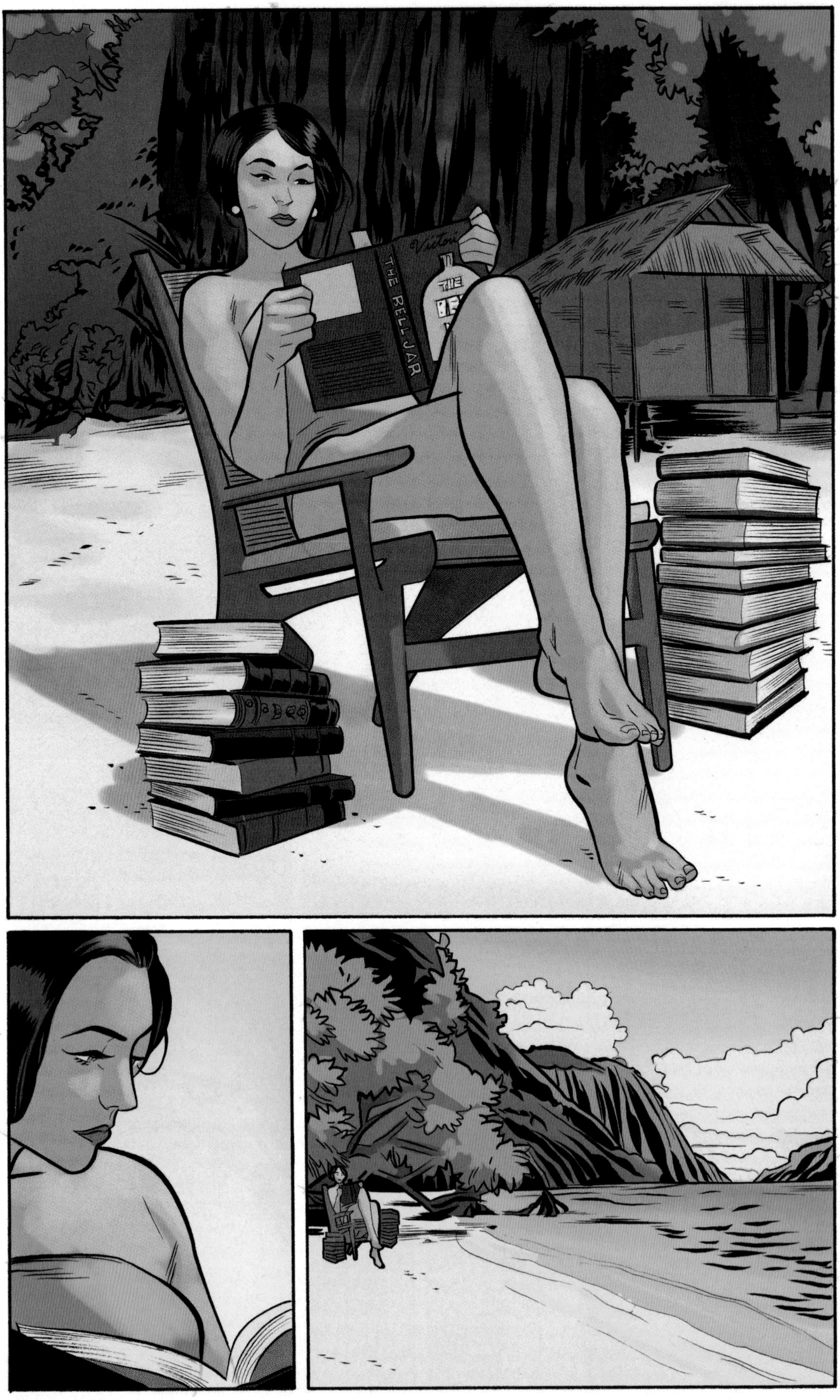
THE BELL JAR

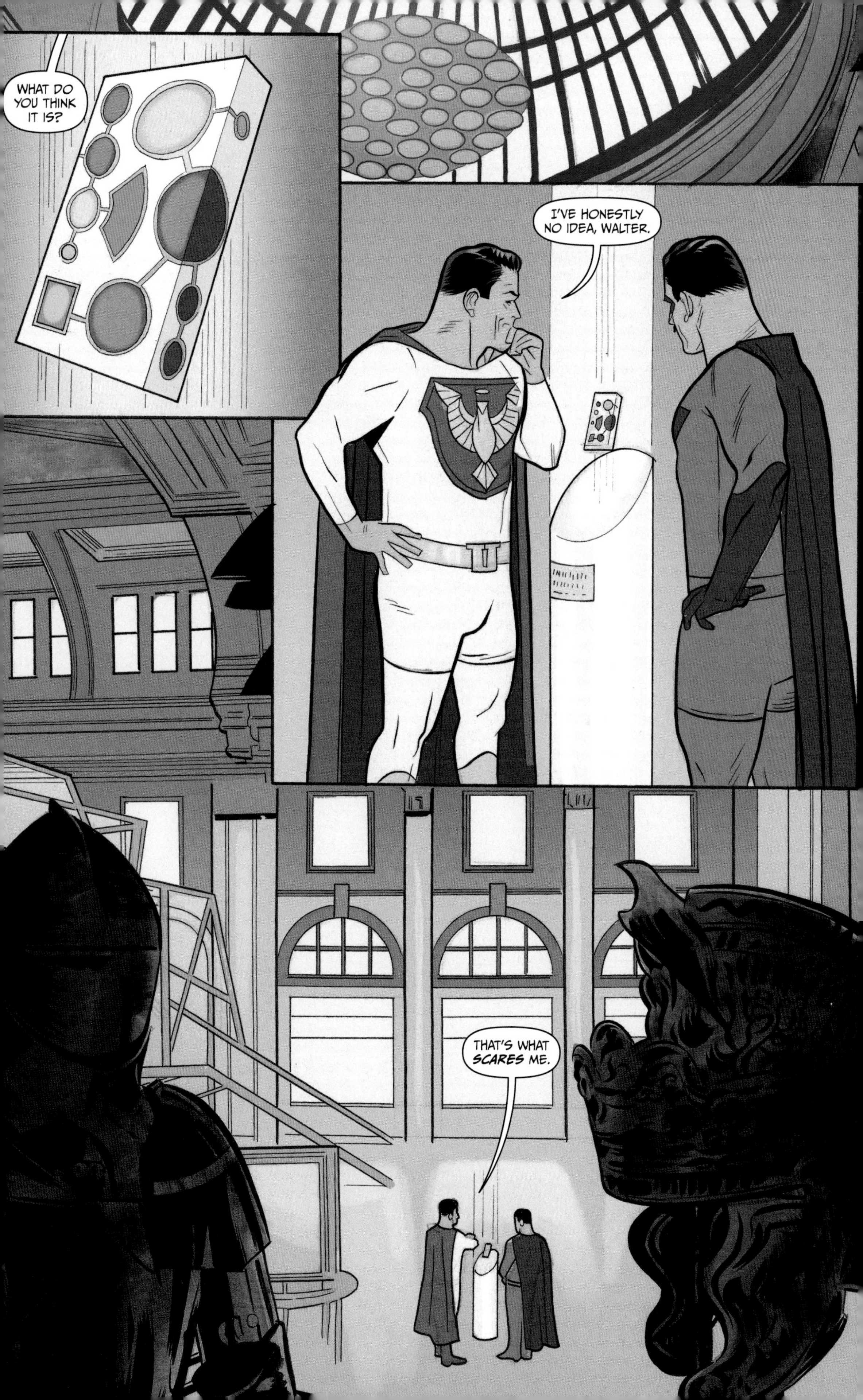
WHAT DO YOU THINK IT IS?
I'VE HONESTLY NO IDEA, WALTER.
THAT'S WHAT SCARES ME.

CHAPTER 2

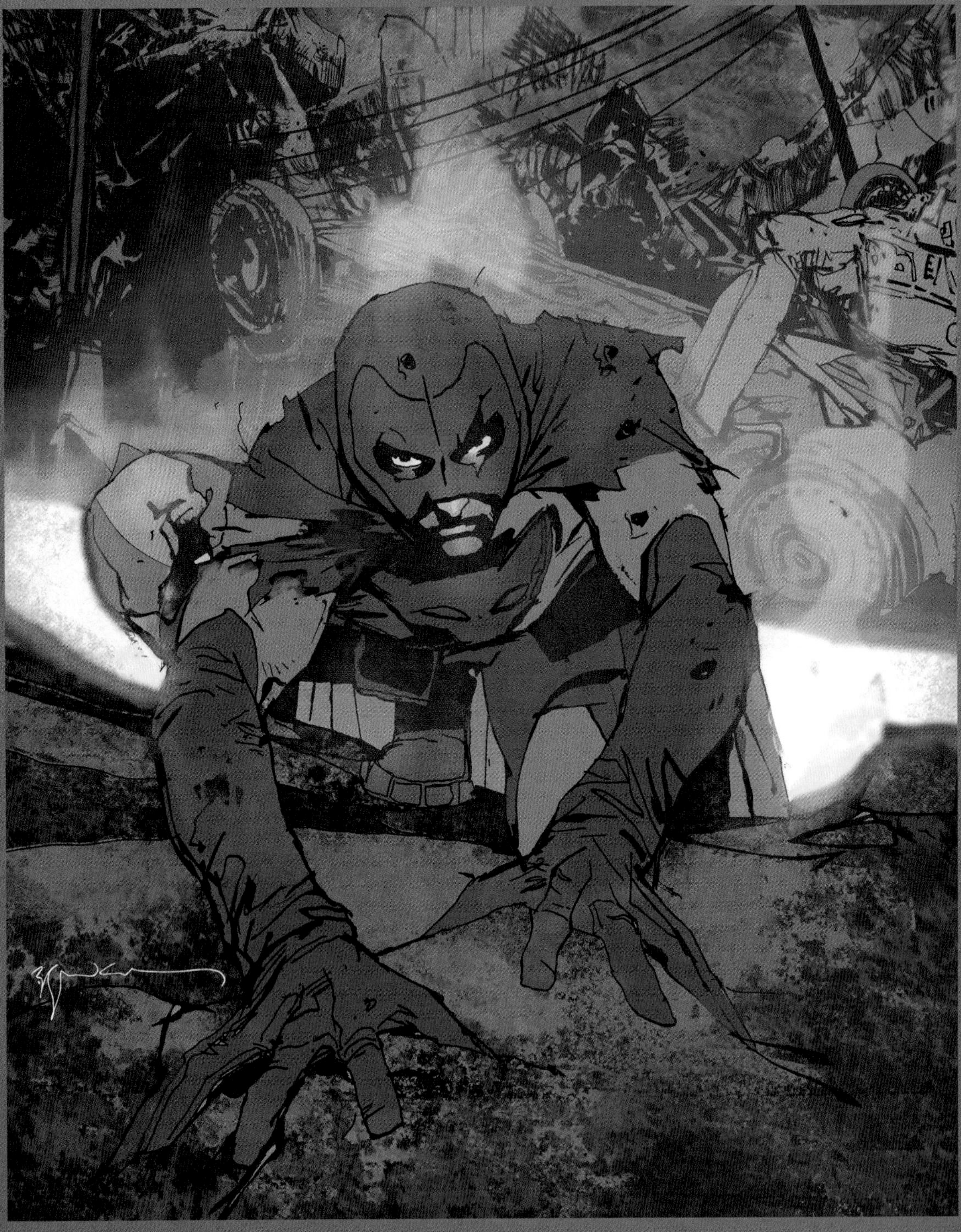

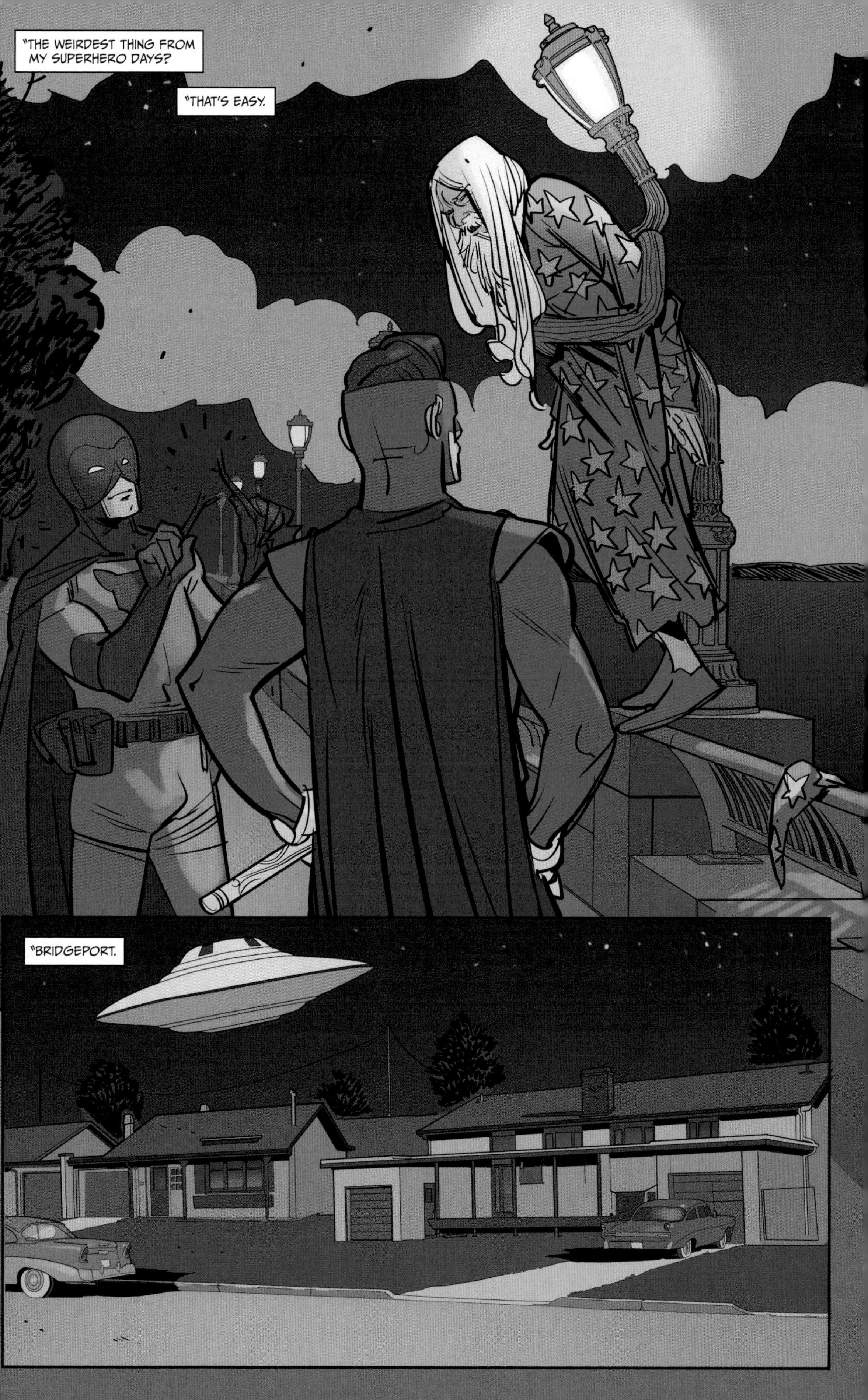
"THE WEIRDEST THING FROM MY SUPERHERO DAYS?
"THAT'S EASY.
"BRIDGEPORT.

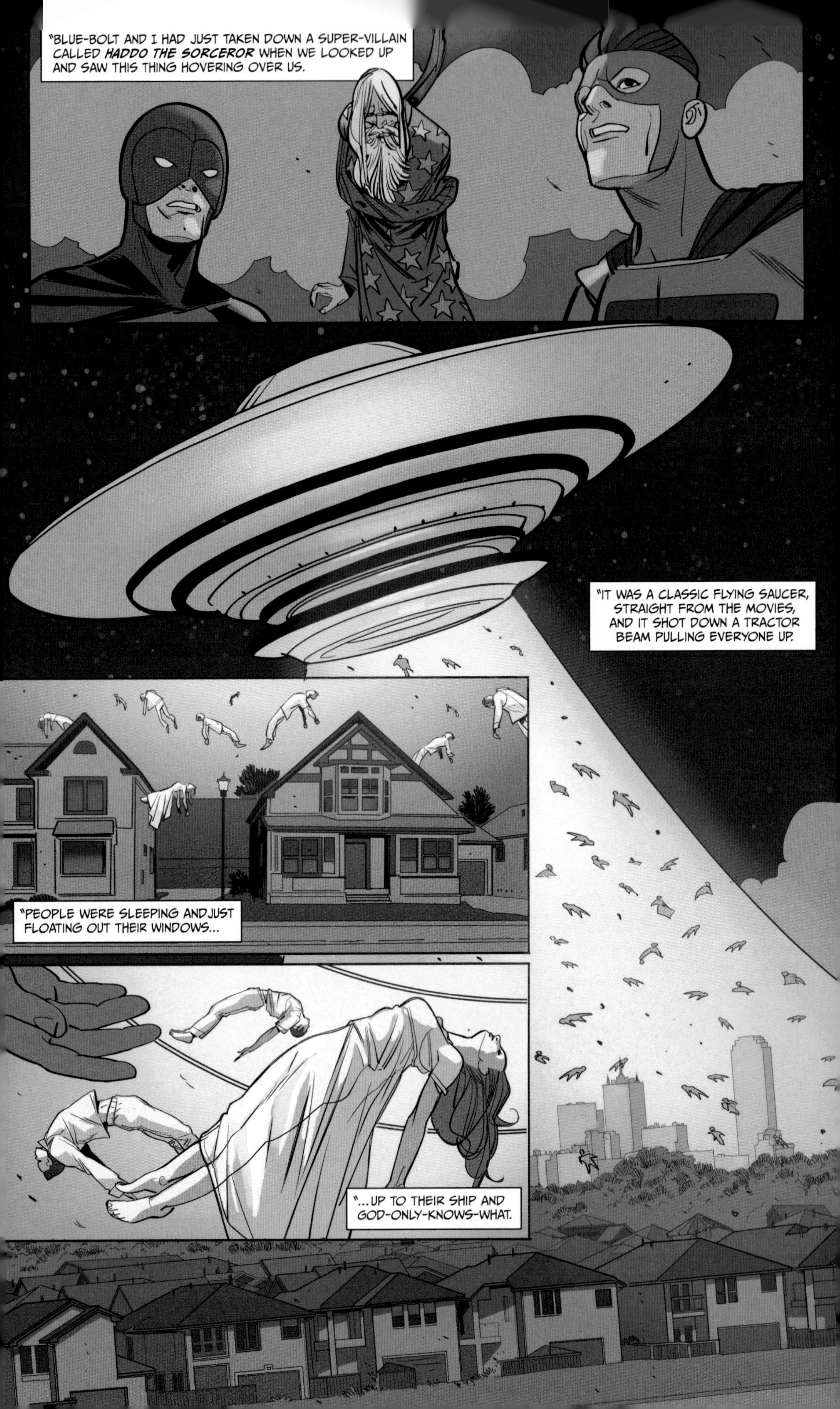
"BLUE-BOLT AND I HAD JUST TAKEN DOWN A SUPER-VILLAIN CALLED ***HADDO THE SORCEROR*** WHEN WE LOOKED UP AND SAW THIS THING HOVERING OVER US.
"IT WAS A CLASSIC FLYING SAUCER, STRAIGHT FROM THE MOVIES, AND IT SHOT DOWN A TRACTOR BEAM PULLING EVERYONE UP.
"PEOPLE WERE SLEEPING AND JUST FLOATING OUT THEIR WINDOWS...
"...UP TO THEIR SHIP AND GOD-ONLY-KNOWS-WHAT.

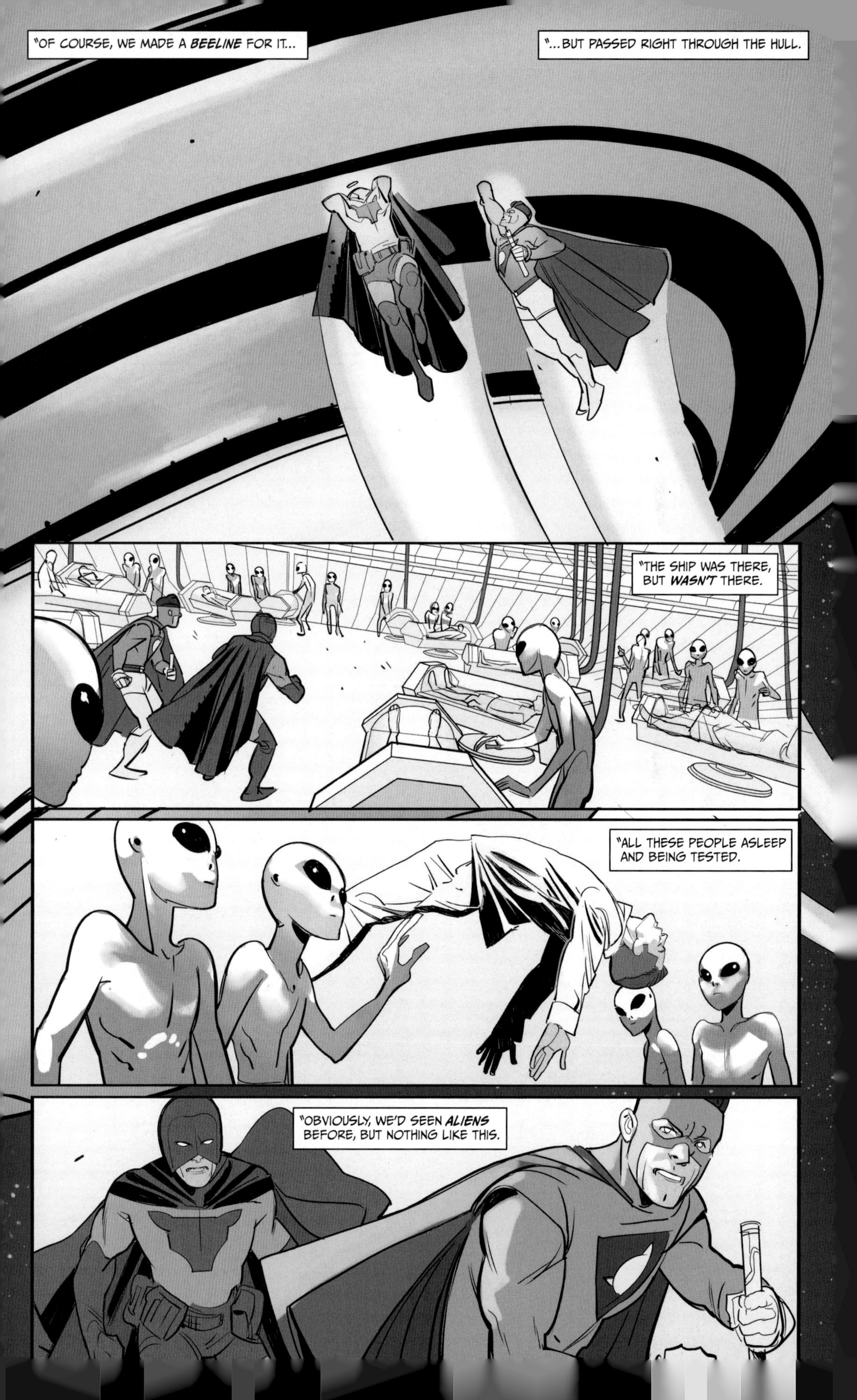
"OF COURSE, WE MADE A BEELINE FOR IT...
"...BUT PASSED RIGHT THROUGH THE HULL.
"THE SHIP WAS THERE, BUT WASN'T THERE.
"ALL THESE PEOPLE ASLEEP AND BEING TESTED.
"OBVIOUSLY, WE'D SEEN ALIENS BEFORE, BUT NOTHING LIKE THIS.

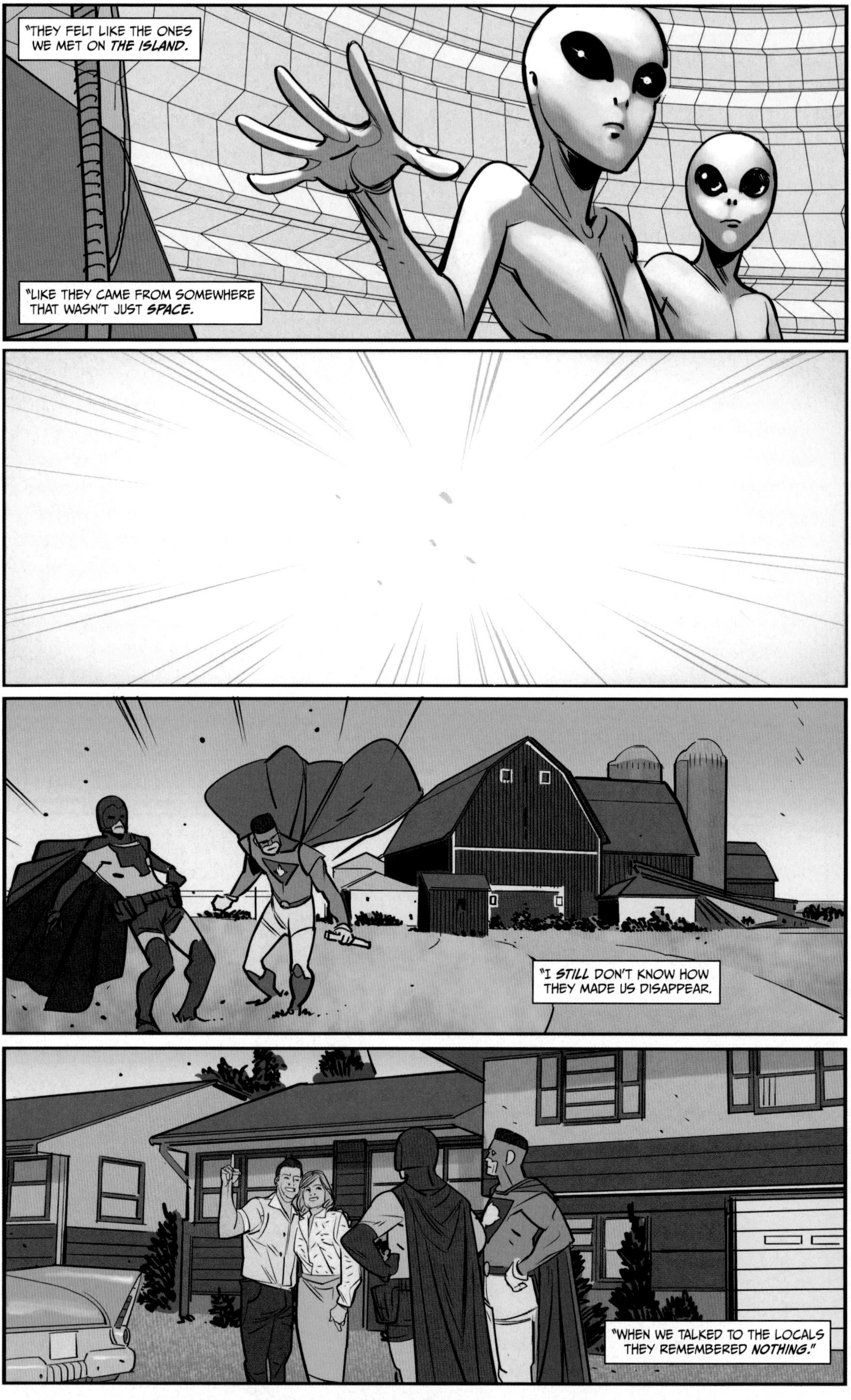
"THEY FELT LIKE THE ONES WE MET ON *THE ISLAND.*
"LIKE THEY CAME FROM SOMEWHERE THAT WASN'T JUST *SPACE.*
"I *STILL* DON'T KNOW HOW THEY MADE US DISAPPEAR.
"WHEN WE TALKED TO THE LOCALS THEY REMEMBERED *NOTHING.*"

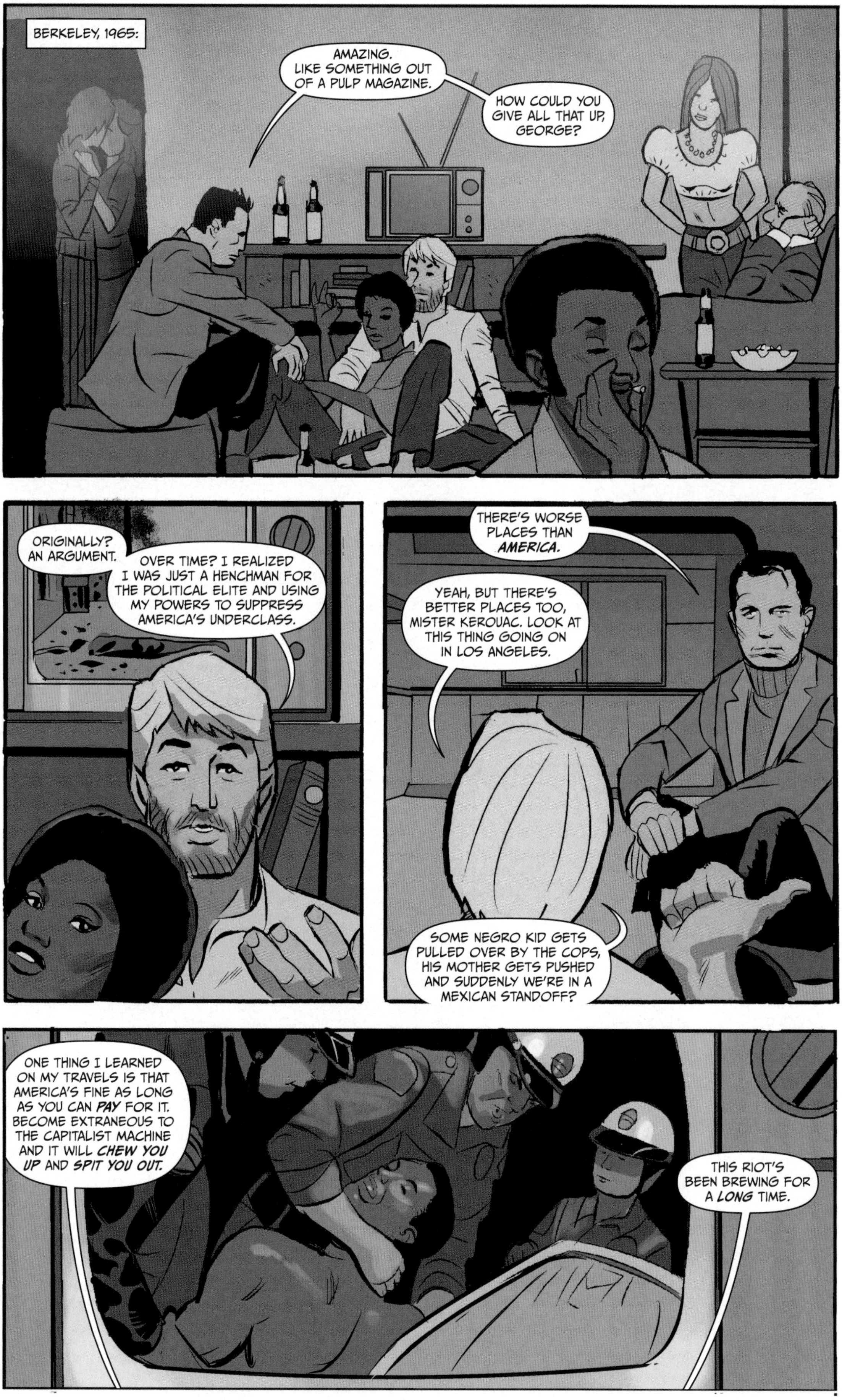
BERKELEY, 1965:
AMAZING. LIKE SOMETHING OUT OF A PULP MAGAZINE.
HOW COULD YOU GIVE ALL THAT UP, GEORGE?
ORIGINALLY? AN ARGUMENT.
OVER TIME? I REALIZED I WAS JUST A HENCHMAN FOR THE POLITICAL ELITE AND USING MY POWERS TO SUPPRESS AMERICA'S UNDERCLASS.
THERE'S WORSE PLACES THAN *AMERICA.*
YEAH, BUT THERE'S BETTER PLACES TOO, MISTER KEROUAC. LOOK AT THIS THING GOING ON IN LOS ANGELES.
SOME NEGRO KID GETS PULLED OVER BY THE COPS, HIS MOTHER GETS PUSHED AND SUDDENLY WE'RE IN A MEXICAN STANDOFF?
ONE THING I LEARNED ON MY TRAVELS IS THAT AMERICA'S FINE AS LONG AS YOU CAN *PAY* FOR IT. BECOME EXTRANEOUS TO THE CAPITALIST MACHINE AND IT WILL *CHEW YOU UP* AND *SPIT YOU OUT.*
THIS RIOT'S BEEN BREWING FOR A *LONG* TIME.

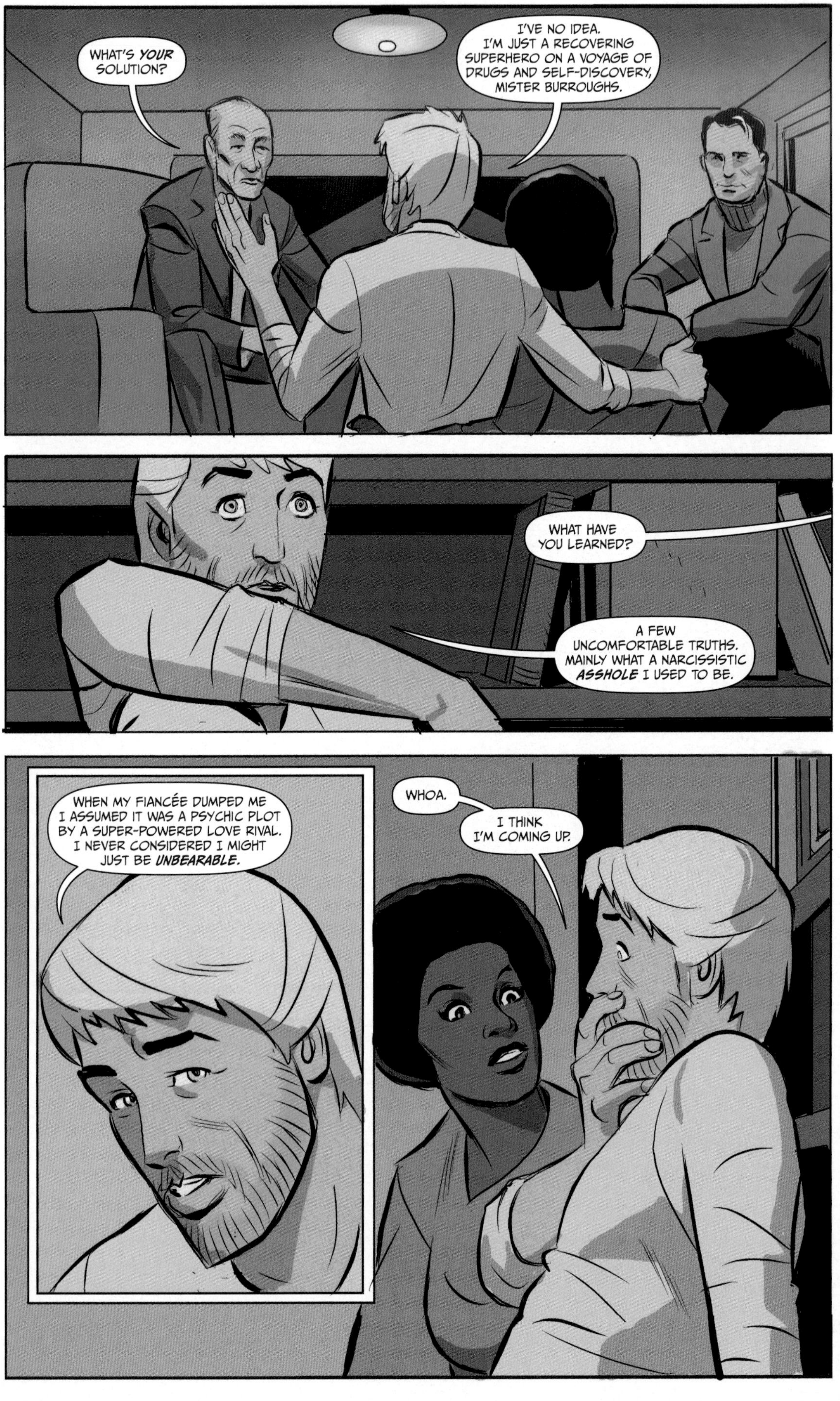
WHAT'S YOUR SOLUTION?
I'VE NO IDEA. I'M JUST A RECOVERING SUPERHERO ON A VOYAGE OF DRUGS AND SELF-DISCOVERY, MISTER BURROUGHS.
WHAT HAVE YOU LEARNED?
A FEW UNCOMFORTABLE TRUTHS. MAINLY WHAT A NARCISSISTIC ASSHOLE I USED TO BE.
WHEN MY FIANCÉE DUMPED ME I ASSUMED IT WAS A PSYCHIC PLOT BY A SUPER-POWERED LOVE RIVAL. I NEVER CONSIDERED I MIGHT JUST BE UNBEARABLE.
WHOA.
I THINK I'M COMING UP.

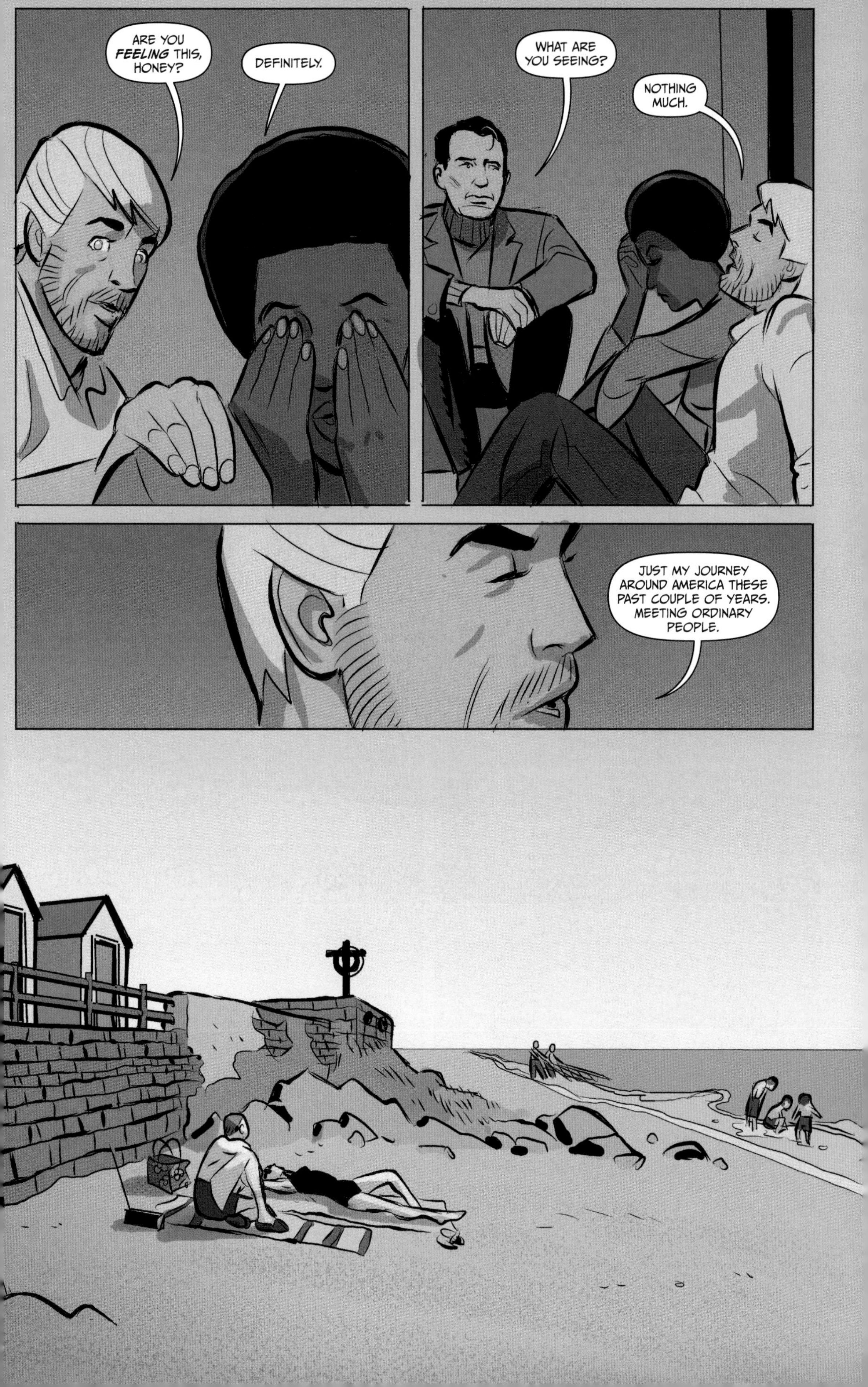
ARE YOU FEELING THIS, HONEY?
DEFINITELY.
WHAT ARE YOU SEEING?
NOTHING MUCH.
JUST MY JOURNEY AROUND AMERICA THESE PAST COUPLE OF YEARS. MEETING ORDINARY PEOPLE.

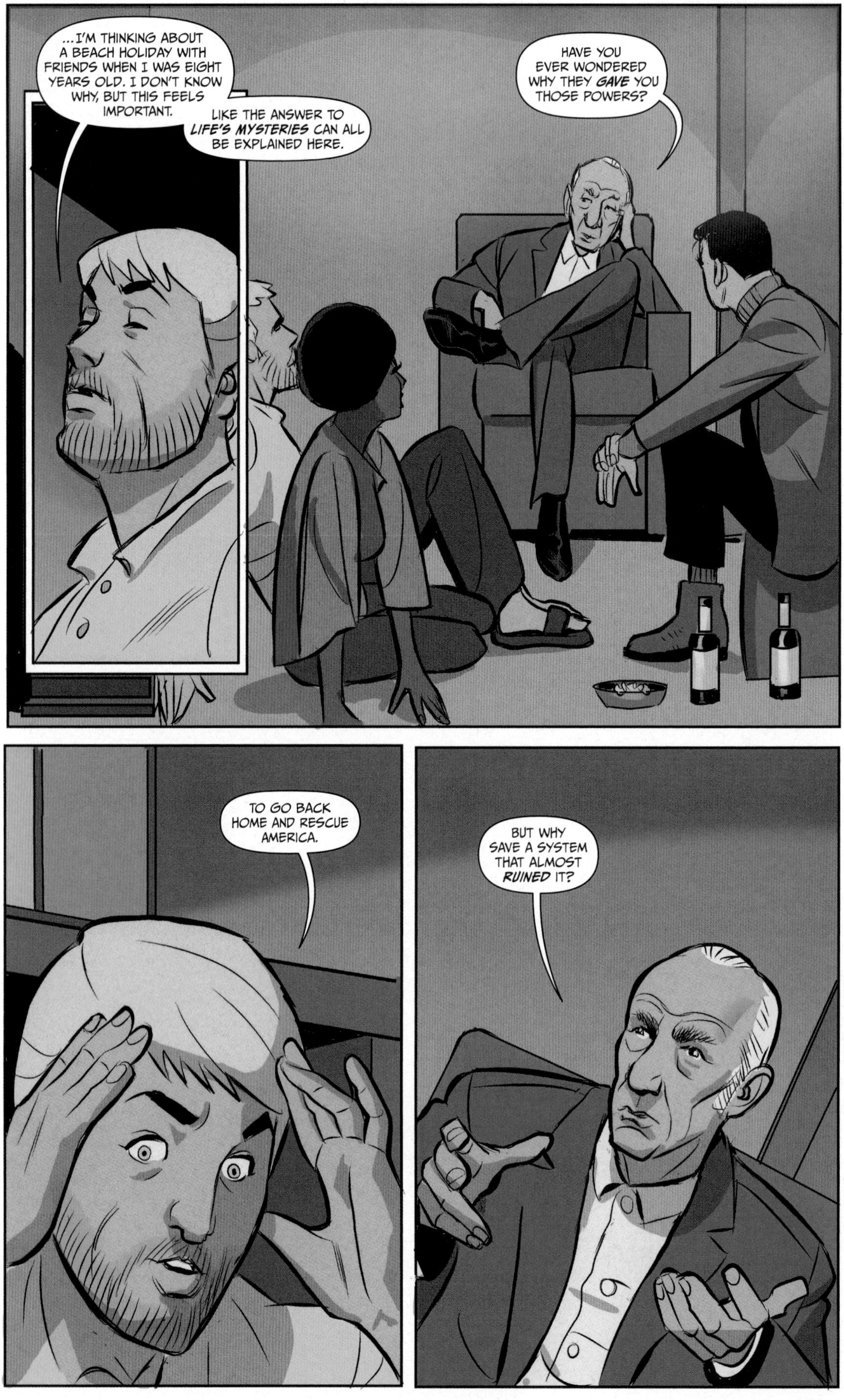
...I'M THINKING ABOUT A BEACH HOLIDAY WITH FRIENDS WHEN I WAS EIGHT YEARS OLD. I DON'T KNOW WHY, BUT THIS FEELS IMPORTANT.
LIKE THE ANSWER TO *LIFE'S MYSTERIES* CAN ALL BE EXPLAINED HERE.
HAVE YOU EVER WONDERED WHY THEY *GAVE* YOU THOSE POWERS?
TO GO BACK HOME AND RESCUE AMERICA.
BUT WHY SAVE A SYSTEM THAT ALMOST *RUINED* IT?

I WISH I HADN'T LEFT GINSBERG IN LONDON. HE'D ARTICULATE THIS SO MUCH BETTER THAN I CAN...

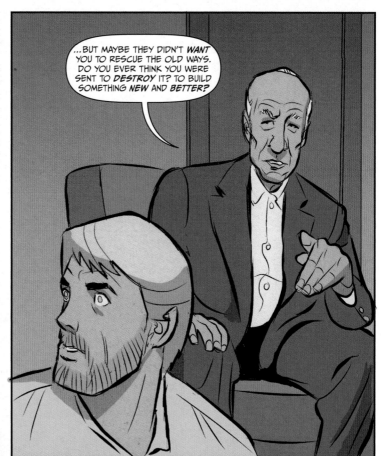

...BUT MAYBE THEY DIDN'T *WANT* YOU TO RESCUE THE OLD WAYS. DO YOU EVER THINK YOU WERE SENT TO *DESTROY* IT? TO BUILD SOMETHING *NEW* AND *BETTER*?

SOMETIMES.

I JUST NEVER HAD THE *NERVE*.

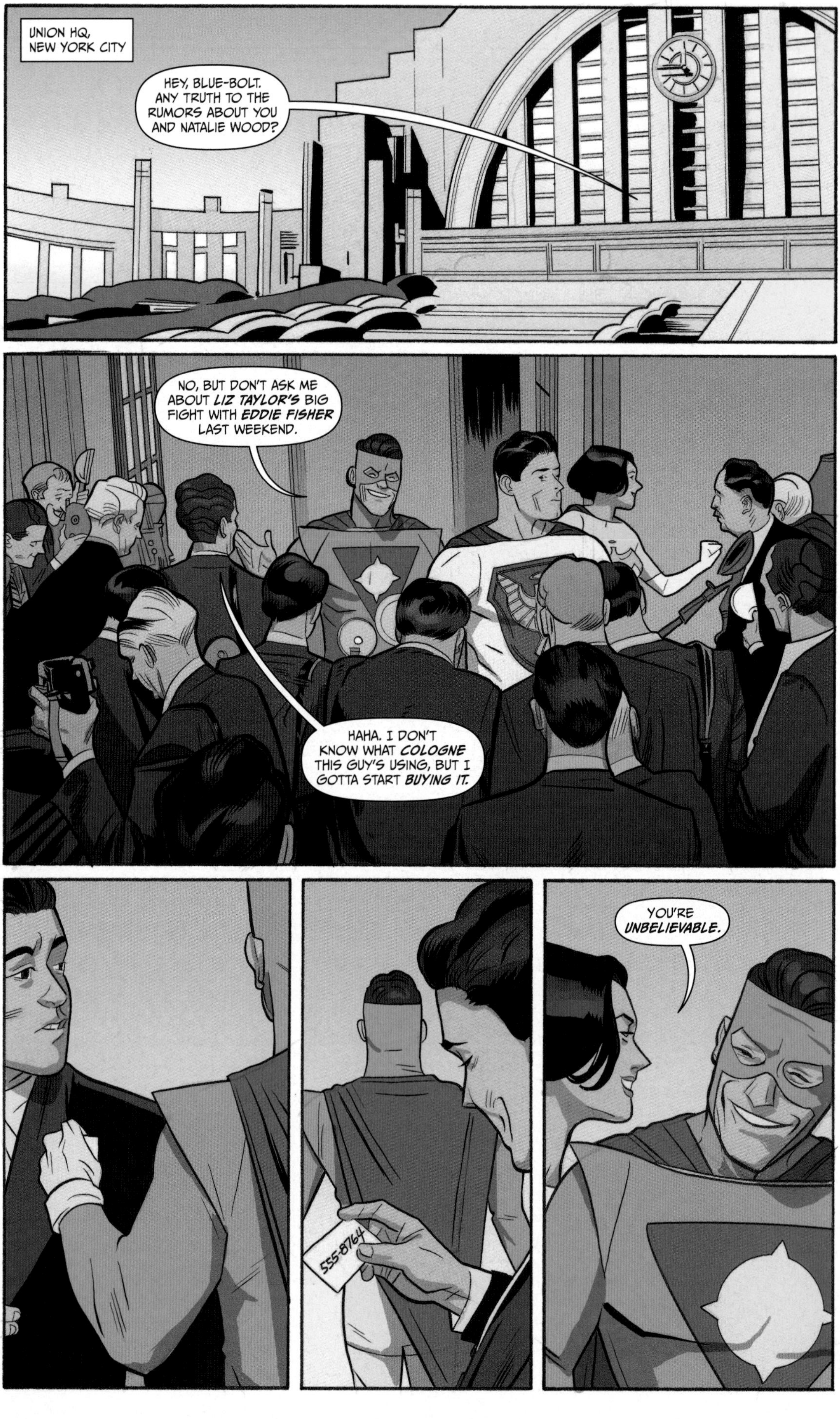
UNION HQ, NEW YORK CITY
HEY, BLUE-BOLT. ANY TRUTH TO THE RUMORS ABOUT YOU AND NATALIE WOOD?
NO, BUT DON'T ASK ME ABOUT LIZ TAYLOR'S BIG FIGHT WITH EDDIE FISHER LAST WEEKEND.
HAHA. I DON'T KNOW WHAT COLOGNE THIS GUY'S USING, BUT I GOTTA START BUYING IT.
555-8764
YOU'RE UNBELIEVABLE.

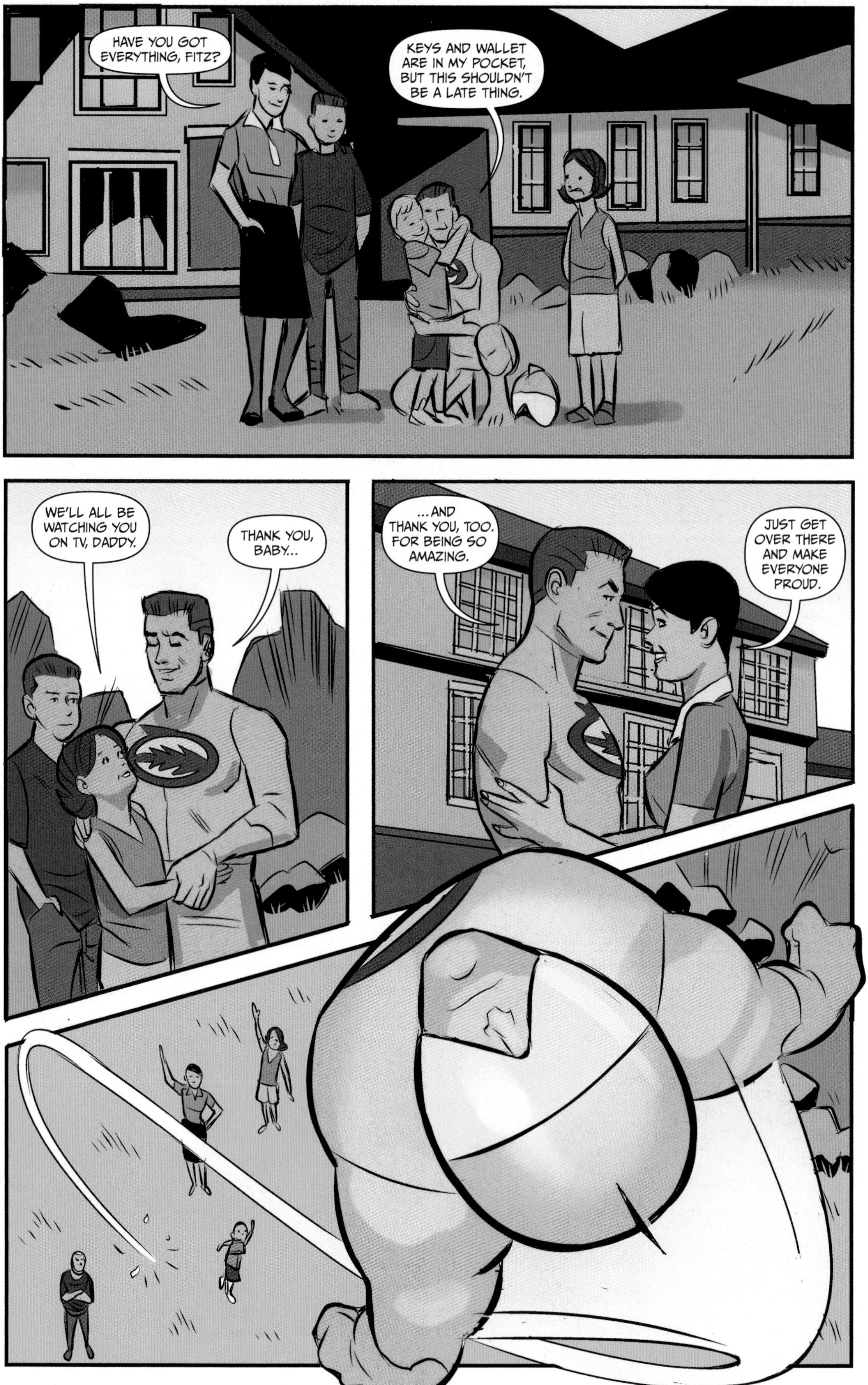
HAVE YOU GOT EVERYTHING, FITZ?
KEYS AND WALLET ARE IN MY POCKET, BUT THIS SHOULDN'T BE A LATE THING.
WE'LL ALL BE WATCHING YOU ON TV, DADDY.
THANK YOU, BABY...
...AND THANK YOU, TOO. FOR BEING SO AMAZING.
JUST GET OVER THERE AND MAKE EVERYONE PROUD.

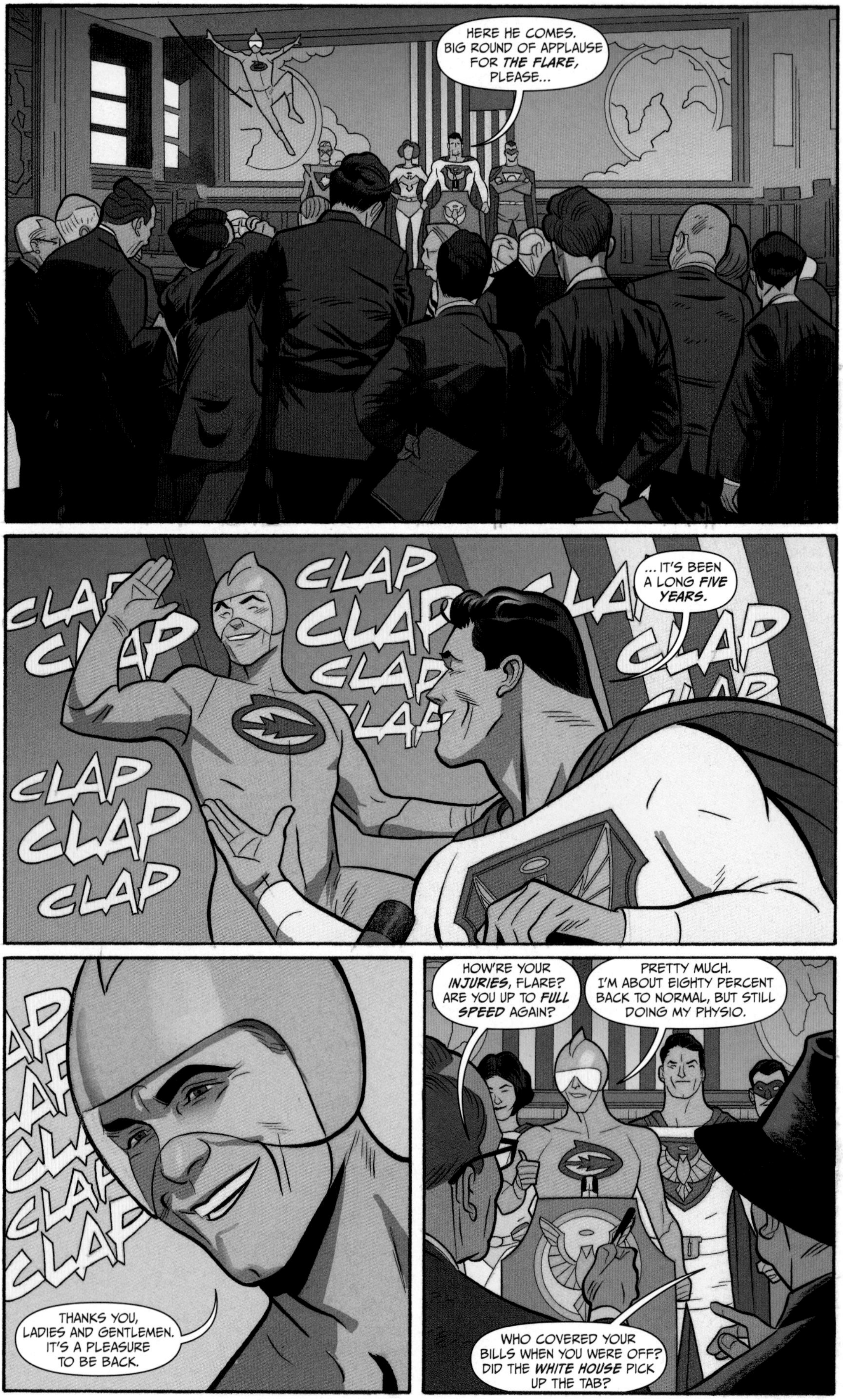
HERE HE COMES. BIG ROUND OF APPLAUSE FOR *THE FLARE,* PLEASE...
CLAP
CLAP
CLAP
CLAP
...IT'S BEEN A LONG *FIVE YEARS.*
CLAP
CLAP
CLAP
CLAP
THANKS YOU, LADIES AND GENTLEMEN. IT'S A PLEASURE TO BE BACK.
HOW'RE YOUR *INJURIES,* FLARE? ARE YOU UP TO *FULL SPEED* AGAIN?
PRETTY MUCH. I'M ABOUT EIGHTY PERCENT BACK TO NORMAL, BUT STILL DOING MY PHYSIO.
WHO COVERED YOUR BILLS WHEN YOU WERE OFF? DID THE *WHITE HOUSE* PICK UP THE TAB?

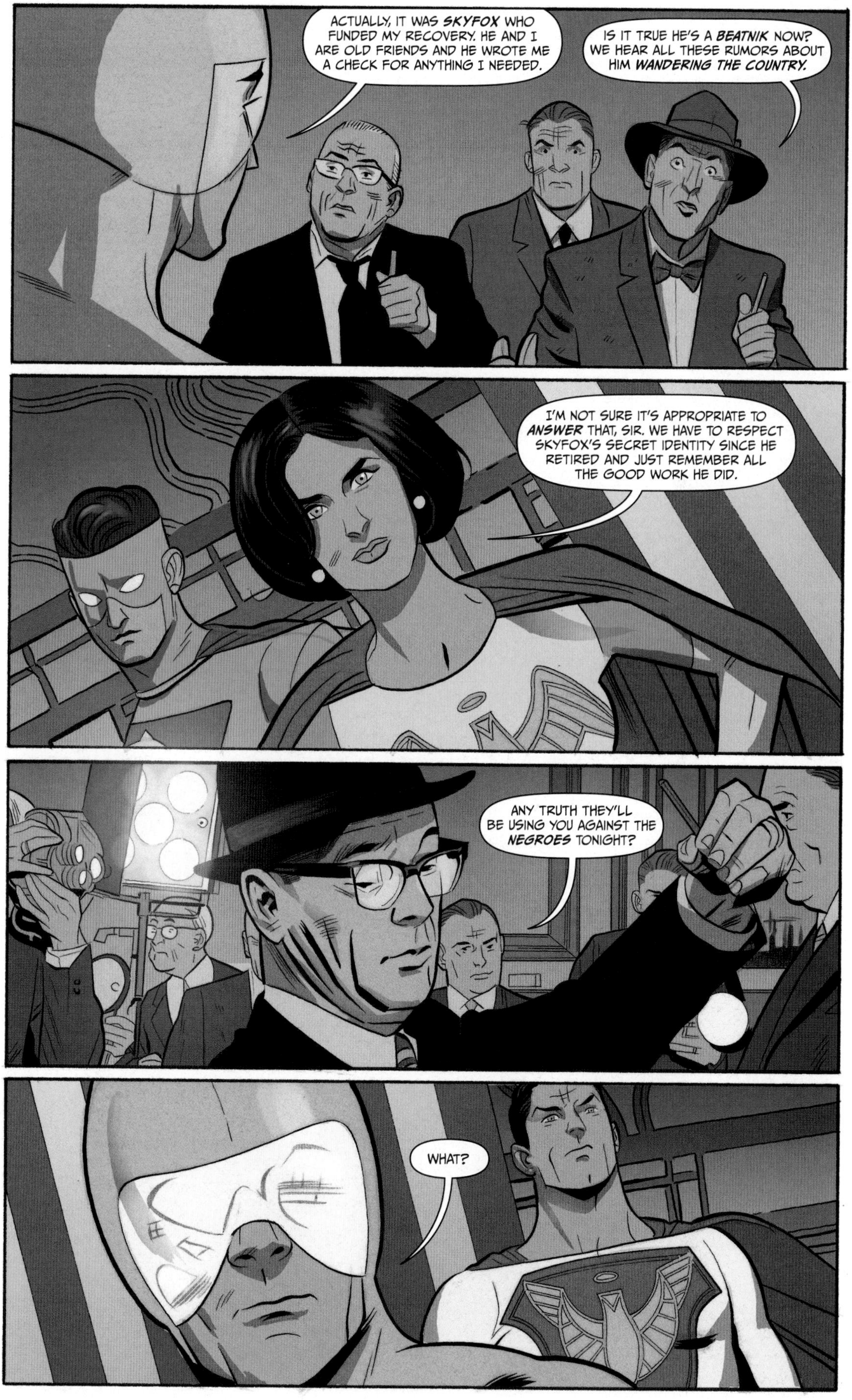
ACTUALLY, IT WAS SKYFOX WHO FUNDED MY RECOVERY. HE AND I ARE OLD FRIENDS AND HE WROTE ME A CHECK FOR ANYTHING I NEEDED.
IS IT TRUE HE'S A BEATNIK NOW? WE HEAR ALL THESE RUMORS ABOUT HIM WANDERING THE COUNTRY.
I'M NOT SURE IT'S APPROPRIATE TO ANSWER THAT, SIR. WE HAVE TO RESPECT SKYFOX'S SECRET IDENTITY SINCE HE RETIRED AND JUST REMEMBER ALL THE GOOD WORK HE DID.
ANY TRUTH THEY'LL BE USING YOU AGAINST THE NEGROES TONIGHT?
WHAT?

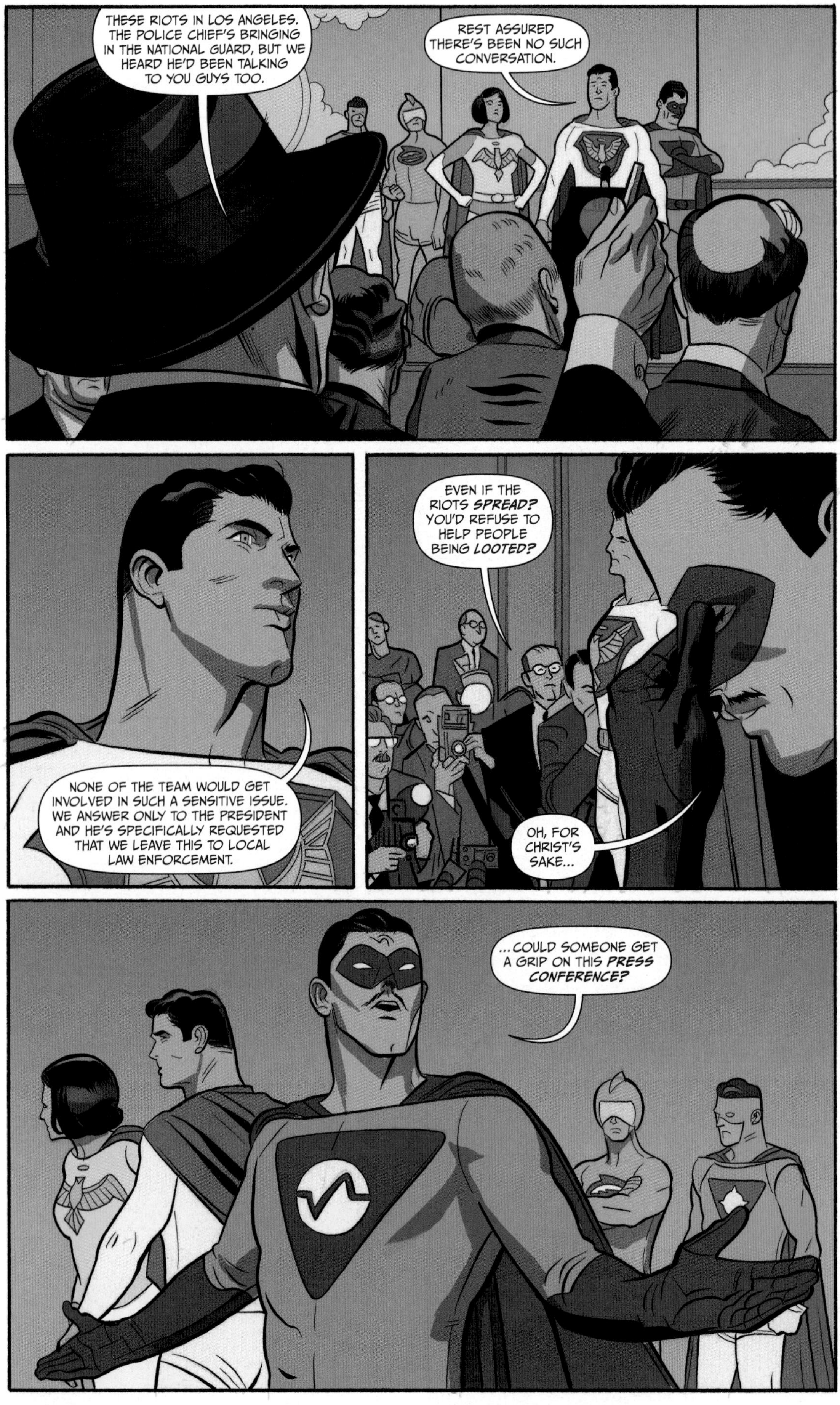
THESE RIOTS IN LOS ANGELES. THE POLICE CHIEF'S BRINGING IN THE NATIONAL GUARD, BUT WE HEARD HE'D BEEN TALKING TO YOU GUYS TOO.
REST ASSURED THERE'S BEEN NO SUCH CONVERSATION.
NONE OF THE TEAM WOULD GET INVOLVED IN SUCH A SENSITIVE ISSUE. WE ANSWER ONLY TO THE PRESIDENT AND HE'S SPECIFICALLY REQUESTED THAT WE LEAVE THIS TO LOCAL LAW ENFORCEMENT.
EVEN IF THE RIOTS *SPREAD?* YOU'D REFUSE TO HELP PEOPLE BEING *LOOTED?*
OH, FOR CHRIST'S SAKE...
...COULD SOMEONE GET A GRIP ON THIS *PRESS CONFERENCE?*

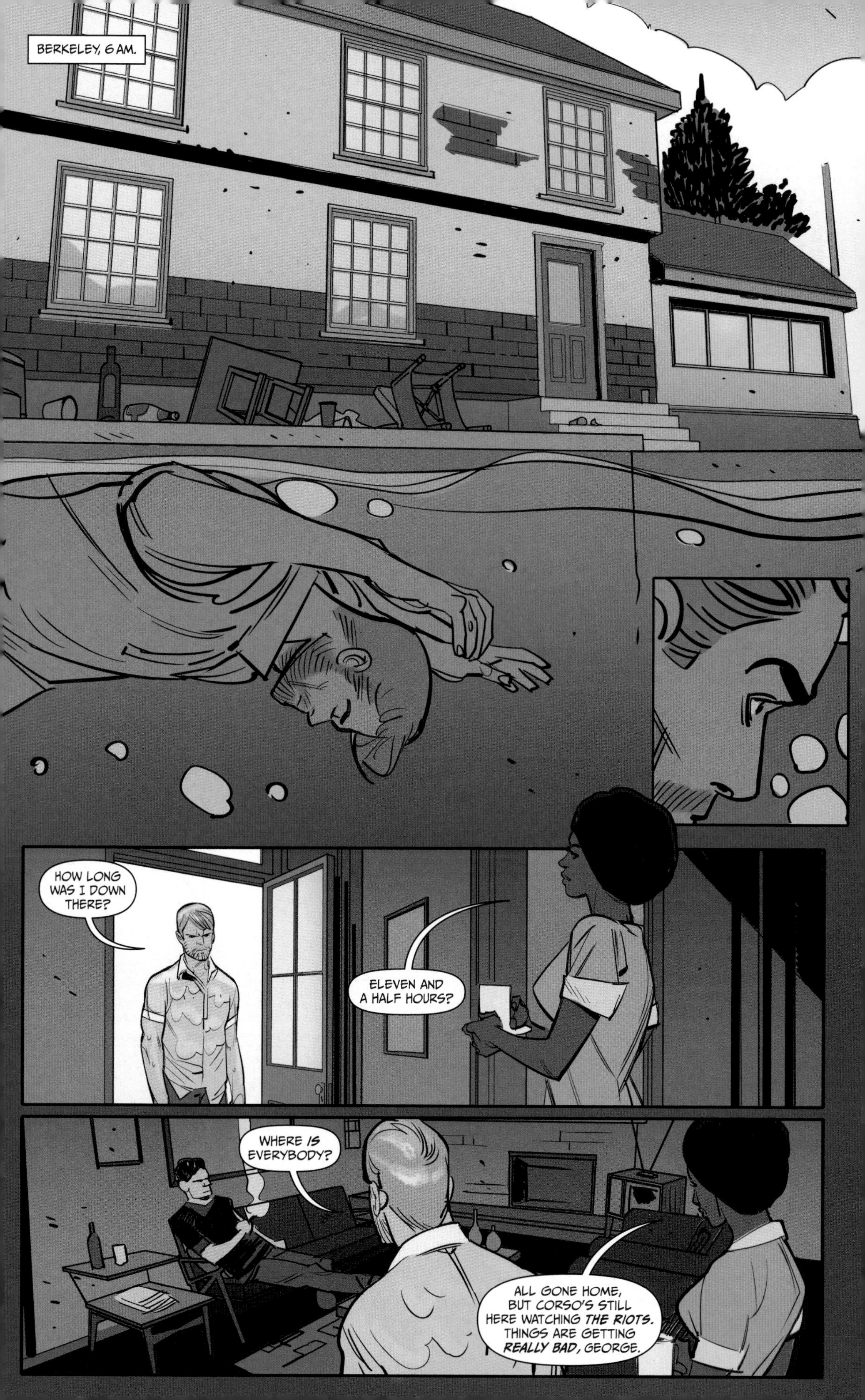
BERKELEY, 6 AM.
HOW LONG WAS I DOWN THERE?
ELEVEN AND A HALF HOURS?
WHERE *IS* EVERYBODY?
ALL GONE HOME, BUT CORSO'S STILL HERE WATCHING ***THE RIOTS.*** THINGS ARE GETTING ***REALLY BAD***, GEORGE.

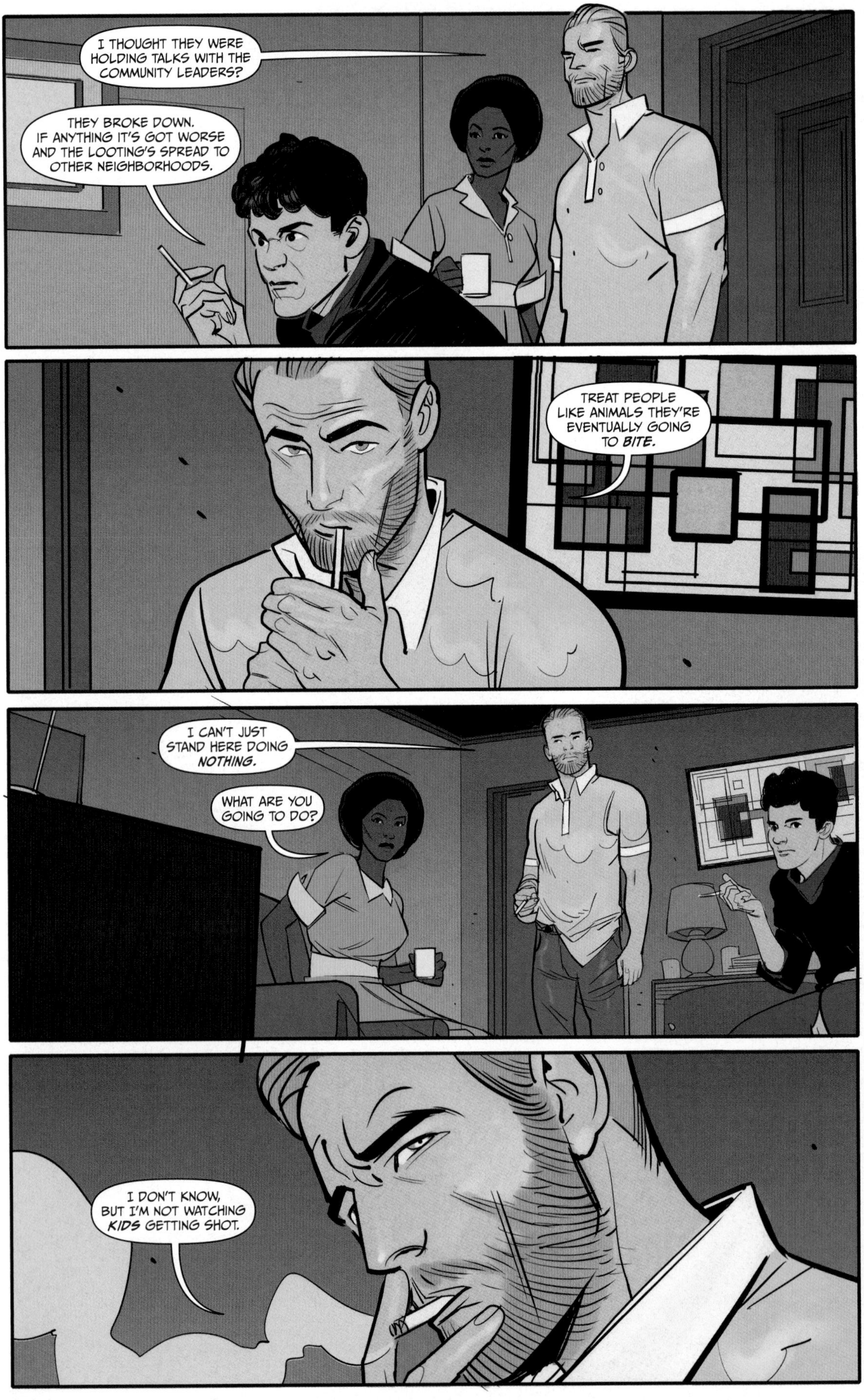
I THOUGHT THEY WERE HOLDING TALKS WITH THE COMMUNITY LEADERS?
THEY BROKE DOWN. IF ANYTHING IT'S GOT WORSE AND THE LOOTING'S SPREAD TO OTHER NEIGHBORHOODS.
TREAT PEOPLE LIKE ANIMALS THEY'RE EVENTUALLY GOING TO *BITE.*
I CAN'T JUST STAND HERE DOING *NOTHING.*
WHAT ARE YOU GOING TO DO?
I DON'T KNOW, BUT I'M NOT WATCHING *KIDS* GETTING SHOT.

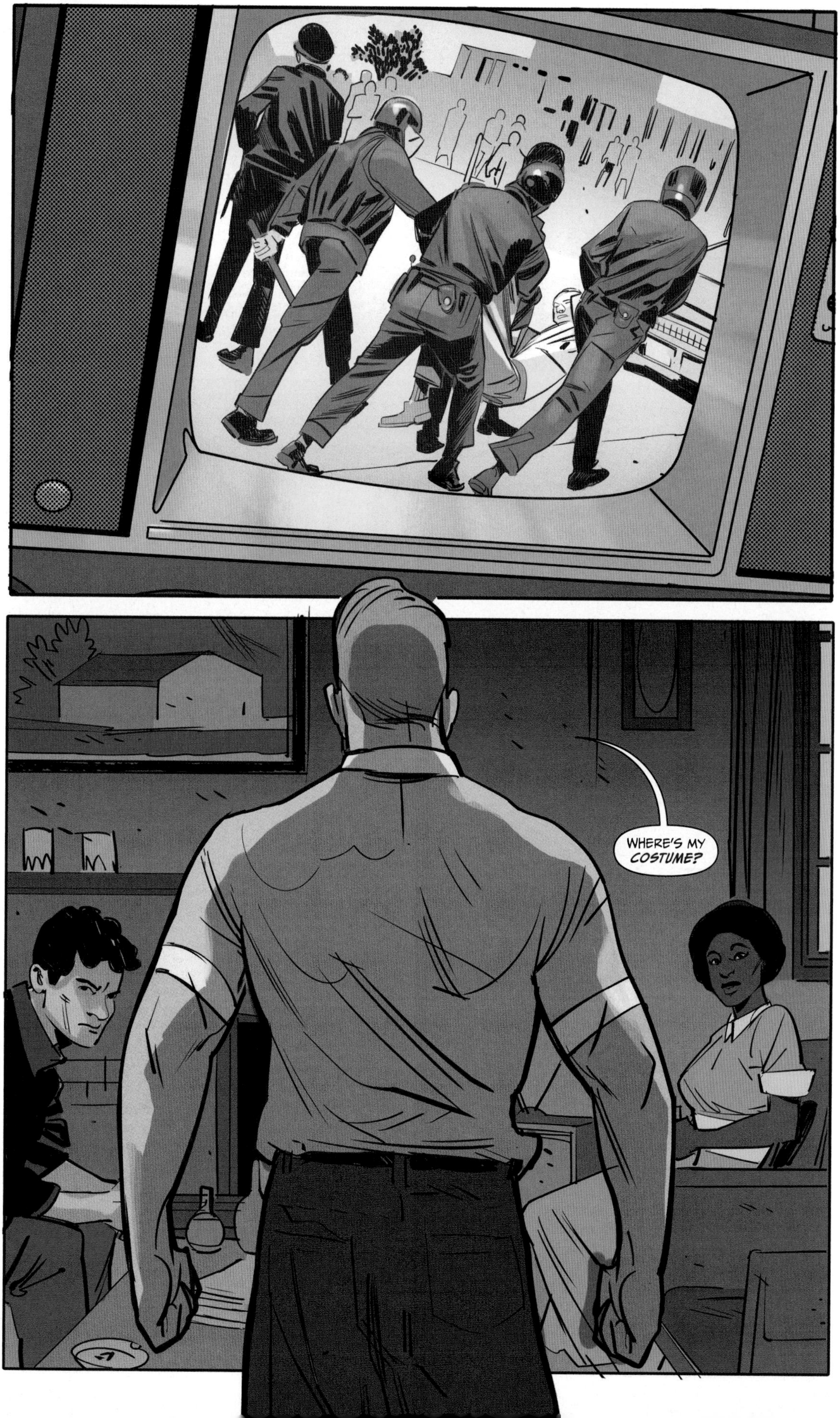
WHERE'S MY *COSTUME?*

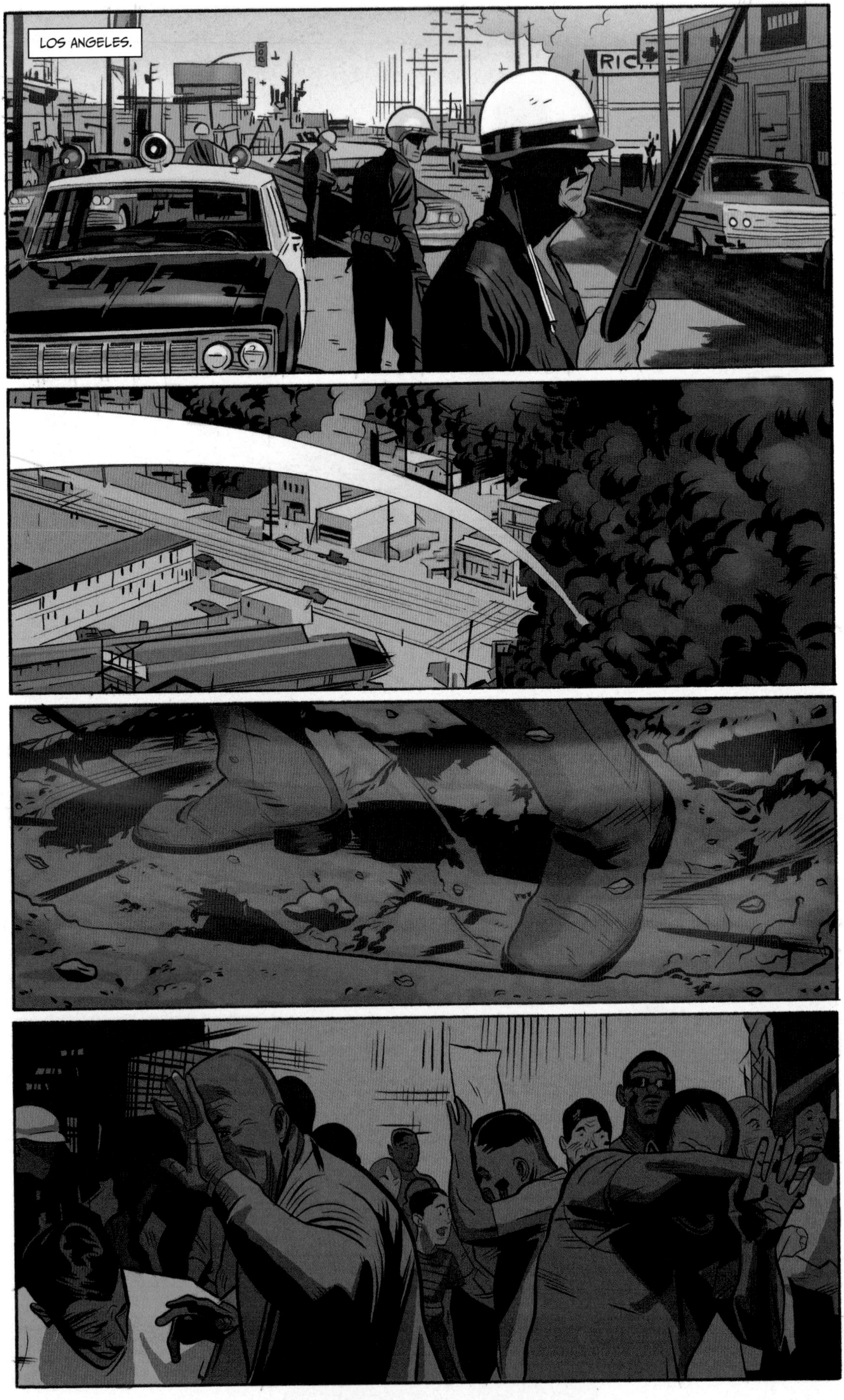
LOS ANGELES.
RIC

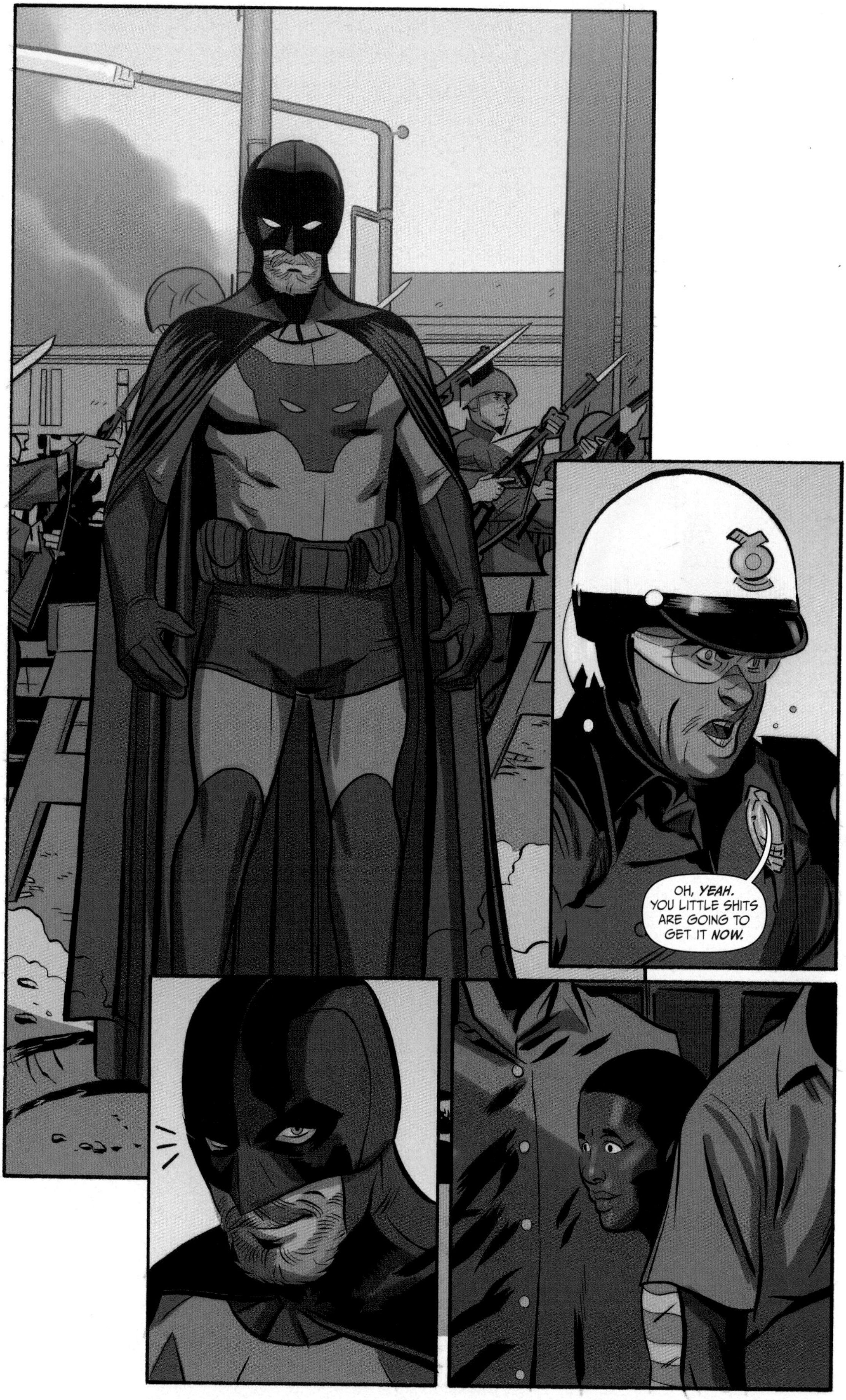
OH, *YEAH.* YOU LITTLE SHITS ARE GOING TO GET IT *NOW.*

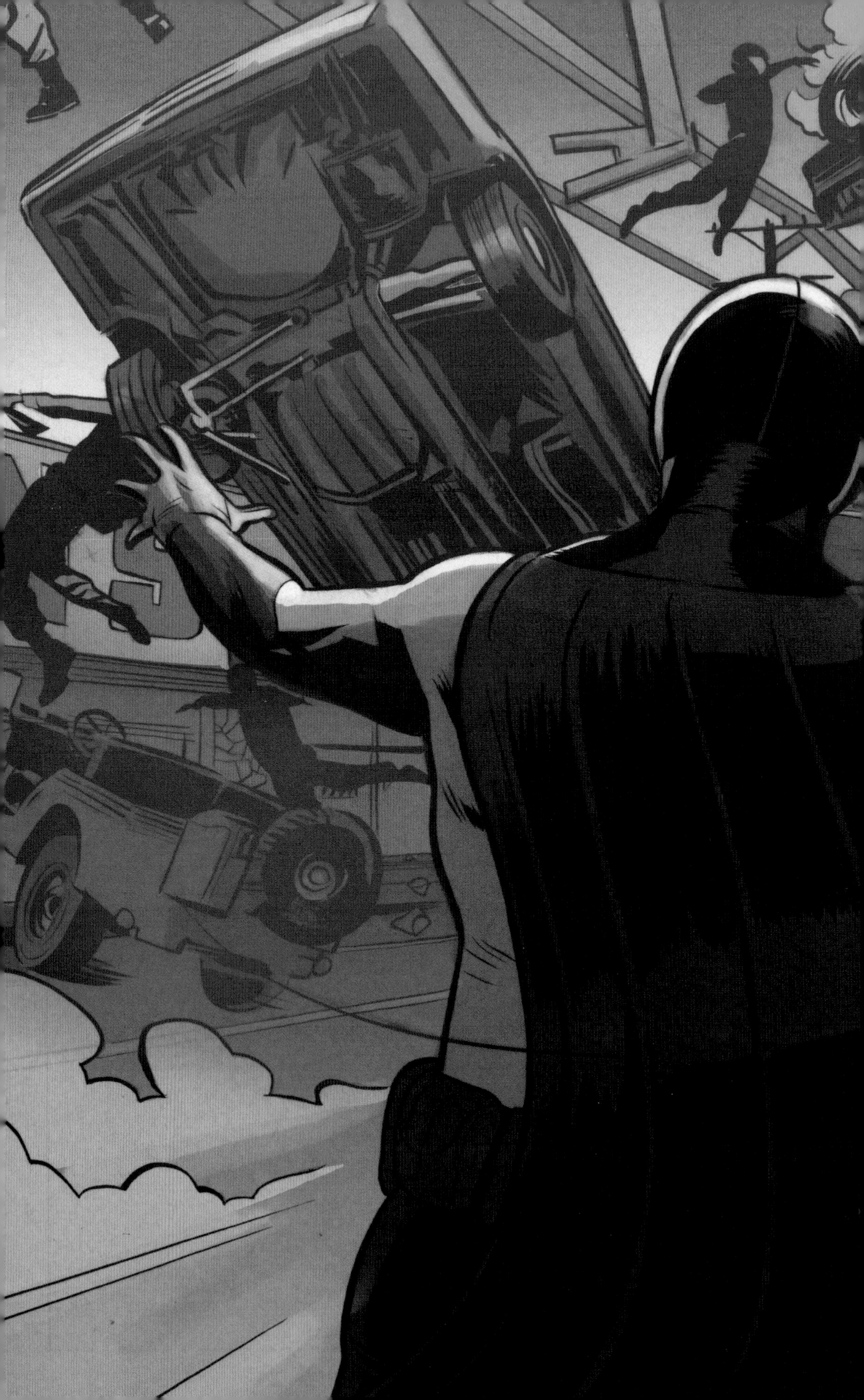

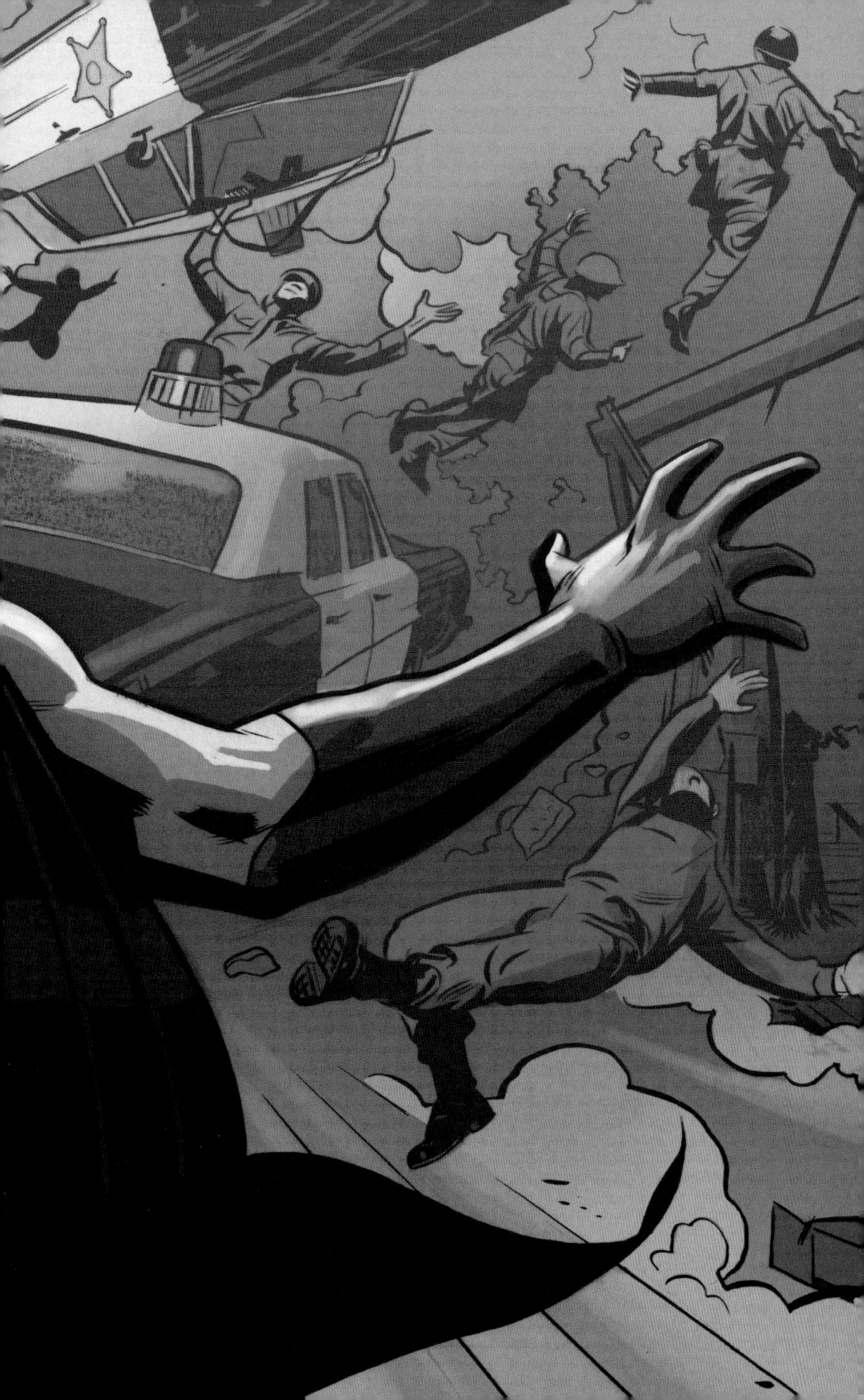

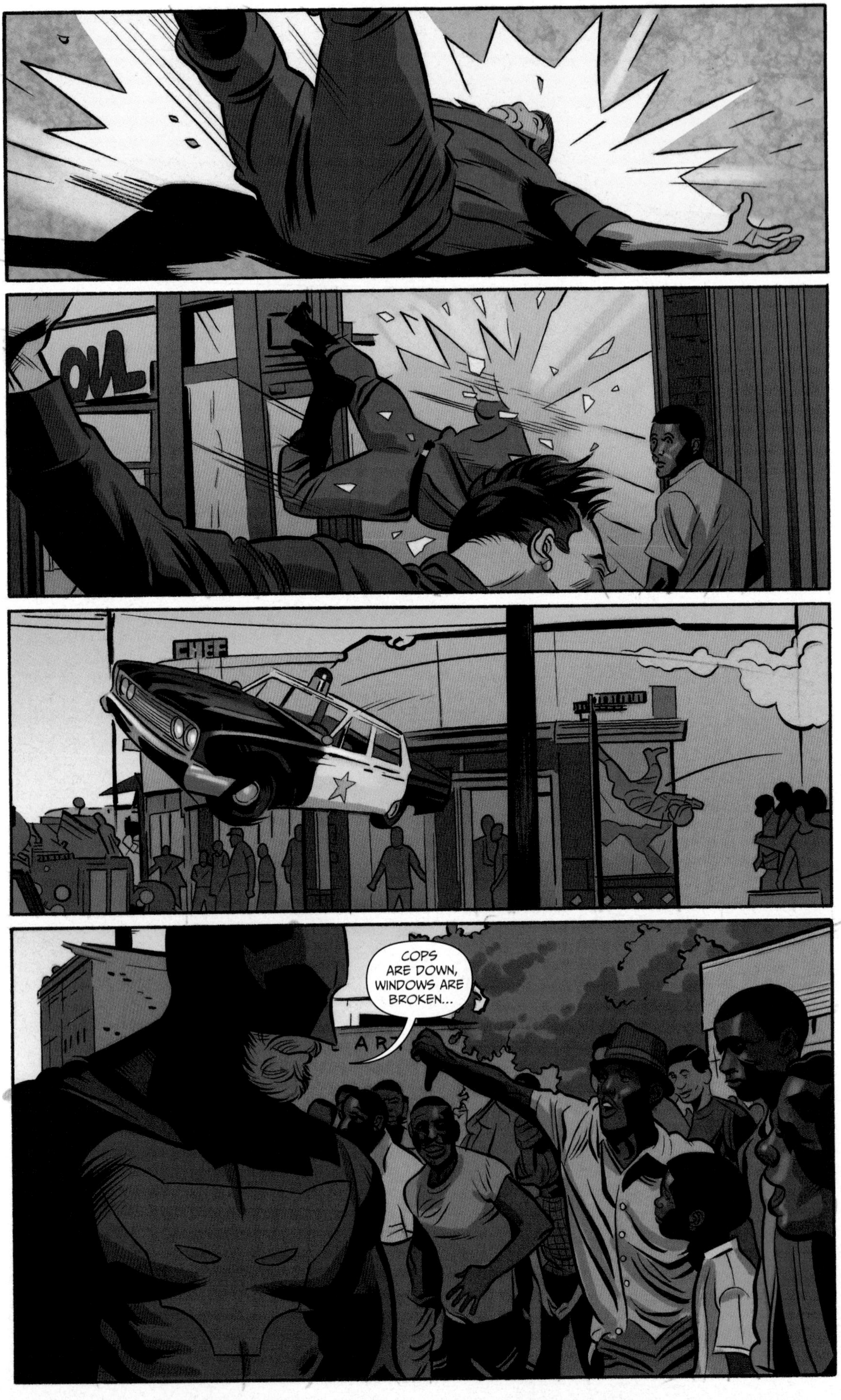
CHEF
COPS ARE DOWN, WINDOWS ARE BROKEN...

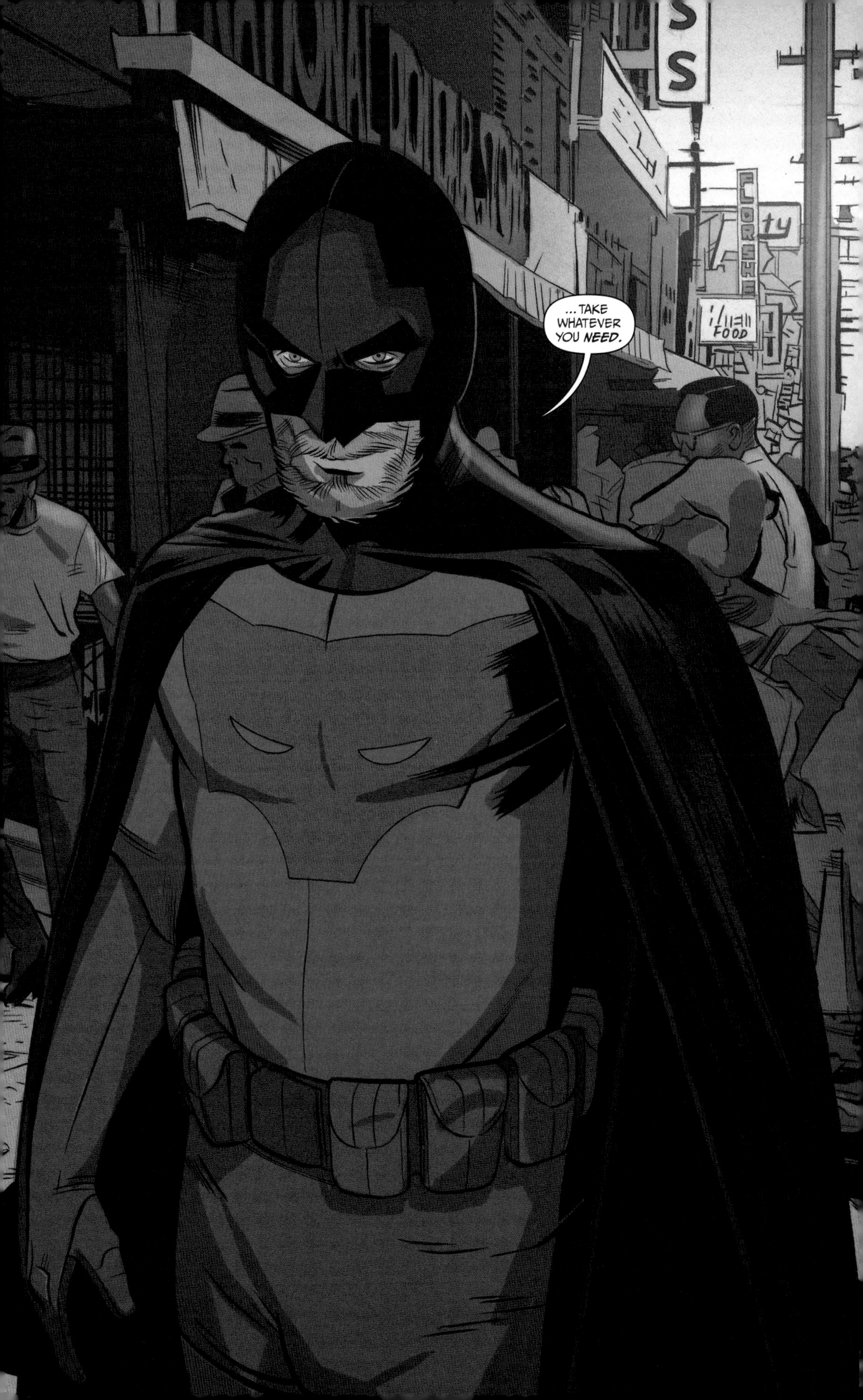
...TAKE WHATEVER YOU NEED.
FOOD

CHAPTER 3

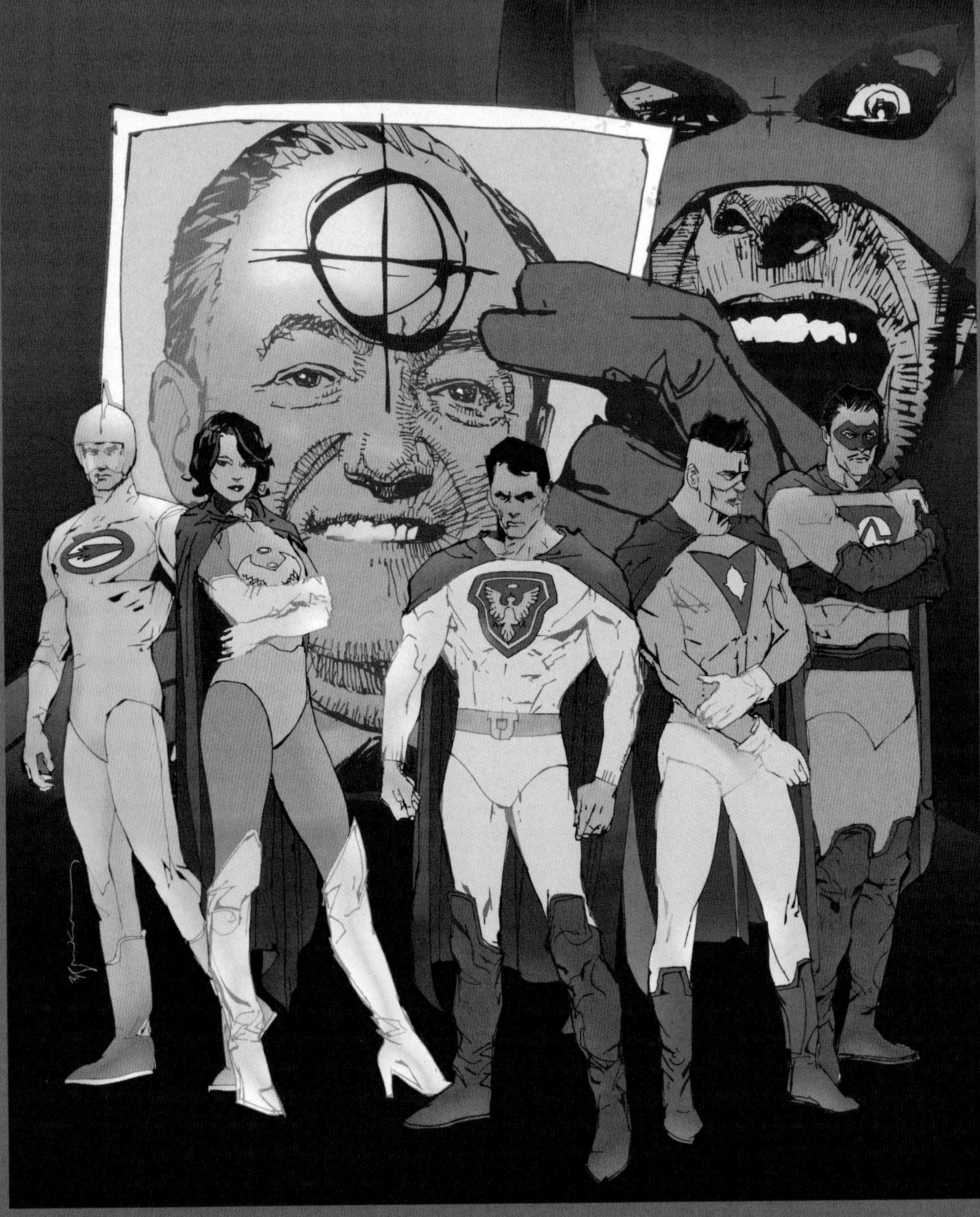

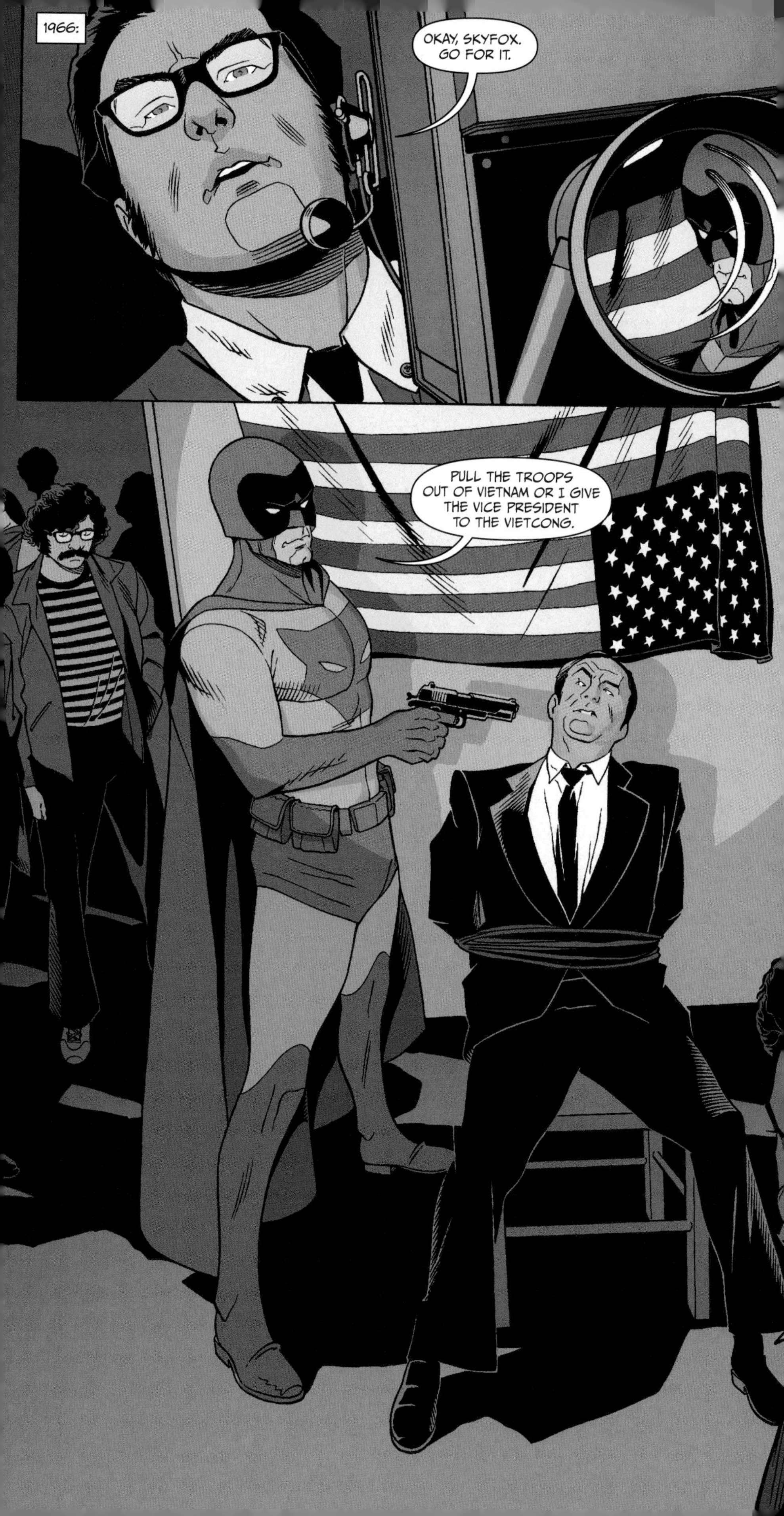
1966:
OKAY, SKYFOX. GO FOR IT.
PULL THE TROOPS OUT OF VIETNAM OR I GIVE THE VICE PRESIDENT TO THE VIETCONG.

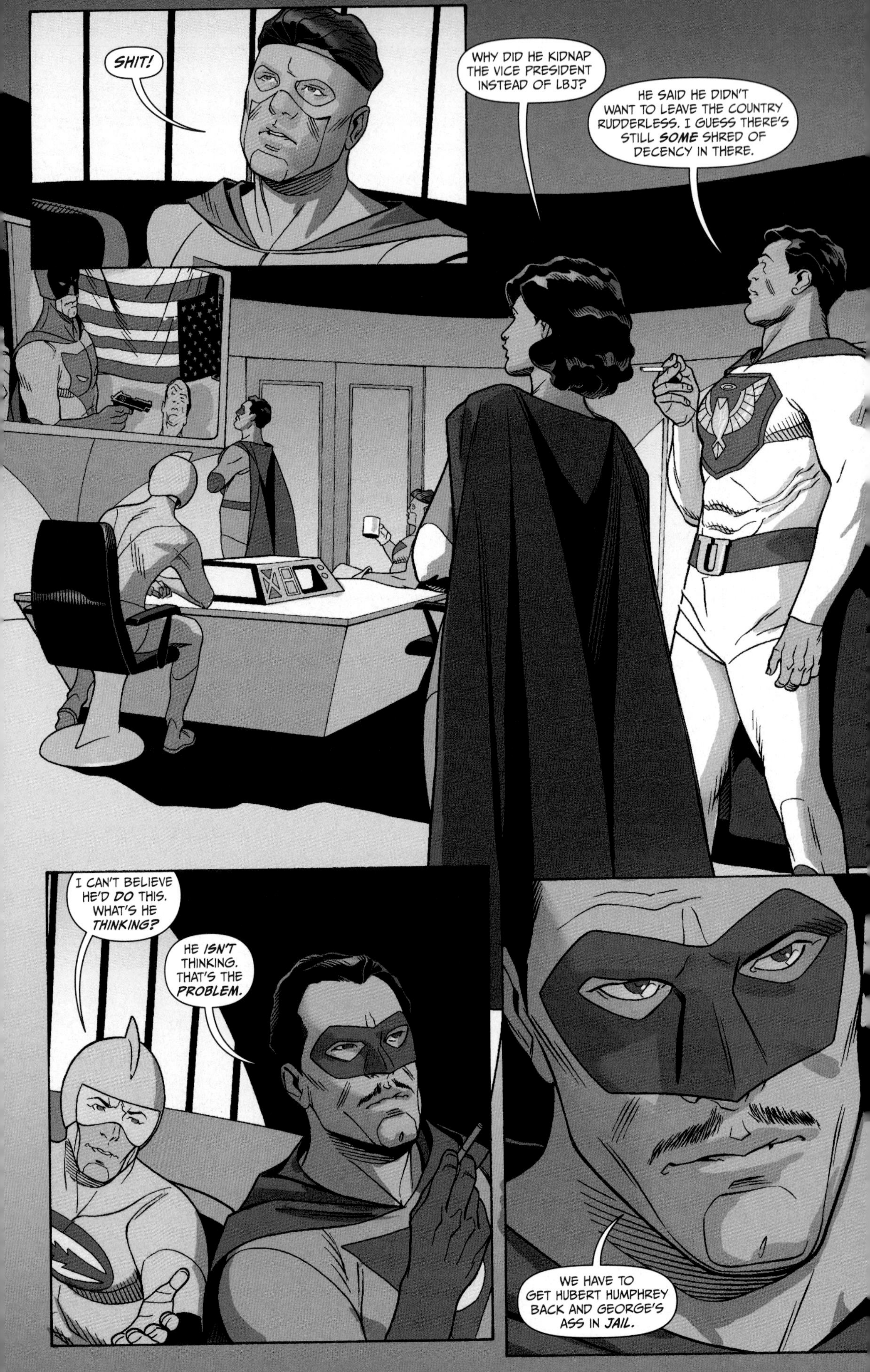

SHIT!
WHY DID HE KIDNAP THE VICE PRESIDENT INSTEAD OF LBJ?
HE SAID HE DIDN'T WANT TO LEAVE THE COUNTRY RUDDERLESS. I GUESS THERE'S STILL SOME SHRED OF DECENCY IN THERE.
I CAN'T BELIEVE HE'D DO THIS. WHAT'S HE THINKING?
HE ISN'T THINKING. THAT'S THE PROBLEM.
WE HAVE TO GET HUBERT HUMPHREY BACK AND GEORGE'S ASS IN JAIL.

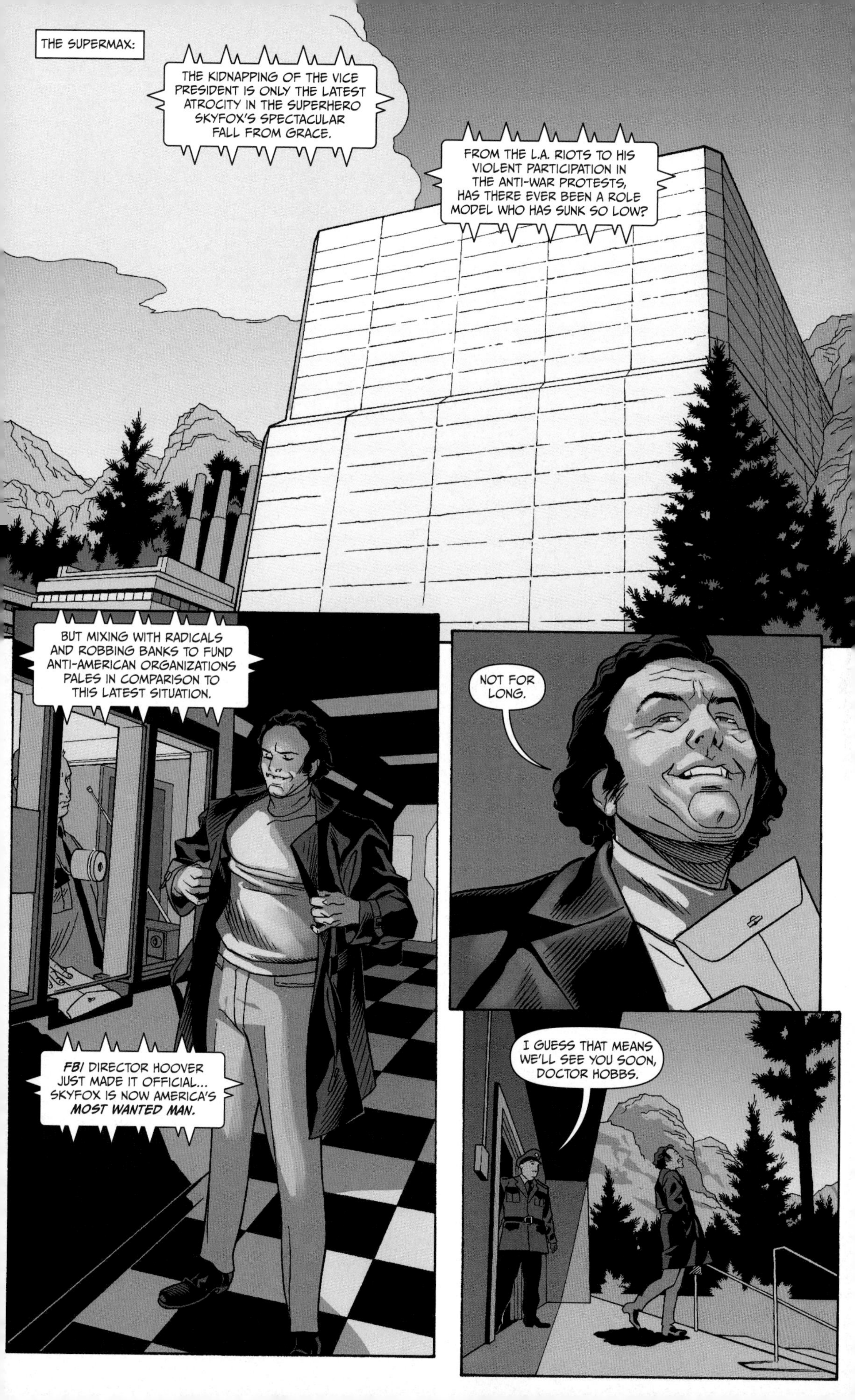

THE SUPERMAX:
THE KIDNAPPING OF THE VICE PRESIDENT IS ONLY THE LATEST ATROCITY IN THE SUPERHERO SKYFOX'S SPECTACULAR FALL FROM GRACE.
FROM THE L.A. RIOTS TO HIS VIOLENT PARTICIPATION IN THE ANTI-WAR PROTESTS, HAS THERE EVER BEEN A ROLE MODEL WHO HAS SUNK SO LOW?
BUT MIXING WITH RADICALS AND ROBBING BANKS TO FUND ANTI-AMERICAN ORGANIZATIONS PALES IN COMPARISON TO THIS LATEST SITUATION.
NOT FOR LONG.
FBI DIRECTOR HOOVER JUST MADE IT OFFICIAL... SKYFOX IS NOW AMERICA'S ***MOST WANTED MAN.***
I GUESS THAT MEANS WE'LL SEE YOU SOON, DOCTOR HOBBS.

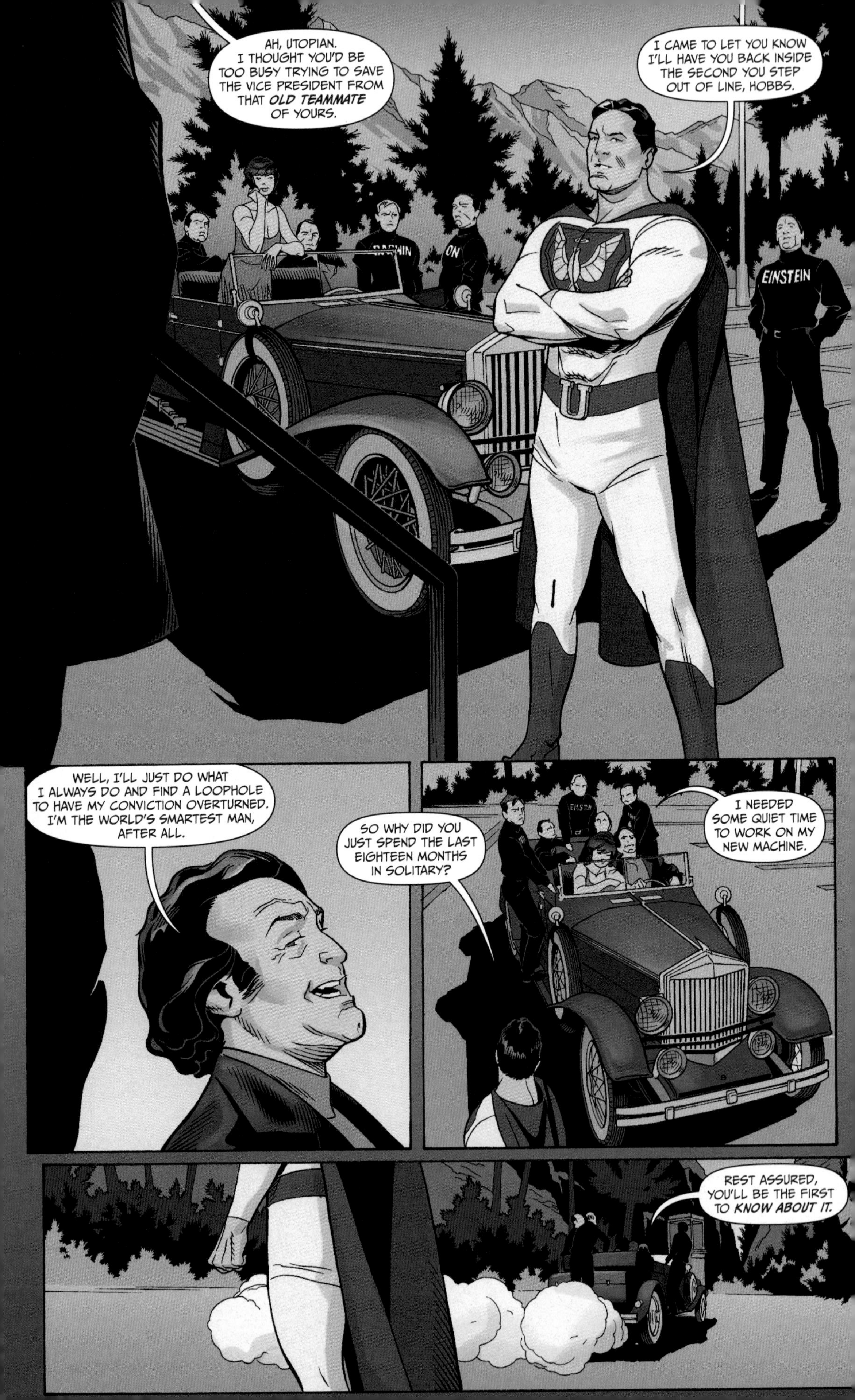

AH, UTOPIAN. I THOUGHT YOU'D BE TOO BUSY TRYING TO SAVE THE VICE PRESIDENT FROM THAT *OLD TEAMMATE* OF YOURS.
I CAME TO LET YOU KNOW I'LL HAVE YOU BACK INSIDE THE SECOND YOU STEP OUT OF LINE, HOBBS.
EINSTEIN
WELL, I'LL JUST DO WHAT I ALWAYS DO AND FIND A LOOPHOLE TO HAVE MY CONVICTION OVERTURNED. I'M THE WORLD'S SMARTEST MAN, AFTER ALL.
SO WHY DID YOU JUST SPEND THE LAST EIGHTEEN MONTHS IN SOLITARY?
I NEEDED SOME QUIET TIME TO WORK ON MY NEW MACHINE.
REST ASSURED, YOU'LL BE THE FIRST TO *KNOW ABOUT IT.*

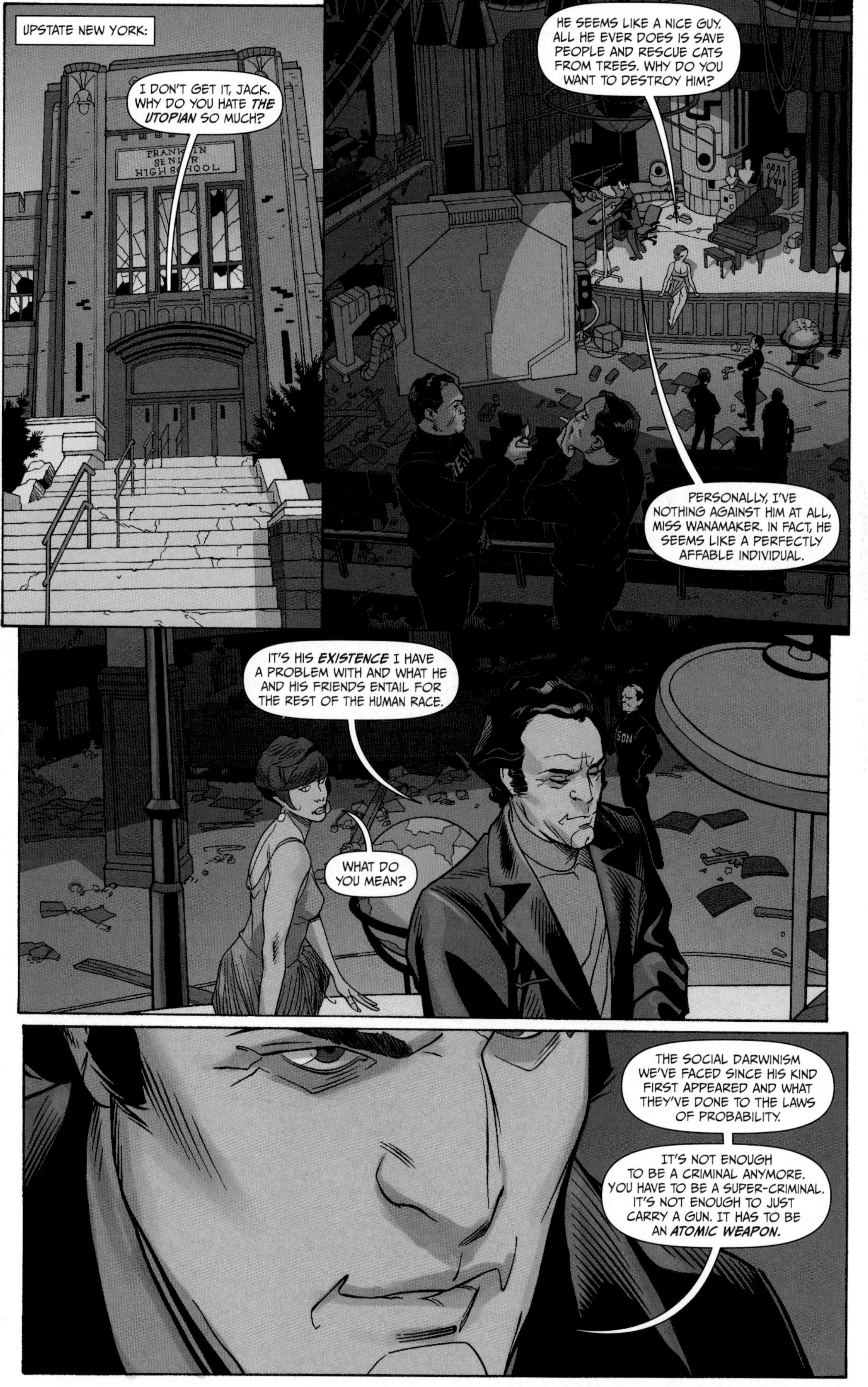
UPSTATE NEW YORK:
FRANKLIN SENDER HIGH SCHOOL
I DON'T GET IT, JACK. WHY DO YOU HATE ***THE UTOPIAN*** SO MUCH?
HE SEEMS LIKE A NICE GUY. ALL HE EVER DOES IS SAVE PEOPLE AND RESCUE CATS FROM TREES. WHY DO YOU WANT TO DESTROY HIM?
PERSONALLY, I'VE NOTHING AGAINST HIM AT ALL, MISS WANAMAKER. IN FACT, HE SEEMS LIKE A PERFECTLY AFFABLE INDIVIDUAL.
IT'S HIS ***EXISTENCE*** I HAVE A PROBLEM WITH AND WHAT HE AND HIS FRIENDS ENTAIL FOR THE REST OF THE HUMAN RACE.
WHAT DO YOU MEAN?
THE SOCIAL DARWINISM WE'VE FACED SINCE HIS KIND FIRST APPEARED AND WHAT THEY'VE DONE TO THE LAWS OF PROBABILITY.
IT'S NOT ENOUGH TO BE A CRIMINAL ANYMORE. YOU HAVE TO BE A SUPER-CRIMINAL. IT'S NOT ENOUGH TO JUST CARRY A GUN. IT HAS TO BE AN ***ATOMIC WEAPON.***

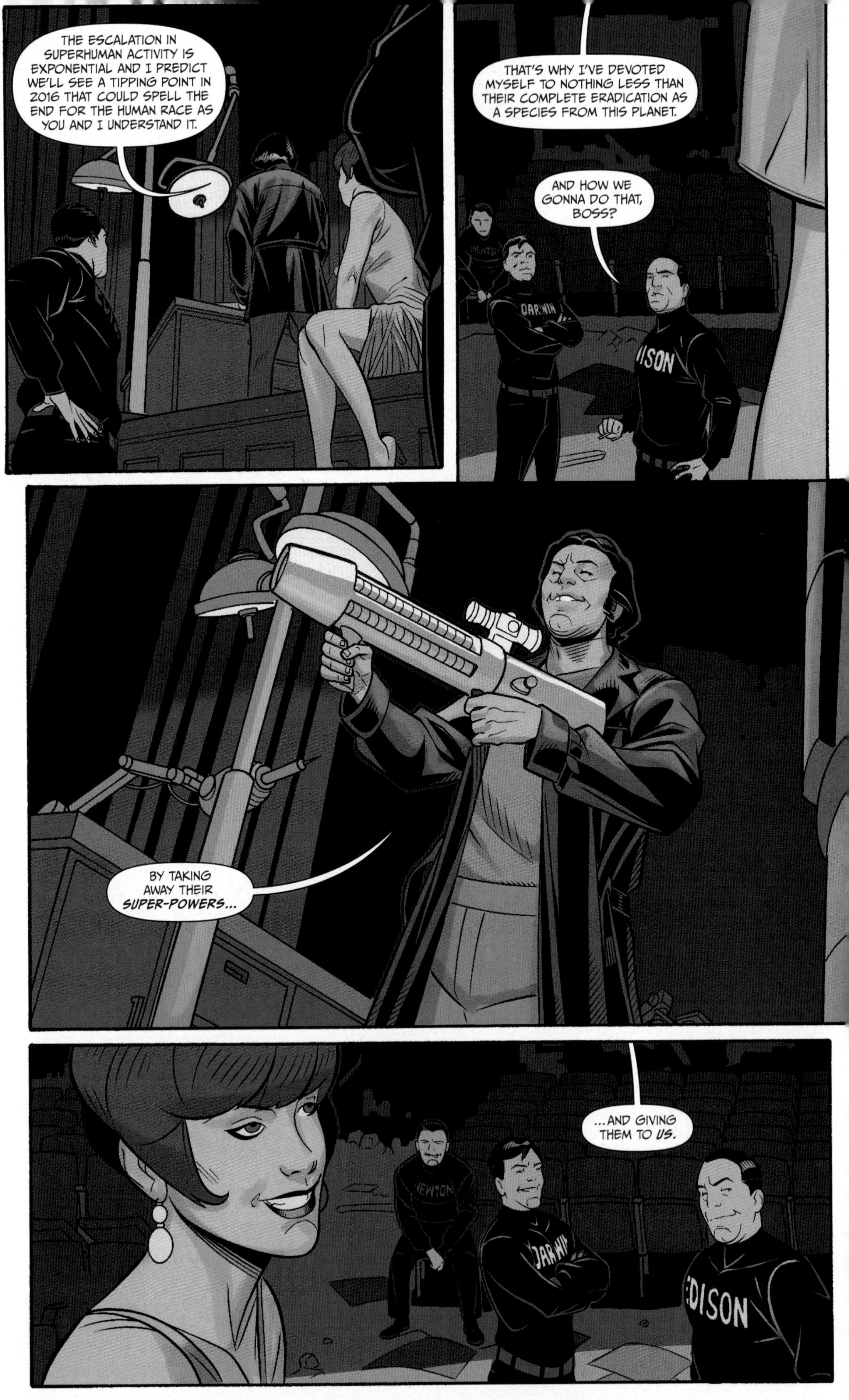
THE ESCALATION IN SUPERHUMAN ACTIVITY IS EXPONENTIAL AND I PREDICT WE'LL SEE A TIPPING POINT IN 2016 THAT COULD SPELL THE END FOR THE HUMAN RACE AS YOU AND I UNDERSTAND IT.
THAT'S WHY I'VE DEVOTED MYSELF TO NOTHING LESS THAN THEIR COMPLETE ERADICATION AS A SPECIES FROM THIS PLANET.
AND HOW WE GONNA DO THAT, BOSS?
DARWIN
ISON
BY TAKING AWAY THEIR SUPER-POWERS...
...AND GIVING THEM TO US.
NEWTON
DARWIN
EDISON

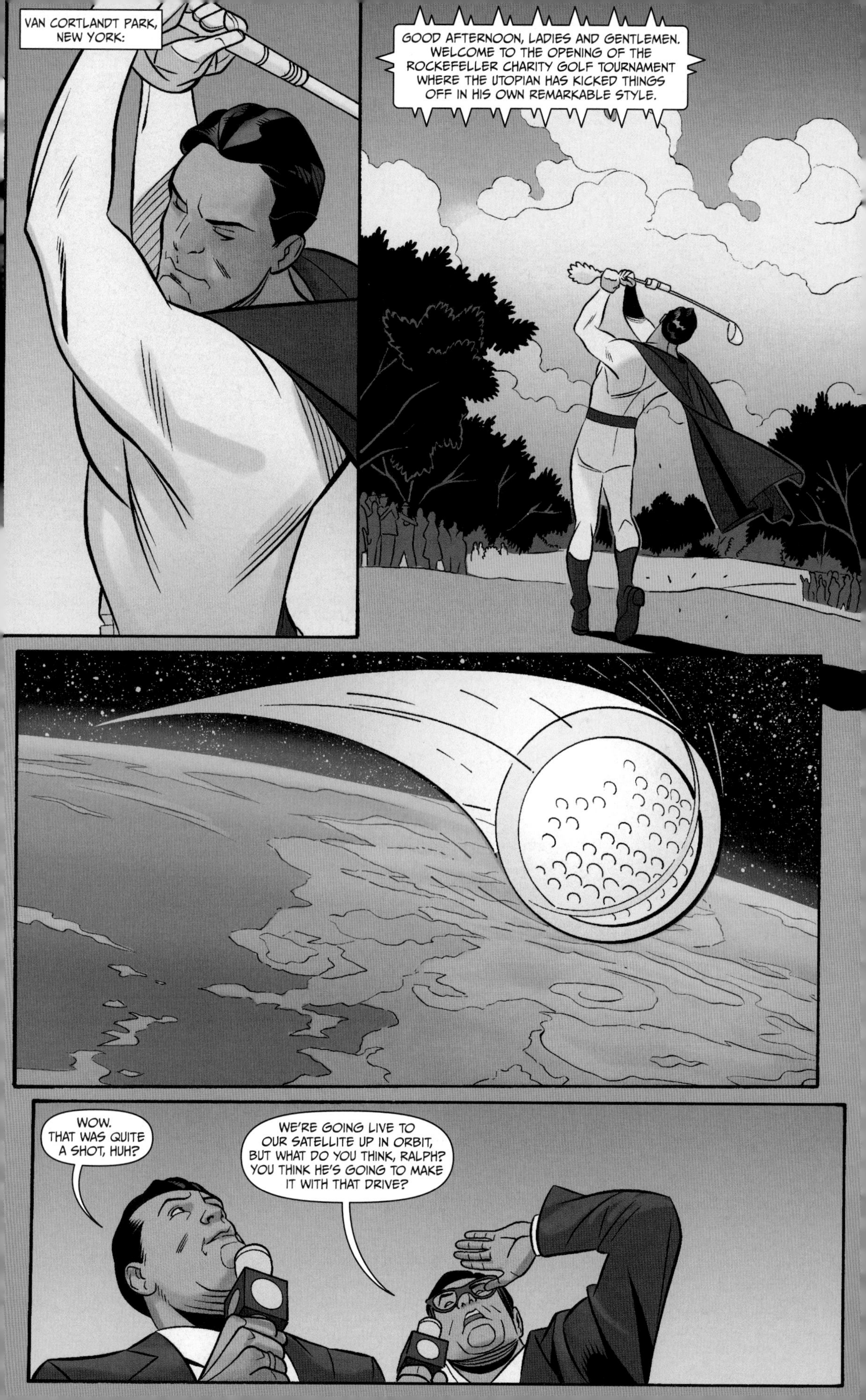
VAN CORTLANDT PARK, NEW YORK:
GOOD AFTERNOON, LADIES AND GENTLEMEN. WELCOME TO THE OPENING OF THE ROCKEFELLER CHARITY GOLF TOURNAMENT WHERE THE UTOPIAN HAS KICKED THINGS OFF IN HIS OWN REMARKABLE STYLE.
WOW. THAT WAS QUITE A SHOT, HUH?
WE'RE GOING LIVE TO OUR SATELLITE UP IN ORBIT, BUT WHAT DO YOU THINK, RALPH? YOU THINK HE'S GOING TO MAKE IT WITH THAT DRIVE?

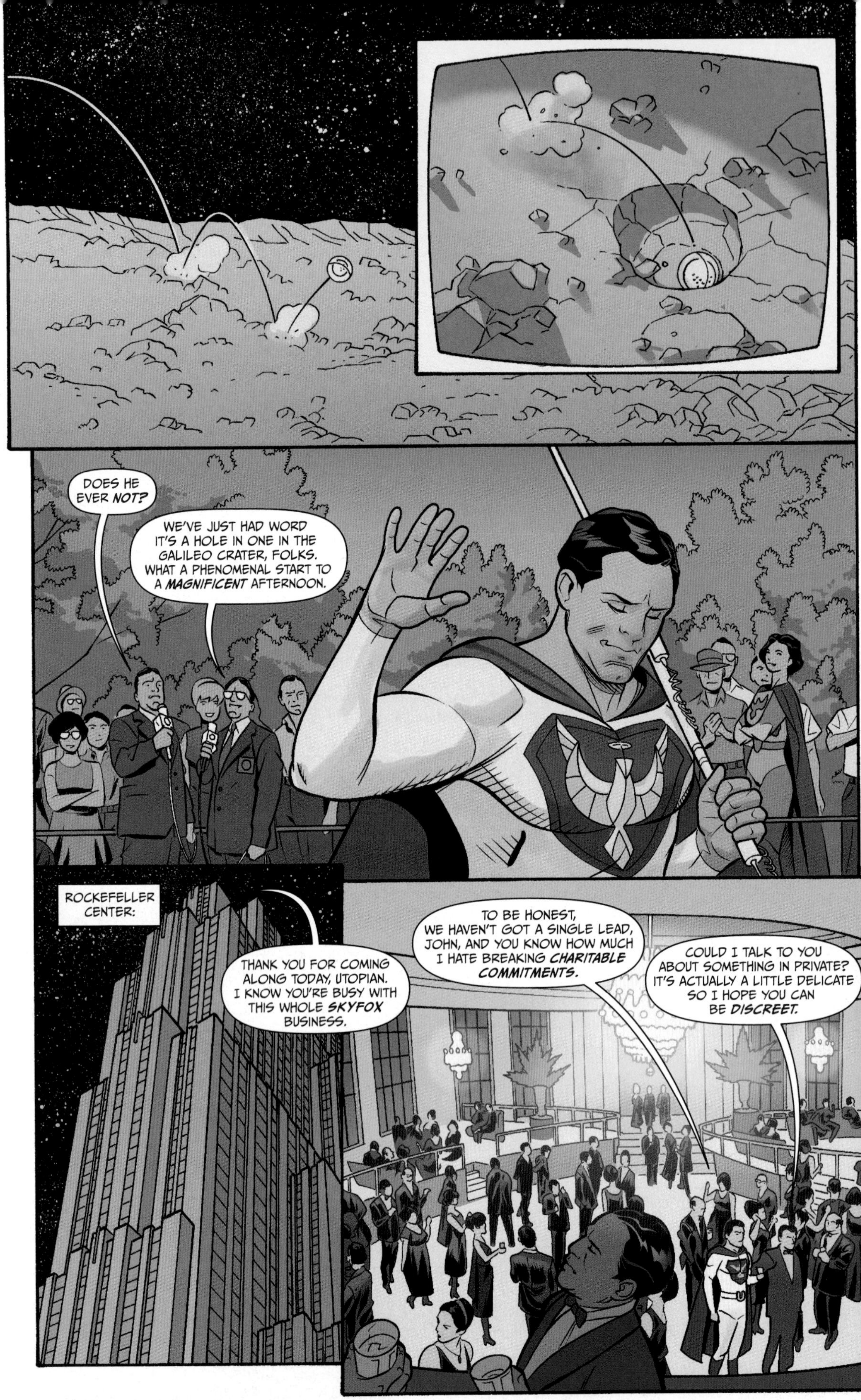
DOES HE EVER *NOT?*
WE'VE JUST HAD WORD IT'S A HOLE IN ONE IN THE GALILEO CRATER, FOLKS. WHAT A PHENOMENAL START TO A *MAGNIFICENT* AFTERNOON.
ROCKEFELLER CENTER:
THANK YOU FOR COMING ALONG TODAY, UTOPIAN. I KNOW YOU'RE BUSY WITH THIS WHOLE *SKYFOX* BUSINESS.
TO BE HONEST, WE HAVEN'T GOT A SINGLE LEAD, JOHN, AND YOU KNOW HOW MUCH I HATE BREAKING *CHARITABLE COMMITMENTS.*
COULD I TALK TO YOU ABOUT SOMETHING IN PRIVATE? IT'S ACTUALLY A LITTLE DELICATE SO I HOPE YOU CAN BE *DISCREET.*

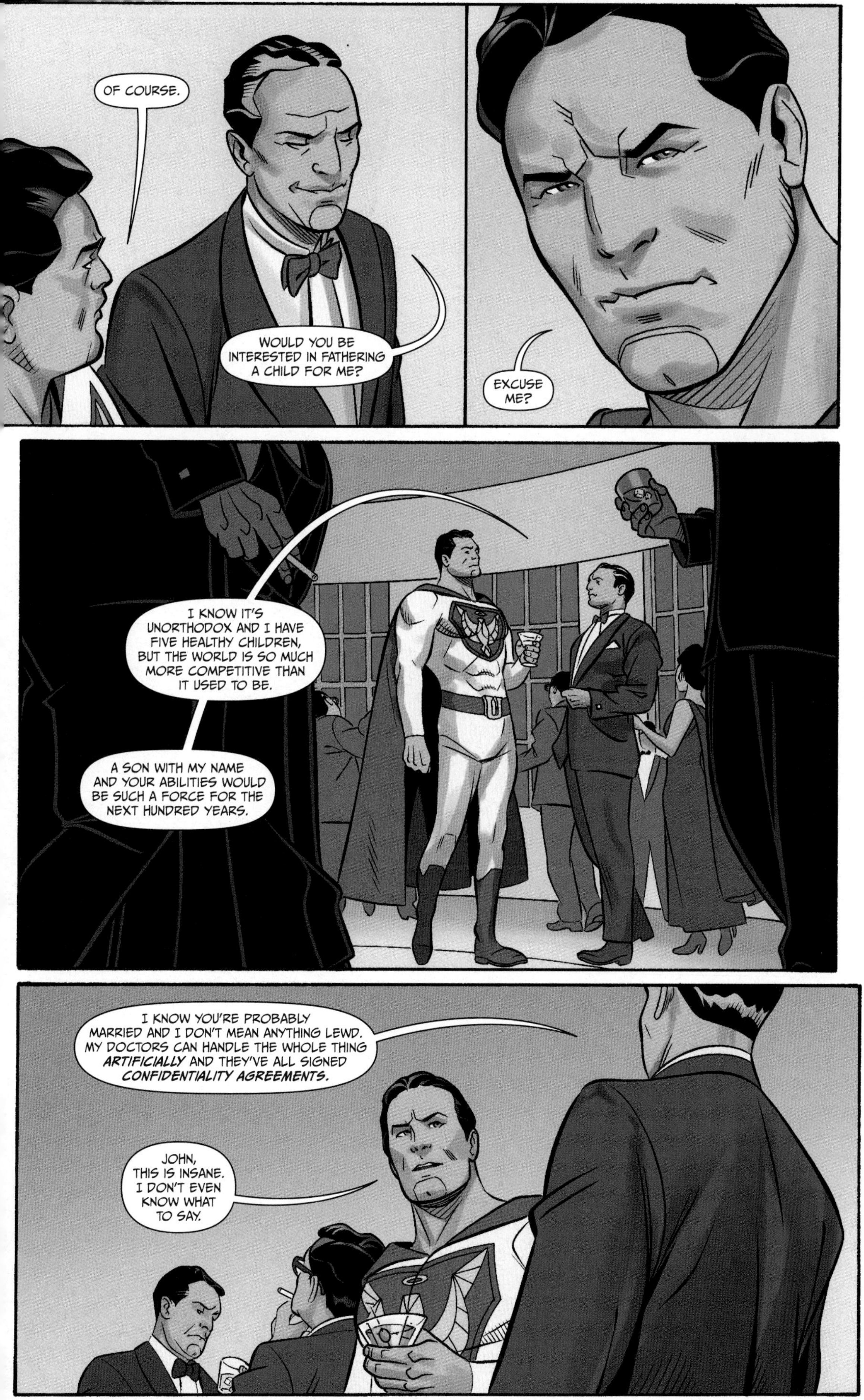
OF COURSE.
WOULD YOU BE INTERESTED IN FATHERING A CHILD FOR ME?
EXCUSE ME?
I KNOW IT'S UNORTHODOX AND I HAVE FIVE HEALTHY CHILDREN, BUT THE WORLD IS SO MUCH MORE COMPETITIVE THAN IT USED TO BE.
A SON WITH MY NAME AND YOUR ABILITIES WOULD BE SUCH A FORCE FOR THE NEXT HUNDRED YEARS.
I KNOW YOU'RE PROBABLY MARRIED AND I DON'T MEAN ANYTHING LEWD. MY DOCTORS CAN HANDLE THE WHOLE THING *ARTIFICIALLY* AND THEY'VE ALL SIGNED *CONFIDENTIALITY AGREEMENTS.*
JOHN, THIS IS INSANE. I DON'T EVEN KNOW WHAT TO SAY.

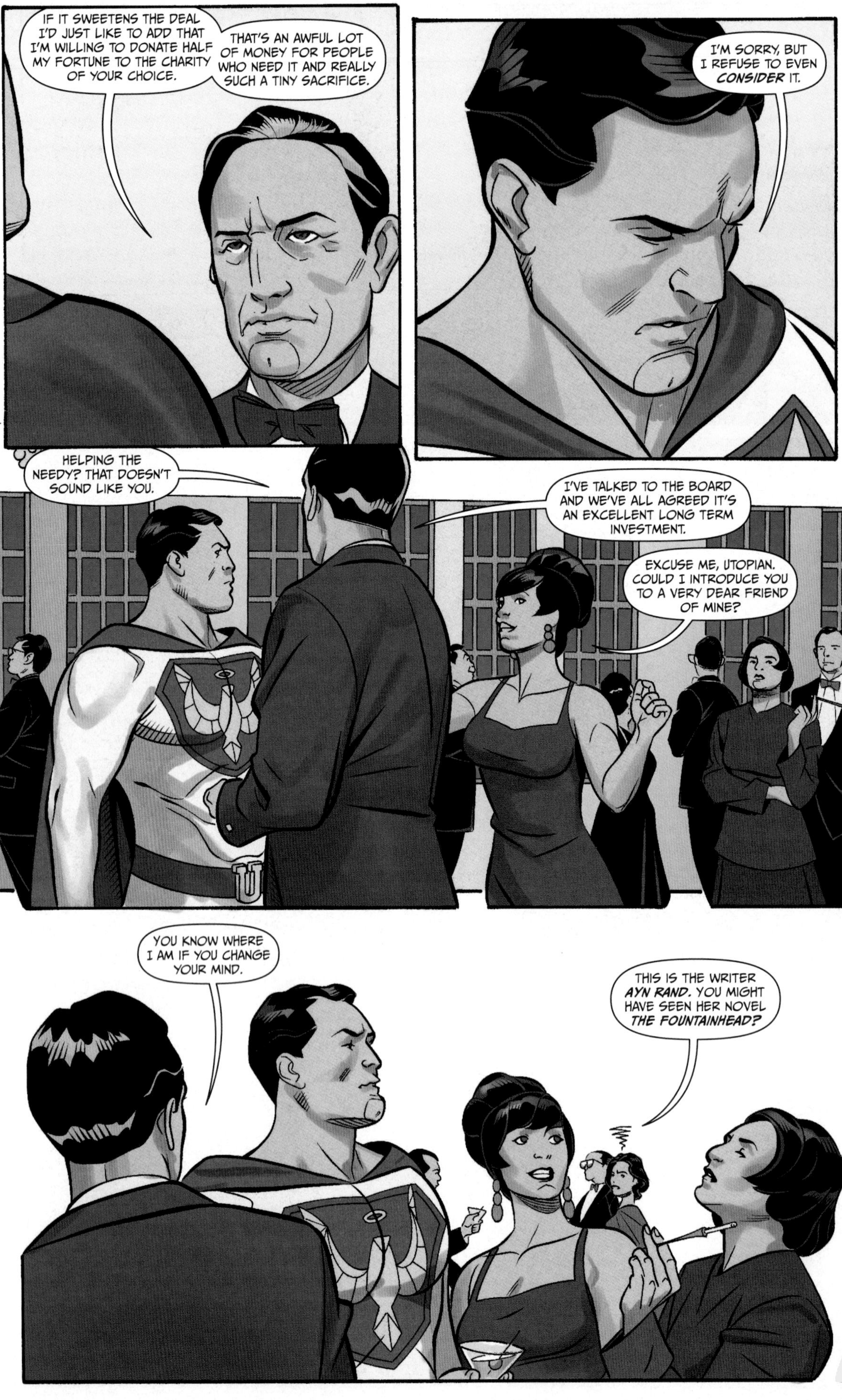
IF IT SWEETENS THE DEAL I'D JUST LIKE TO ADD THAT I'M WILLING TO DONATE HALF MY FORTUNE TO THE CHARITY OF YOUR CHOICE.
THAT'S AN AWFUL LOT OF MONEY FOR PEOPLE WHO NEED IT AND REALLY SUCH A TINY SACRIFICE.
I'M SORRY, BUT I REFUSE TO EVEN ***CONSIDER*** IT.
HELPING THE NEEDY? THAT DOESN'T SOUND LIKE YOU.
I'VE TALKED TO THE BOARD AND WE'VE ALL AGREED IT'S AN EXCELLENT LONG TERM INVESTMENT.
EXCUSE ME, UTOPIAN. COULD I INTRODUCE YOU TO A VERY DEAR FRIEND OF MINE?
YOU KNOW WHERE I AM IF YOU CHANGE YOUR MIND.
THIS IS THE WRITER ***AYN RAND.*** YOU MIGHT HAVE SEEN HER NOVEL ***THE FOUNTAINHEAD?***

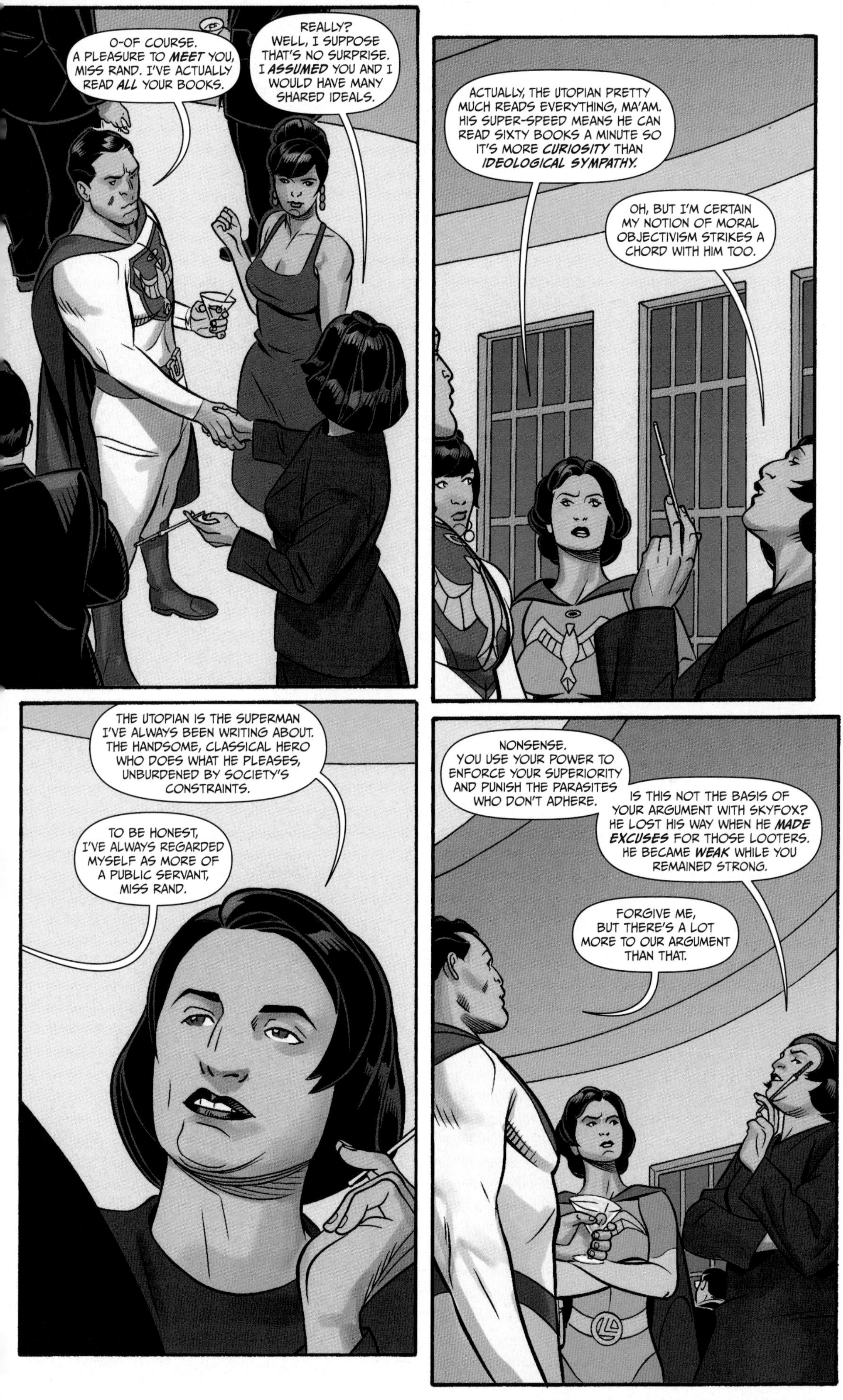
O-OF COURSE. A PLEASURE TO MEET YOU, MISS RAND. I'VE ACTUALLY READ ALL YOUR BOOKS.
REALLY? WELL, I SUPPOSE THAT'S NO SURPRISE. I ASSUMED YOU AND I WOULD HAVE MANY SHARED IDEALS.
ACTUALLY, THE UTOPIAN PRETTY MUCH READS EVERYTHING, MA'AM. HIS SUPER-SPEED MEANS HE CAN READ SIXTY BOOKS A MINUTE SO IT'S MORE CURIOSITY THAN IDEOLOGICAL SYMPATHY.
OH, BUT I'M CERTAIN MY NOTION OF MORAL OBJECTIVISM STRIKES A CHORD WITH HIM TOO.
THE UTOPIAN IS THE SUPERMAN I'VE ALWAYS BEEN WRITING ABOUT. THE HANDSOME, CLASSICAL HERO WHO DOES WHAT HE PLEASES, UNBURDENED BY SOCIETY'S CONSTRAINTS.
TO BE HONEST, I'VE ALWAYS REGARDED MYSELF AS MORE OF A PUBLIC SERVANT, MISS RAND.
NONSENSE. YOU USE YOUR POWER TO ENFORCE YOUR SUPERIORITY AND PUNISH THE PARASITES WHO DON'T ADHERE.
IS THIS NOT THE BASIS OF YOUR ARGUMENT WITH SKYFOX? HE LOST HIS WAY WHEN HE MADE EXCUSES FOR THOSE LOOTERS. HE BECAME WEAK WHILE YOU REMAINED STRONG.
FORGIVE ME, BUT THERE'S A LOT MORE TO OUR ARGUMENT THAN THAT.

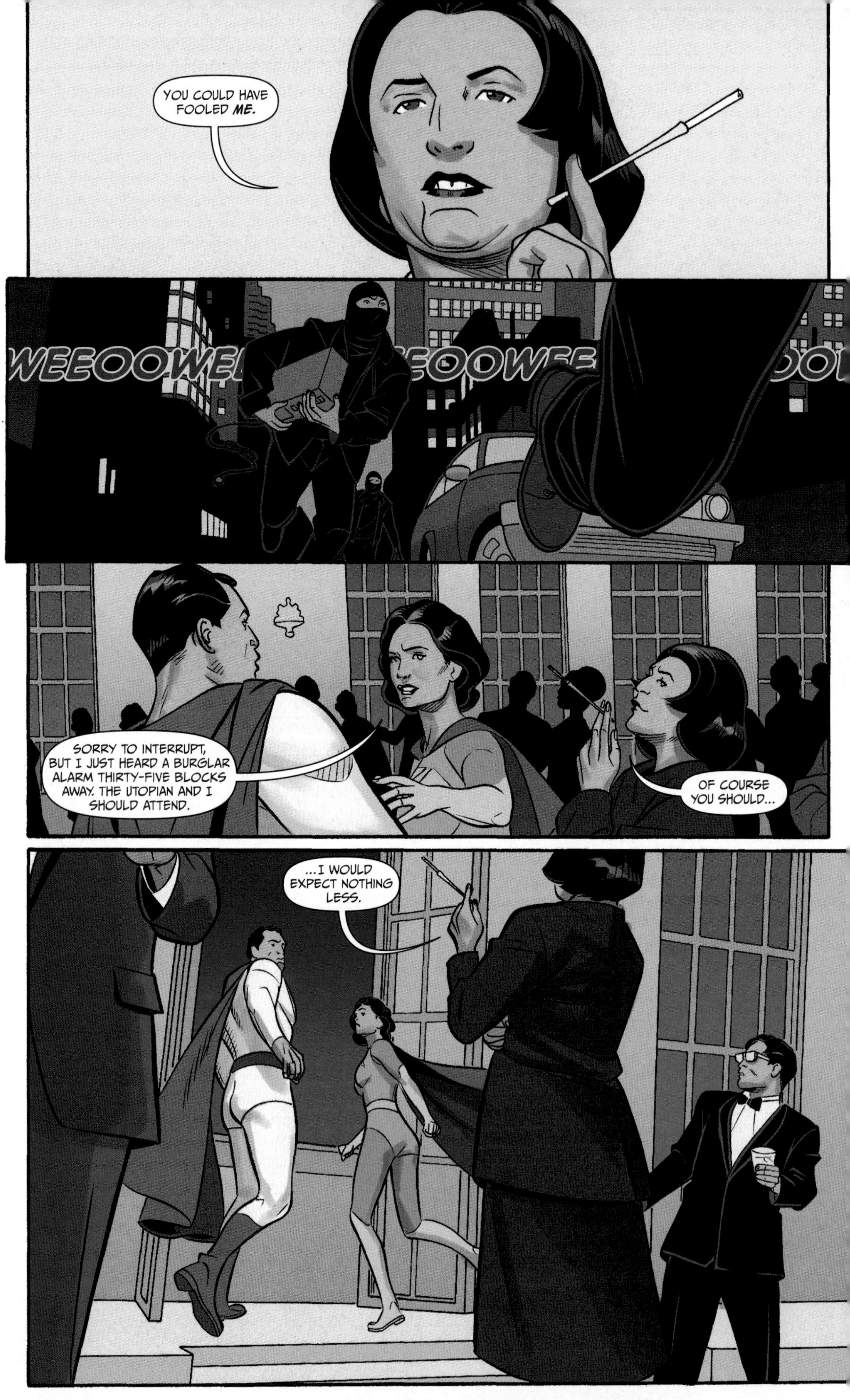
YOU COULD HAVE FOOLED ME.
WEEOOWEE
SORRY TO INTERRUPT, BUT I JUST HEARD A BURGLAR ALARM THIRTY-FIVE BLOCKS AWAY. THE UTOPIAN AND I SHOULD ATTEND.
OF COURSE YOU SHOULD...
...I WOULD EXPECT NOTHING LESS.

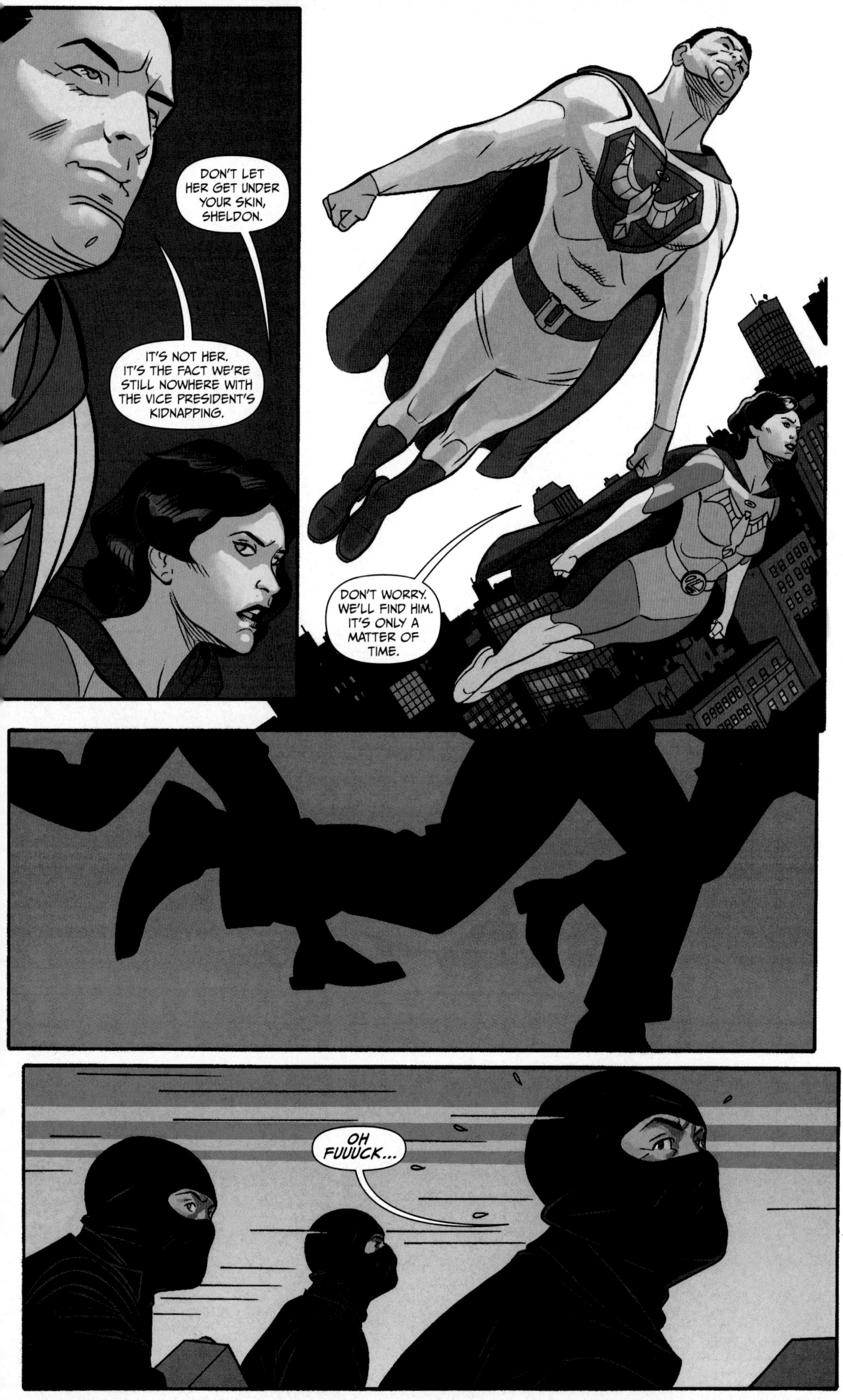
DON'T LET HER GET UNDER YOUR SKIN, SHELDON.
IT'S NOT HER. IT'S THE FACT WE'RE STILL NOWHERE WITH THE VICE PRESIDENT'S KIDNAPPING.
DON'T WORRY. WE'LL FIND HIM. IT'S ONLY A MATTER OF TIME.
OH FUUUCK...

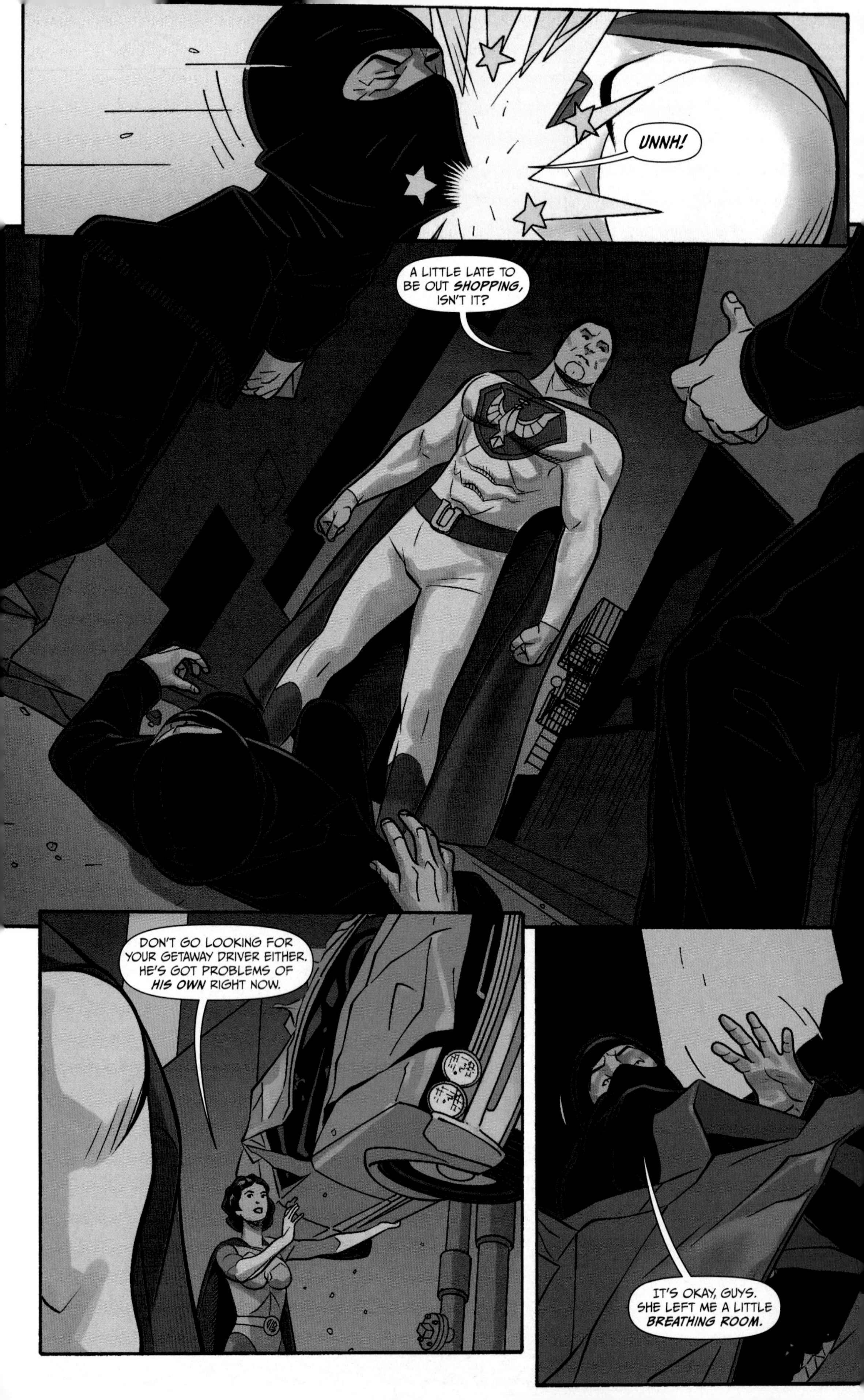
UNNH!
A LITTLE LATE TO BE OUT SHOPPING, ISN'T IT?
DON'T GO LOOKING FOR YOUR GETAWAY DRIVER EITHER. HE'S GOT PROBLEMS OF HIS OWN RIGHT NOW.
IT'S OKAY, GUYS. SHE LEFT ME A LITTLE BREATHING ROOM.

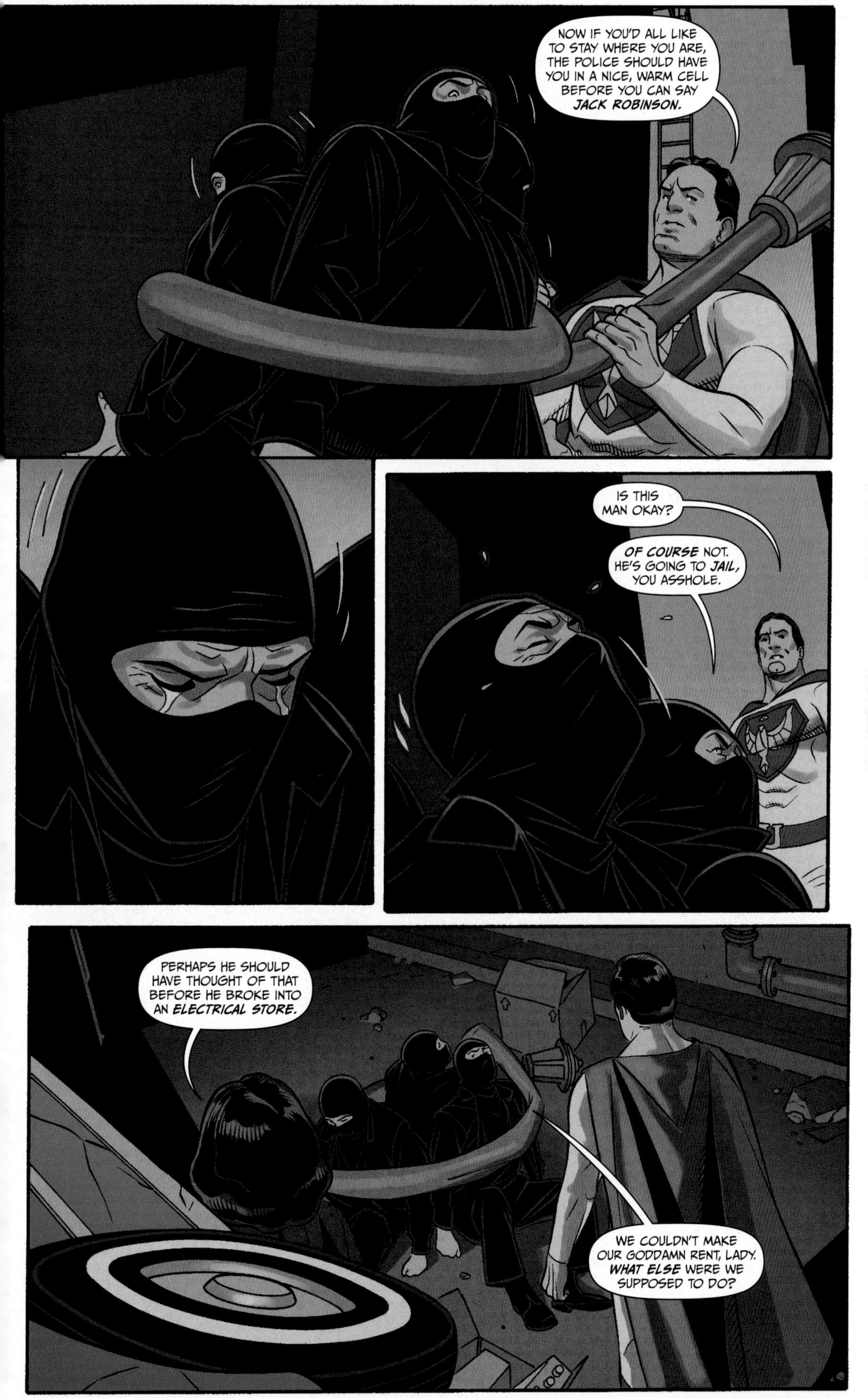
NOW IF YOU'D ALL LIKE TO STAY WHERE YOU ARE, THE POLICE SHOULD HAVE YOU IN A NICE, WARM CELL BEFORE YOU CAN SAY ***JACK ROBINSON.***
IS THIS MAN OKAY?
OF COURSE NOT. HE'S GOING TO ***JAIL,*** YOU ASSHOLE.
PERHAPS HE SHOULD HAVE THOUGHT OF THAT BEFORE HE BROKE INTO AN ***ELECTRICAL STORE.***
WE COULDN'T MAKE OUR GODDAMN RENT, LADY. ***WHAT ELSE*** WERE WE SUPPOSED TO DO?

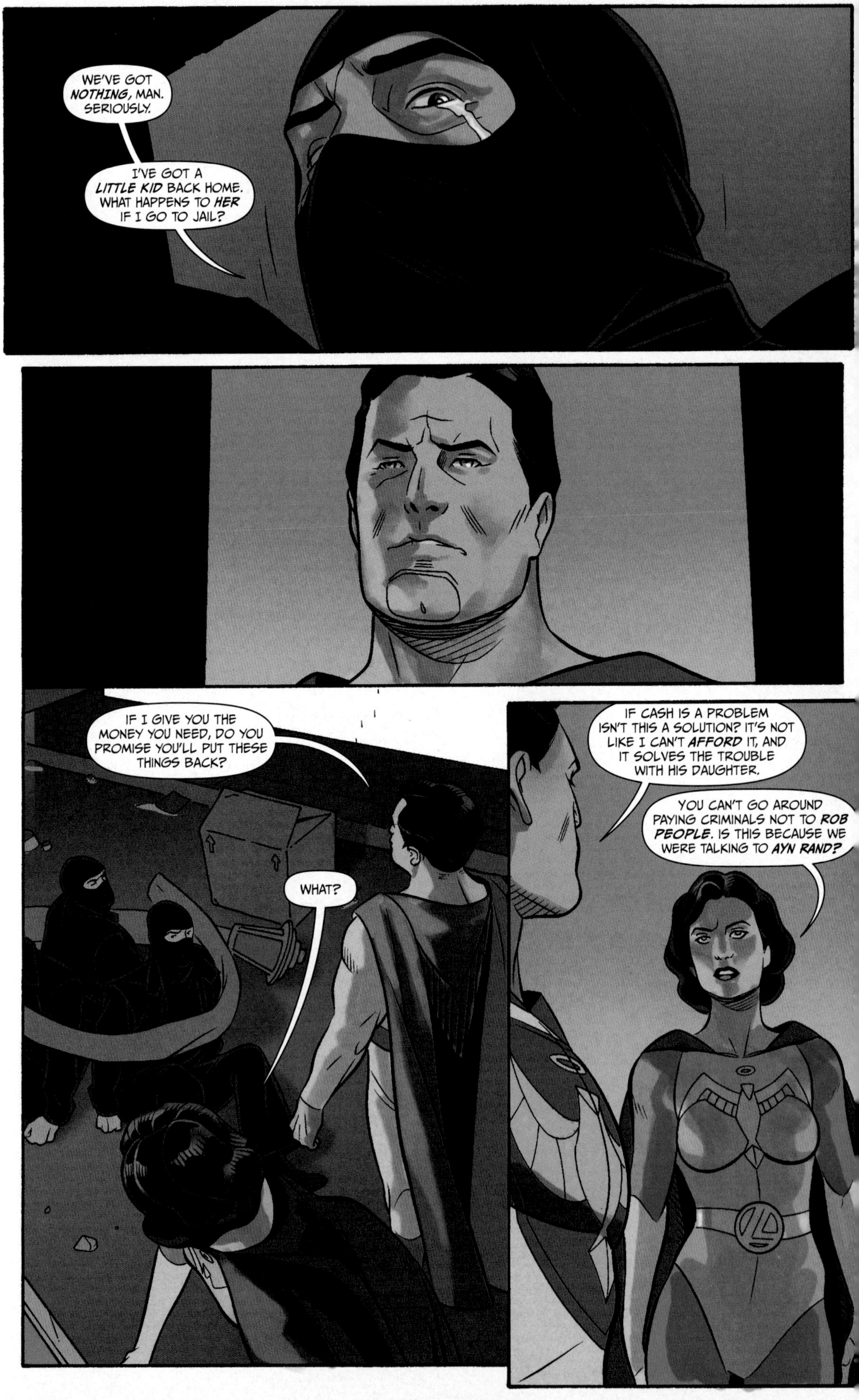
WE'VE GOT NOTHING, MAN. SERIOUSLY.
I'VE GOT A LITTLE KID BACK HOME. WHAT HAPPENS TO HER IF I GO TO JAIL?
IF I GIVE YOU THE MONEY YOU NEED, DO YOU PROMISE YOU'LL PUT THESE THINGS BACK?
WHAT?
IF CASH IS A PROBLEM ISN'T THIS A SOLUTION? IT'S NOT LIKE I CAN'T AFFORD IT, AND IT SOLVES THE TROUBLE WITH HIS DAUGHTER.
YOU CAN'T GO AROUND PAYING CRIMINALS NOT TO ROB PEOPLE. IS THIS BECAUSE WE WERE TALKING TO AYN RAND?

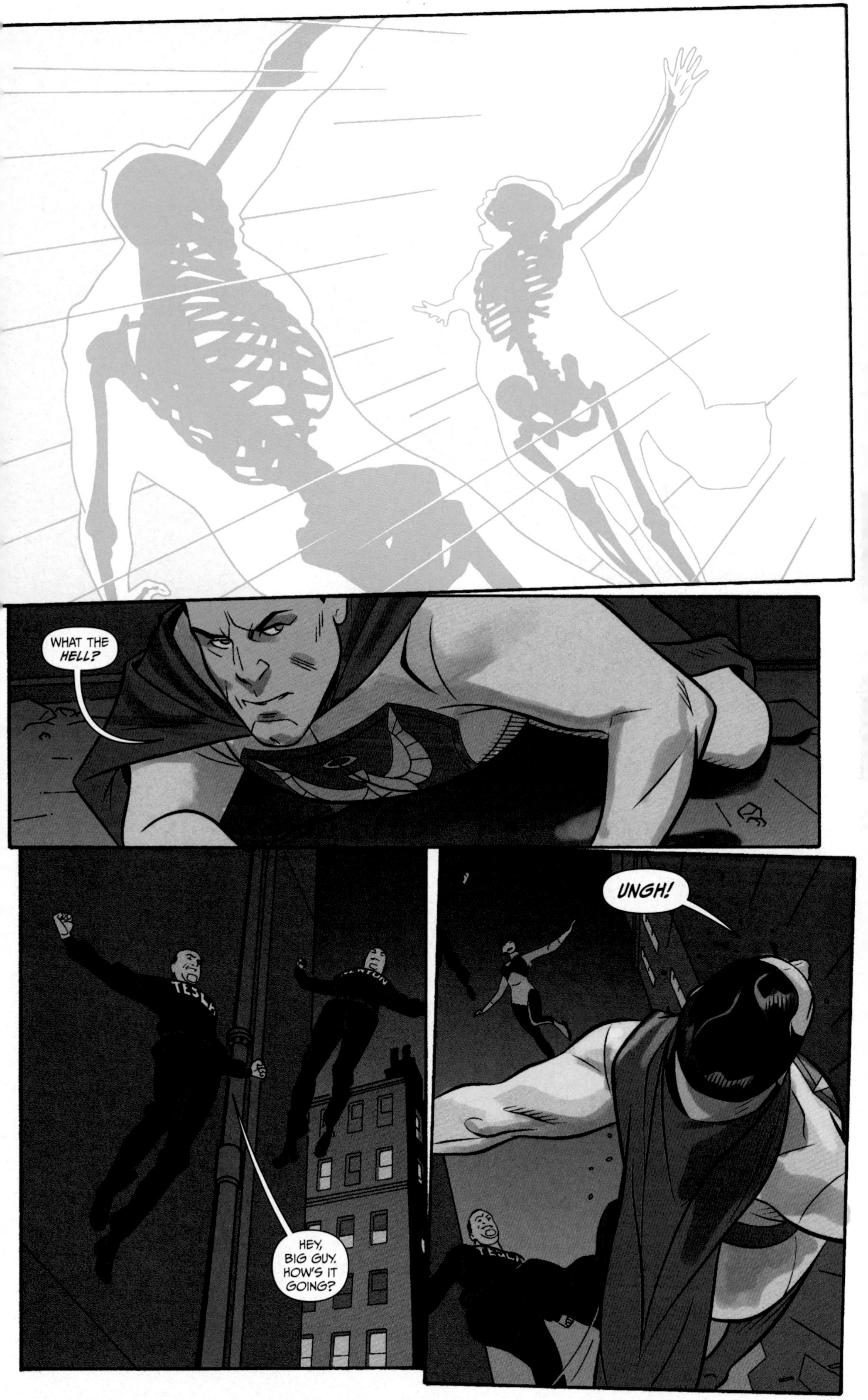
WHAT THE HELL?
HEY, BIG GUY. HOW'S IT GOING?
UNGH!

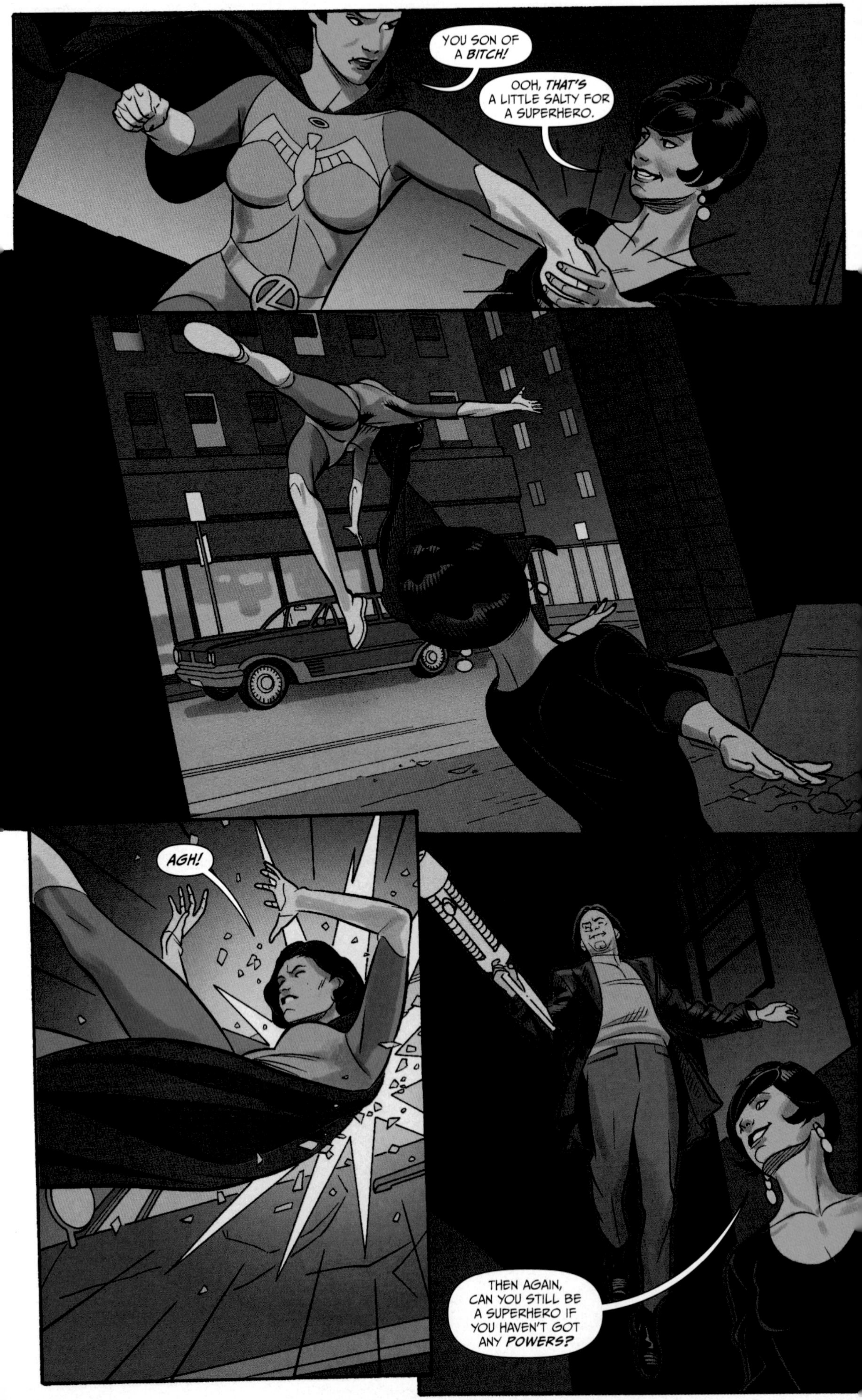
YOU SON OF A *BITCH!*
OOH, *THAT'S* A LITTLE SALTY FOR A SUPERHERO.
AGH!
THEN AGAIN, CAN YOU STILL BE A SUPERHERO IF YOU HAVEN'T GOT ANY *POWERS?*

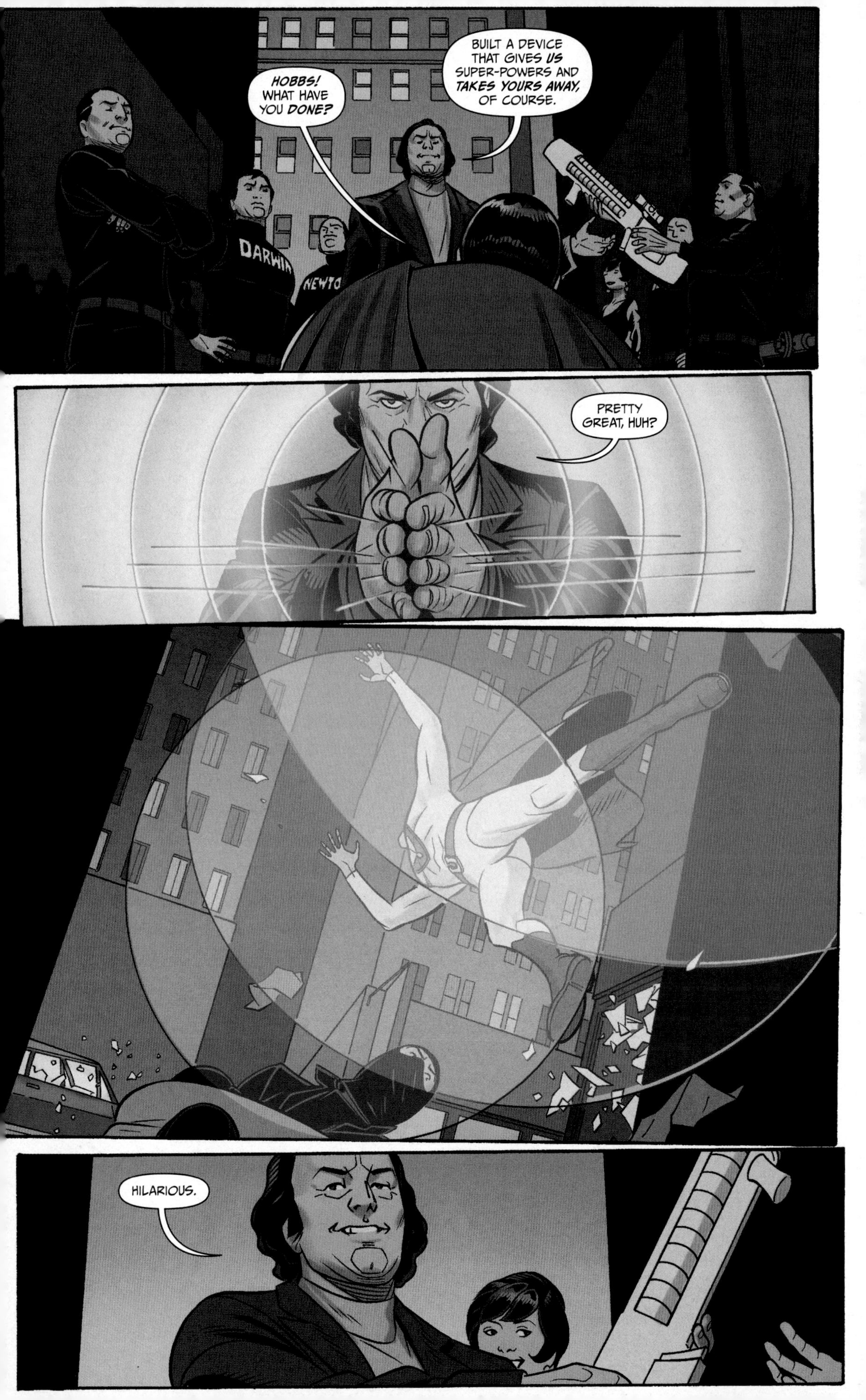
HOBBS! WHAT HAVE YOU DONE?
BUILT A DEVICE THAT GIVES US SUPER-POWERS AND TAKES YOURS AWAY, OF COURSE.
DARWIN
NEWTO
PRETTY GREAT, HUH?
HILARIOUS.

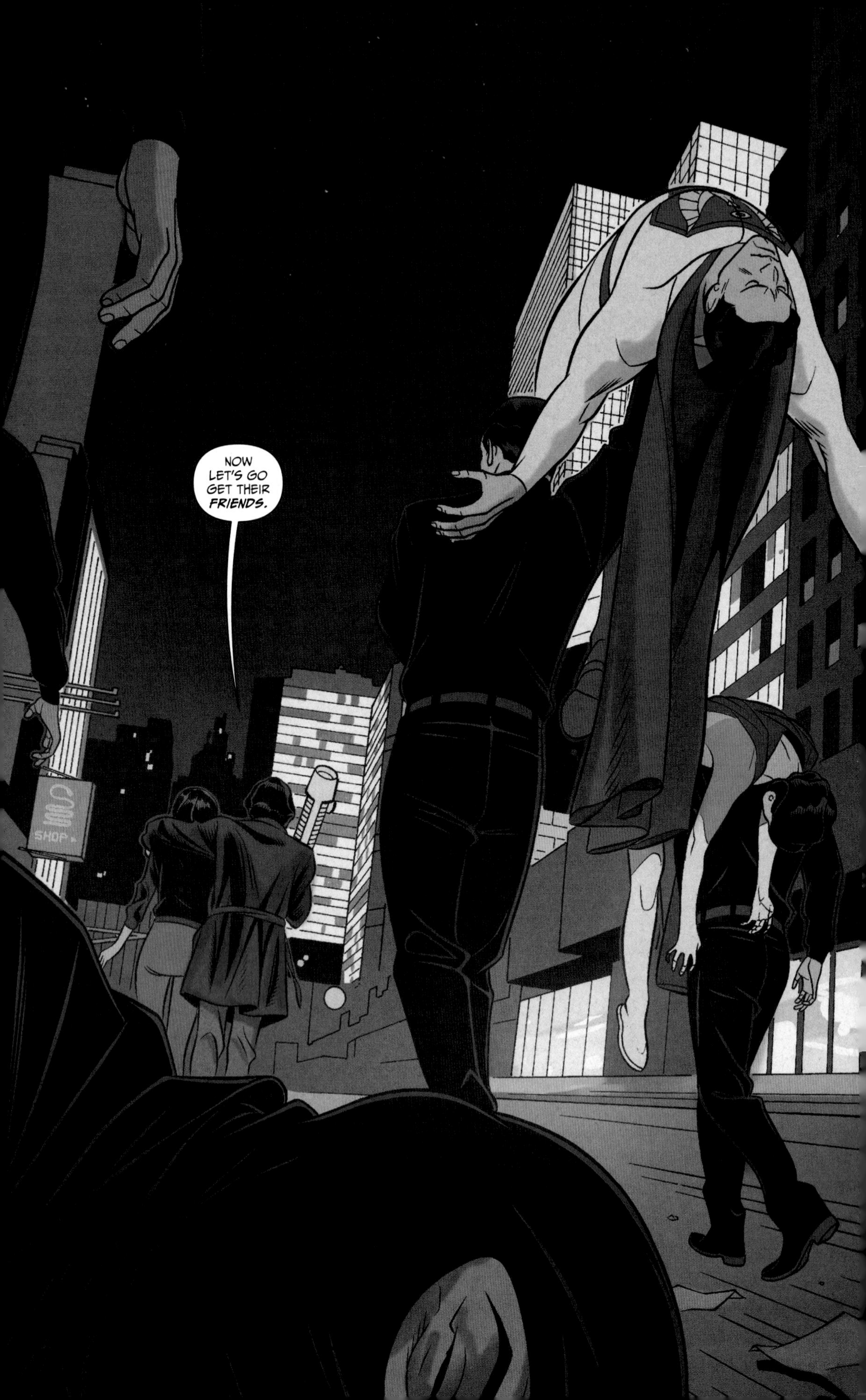
NOW LET'S GO GET THEIR FRIENDS.
SHOP

Chapter 4

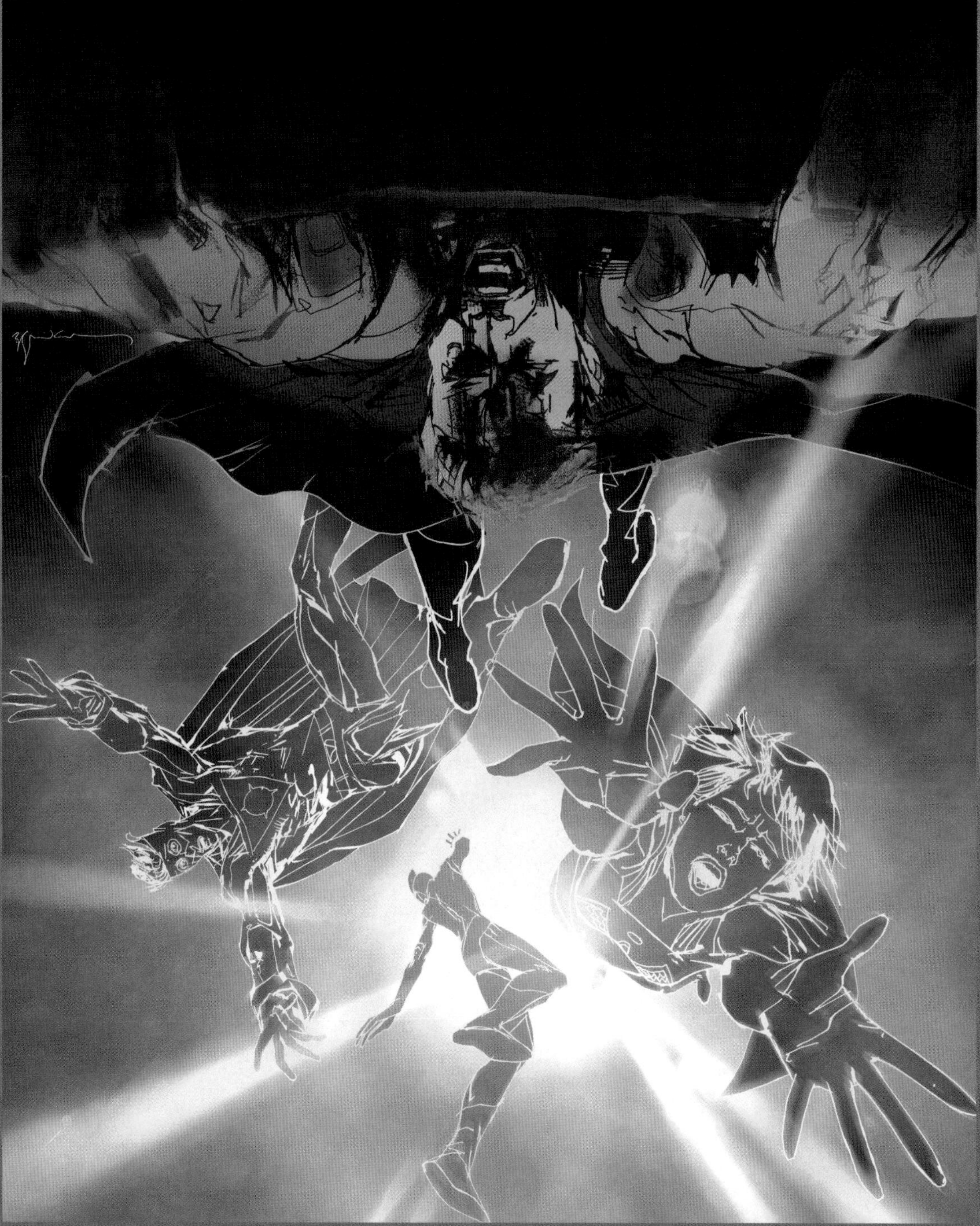

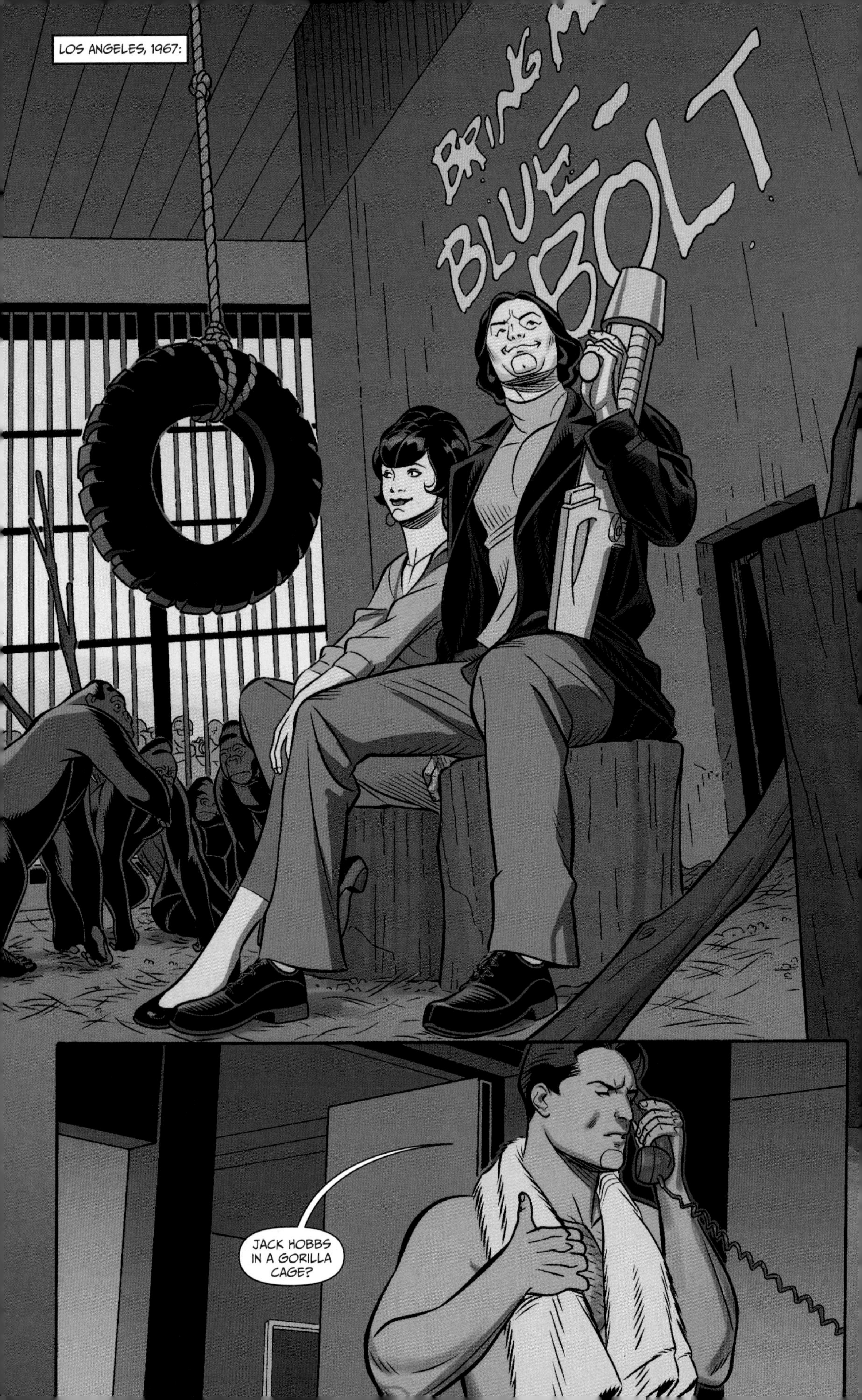
LOS ANGELES, 1967:
BRING
BLUE-BOLT
JACK HOBBS IN A GORILLA CAGE?

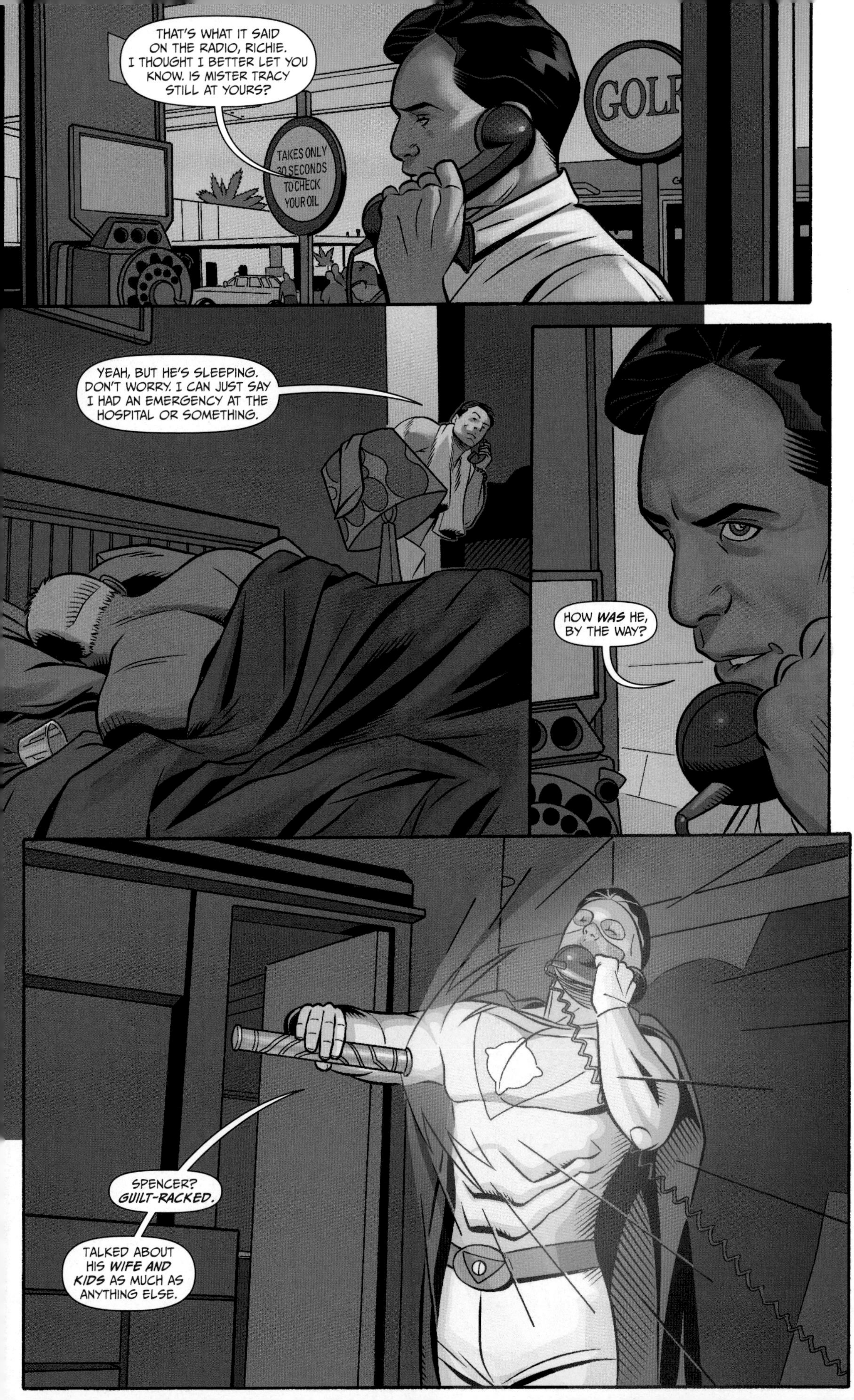
THAT'S WHAT IT SAID ON THE RADIO, RICHIE. I THOUGHT I BETTER LET YOU KNOW. IS MISTER TRACY STILL AT YOURS?
TAKES ONLY 30 SECONDS TO CHECK YOUR OIL
YEAH, BUT HE'S SLEEPING. DON'T WORRY. I CAN JUST SAY I HAD AN EMERGENCY AT THE HOSPITAL OR SOMETHING.
HOW *WAS* HE, BY THE WAY?
SPENCER? *GUILT-RACKED.*
TALKED ABOUT HIS *WIFE AND KIDS* AS MUCH AS ANYTHING ELSE.

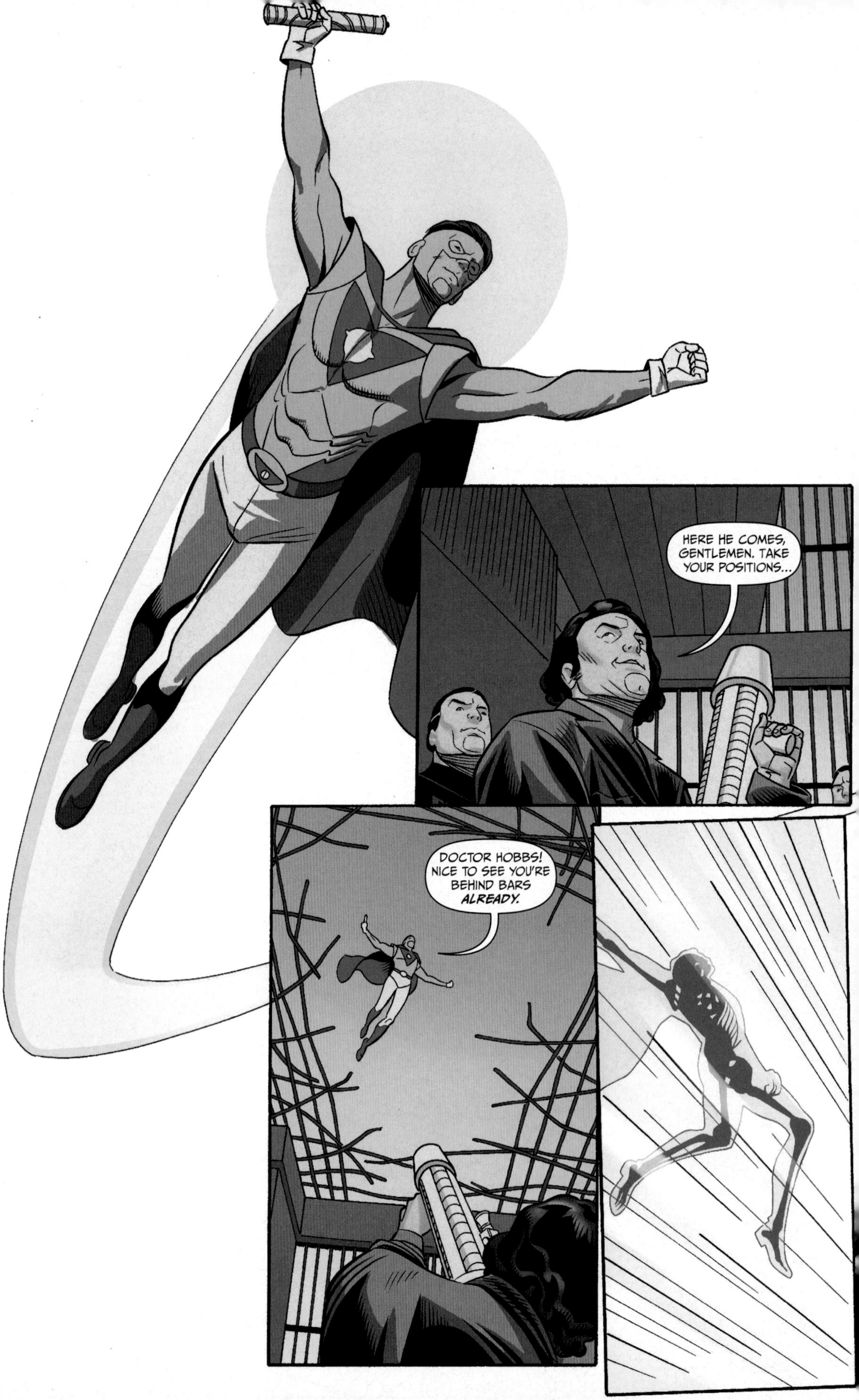
HERE HE COMES, GENTLEMEN. TAKE YOUR POSITIONS...
DOCTOR HOBBS! NICE TO SEE YOU'RE BEHIND BARS *ALREADY.*

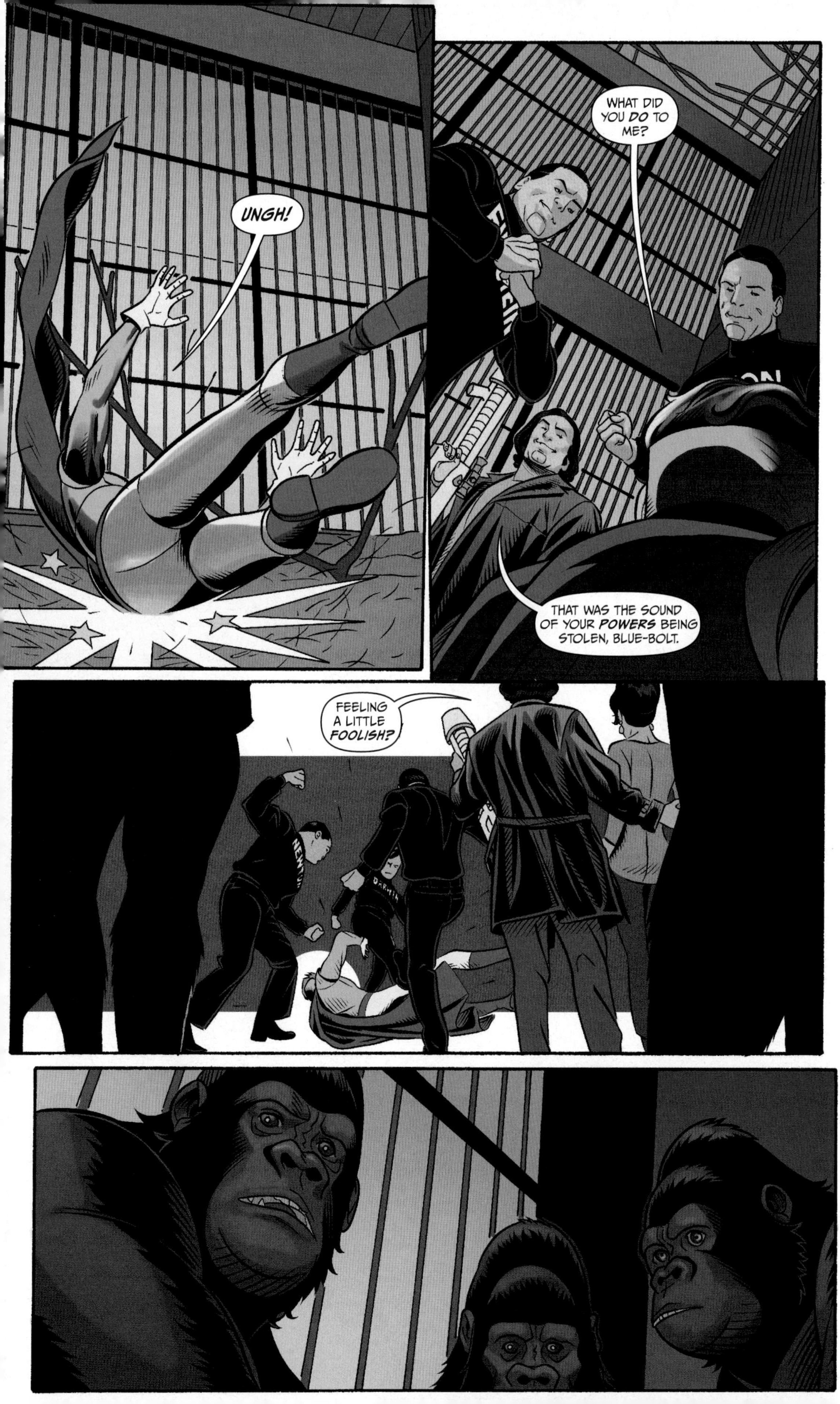
UNGH!
WHAT DID YOU DO TO ME?
THAT WAS THE SOUND OF YOUR POWERS BEING STOLEN, BLUE-BOLT.
FEELING A LITTLE FOOLISH?

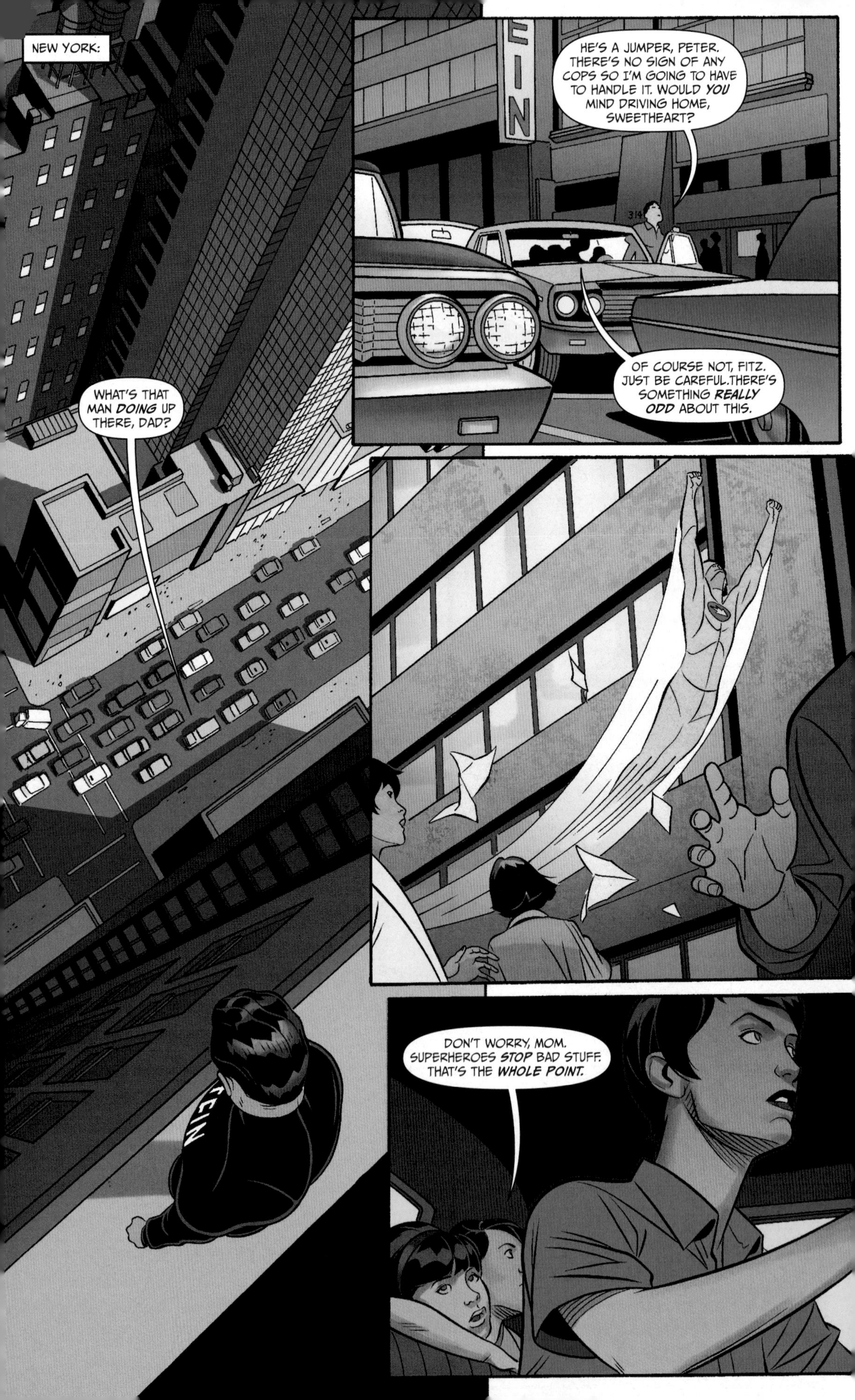
NEW YORK:
WHAT'S THAT MAN DOING UP THERE, DAD?
HE'S A JUMPER, PETER. THERE'S NO SIGN OF ANY COPS SO I'M GOING TO HAVE TO HANDLE IT. WOULD YOU MIND DRIVING HOME, SWEETHEART?
OF COURSE NOT, FITZ. JUST BE CAREFUL.THERE'S SOMETHING REALLY ODD ABOUT THIS.
DON'T WORRY, MOM. SUPERHEROES STOP BAD STUFF. THAT'S THE WHOLE POINT.

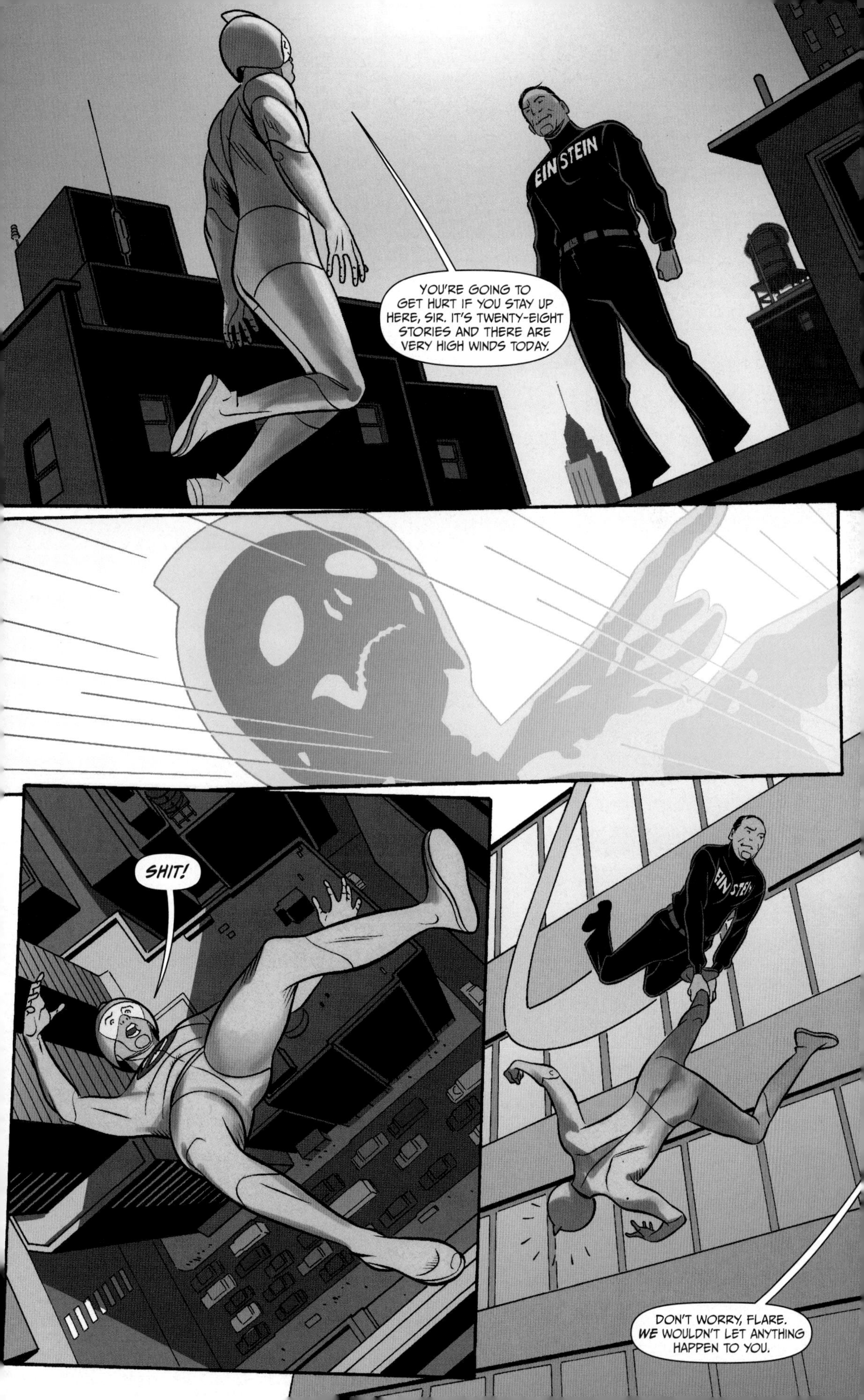
EIN STEIN
YOU'RE GOING TO GET HURT IF YOU STAY UP HERE, SIR. IT'S TWENTY-EIGHT STORIES AND THERE ARE VERY HIGH WINDS TODAY.
SHIT!
EIN STEIN
DON'T WORRY, FLARE. *WE* WOULDN'T LET ANYTHING HAPPEN TO YOU.

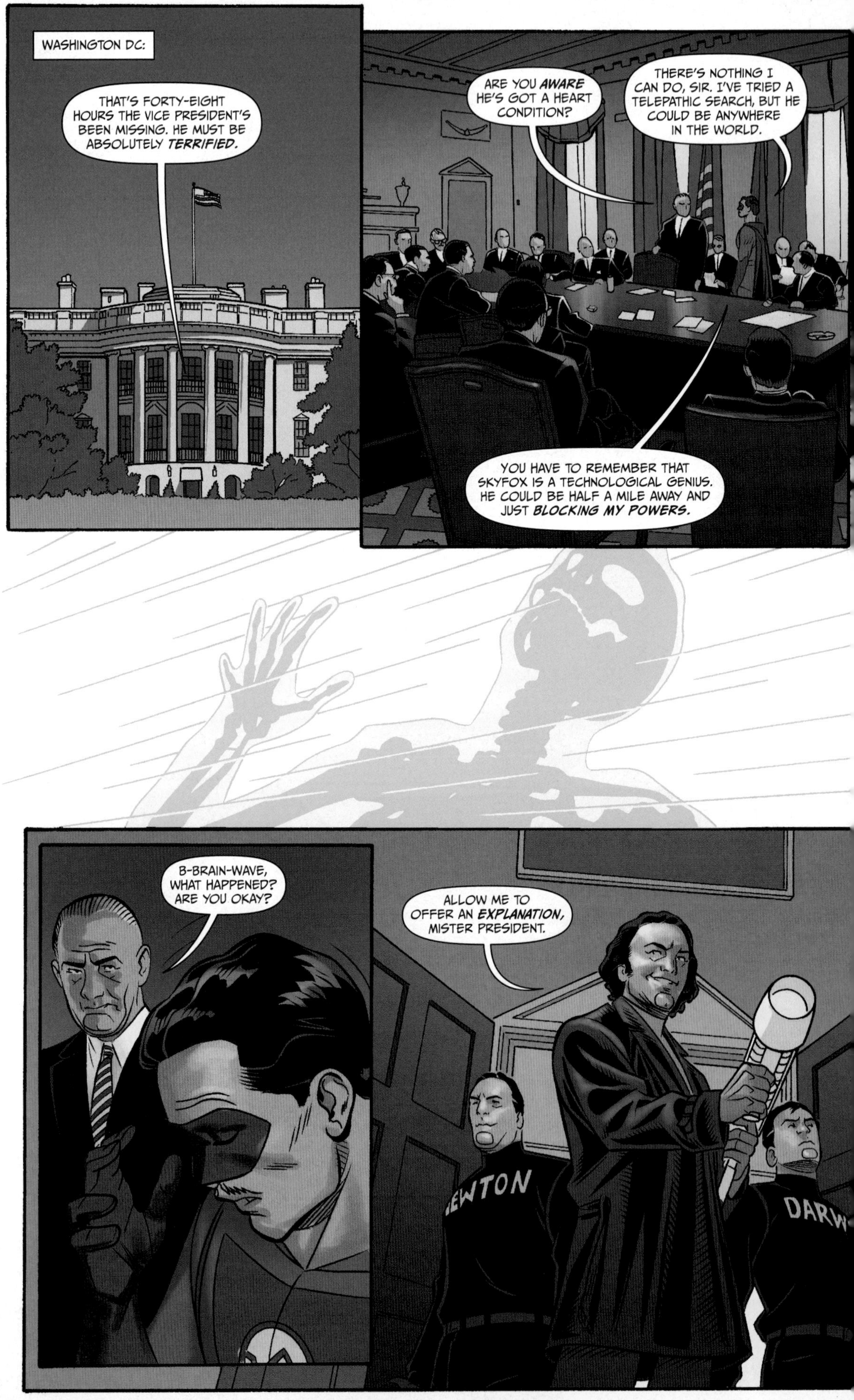
WASHINGTON DC:
THAT'S FORTY-EIGHT HOURS THE VICE PRESIDENT'S BEEN MISSING. HE MUST BE ABSOLUTELY TERRIFIED.
ARE YOU AWARE HE'S GOT A HEART CONDITION?
THERE'S NOTHING I CAN DO, SIR. I'VE TRIED A TELEPATHIC SEARCH, BUT HE COULD BE ANYWHERE IN THE WORLD.
YOU HAVE TO REMEMBER THAT SKYFOX IS A TECHNOLOGICAL GENIUS. HE COULD BE HALF A MILE AWAY AND JUST BLOCKING MY POWERS.
B-BRAIN-WAVE, WHAT HAPPENED? ARE YOU OKAY?
ALLOW ME TO OFFER AN EXPLANATION, MISTER PRESIDENT.
NEWTON
DARW

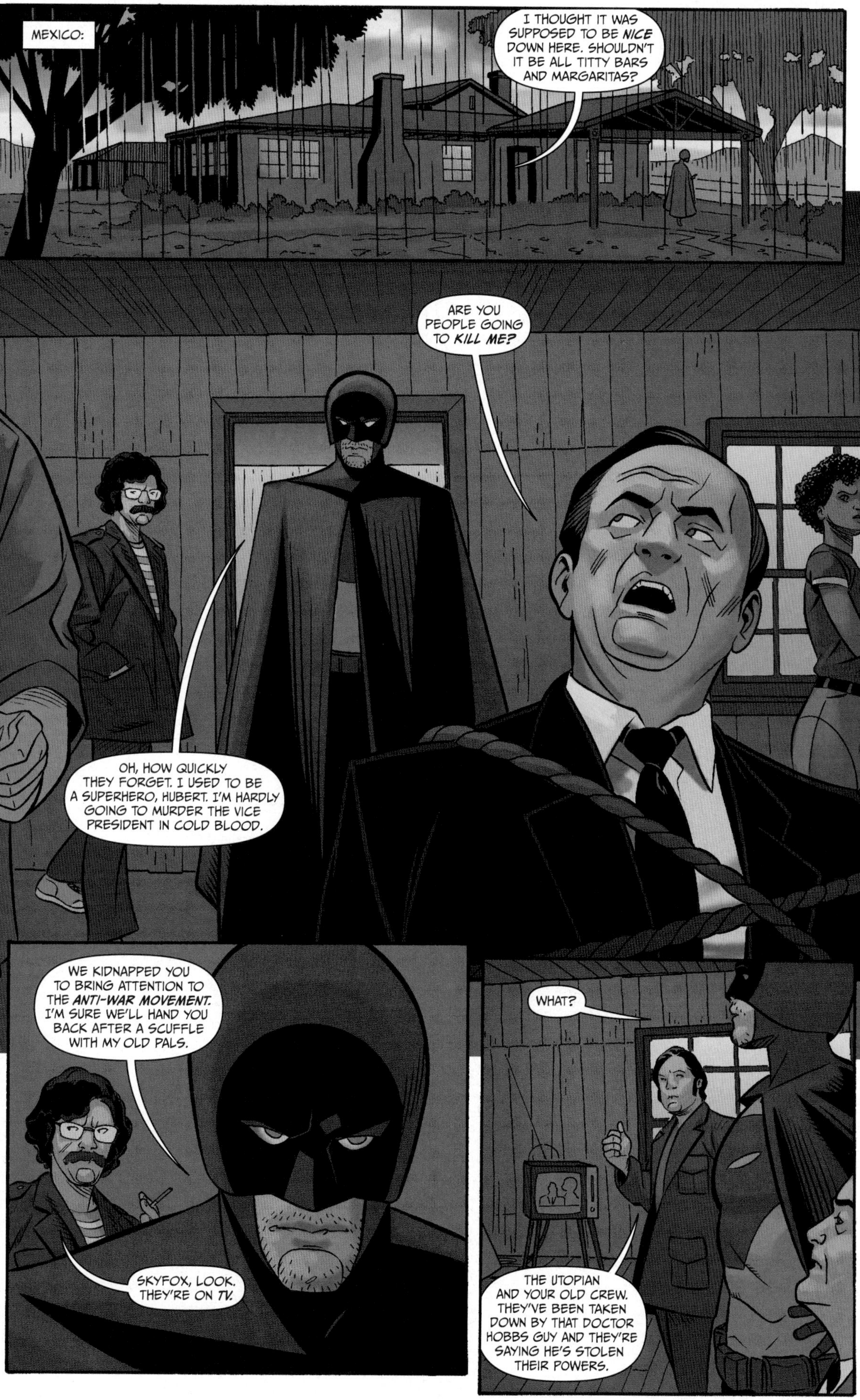
MEXICO:
I THOUGHT IT WAS SUPPOSED TO BE *NICE* DOWN HERE. SHOULDN'T IT BE ALL TITTY BARS AND MARGARITAS?
ARE YOU PEOPLE GOING TO *KILL ME?*
OH, HOW QUICKLY THEY FORGET. I USED TO BE A SUPERHERO, HUBERT. I'M HARDLY GOING TO MURDER THE VICE PRESIDENT IN COLD BLOOD.
WE KIDNAPPED YOU TO BRING ATTENTION TO THE *ANTI-WAR MOVEMENT.* I'M SURE WE'LL HAND YOU BACK AFTER A SCUFFLE WITH MY OLD PALS.
SKYFOX, LOOK. THEY'RE ON *TV.*
WHAT?
THE UTOPIAN AND YOUR OLD CREW. THEY'VE BEEN TAKEN DOWN BY THAT DOCTOR HOBBS GUY AND THEY'RE SAYING HE'S STOLEN THEIR POWERS.

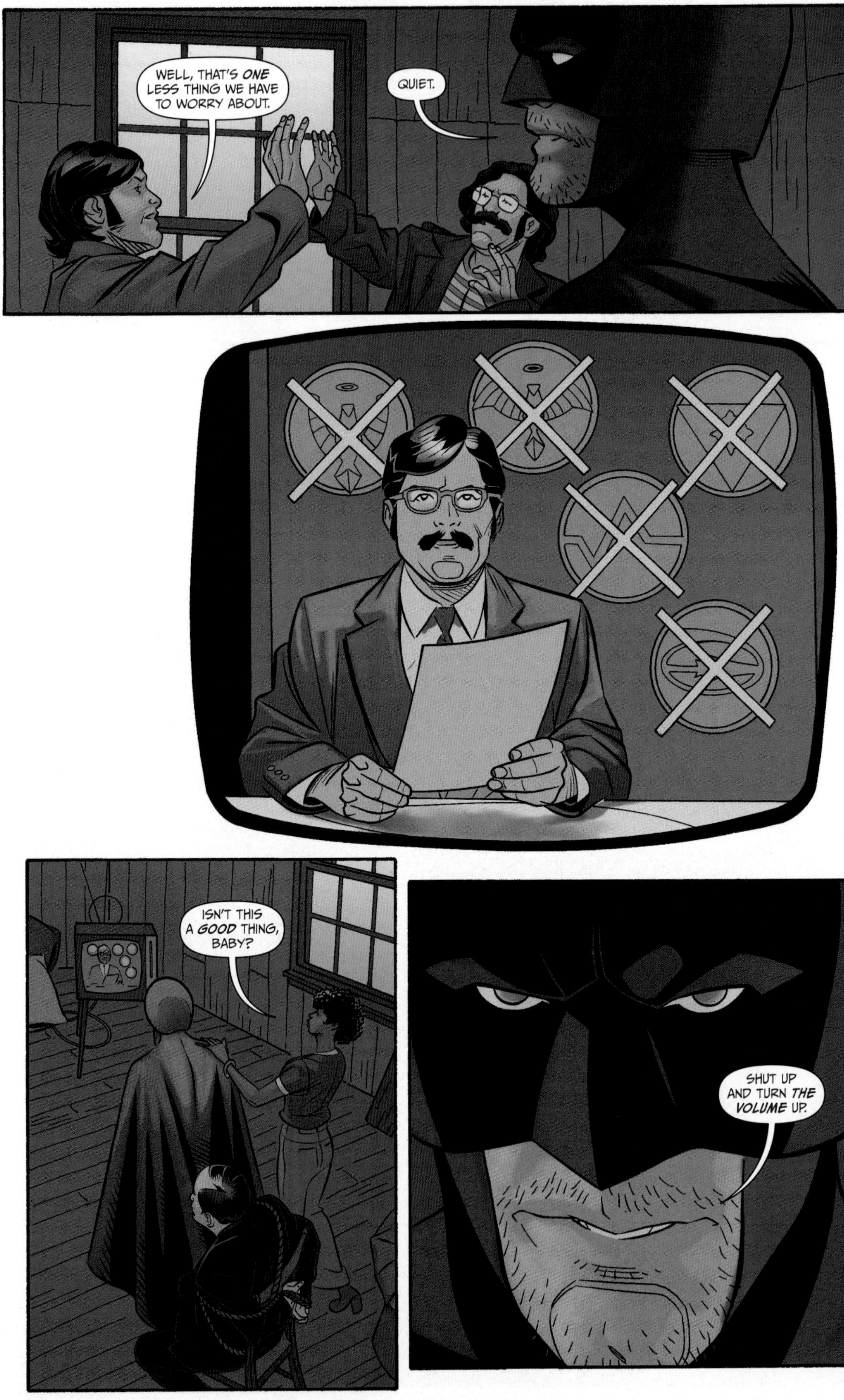
WELL, THAT'S ONE LESS THING WE HAVE TO WORRY ABOUT.
QUIET.
ISN'T THIS A GOOD THING, BABY?
SHUT UP AND TURN THE VOLUME UP.

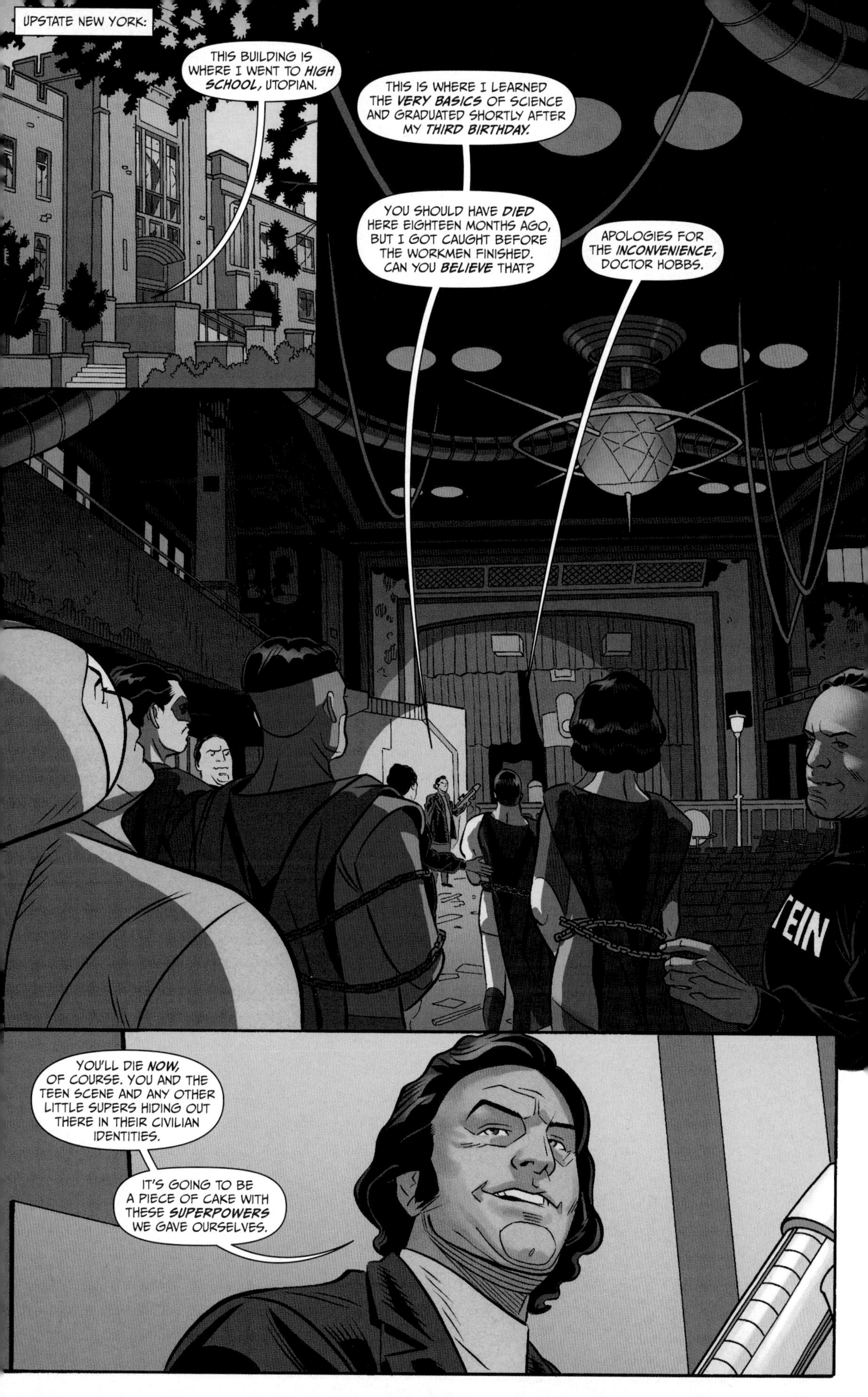
UPSTATE NEW YORK:
THIS BUILDING IS WHERE I WENT TO HIGH SCHOOL, UTOPIAN.
THIS IS WHERE I LEARNED THE VERY BASICS OF SCIENCE AND GRADUATED SHORTLY AFTER MY THIRD BIRTHDAY.
YOU SHOULD HAVE DIED HERE EIGHTEEN MONTHS AGO, BUT I GOT CAUGHT BEFORE THE WORKMEN FINISHED. CAN YOU BELIEVE THAT?
APOLOGIES FOR THE INCONVENIENCE, DOCTOR HOBBS.
TEIN
YOU'LL DIE NOW, OF COURSE. YOU AND THE TEEN SCENE AND ANY OTHER LITTLE SUPERS HIDING OUT THERE IN THEIR CIVILIAN IDENTITIES.
IT'S GOING TO BE A PIECE OF CAKE WITH THESE SUPERPOWERS WE GAVE OURSELVES.

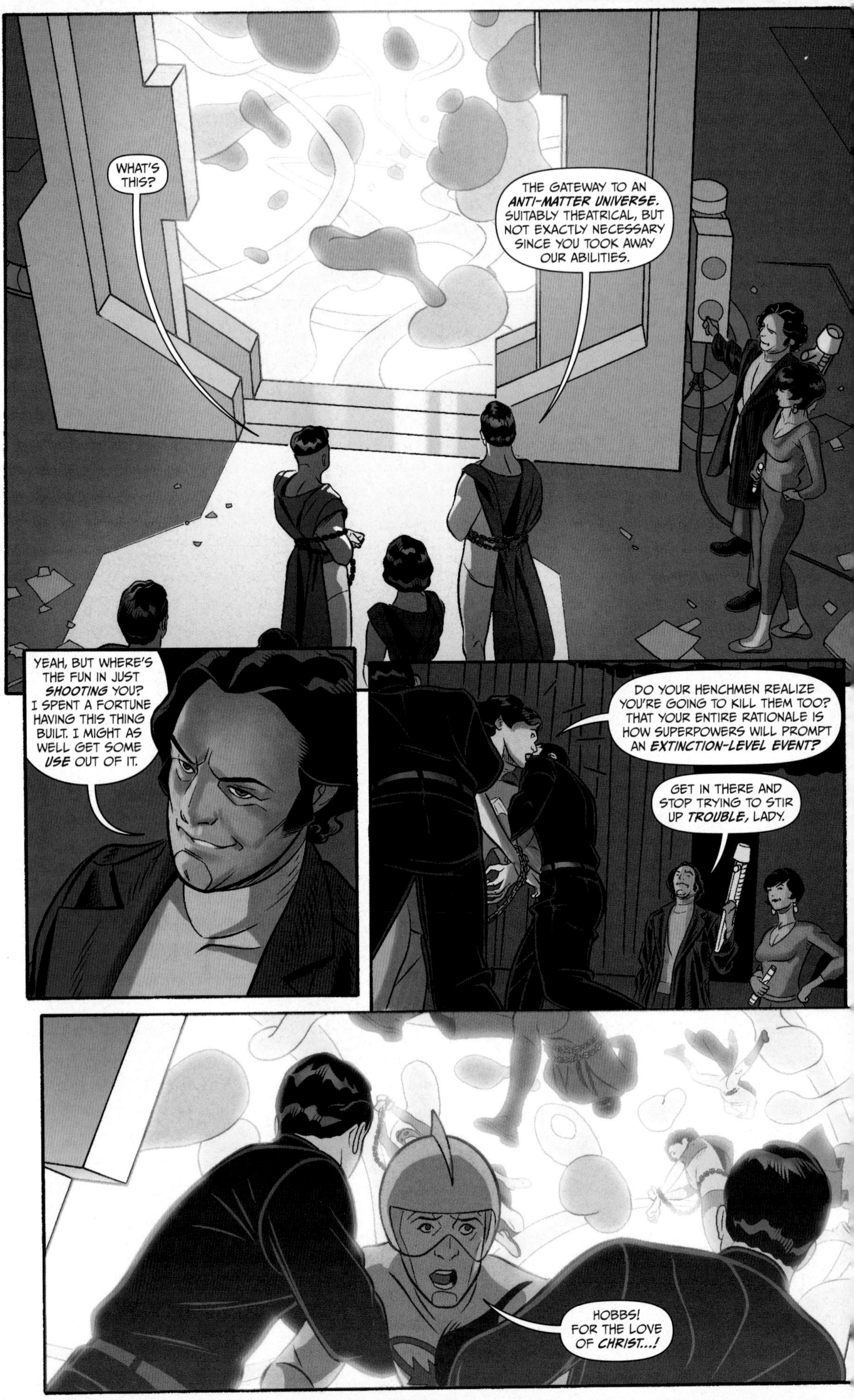
WHAT'S THIS?
THE GATEWAY TO AN ANTI-MATTER UNIVERSE. SUITABLY THEATRICAL, BUT NOT EXACTLY NECESSARY SINCE YOU TOOK AWAY OUR ABILITIES.
YEAH, BUT WHERE'S THE FUN IN JUST SHOOTING YOU? I SPENT A FORTUNE HAVING THIS THING BUILT. I MIGHT AS WELL GET SOME USE OUT OF IT.
DO YOUR HENCHMEN REALIZE YOU'RE GOING TO KILL THEM TOO? THAT YOUR ENTIRE RATIONALE IS HOW SUPERPOWERS WILL PROMPT AN EXTINCTION-LEVEL EVENT?
GET IN THERE AND STOP TRYING TO STIR UP TROUBLE, LADY.
HOBBS! FOR THE LOVE OF CHRIST...!

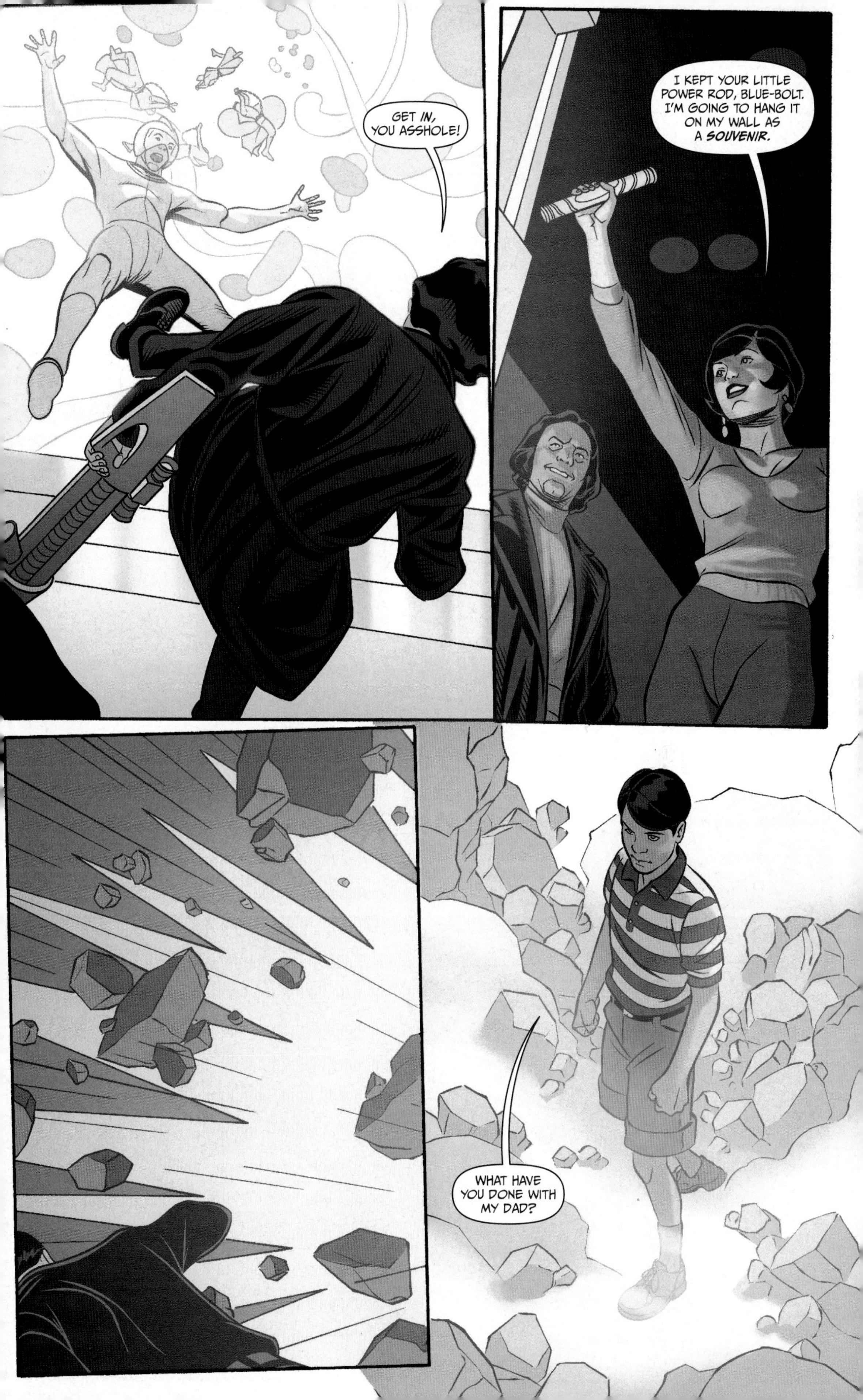
GET *IN*, YOU ASSHOLE!
I KEPT YOUR LITTLE POWER ROD, BLUE-BOLT. I'M GOING TO HANG IT ON MY WALL AS A *SOUVENIR.*
WHAT HAVE YOU DONE WITH MY DAD?

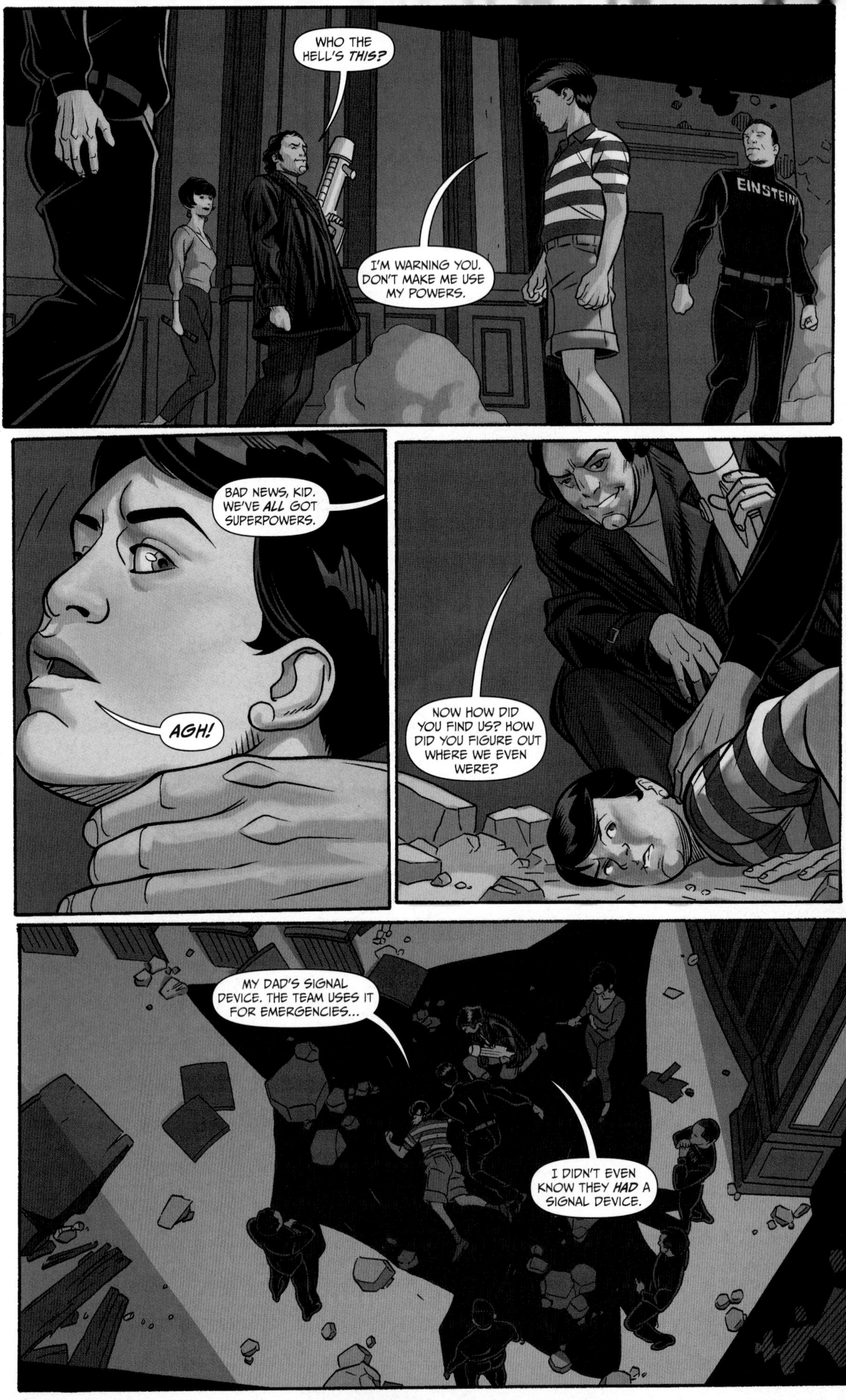
WHO THE HELL'S *THIS?*
I'M WARNING YOU. DON'T MAKE ME USE MY POWERS.
EINSTEIN
BAD NEWS, KID. WE'VE *ALL* GOT SUPERPOWERS.
AGH!
NOW HOW DID YOU FIND US? HOW DID YOU FIGURE OUT WHERE WE EVEN WERE?
MY DAD'S SIGNAL DEVICE. THE TEAM USES IT FOR EMERGENCIES...
I DIDN'T EVEN KNOW THEY *HAD* A SIGNAL DEVICE.

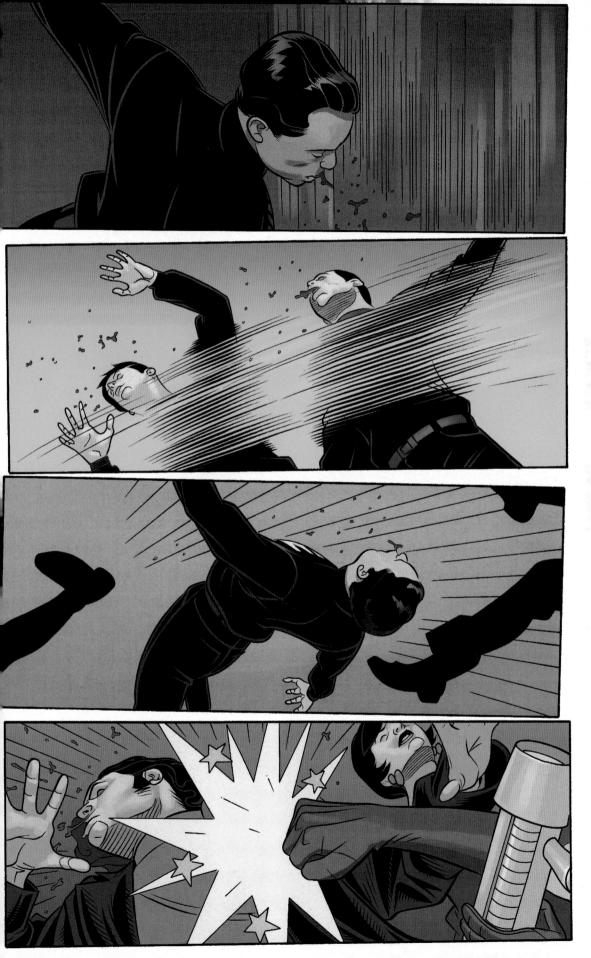

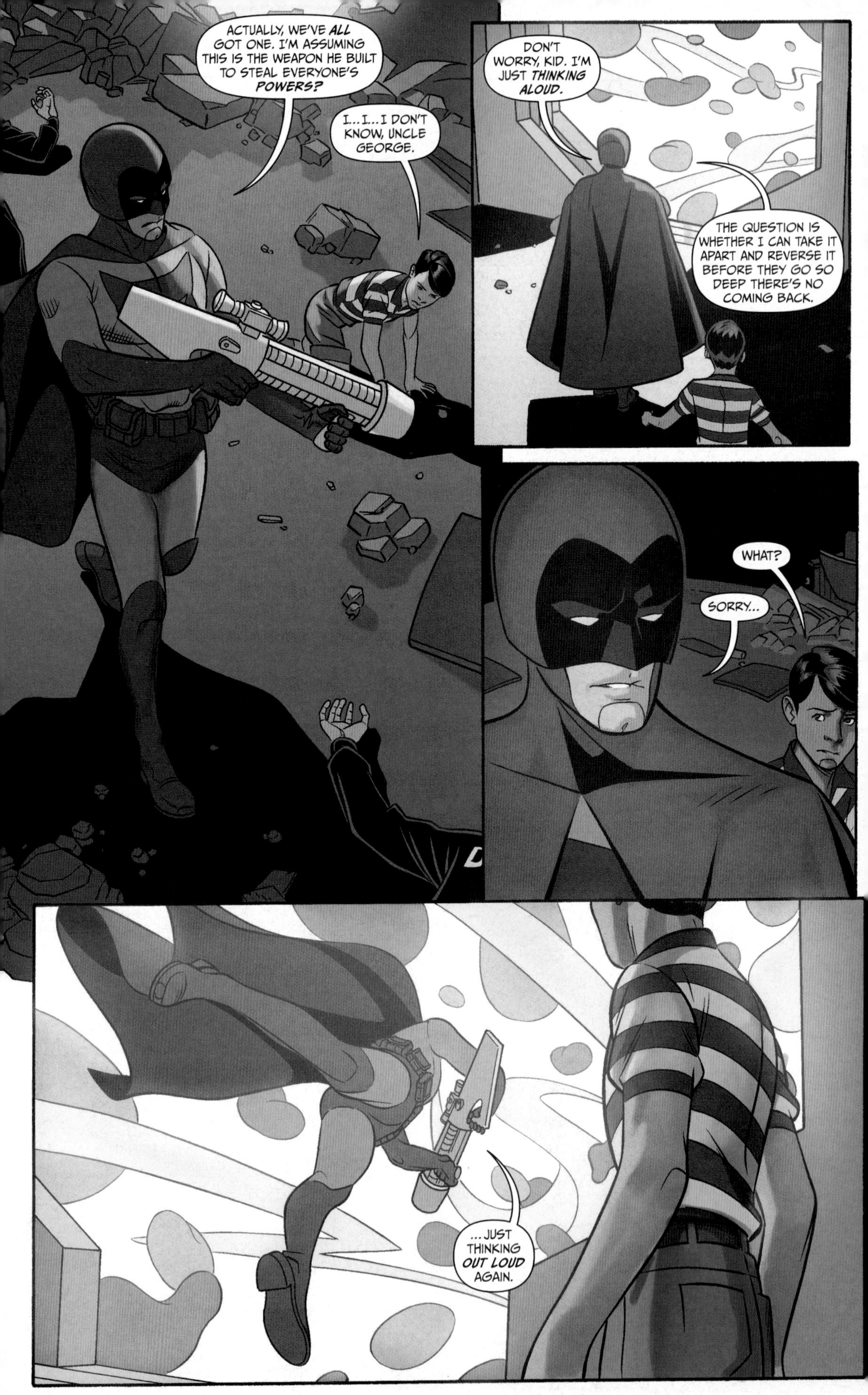

ACTUALLY, WE'VE ALL GOT ONE. I'M ASSUMING THIS IS THE WEAPON HE BUILT TO STEAL EVERYONE'S POWERS?
I...I...I DON'T KNOW, UNCLE GEORGE.
DON'T WORRY, KID. I'M JUST THINKING ALOUD.
THE QUESTION IS WHETHER I CAN TAKE IT APART AND REVERSE IT BEFORE THEY GO SO DEEP THERE'S NO COMING BACK.
WHAT?
SORRY...
...JUST THINKING OUT LOUD AGAIN.

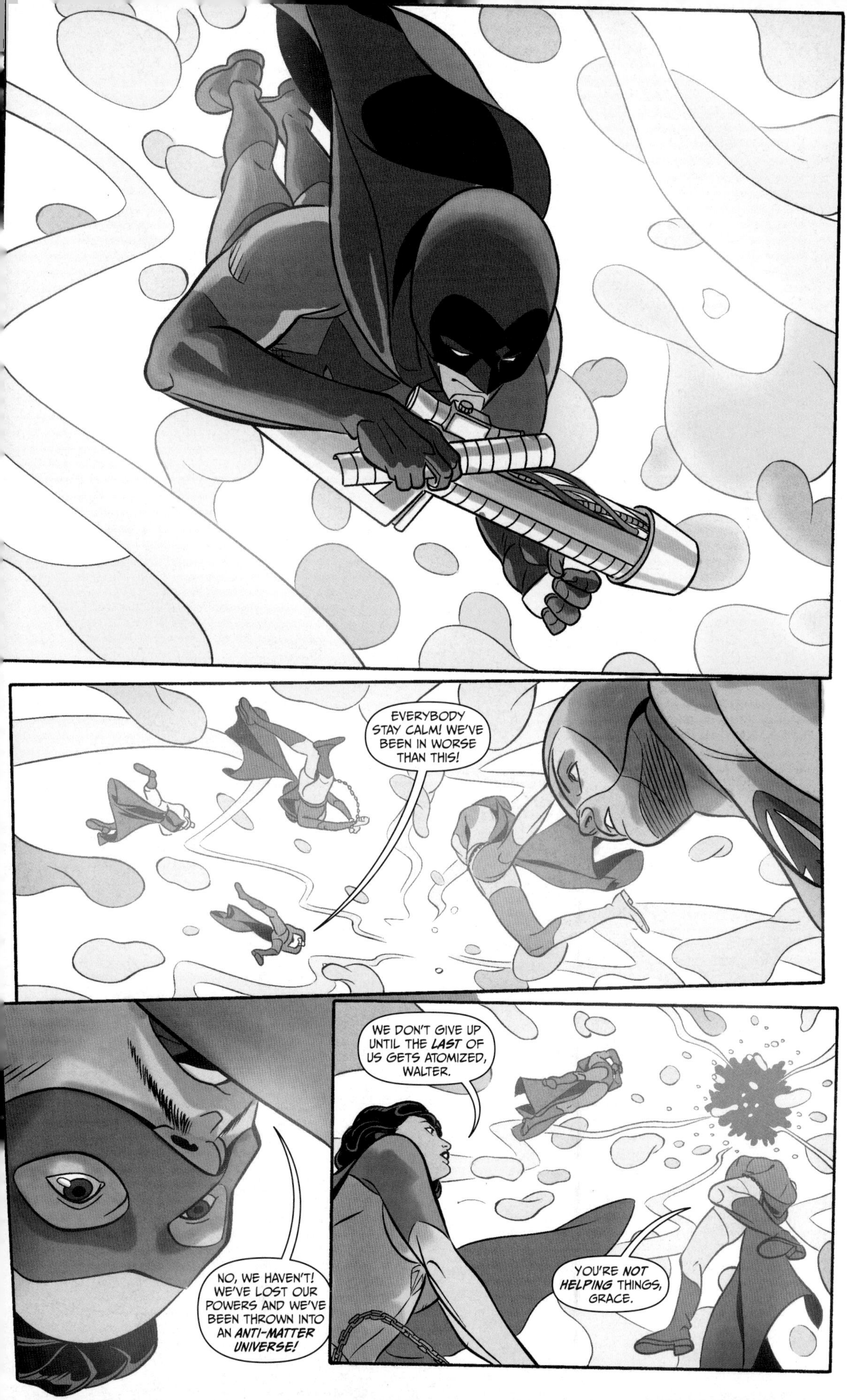
EVERYBODY STAY CALM! WE'VE BEEN IN WORSE THAN THIS!
NO, WE HAVEN'T! WE'VE LOST OUR POWERS AND WE'VE BEEN THROWN INTO AN ANTI-MATTER UNIVERSE!
WE DON'T GIVE UP UNTIL THE LAST OF US GETS ATOMIZED, WALTER.
YOU'RE NOT HELPING THINGS, GRACE.

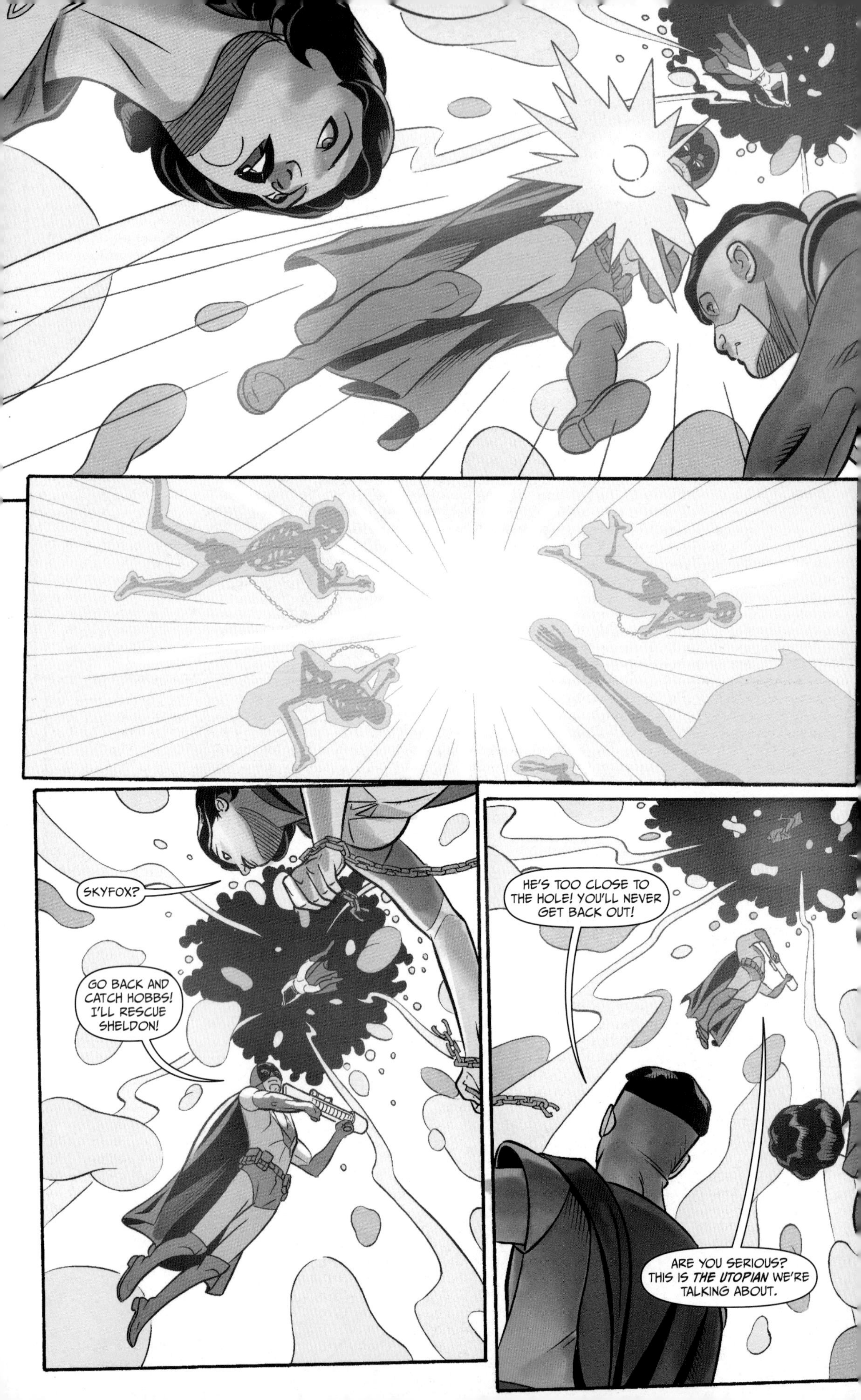
SKYFOX?
GO BACK AND CATCH HOBBS! I'LL RESCUE SHELDON!
HE'S TOO CLOSE TO THE HOLE! YOU'LL NEVER GET BACK OUT!
ARE YOU SERIOUS? THIS IS *THE UTOPIAN* WE'RE TALKING ABOUT.

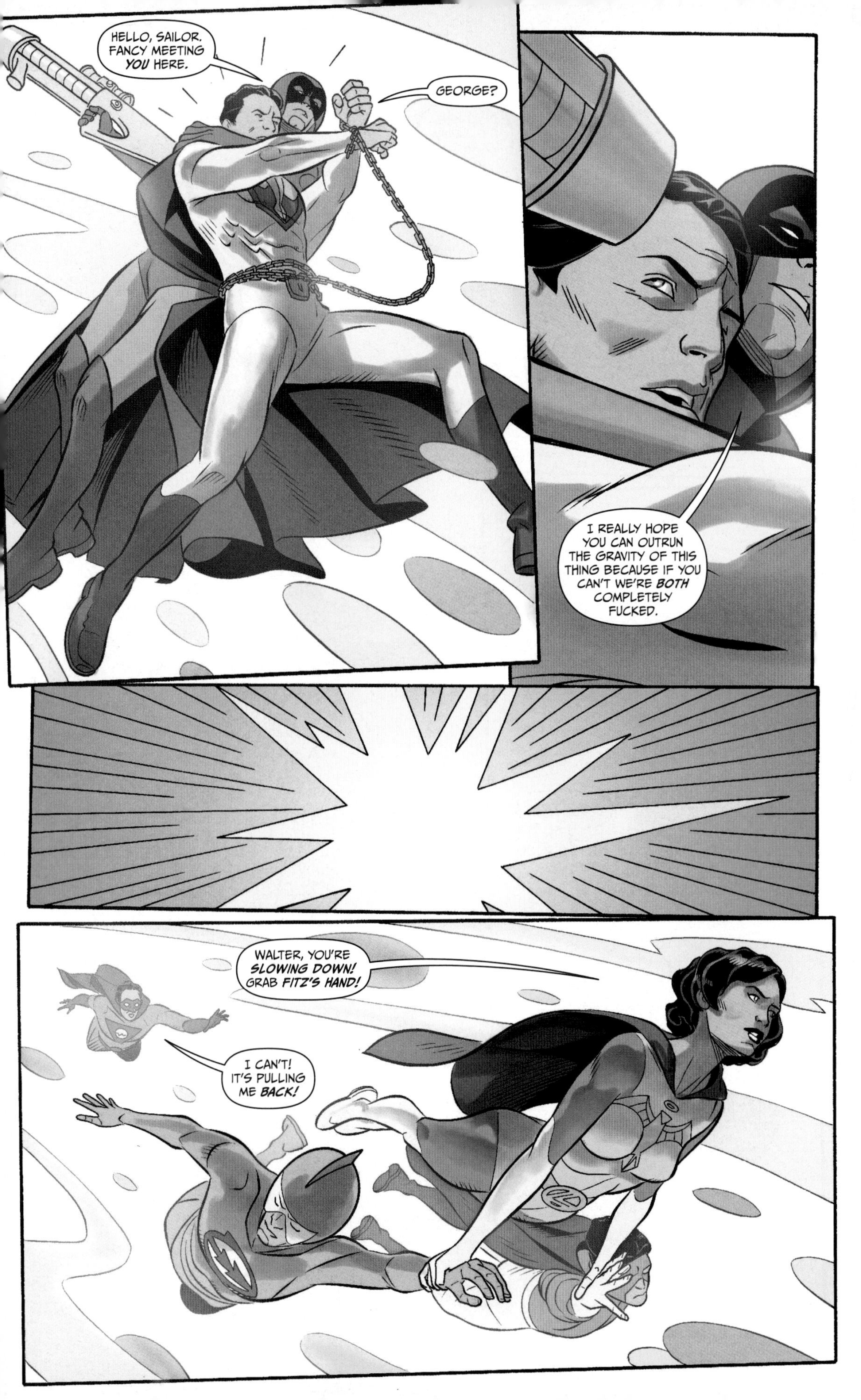
HELLO, SAILOR. FANCY MEETING *YOU* HERE.
GEORGE?
I REALLY HOPE YOU CAN OUTRUN THE GRAVITY OF THIS THING BECAUSE IF YOU CAN'T WE'RE *BOTH* COMPLETELY FUCKED.
WALTER, YOU'RE *SLOWING DOWN!* GRAB *FITZ'S HAND!*
I CAN'T! IT'S PULLING ME *BACK!*

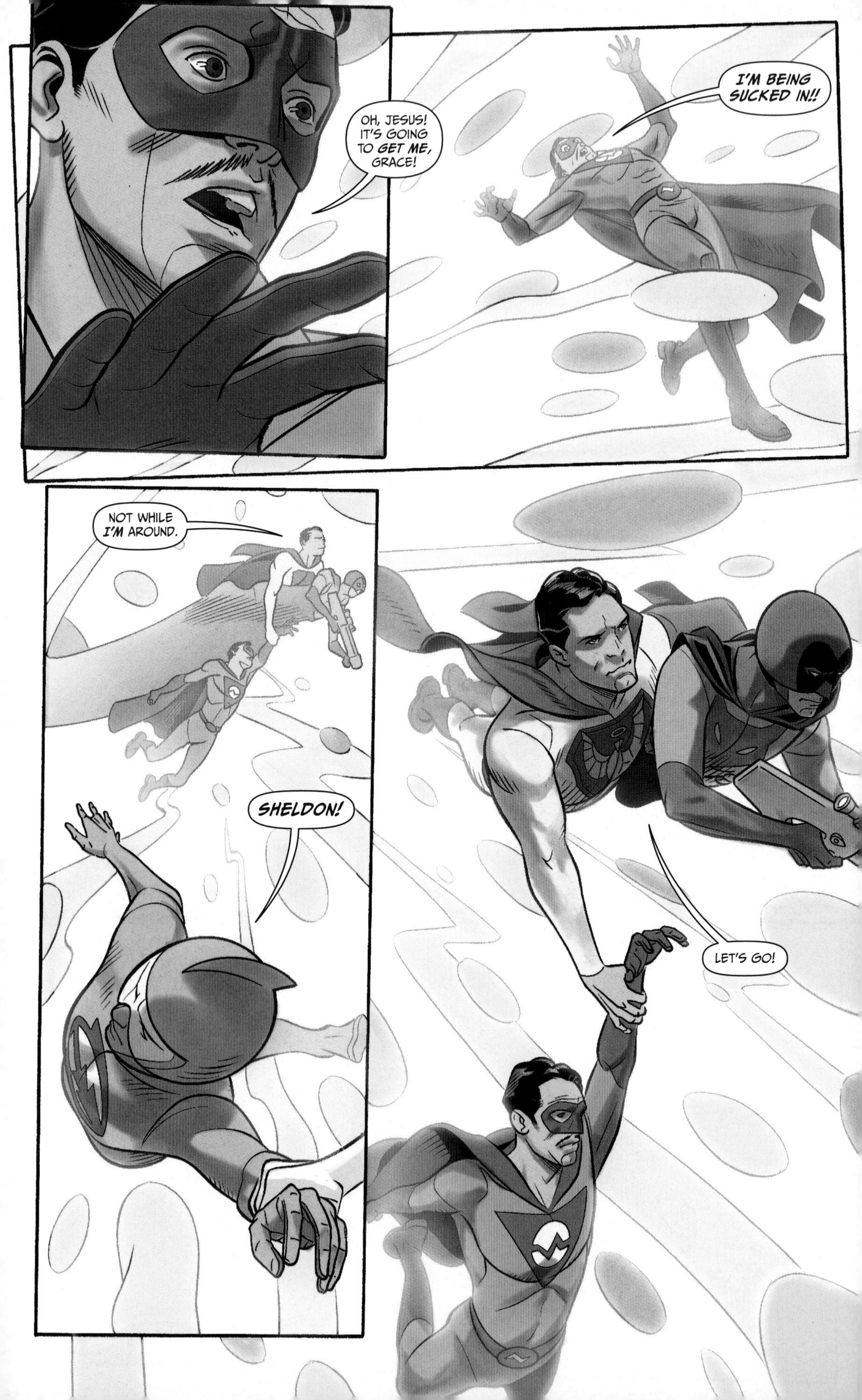
OH, JESUS! IT'S GOING TO GET ME, GRACE!
I'M BEING SUCKED IN!!
NOT WHILE I'M AROUND.
SHELDON!
LET'S GO!

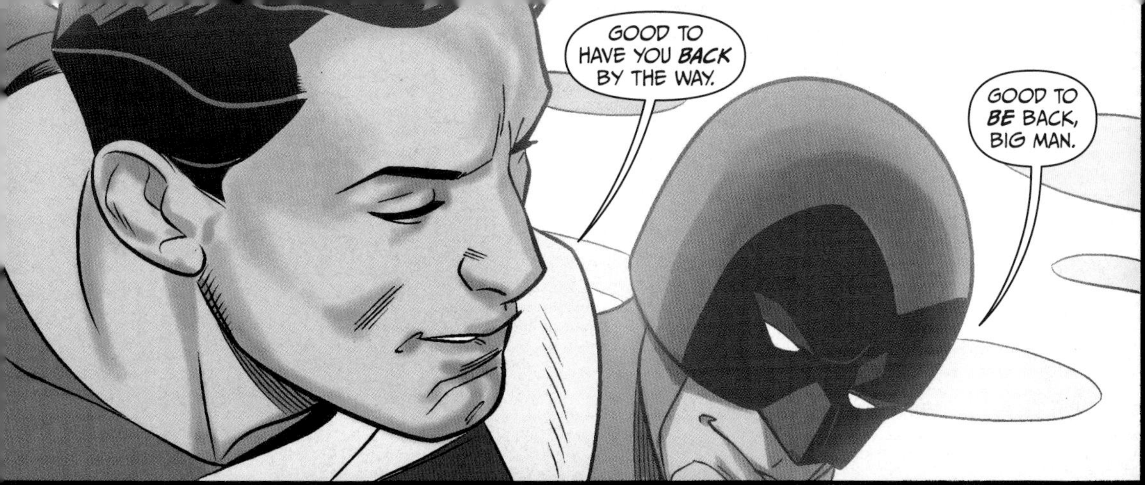
GOOD TO HAVE YOU BACK BY THE WAY.
GOOD TO BE BACK, BIG MAN.

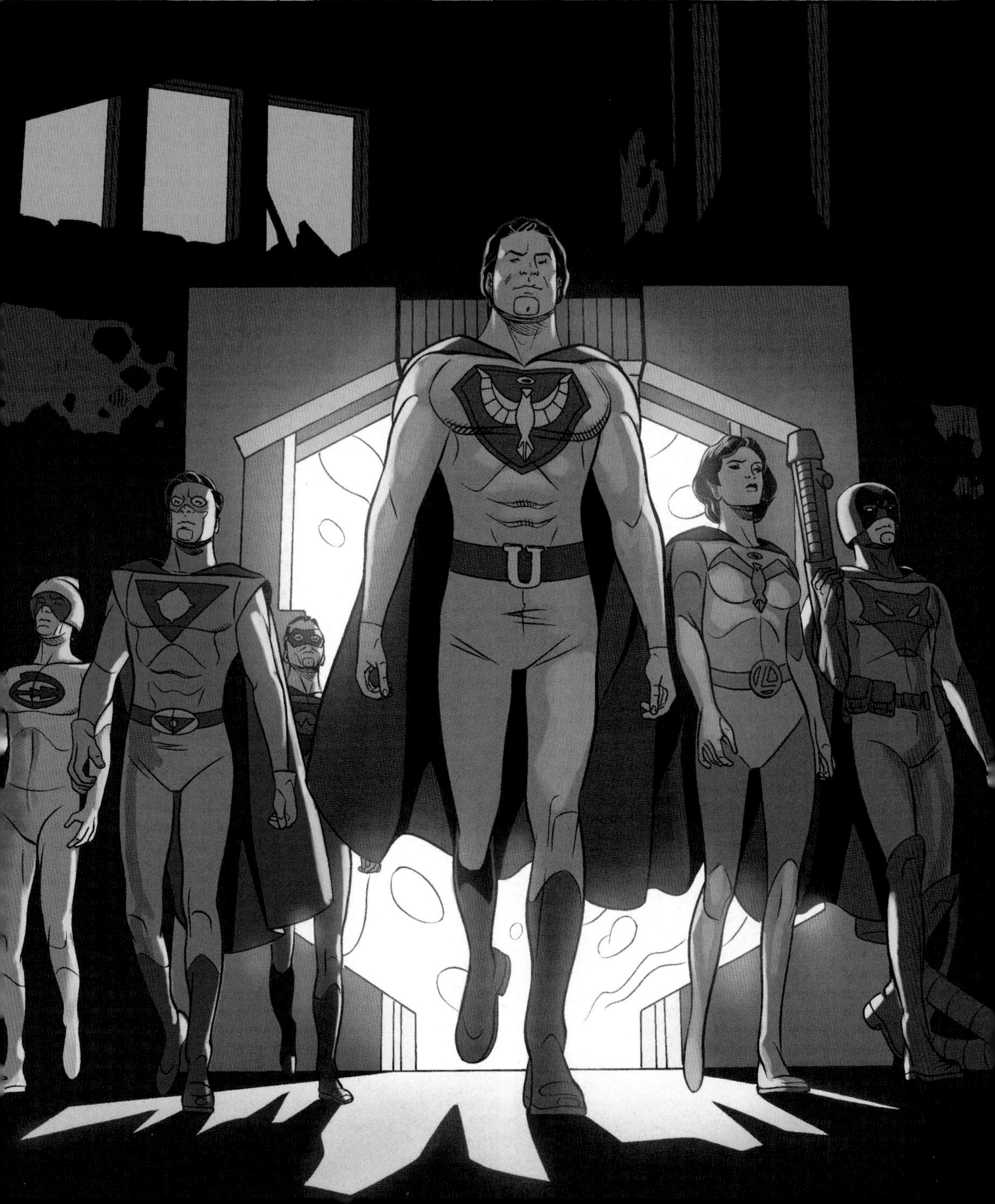

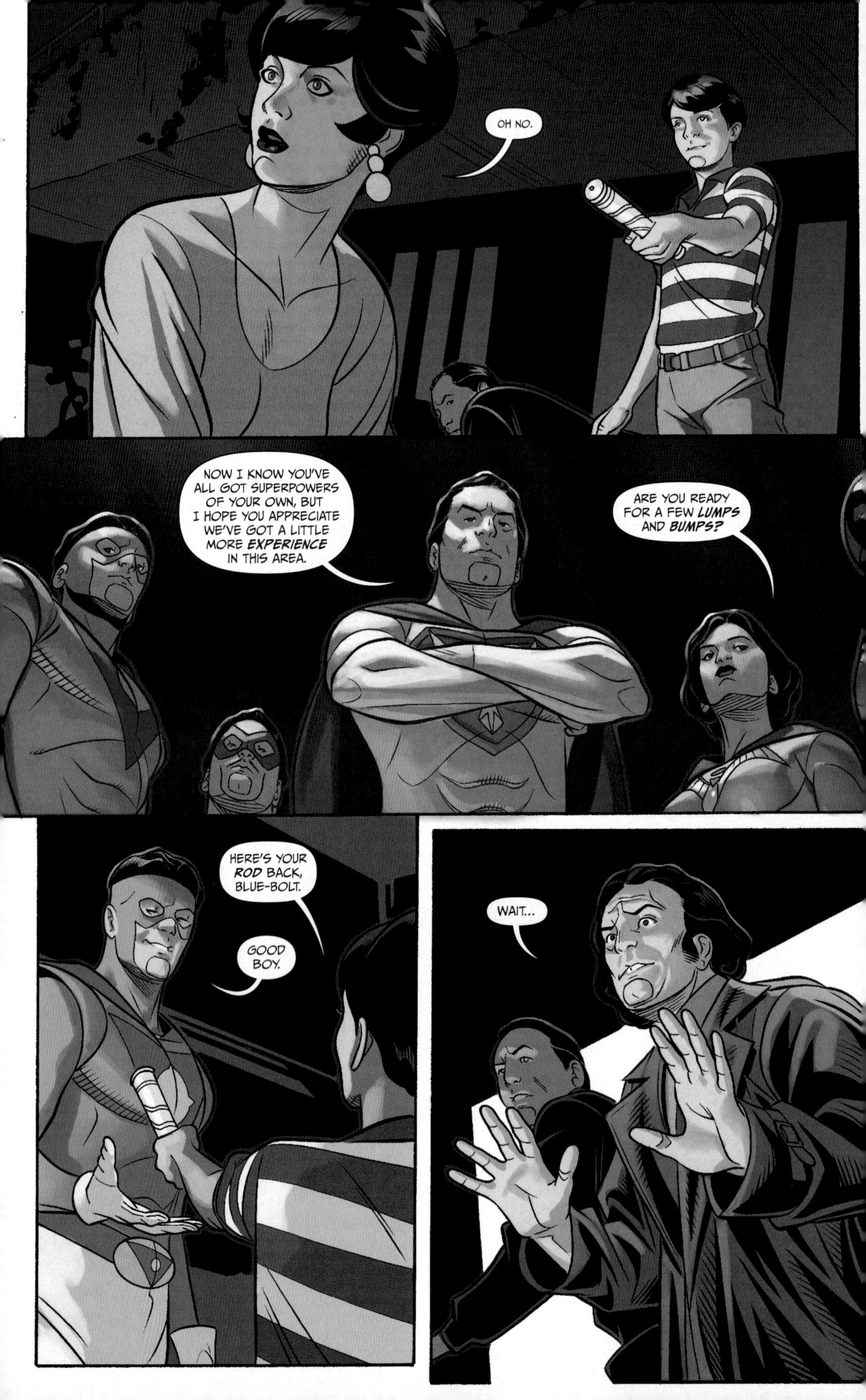
OH NO.
NOW I KNOW YOU'VE ALL GOT SUPERPOWERS OF YOUR OWN, BUT I HOPE YOU APPRECIATE WE'VE GOT A LITTLE MORE EXPERIENCE IN THIS AREA.
ARE YOU READY FOR A FEW LUMPS AND BUMPS?
HERE'S YOUR ROD BACK, BLUE-BOLT.
GOOD BOY.
WAIT...

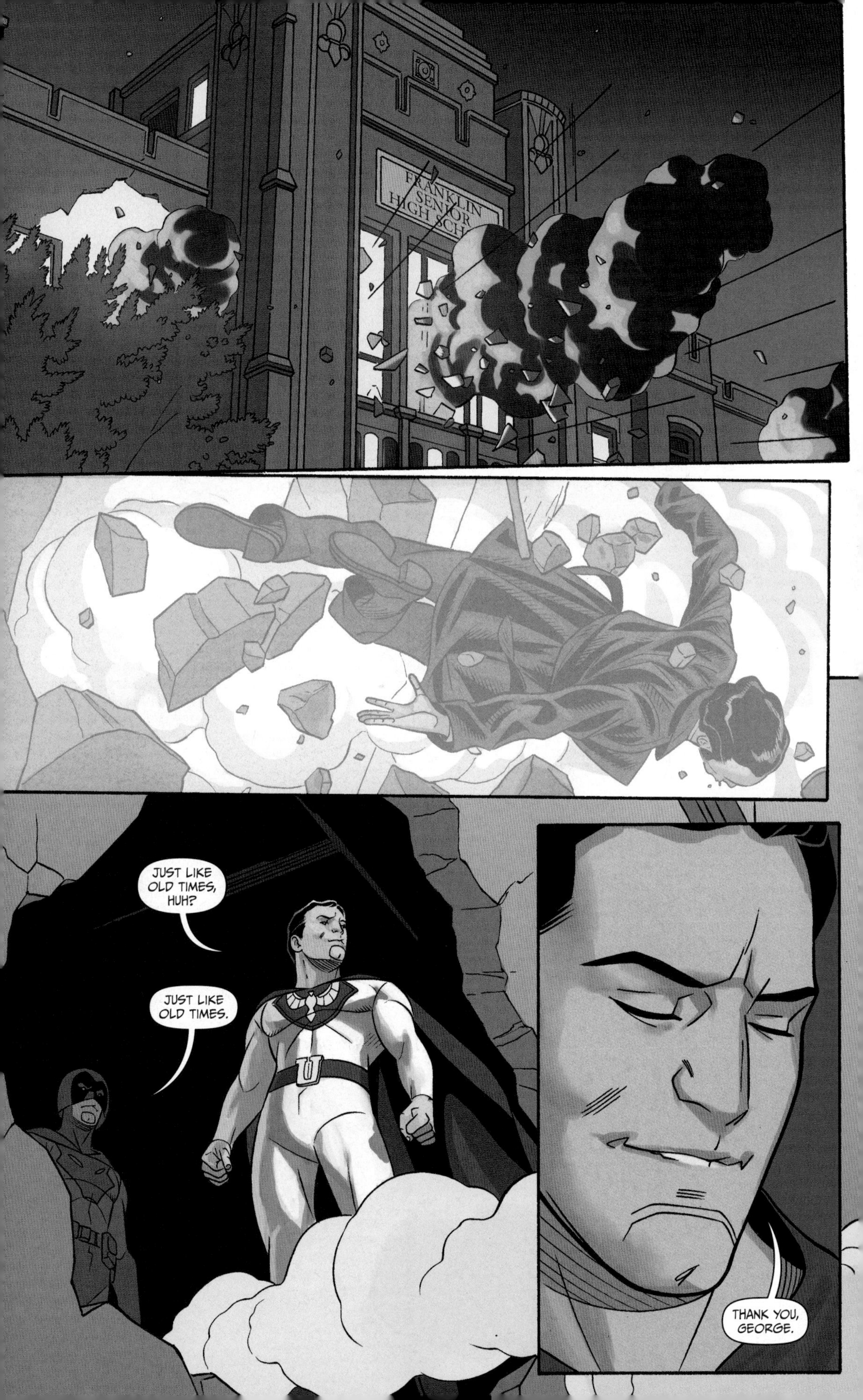
FRANKLIN SENIOR HIGH SCH
JUST LIKE OLD TIMES, HUH?
JUST LIKE OLD TIMES.
THANK YOU, GEORGE.

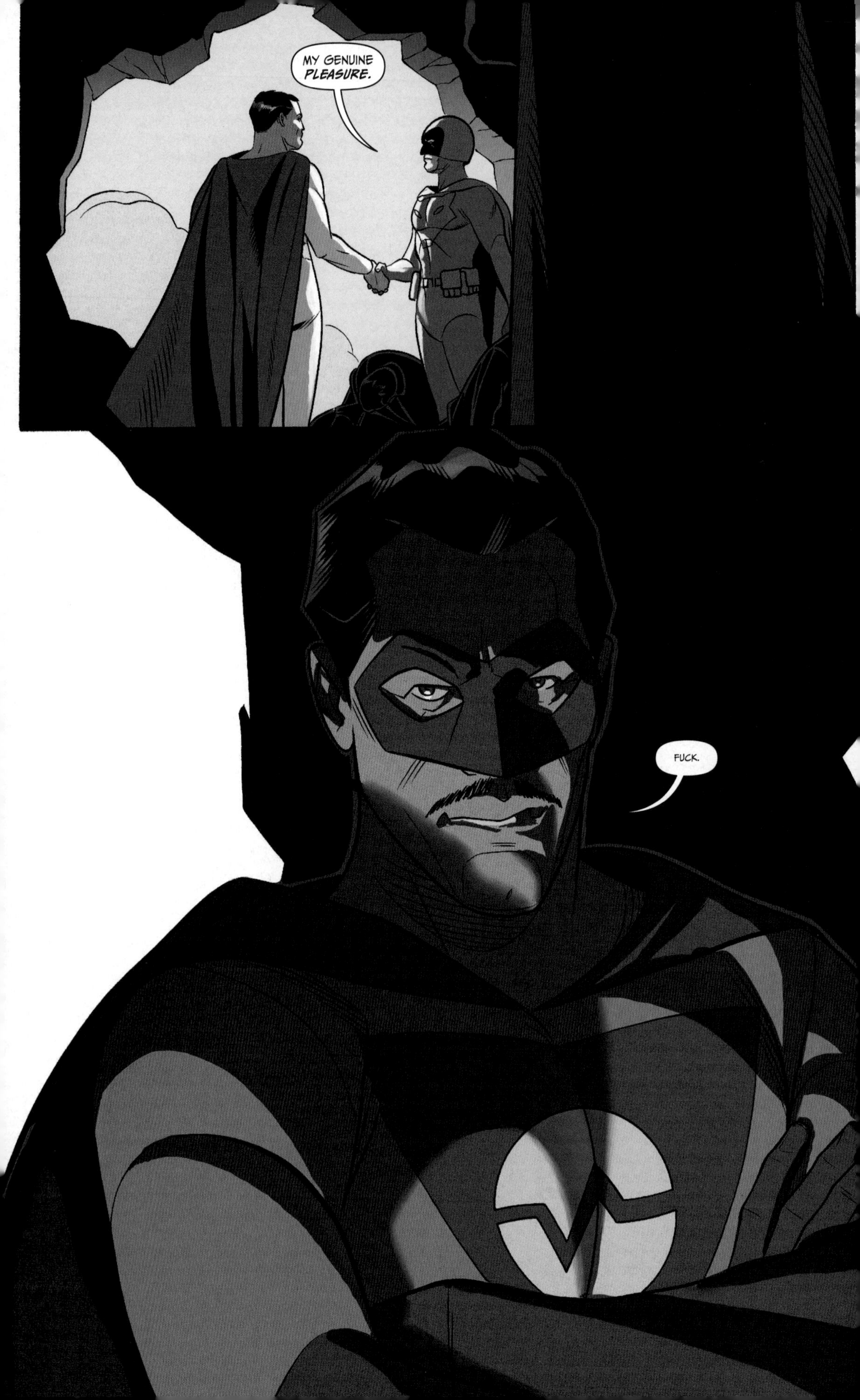
MY GENUINE PLEASURE.
FUCK.

CHAPTER 5

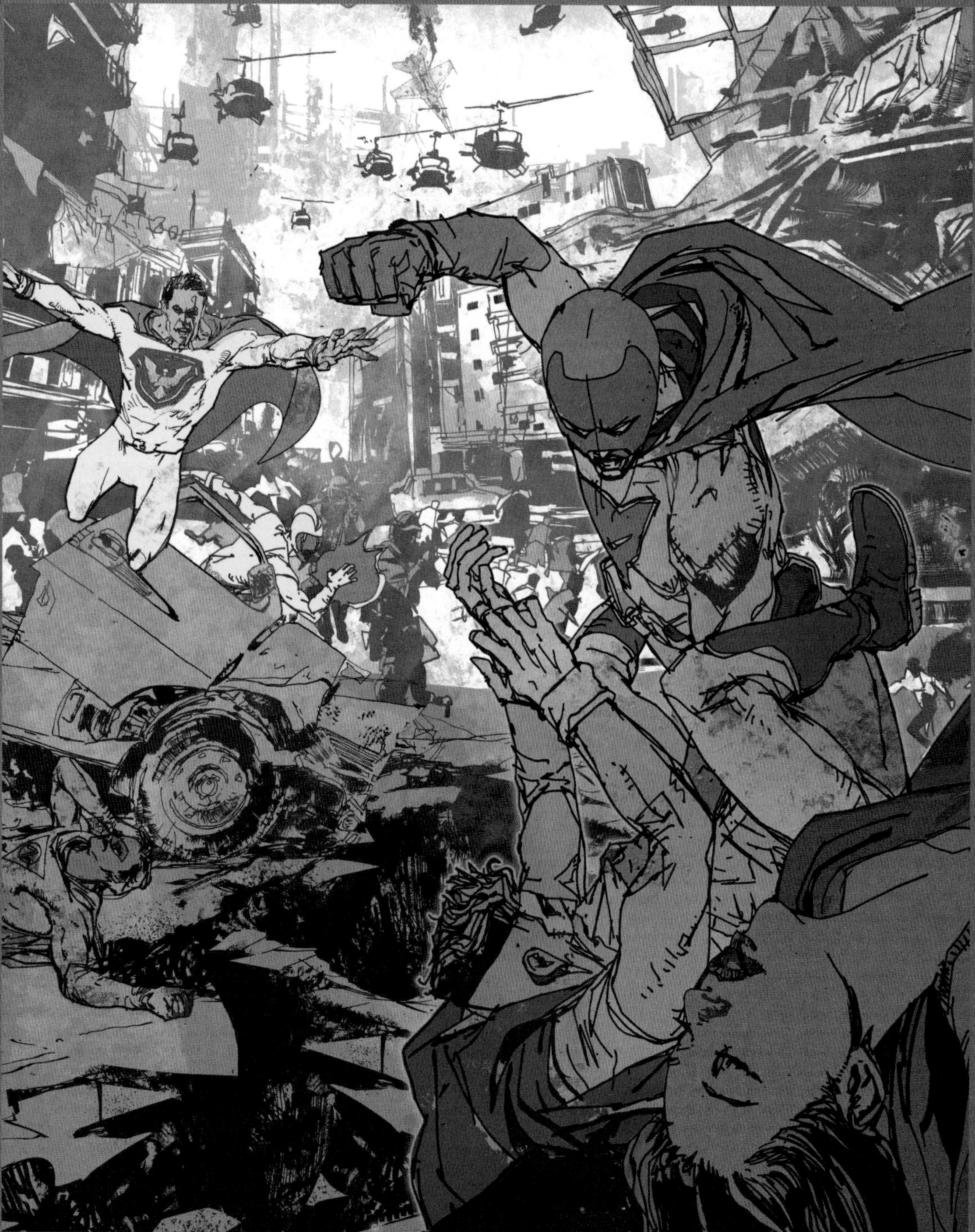

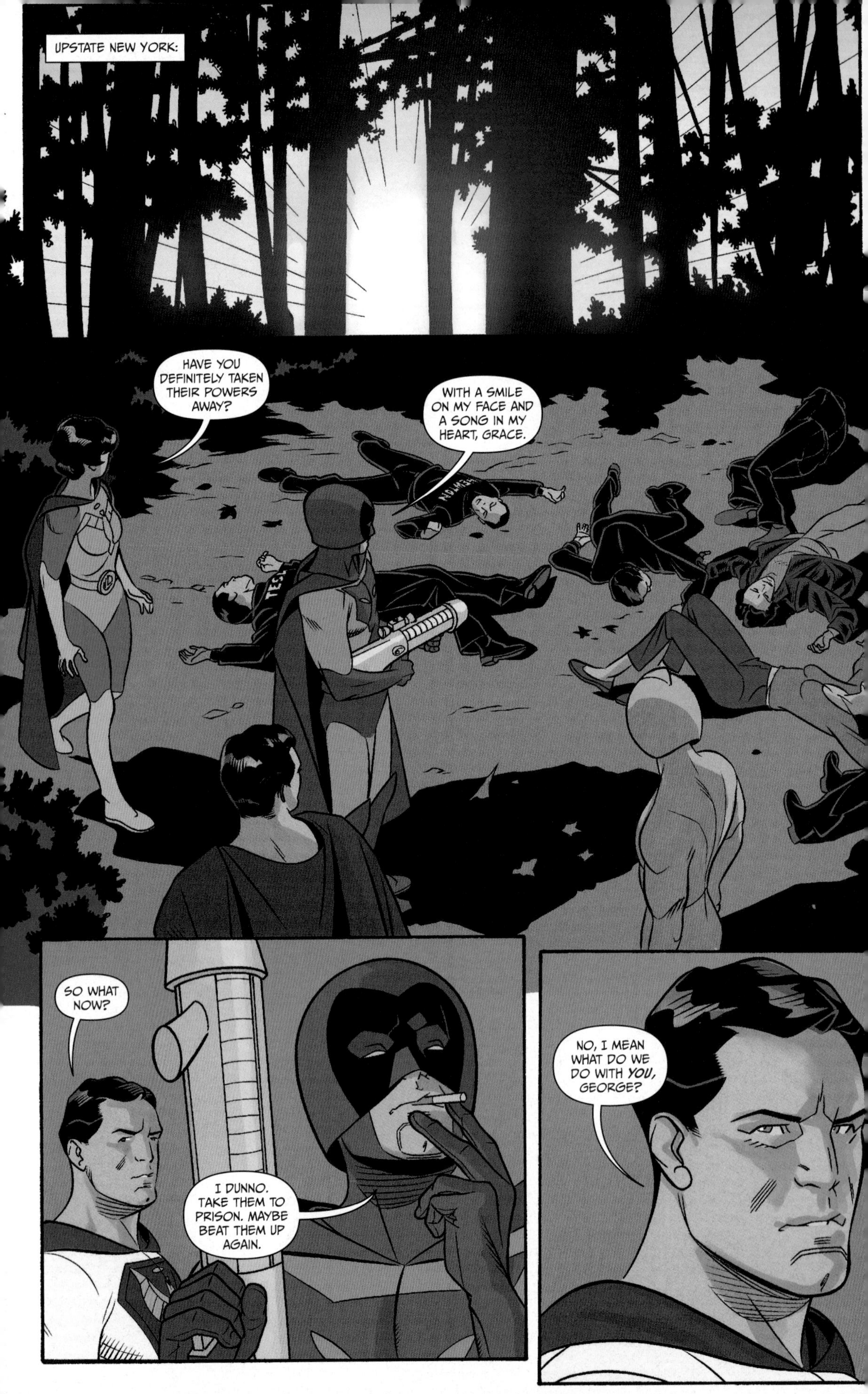

UPSTATE NEW YORK:
HAVE YOU DEFINITELY TAKEN THEIR POWERS AWAY?
WITH A SMILE ON MY FACE AND A SONG IN MY HEART, GRACE.
SO WHAT NOW?
I DUNNO. TAKE THEM TO PRISON. MAYBE BEAT THEM UP AGAIN.
NO, I MEAN WHAT DO WE DO WITH *YOU*, GEORGE?

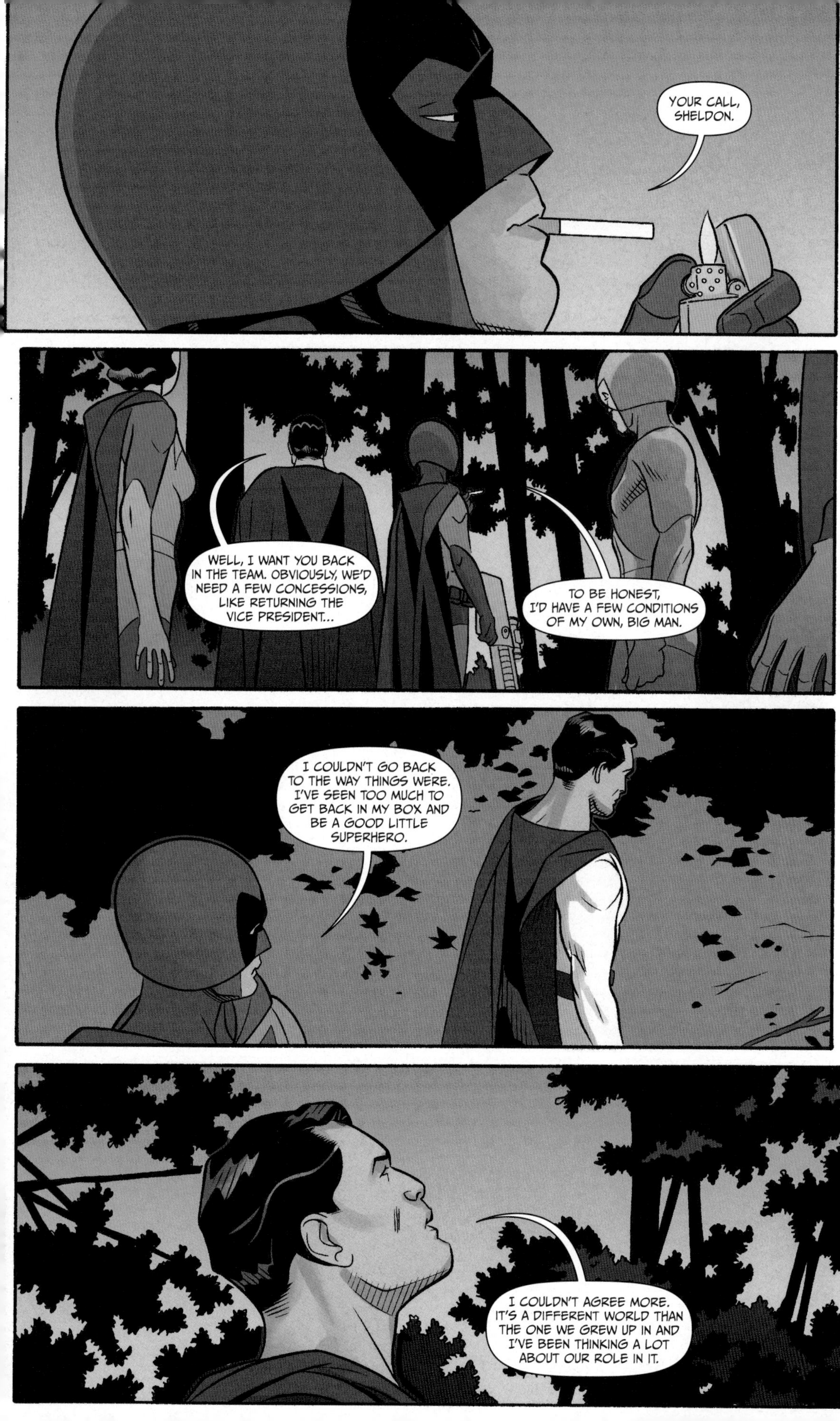
YOUR CALL, SHELDON.
WELL, I WANT YOU BACK IN THE TEAM. OBVIOUSLY, WE'D NEED A FEW CONCESSIONS, LIKE RETURNING THE VICE PRESIDENT...
TO BE HONEST, I'D HAVE A FEW CONDITIONS OF MY OWN, BIG MAN.
I COULDN'T GO BACK TO THE WAY THINGS WERE. I'VE SEEN TOO MUCH TO GET BACK IN MY BOX AND BE A GOOD LITTLE SUPERHERO.
I COULDN'T AGREE MORE. IT'S A DIFFERENT WORLD THAN THE ONE WE GREW UP IN AND I'VE BEEN THINKING A LOT ABOUT OUR ROLE IN IT.

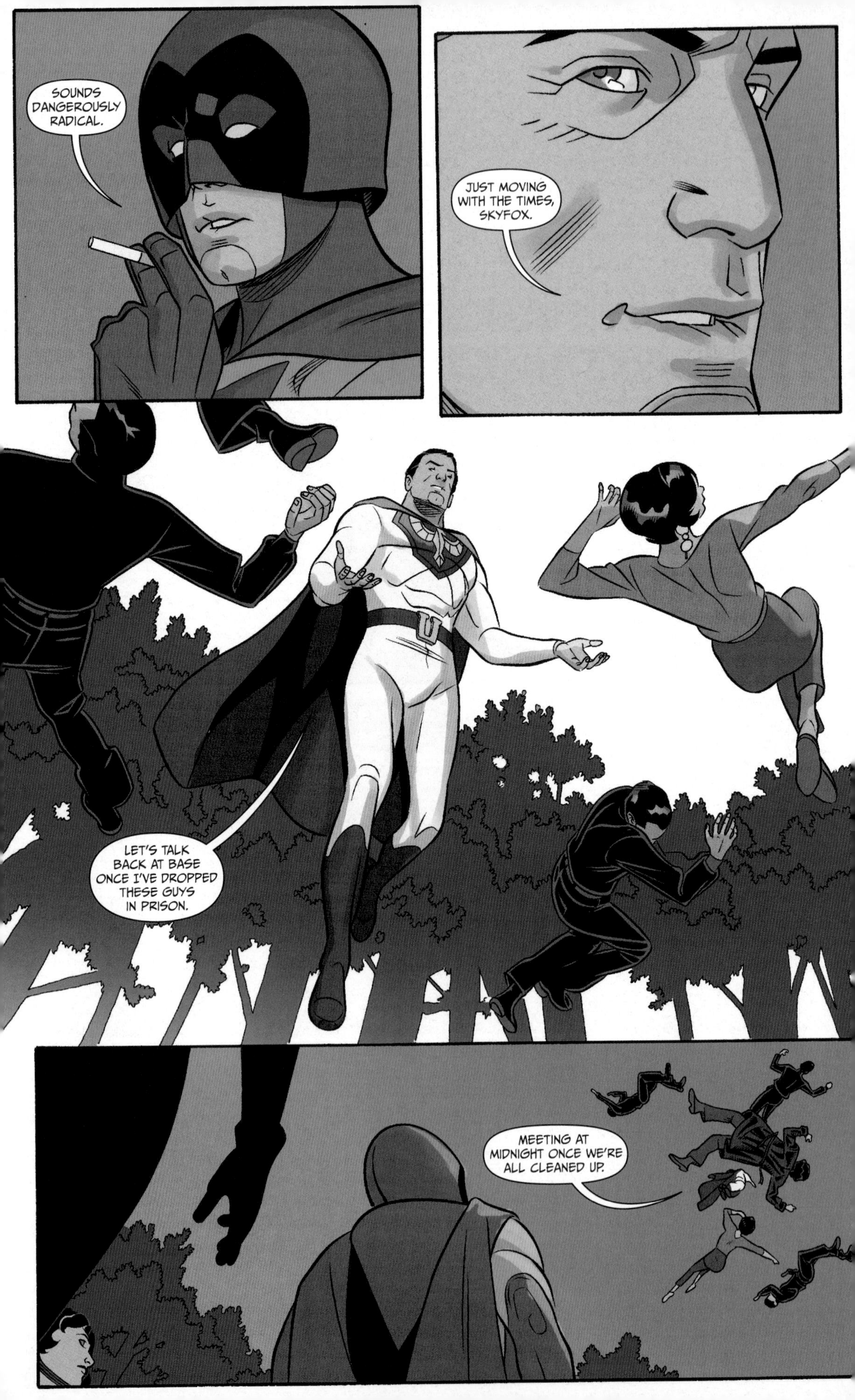
SOUNDS DANGEROUSLY RADICAL.
JUST MOVING WITH THE TIMES, SKYFOX.
LET'S TALK BACK AT BASE ONCE I'VE DROPPED THESE GUYS IN PRISON.
MEETING AT MIDNIGHT ONCE WE'RE ALL CLEANED UP.

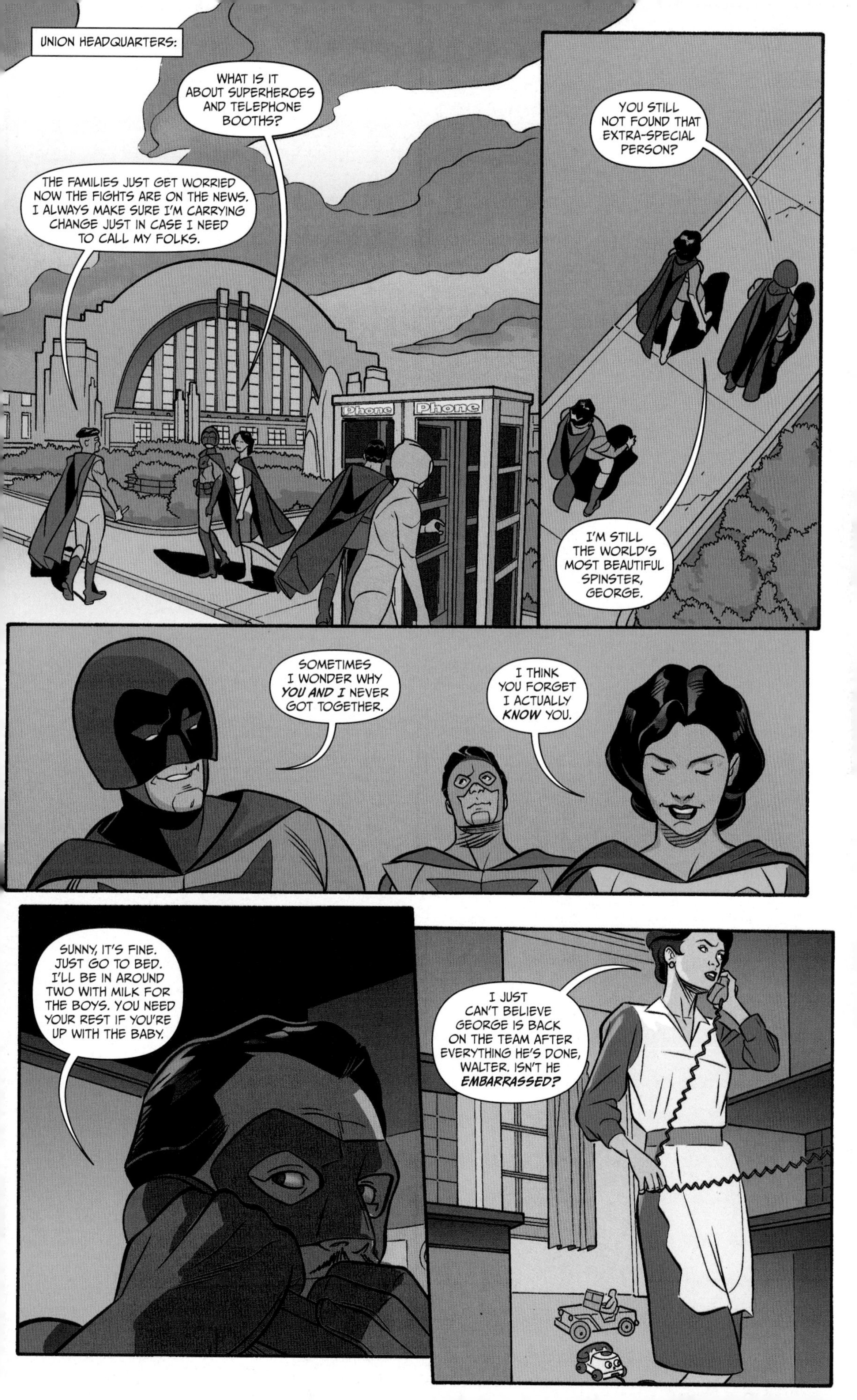
UNION HEADQUARTERS:
WHAT IS IT ABOUT SUPERHEROES AND TELEPHONE BOOTHS?
THE FAMILIES JUST GET WORRIED NOW THE FIGHTS ARE ON THE NEWS. I ALWAYS MAKE SURE I'M CARRYING CHANGE JUST IN CASE I NEED TO CALL MY FOLKS.
Phone
Phone
YOU STILL NOT FOUND THAT EXTRA-SPECIAL PERSON?
I'M STILL THE WORLD'S MOST BEAUTIFUL SPINSTER, GEORGE.
SOMETIMES I WONDER WHY ***YOU AND I*** NEVER GOT TOGETHER.
I THINK YOU FORGET I ACTUALLY ***KNOW*** YOU.
SUNNY, IT'S FINE. JUST GO TO BED. I'LL BE IN AROUND TWO WITH MILK FOR THE BOYS. YOU NEED YOUR REST IF YOU'RE UP WITH THE BABY.
I JUST CAN'T BELIEVE GEORGE IS BACK ON THE TEAM AFTER EVERYTHING HE'S DONE, WALTER. ISN'T HE ***EMBARRASSED?***

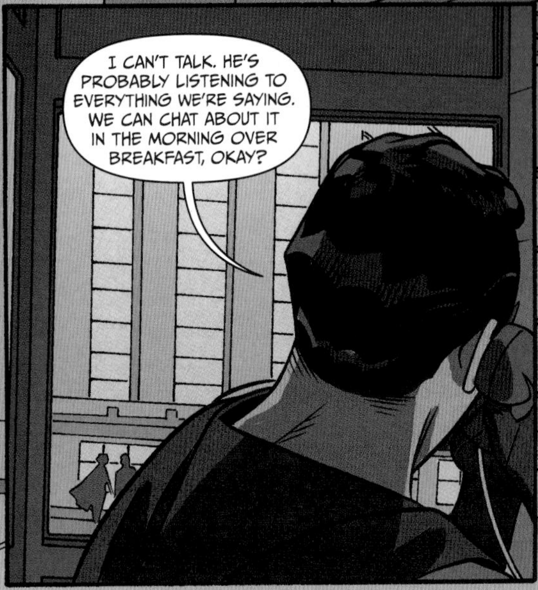
I CAN'T TALK. HE'S PROBABLY LISTENING TO EVERYTHING WE'RE SAYING. WE CAN CHAT ABOUT IT IN THE MORNING OVER BREAKFAST, OKAY?

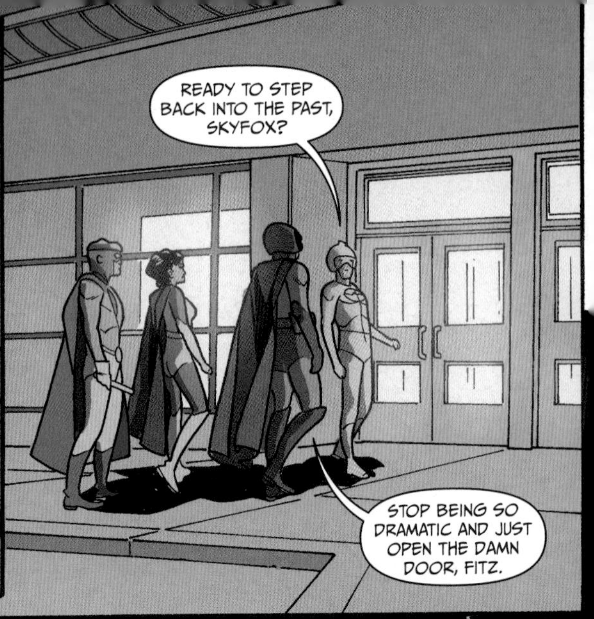
READY TO STEP BACK INTO THE PAST, SKYFOX?
STOP BEING SO DRAMATIC AND JUST OPEN THE DAMN DOOR, FITZ.

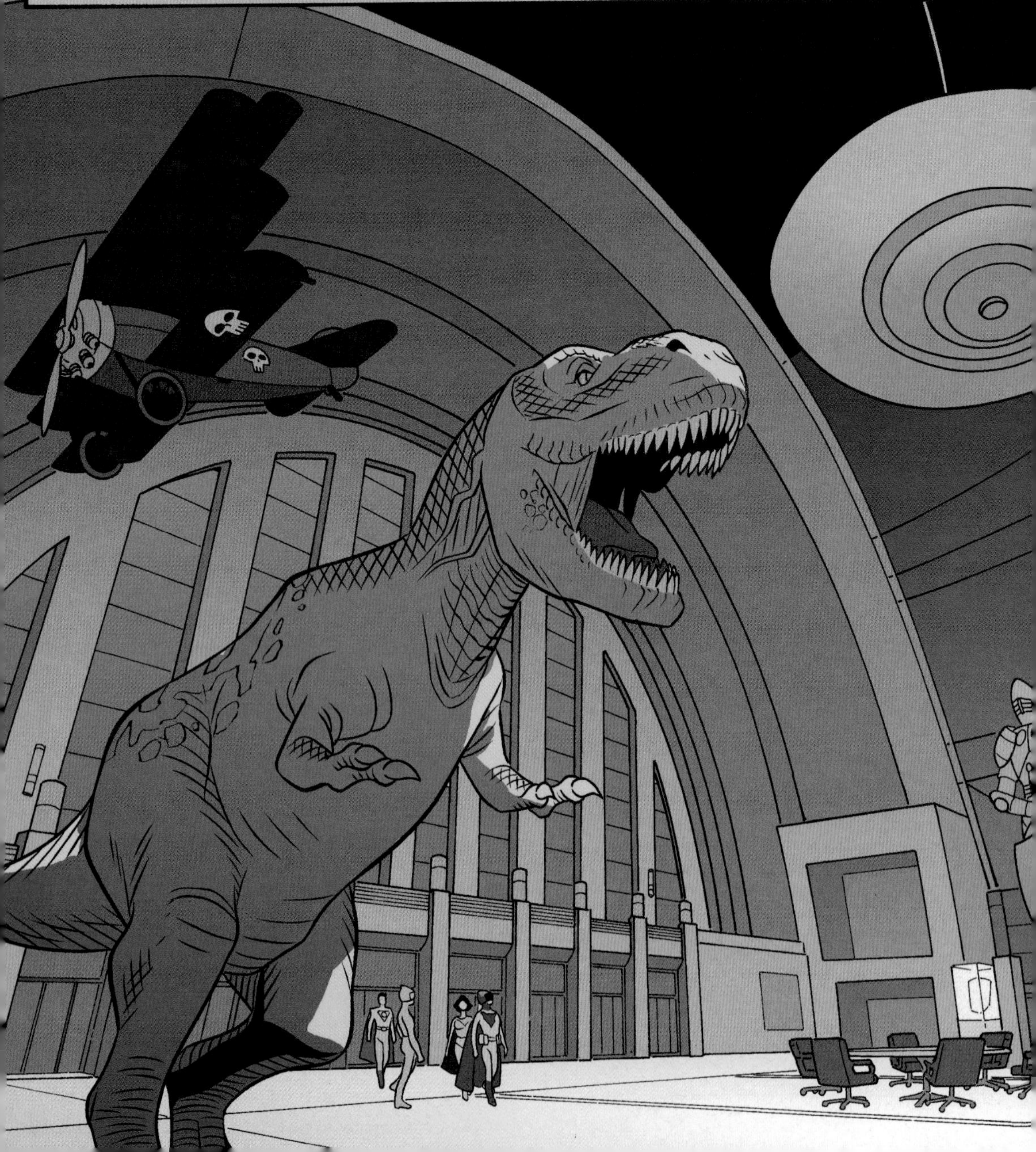

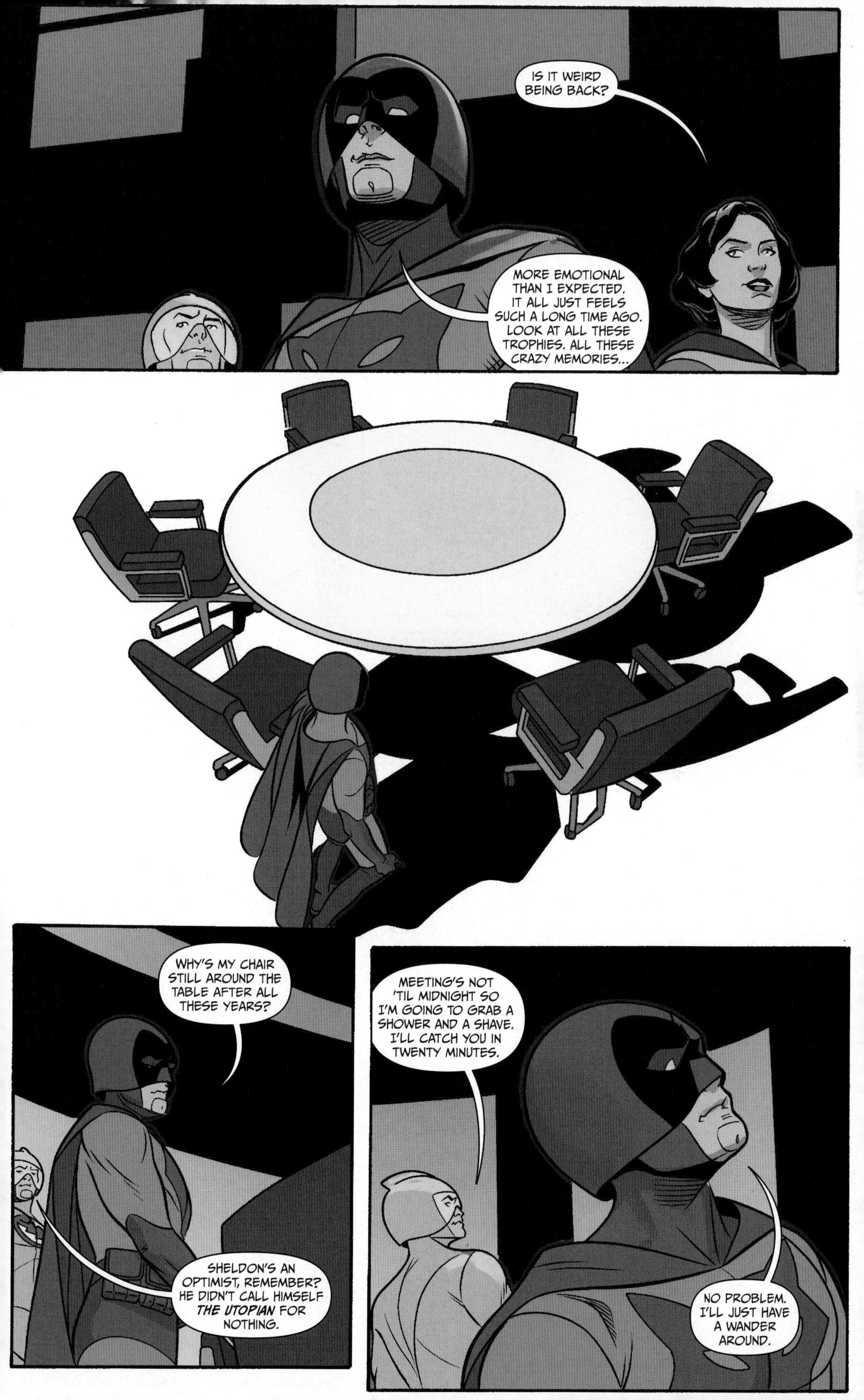
IS IT WEIRD BEING BACK?
MORE EMOTIONAL THAN I EXPECTED. IT ALL JUST FEELS SUCH A LONG TIME AGO. LOOK AT ALL THESE TROPHIES. ALL THESE CRAZY MEMORIES...
WHY'S MY CHAIR STILL AROUND THE TABLE AFTER ALL THESE YEARS?
SHELDON'S AN OPTIMIST, REMEMBER? HE DIDN'T CALL HIMSELF ***THE UTOPIAN*** FOR NOTHING.
MEETING'S NOT 'TIL MIDNIGHT SO I'M GOING TO GRAB A SHOWER AND A SHAVE. I'LL CATCH YOU IN TWENTY MINUTES.
NO PROBLEM. I'LL JUST HAVE A WANDER AROUND.

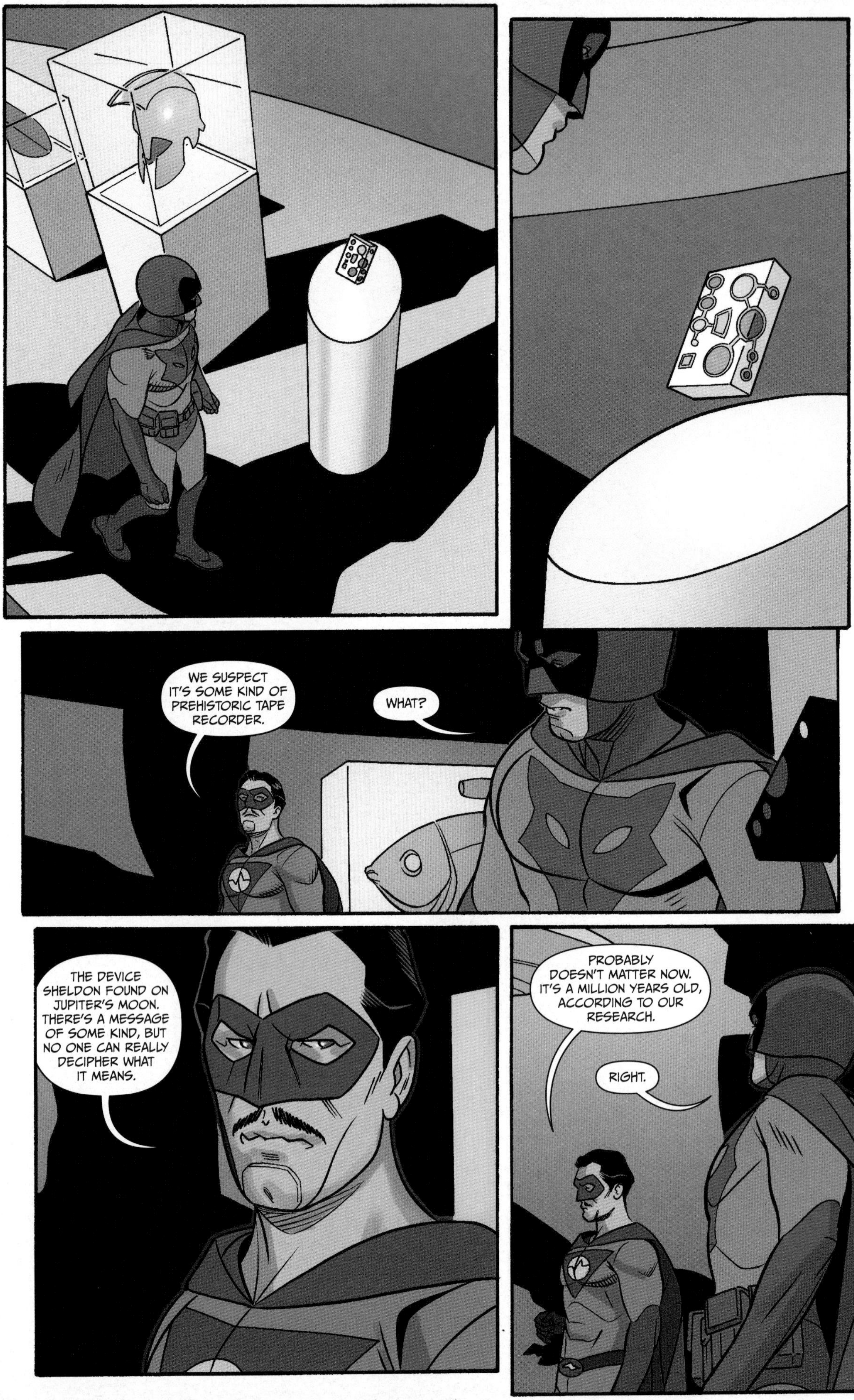
WE SUSPECT IT'S SOME KIND OF PREHISTORIC TAPE RECORDER.
WHAT?
THE DEVICE SHELDON FOUND ON JUPITER'S MOON. THERE'S A MESSAGE OF SOME KIND, BUT NO ONE CAN REALLY DECIPHER WHAT IT MEANS.
PROBABLY DOESN'T MATTER NOW. IT'S A MILLION YEARS OLD, ACCORDING TO OUR RESEARCH.
RIGHT.

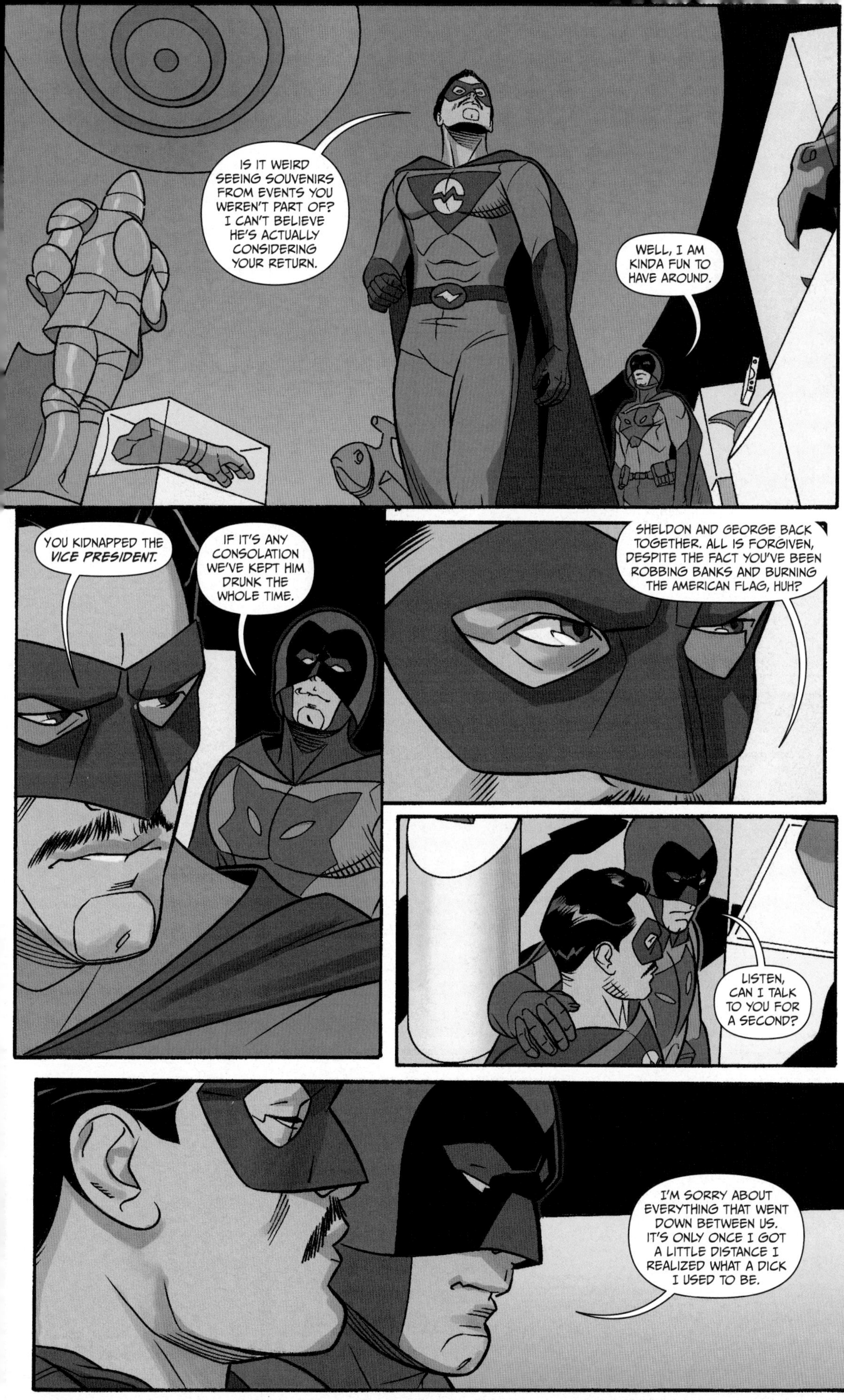
IS IT WEIRD SEEING SOUVENIRS FROM EVENTS YOU WEREN'T PART OF? I CAN'T BELIEVE HE'S ACTUALLY CONSIDERING YOUR RETURN.
WELL, I AM KINDA FUN TO HAVE AROUND.
YOU KIDNAPPED THE *VICE PRESIDENT.*
IF IT'S ANY CONSOLATION WE'VE KEPT HIM DRUNK THE WHOLE TIME.
SHELDON AND GEORGE BACK TOGETHER. ALL IS FORGIVEN, DESPITE THE FACT YOU'VE BEEN ROBBING BANKS AND BURNING THE AMERICAN FLAG, HUH?
LISTEN, CAN I TALK TO YOU FOR A SECOND?
I'M SORRY ABOUT EVERYTHING THAT WENT DOWN BETWEEN US. IT'S ONLY ONCE I GOT A LITTLE DISTANCE I REALIZED WHAT A DICK I USED TO BE.

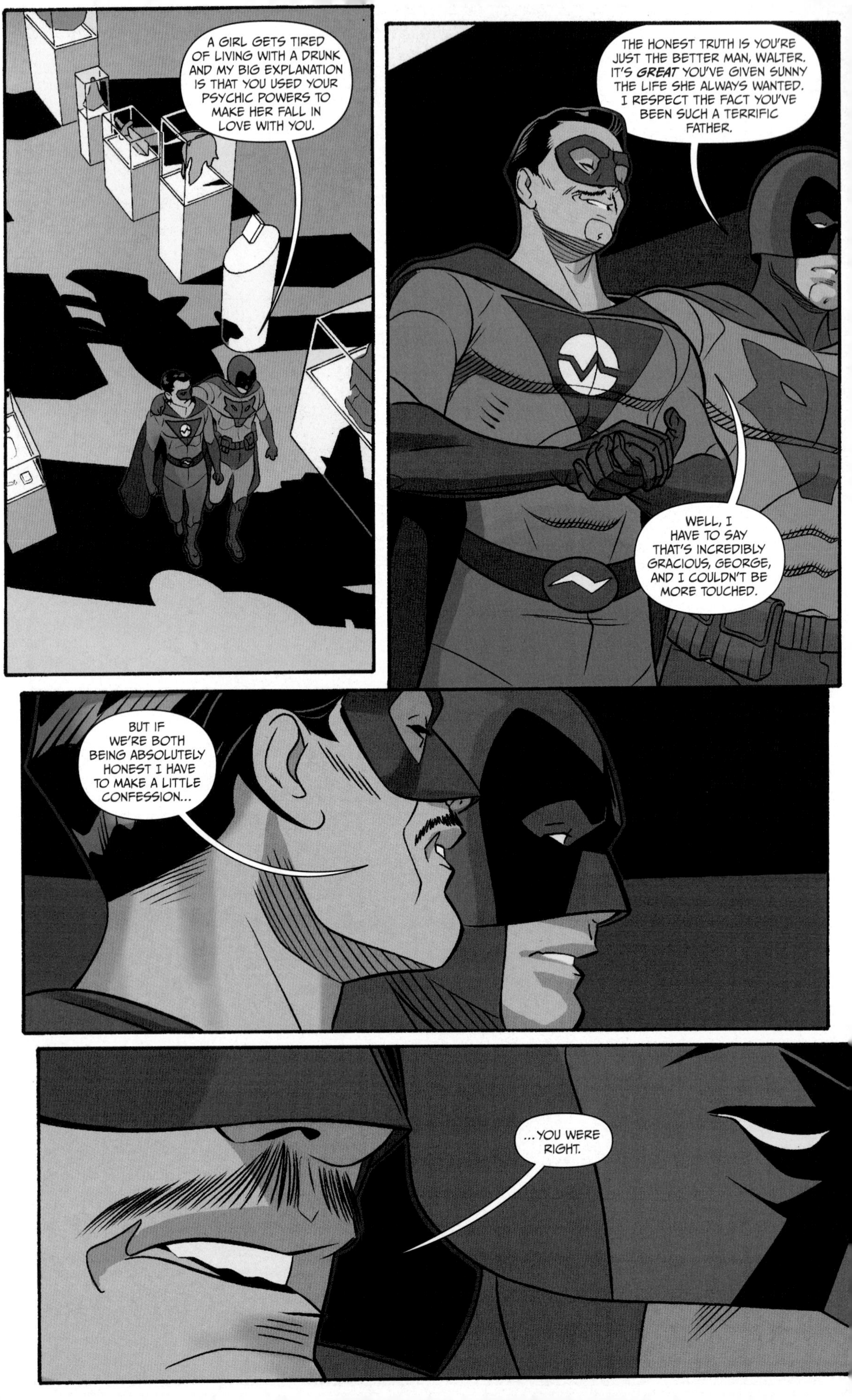
A GIRL GETS TIRED OF LIVING WITH A DRUNK AND MY BIG EXPLANATION IS THAT YOU USED YOUR PSYCHIC POWERS TO MAKE HER FALL IN LOVE WITH YOU.
THE HONEST TRUTH IS YOU'RE JUST THE BETTER MAN, WALTER. IT'S *GREAT* YOU'VE GIVEN SUNNY THE LIFE SHE ALWAYS WANTED. I RESPECT THE FACT YOU'VE BEEN SUCH A TERRIFIC FATHER.
WELL, I HAVE TO SAY THAT'S INCREDIBLY GRACIOUS, GEORGE, AND I COULDN'T BE MORE TOUCHED.
BUT IF WE'RE BOTH BEING ABSOLUTELY HONEST I HAVE TO MAKE A LITTLE CONFESSION...
...YOU WERE RIGHT.

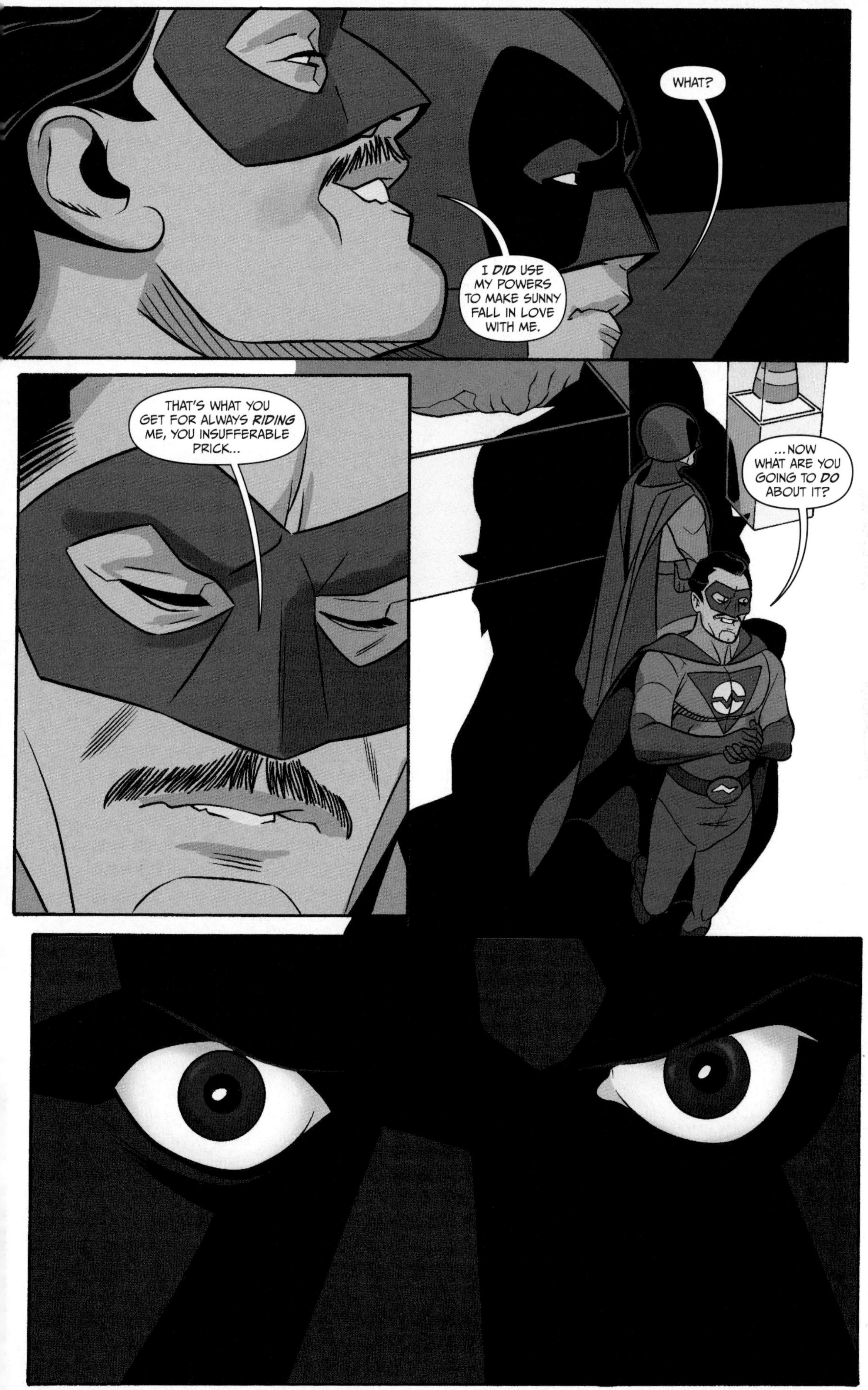
WHAT?
I DID USE MY POWERS TO MAKE SUNNY FALL IN LOVE WITH ME.
THAT'S WHAT YOU GET FOR ALWAYS RIDING ME, YOU INSUFFERABLE PRICK...
...NOW WHAT ARE YOU GOING TO DO ABOUT IT?

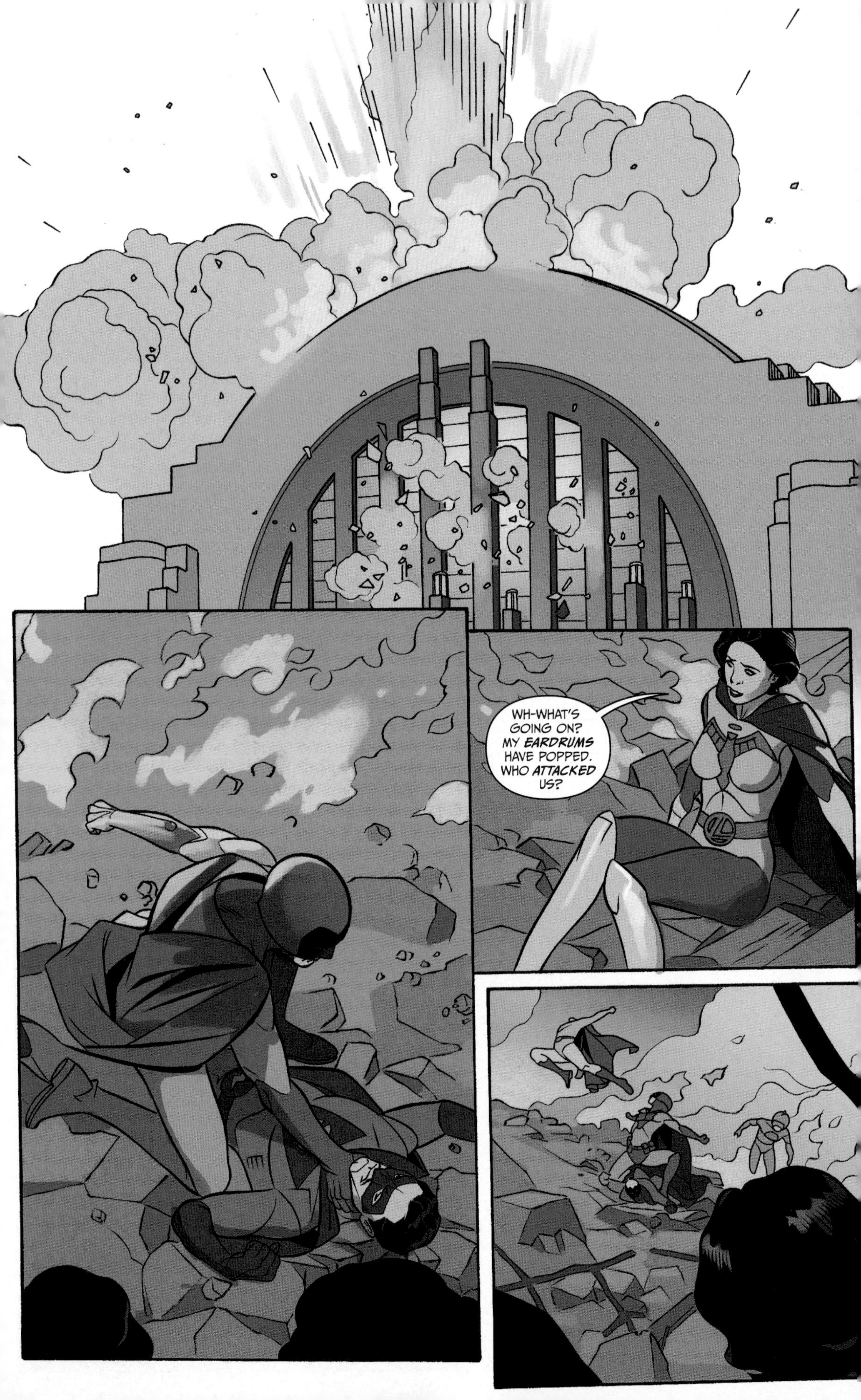
WH-WHAT'S GOING ON? MY EARDRUMS HAVE POPPED. WHO ATTACKED US?

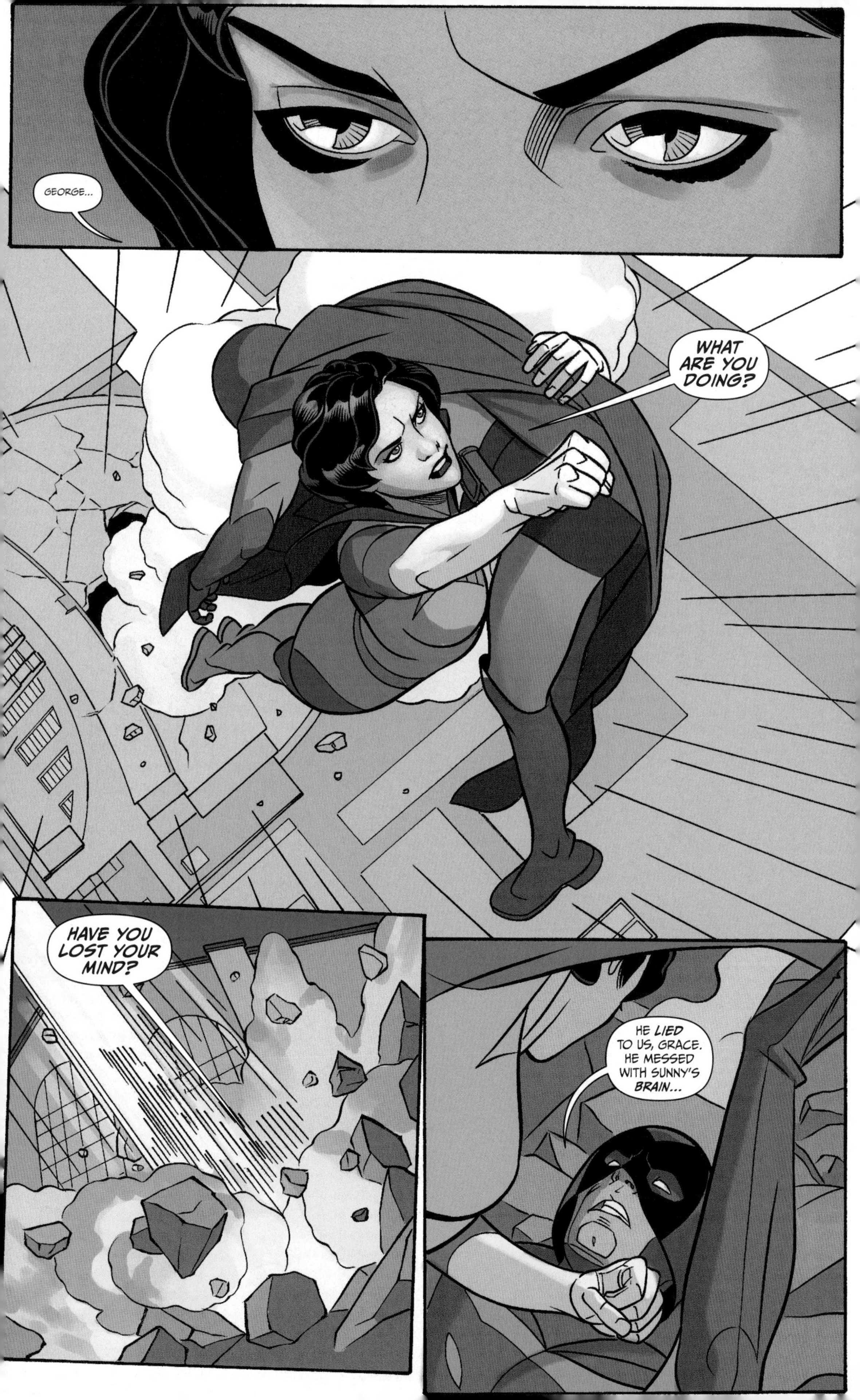
GEORGE...
WHAT ARE YOU DOING?
HAVE YOU LOST YOUR MIND?
HE *LIED* TO US, GRACE. HE MESSED WITH SUNNY'S *BRAIN*...

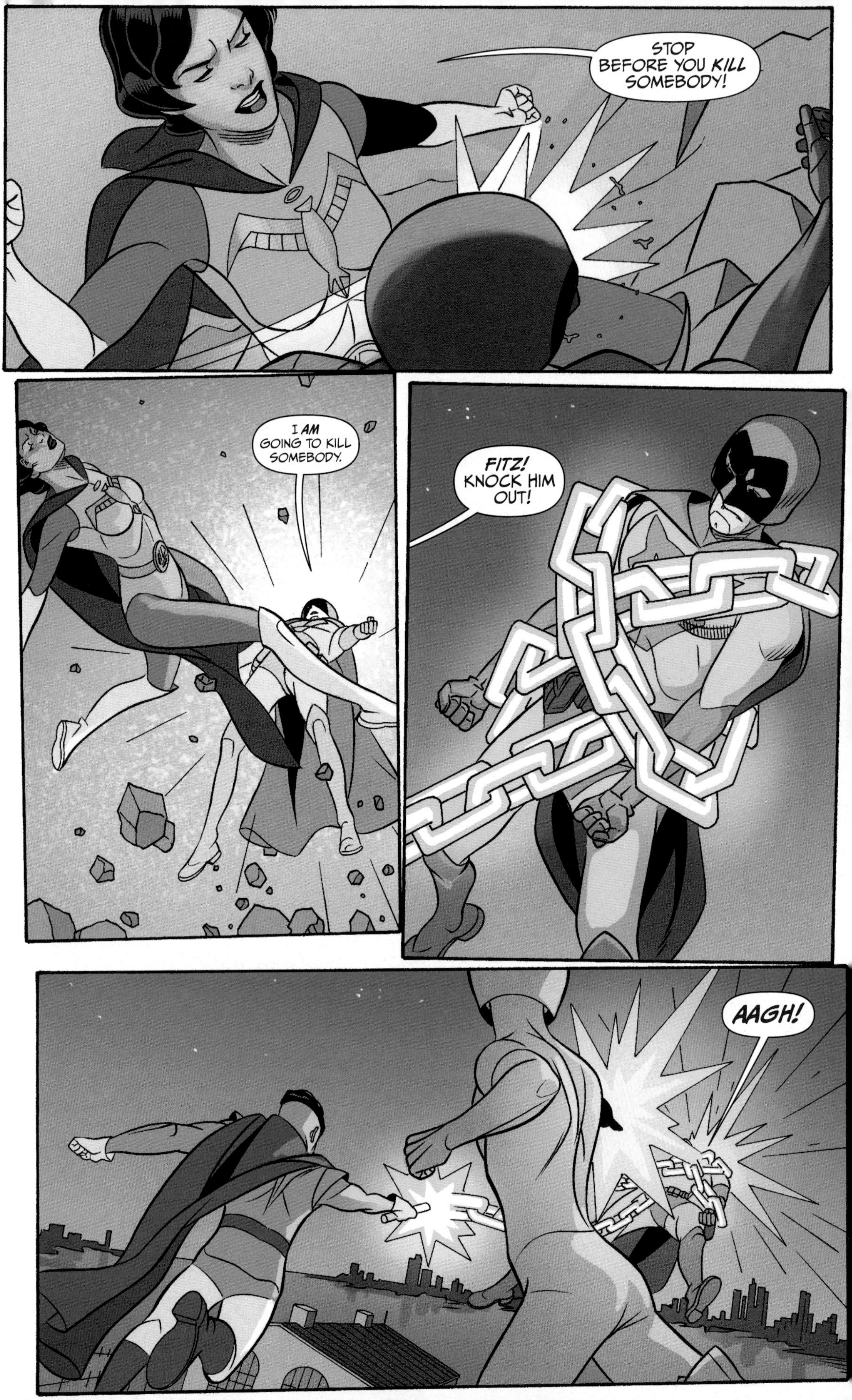
STOP BEFORE YOU KILL SOMEBODY!
I AM GOING TO KILL SOMEBODY.
FITZ! KNOCK HIM OUT!
AAGH!

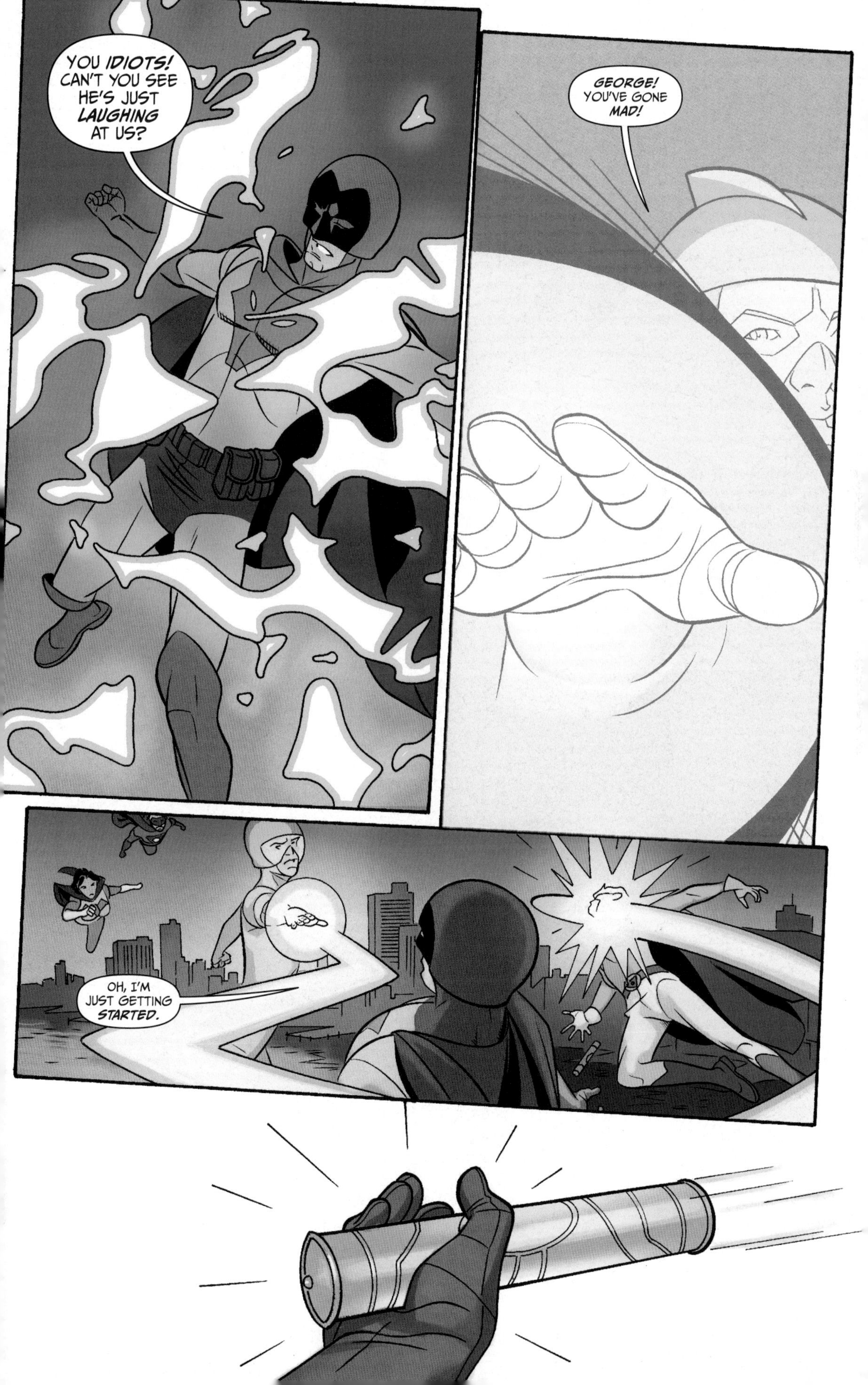
YOU IDIOTS! CAN'T YOU SEE HE'S JUST LAUGHING AT US?
GEORGE! YOU'VE GONE MAD!
OH, I'M JUST GETTING STARTED.

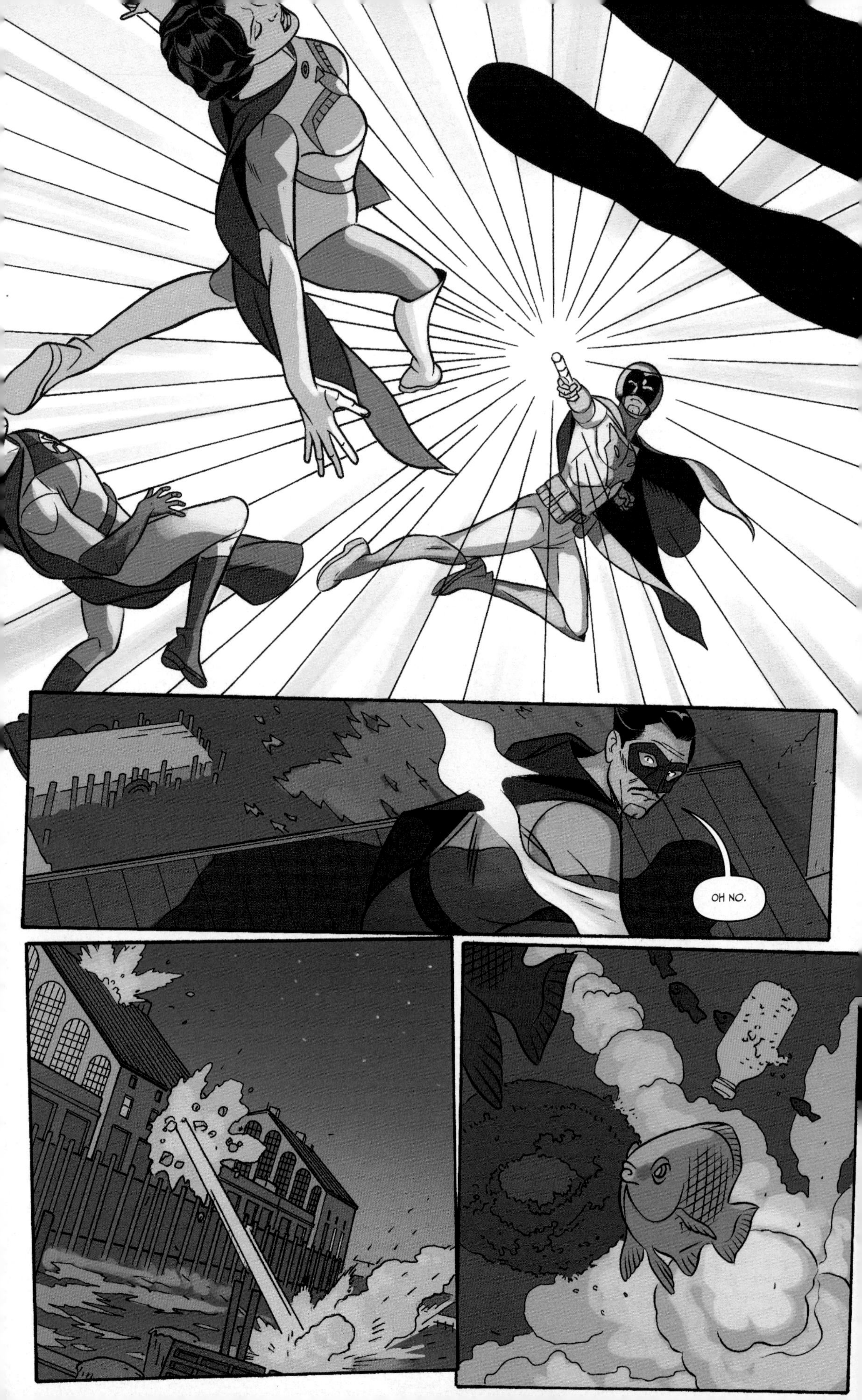
OH NO.

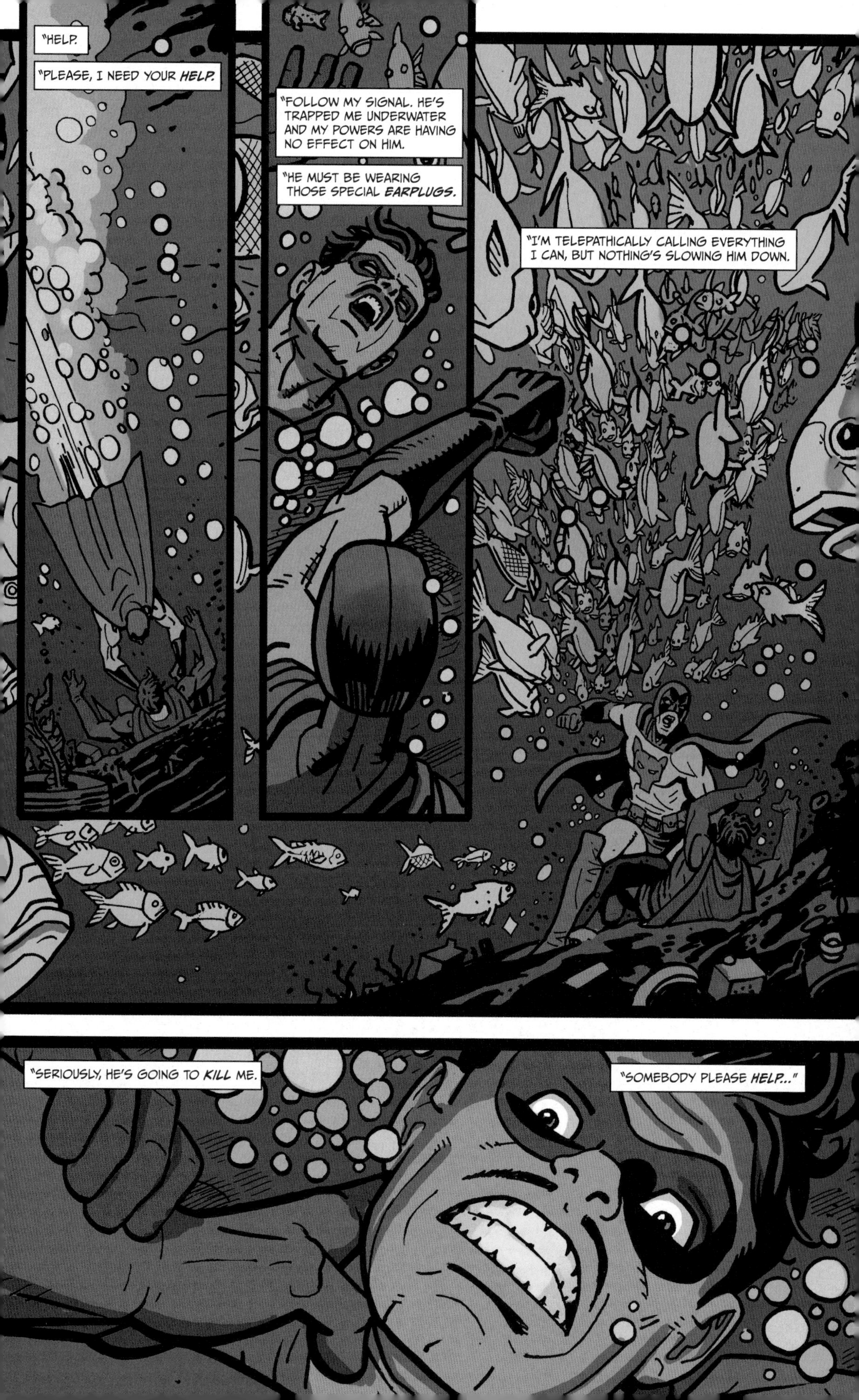
"HELP.
"PLEASE, I NEED YOUR HELP.
"FOLLOW MY SIGNAL. HE'S TRAPPED ME UNDERWATER AND MY POWERS ARE HAVING NO EFFECT ON HIM.
"HE MUST BE WEARING THOSE SPECIAL EARPLUGS.
"I'M TELEPATHICALLY CALLING EVERYTHING I CAN, BUT NOTHING'S SLOWING HIM DOWN.
"SERIOUSLY, HE'S GOING TO KILL ME.
"SOMEBODY PLEASE HELP..."

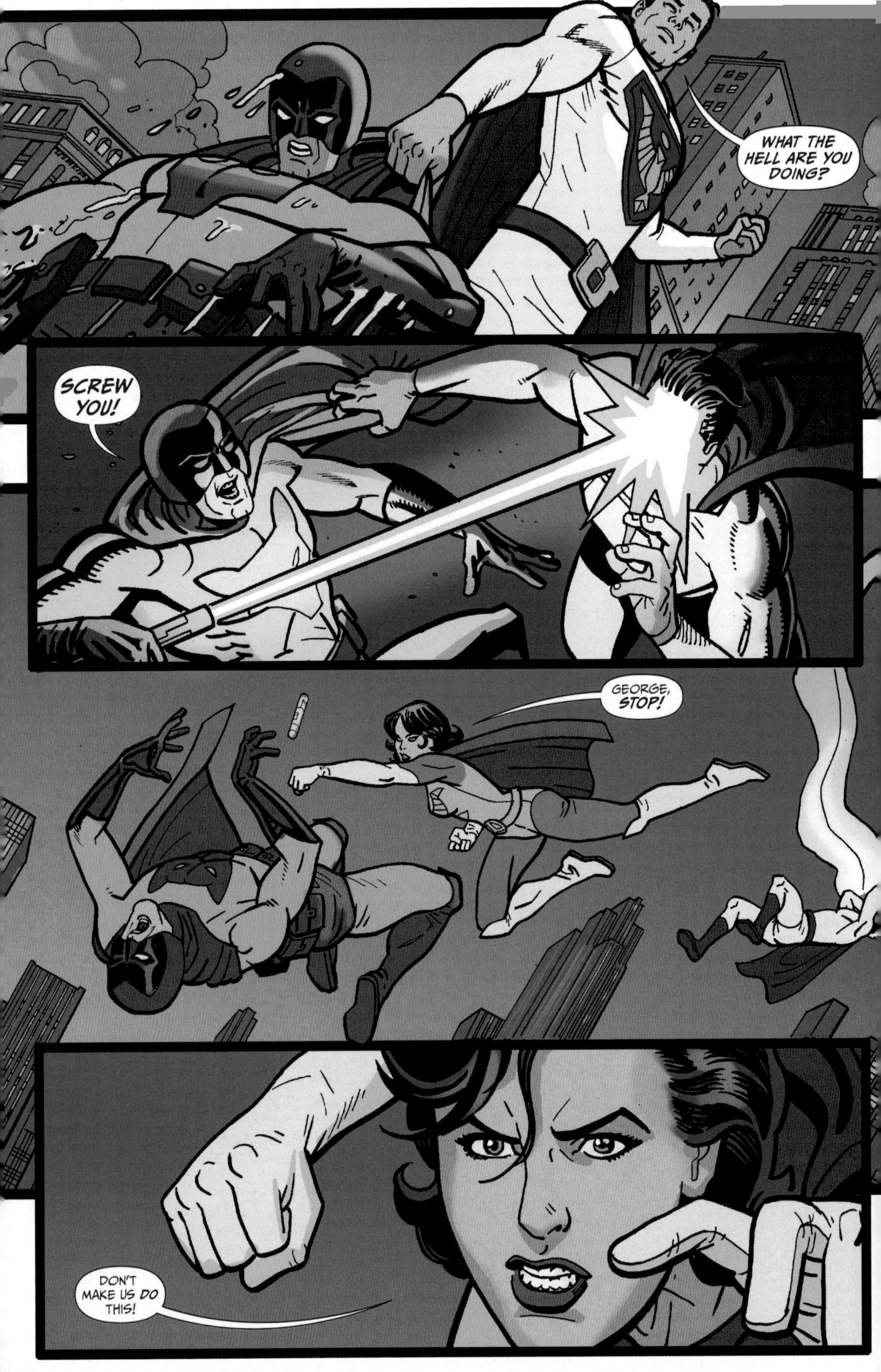
WHAT THE HELL ARE YOU DOING?
SCREW YOU!
GEORGE, STOP!
DON'T MAKE US DO THIS!

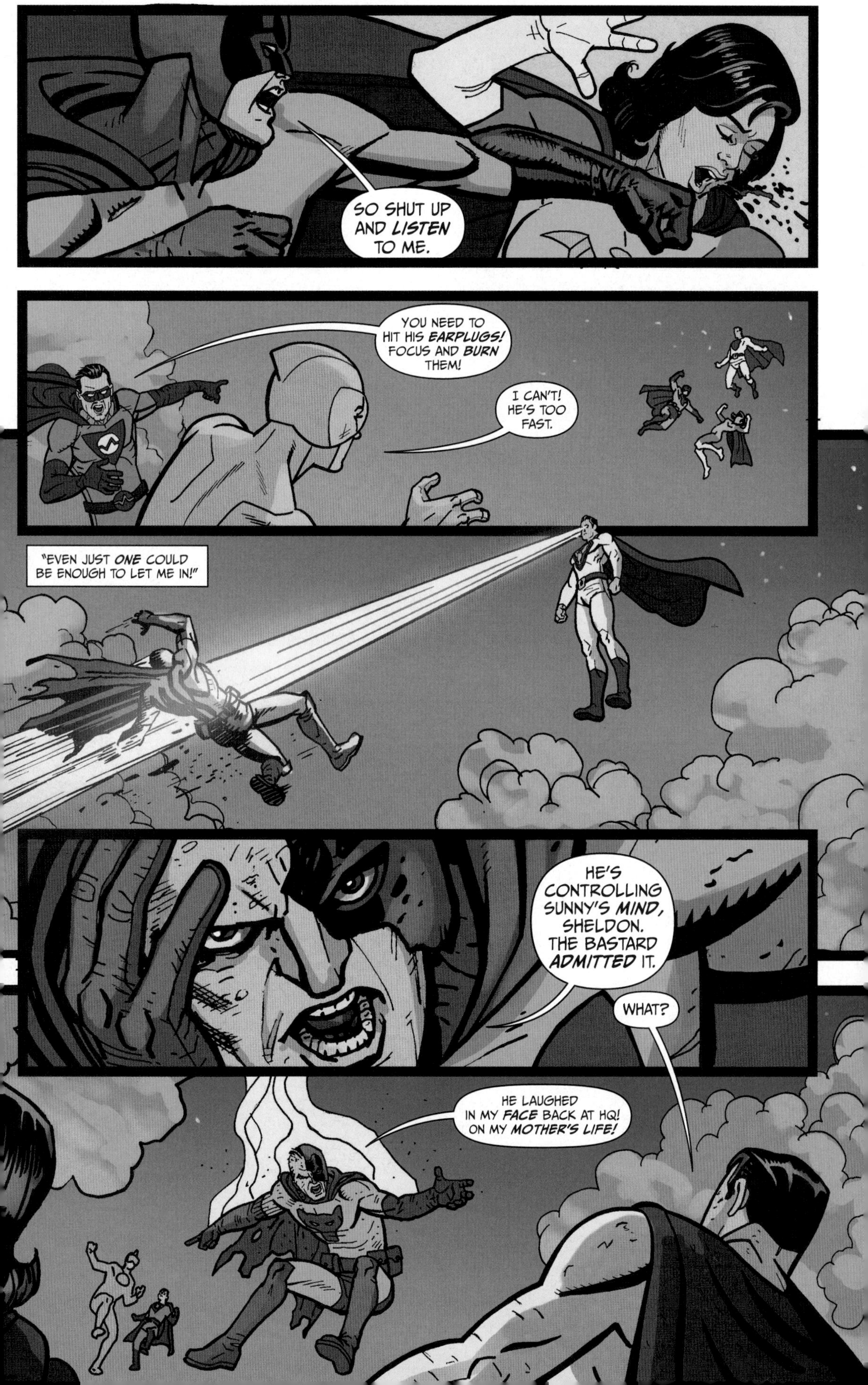
SO SHUT UP AND LISTEN TO ME.
YOU NEED TO HIT HIS EARPLUGS! FOCUS AND BURN THEM!
I CAN'T! HE'S TOO FAST.
"EVEN JUST ONE COULD BE ENOUGH TO LET ME IN!"
HE'S CONTROLLING SUNNY'S MIND, SHELDON. THE BASTARD ADMITTED IT.
WHAT?
HE LAUGHED IN MY FACE BACK AT HQ! ON MY MOTHER'S LIFE!

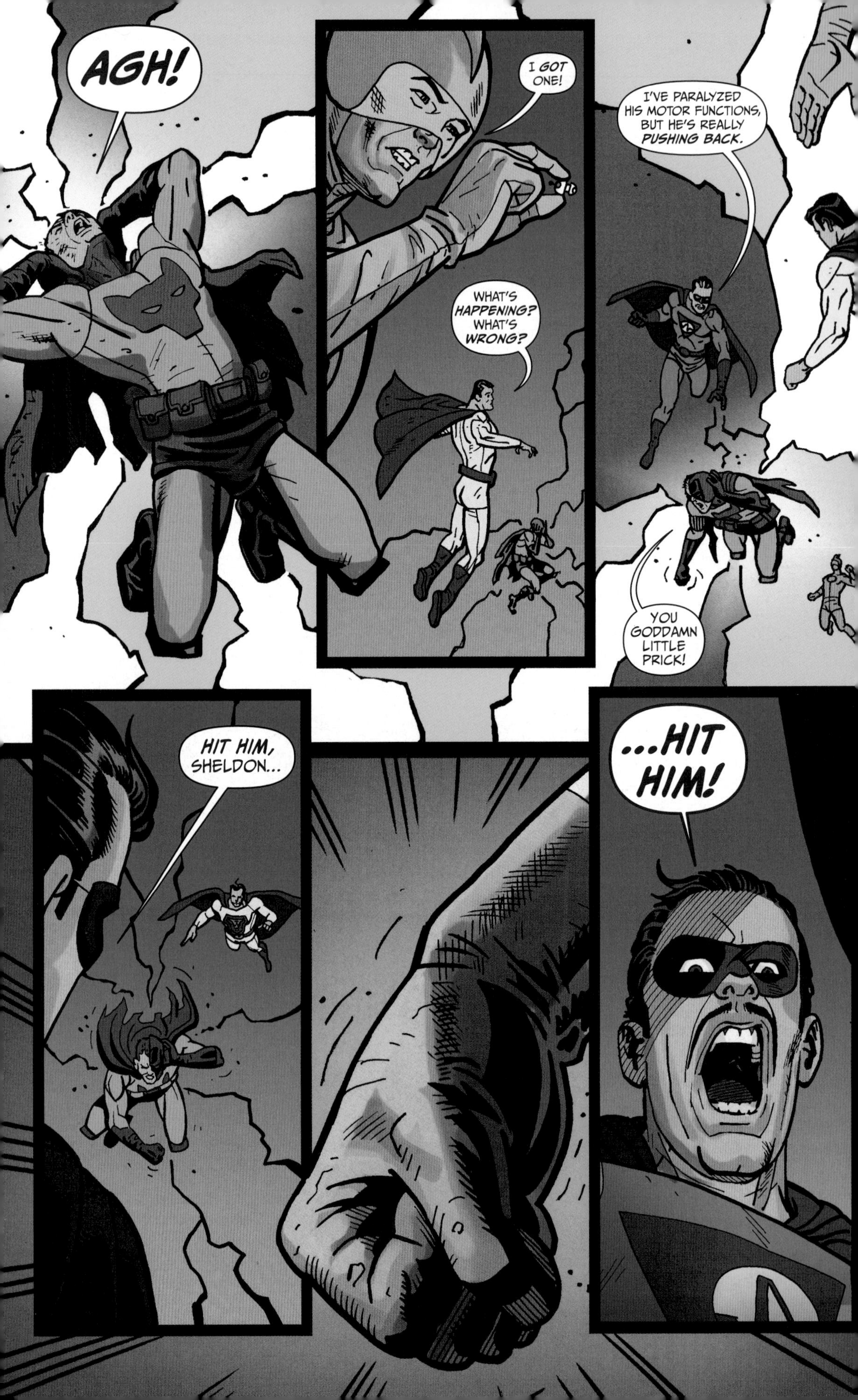
AGH!
I GOT ONE!
WHAT'S HAPPENING? WHAT'S WRONG?
I'VE PARALYZED HIS MOTOR FUNCTIONS, BUT HE'S REALLY PUSHING BACK.
YOU GODDAMN LITTLE PRICK!
HIT HIM, SHELDON...
...HIT HIM!

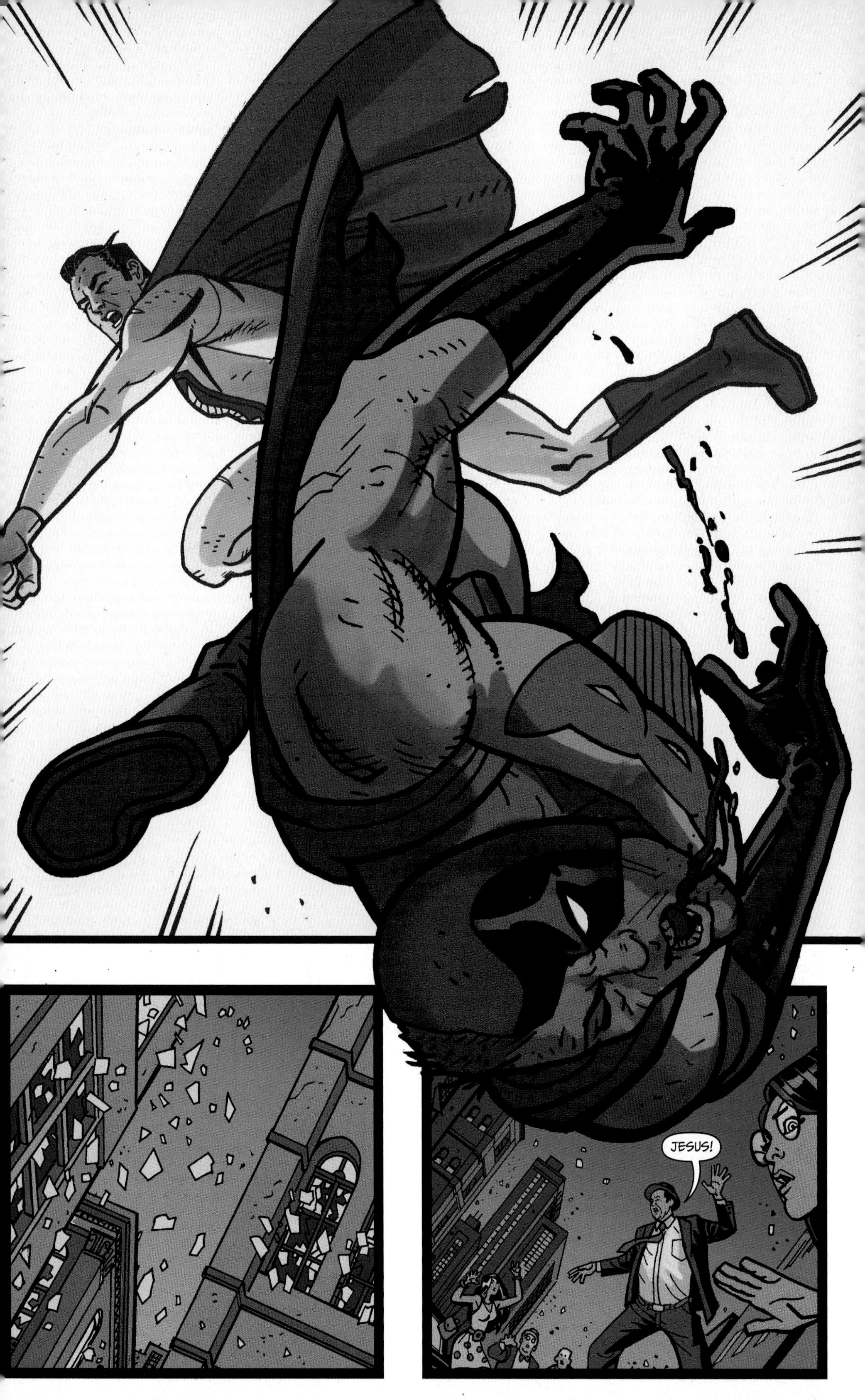
JESUS!

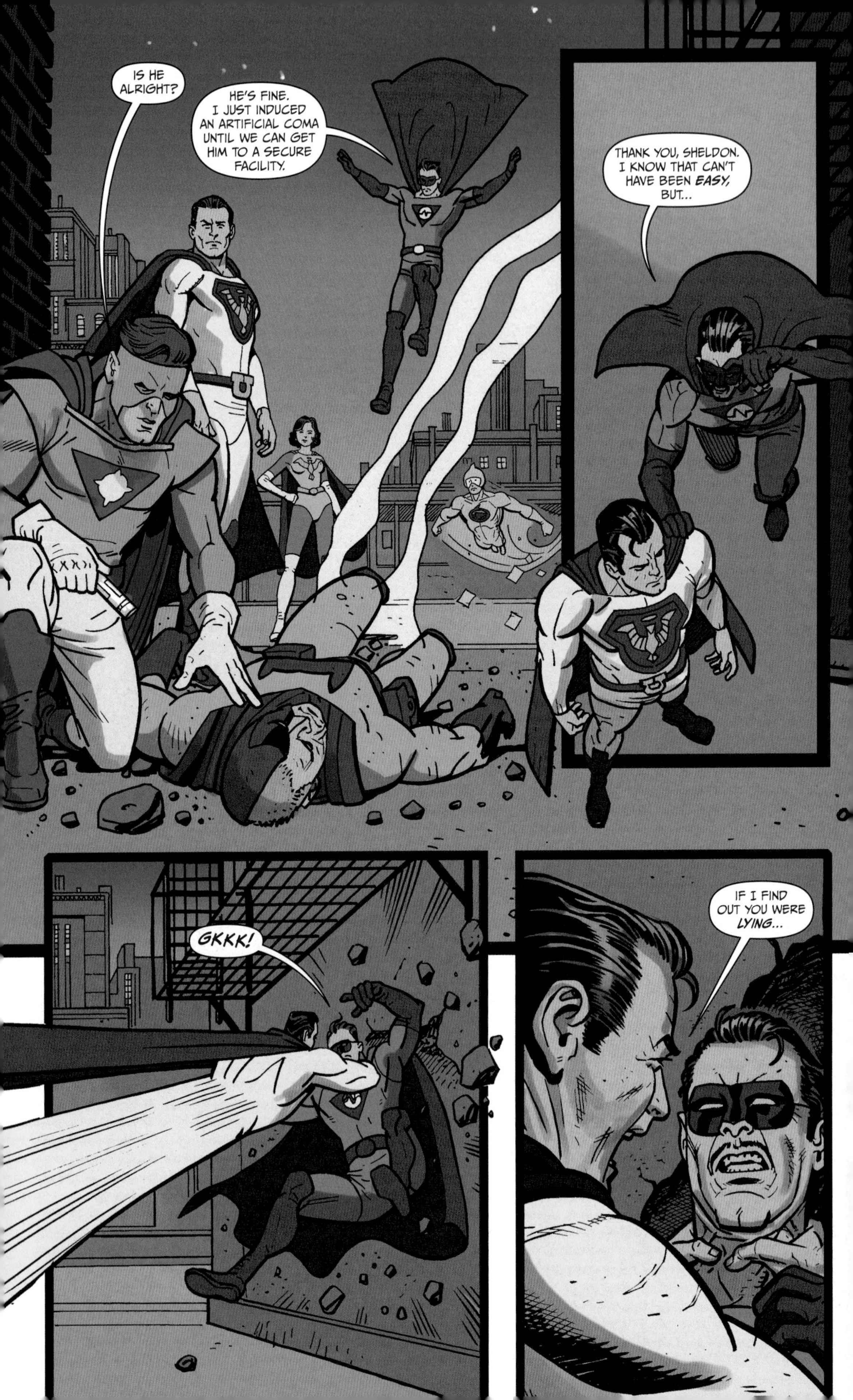
IS HE ALRIGHT?
HE'S FINE. I JUST INDUCED AN ARTIFICIAL COMA UNTIL WE CAN GET HIM TO A SECURE FACILITY.
THANK YOU, SHELDON. I KNOW THAT CAN'T HAVE BEEN *EASY,* BUT...
GKKK!
IF I FIND OUT YOU WERE *LYING*...

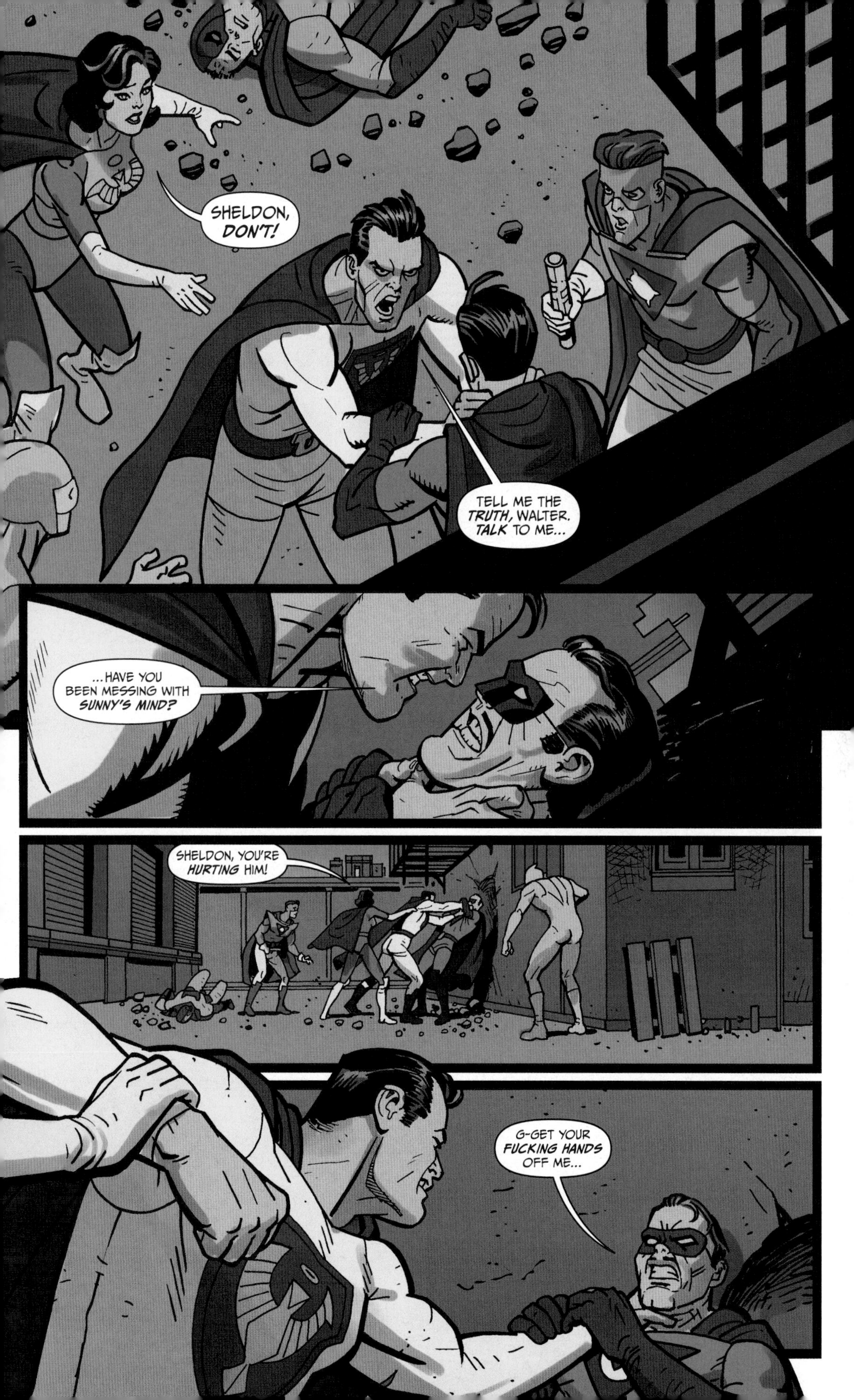
SHELDON, DON'T!
TELL ME THE TRUTH, WALTER. TALK TO ME...
...HAVE YOU BEEN MESSING WITH SUNNY'S MIND?
SHELDON, YOU'RE HURTING HIM!
G-GET YOUR FUCKING HANDS OFF ME...

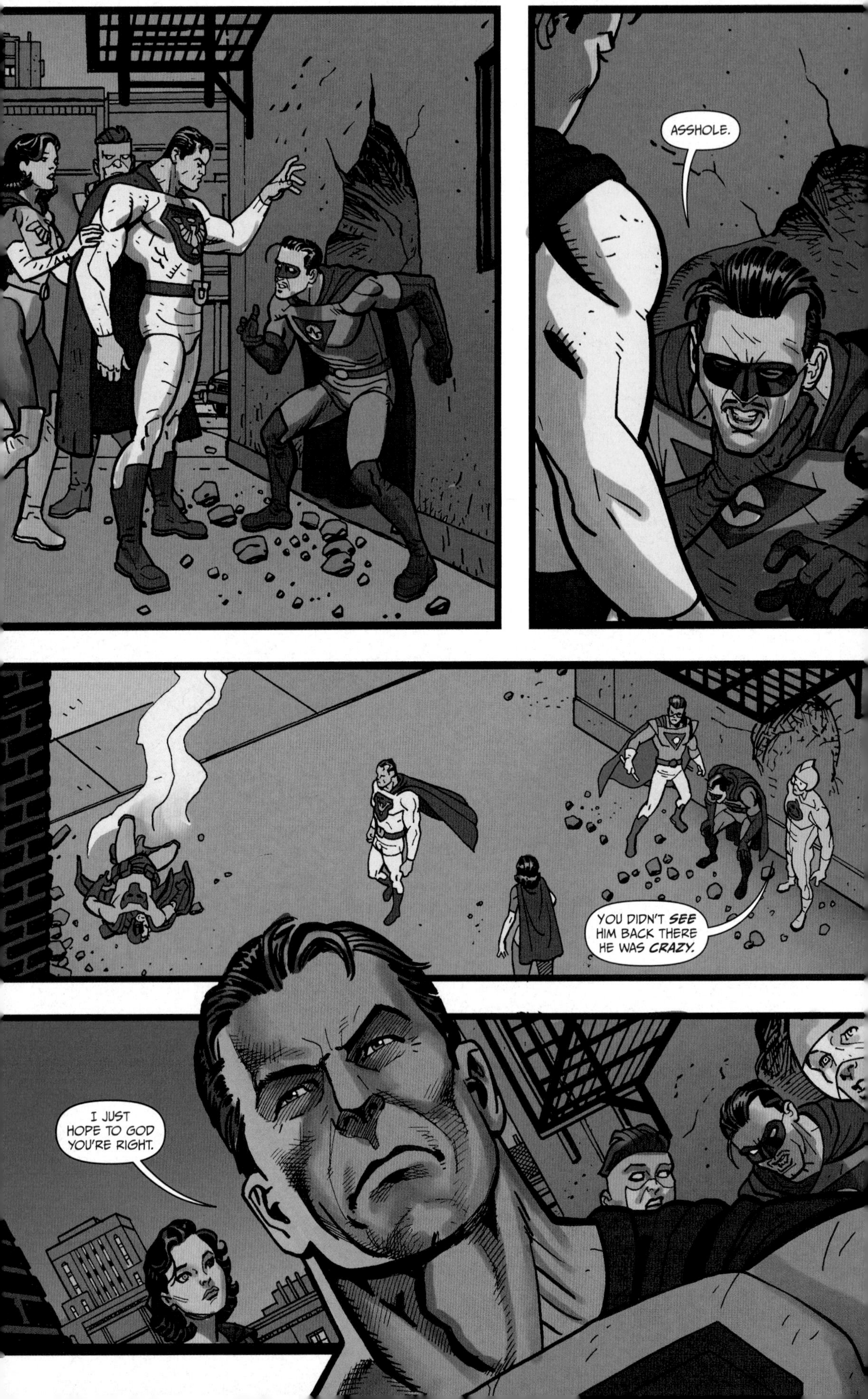
ASSHOLE.
YOU DIDN'T SEE HIM BACK THERE HE WAS CRAZY.
I JUST HOPE TO GOD YOU'RE RIGHT.

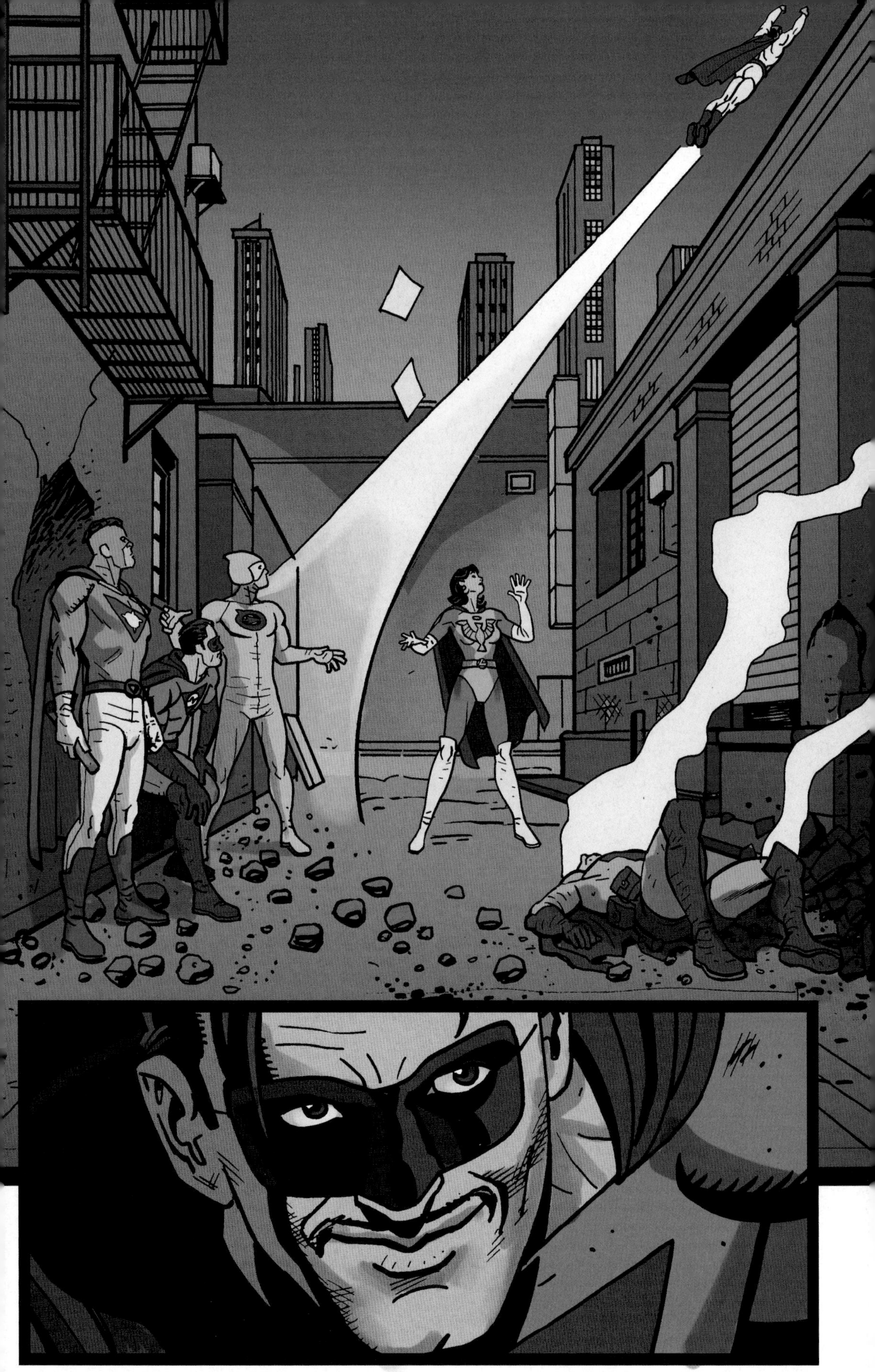

CHAPTER 6

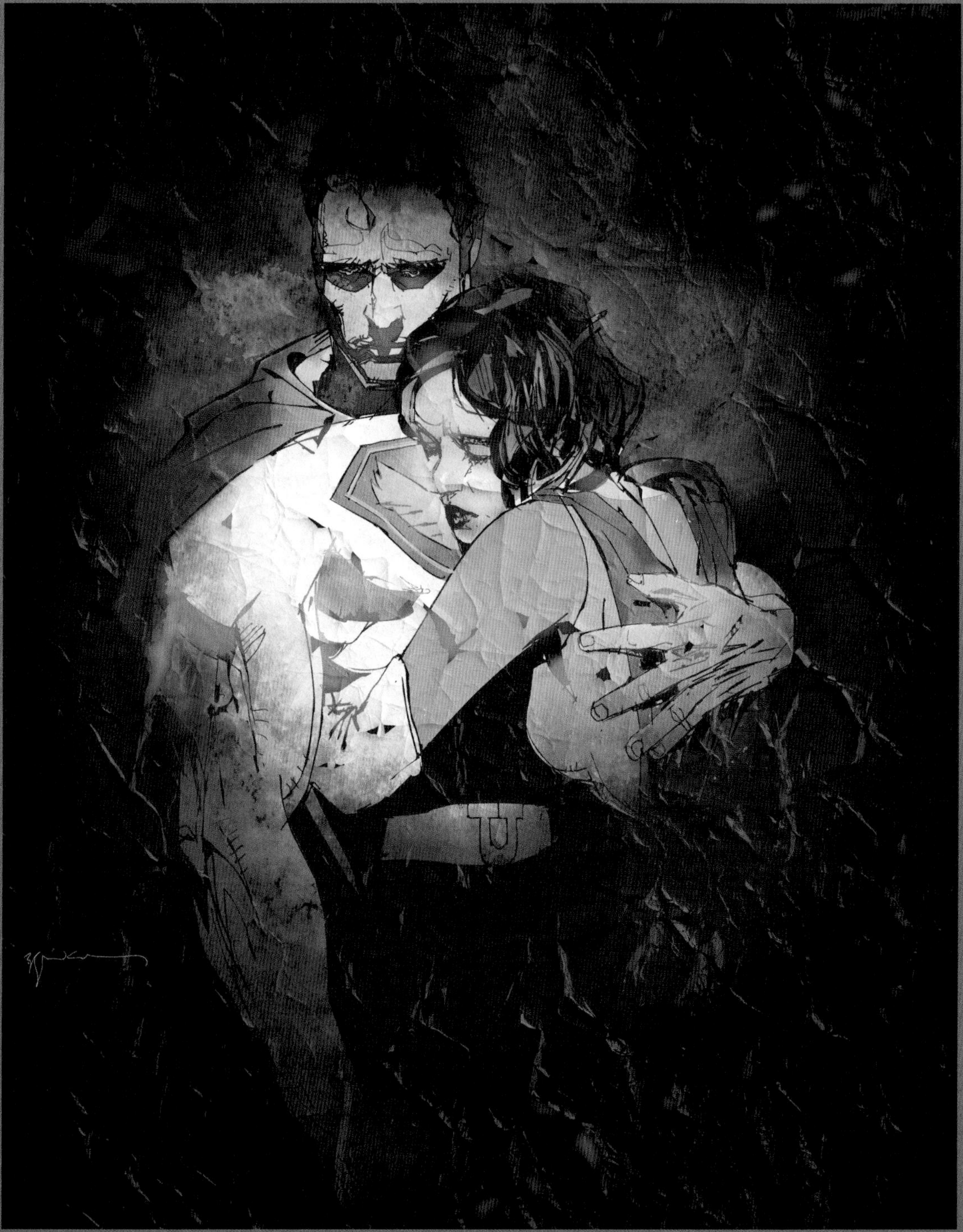

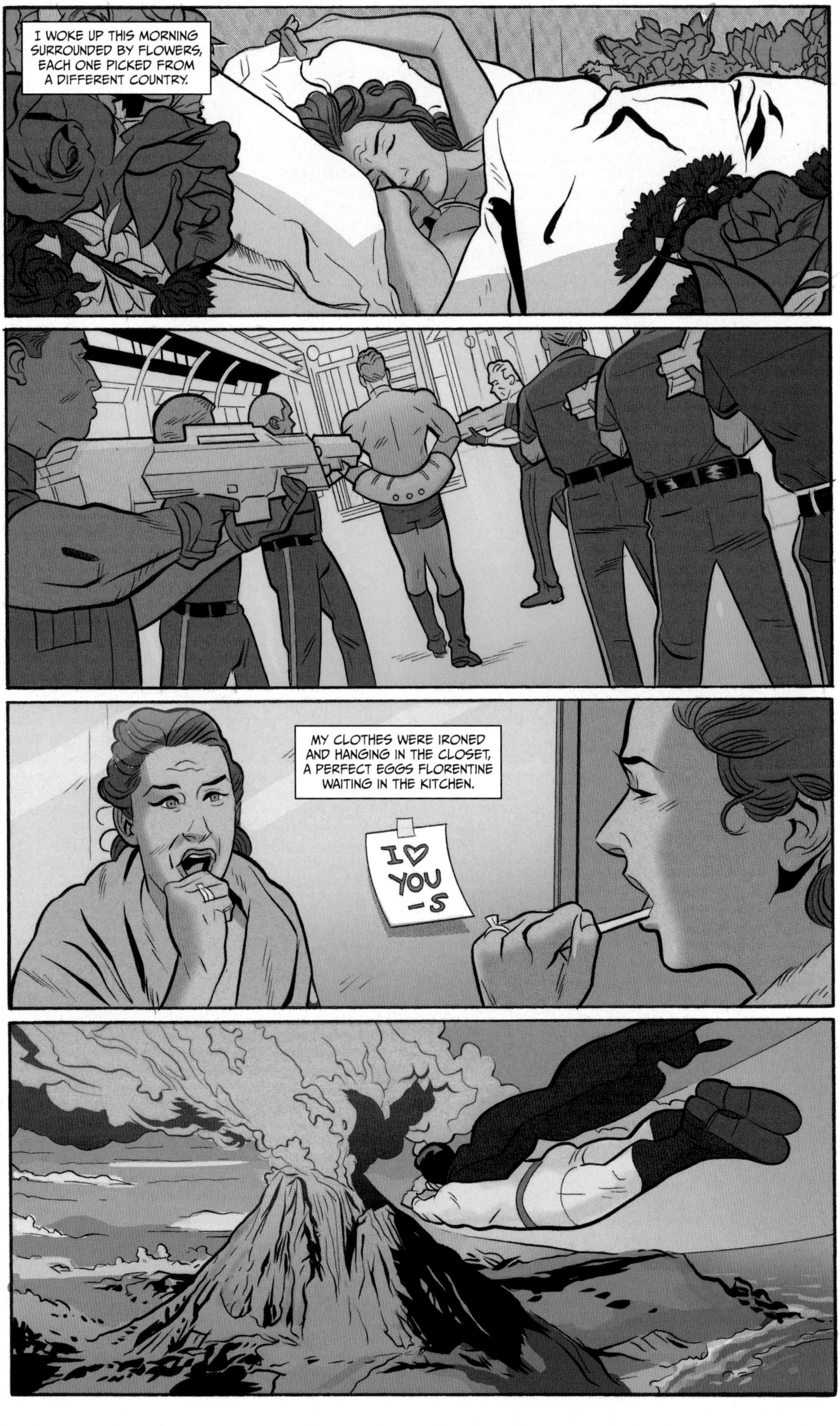
I WOKE UP THIS MORNING SURROUNDED BY FLOWERS, EACH ONE PICKED FROM A DIFFERENT COUNTRY.
MY CLOTHES WERE IRONED AND HANGING IN THE CLOSET, A PERFECT EGGS FLORENTINE WAITING IN THE KITCHEN.
I ♥ YOU -S

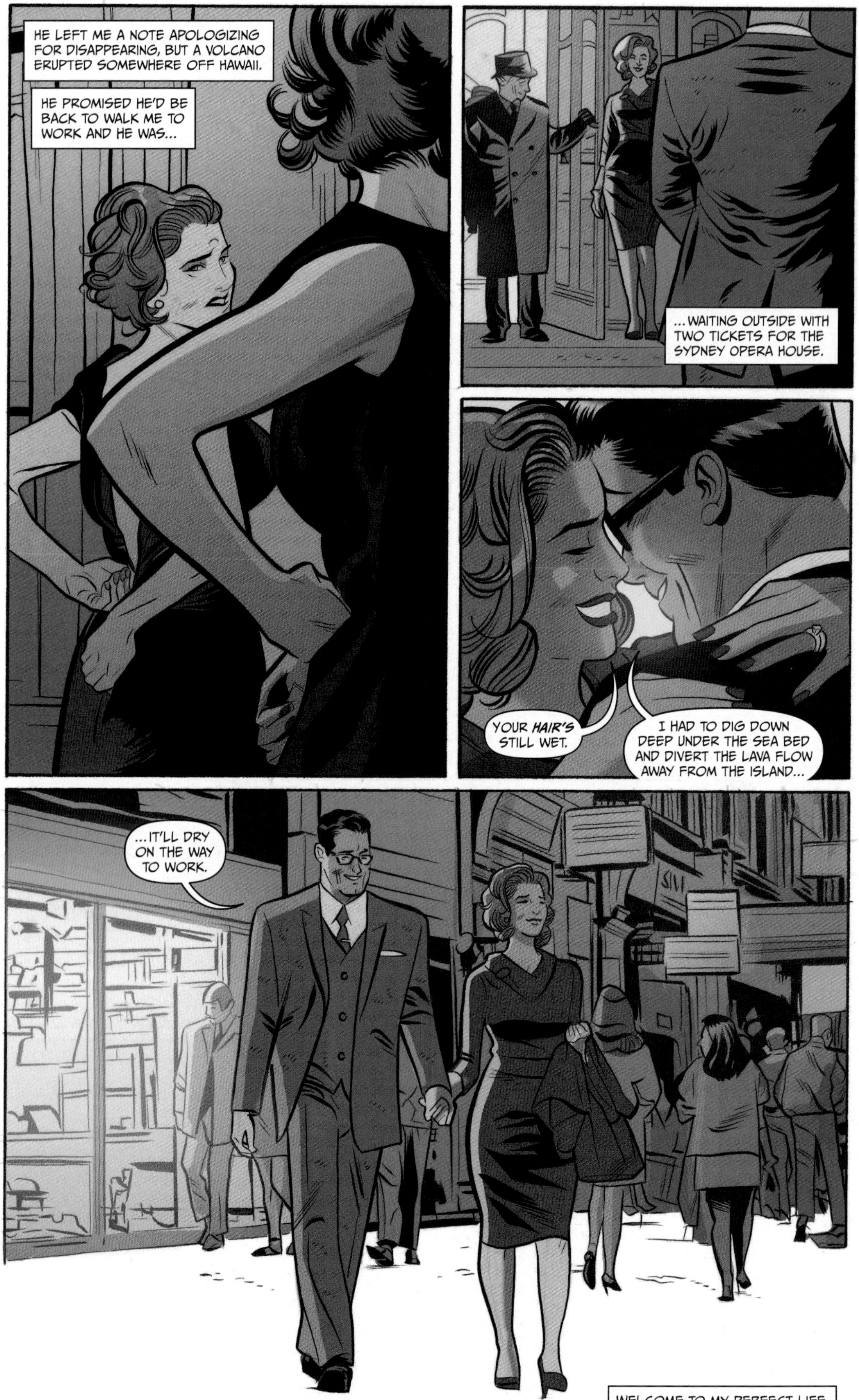
HE LEFT ME A NOTE APOLOGIZING FOR DISAPPEARING, BUT A VOLCANO ERUPTED SOMEWHERE OFF HAWAII.
HE PROMISED HE'D BE BACK TO WALK ME TO WORK AND HE WAS...
...WAITING OUTSIDE WITH TWO TICKETS FOR THE SYDNEY OPERA HOUSE.
YOUR HAIR'S STILL WET.
I HAD TO DIG DOWN DEEP UNDER THE SEA BED AND DIVERT THE LAVA FLOW AWAY FROM THE ISLAND...
...IT'LL DRY ON THE WAY TO WORK.
WELCOME TO MY PERFECT LIFE.

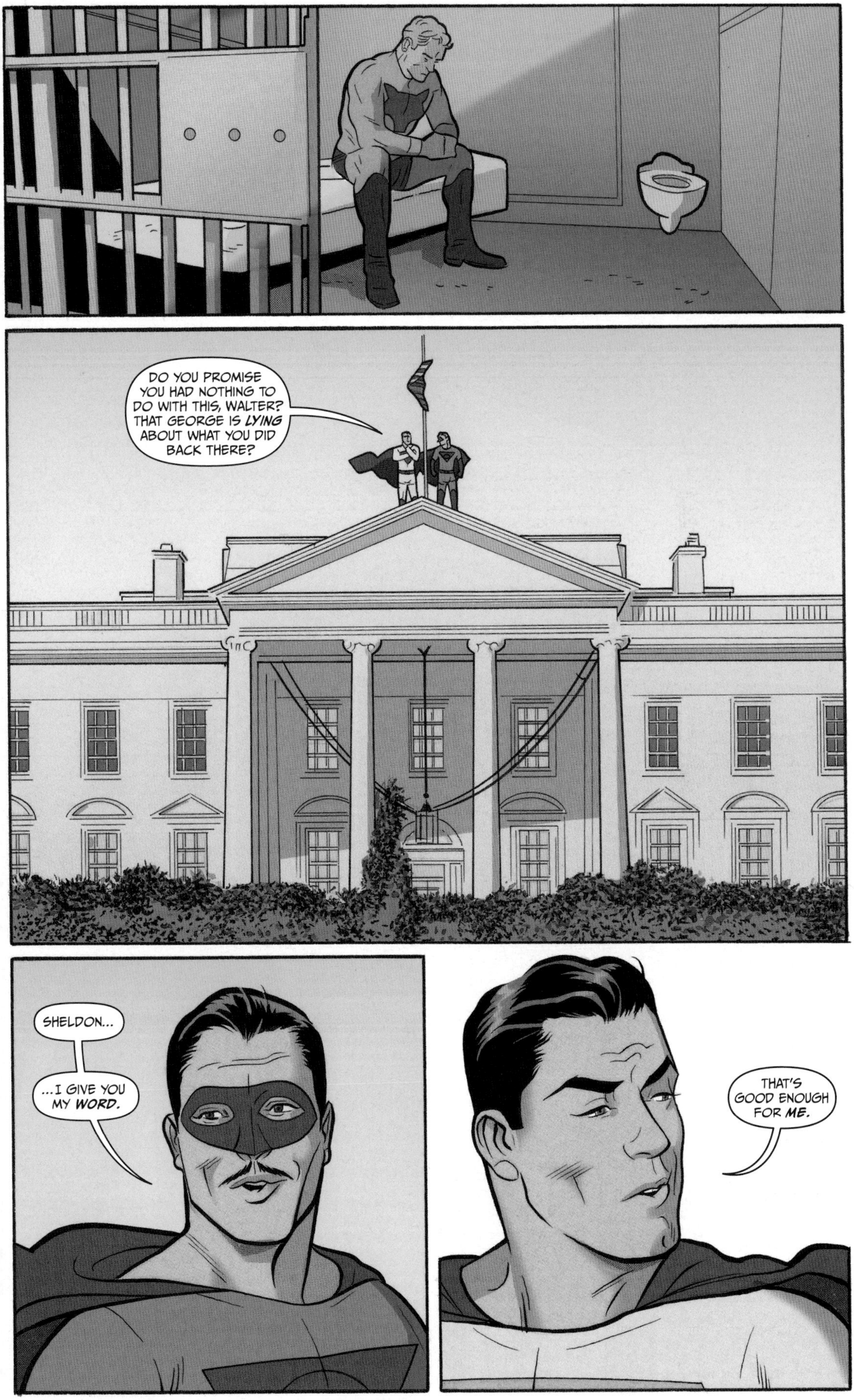
DO YOU PROMISE YOU HAD NOTHING TO DO WITH THIS, WALTER? THAT GEORGE IS ***LYING*** ABOUT WHAT YOU DID BACK THERE?
SHELDON...
...I GIVE YOU MY ***WORD.***
THAT'S GOOD ENOUGH FOR ***ME.***

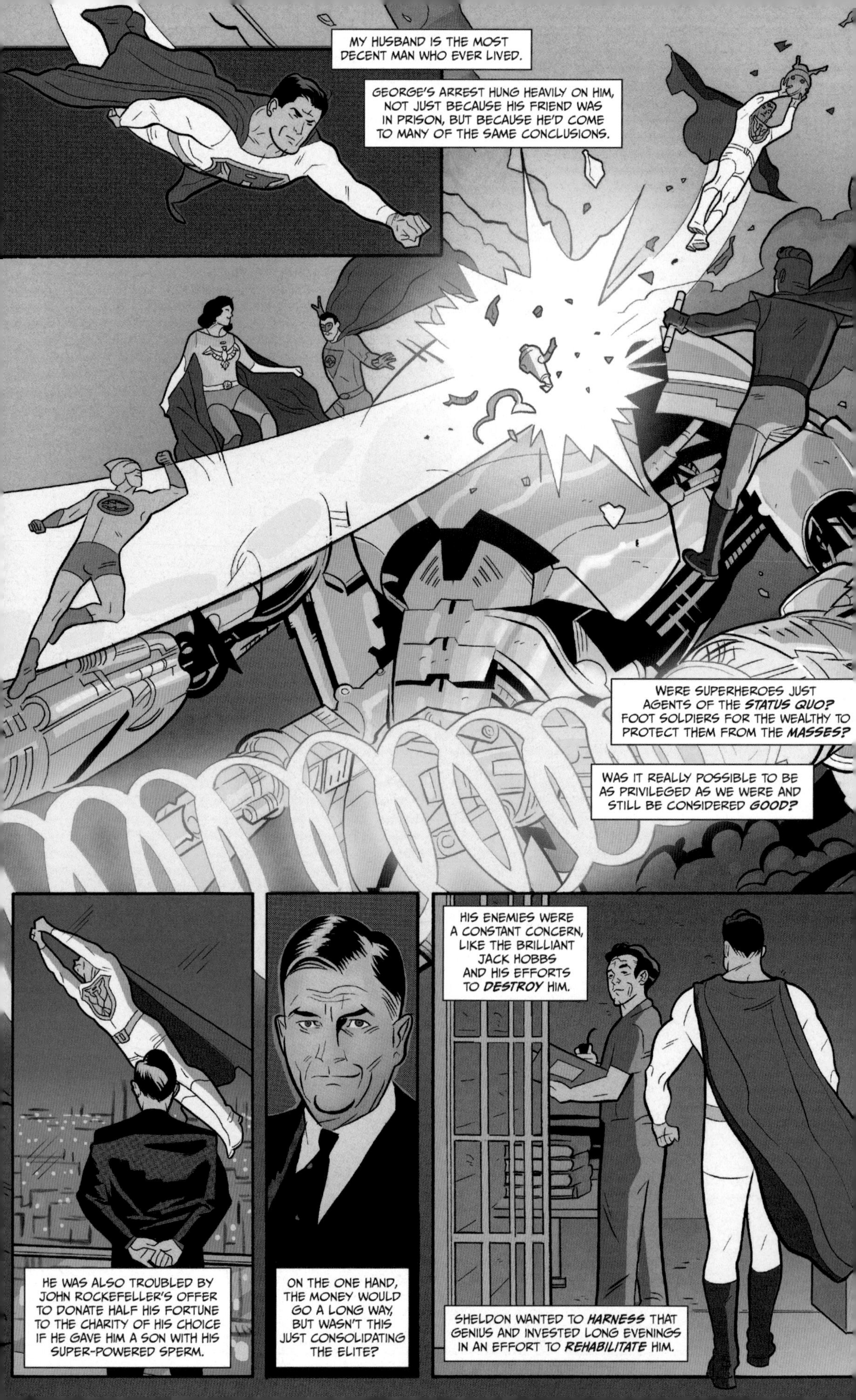
MY HUSBAND IS THE MOST DECENT MAN WHO EVER LIVED.
GEORGE'S ARREST HUNG HEAVILY ON HIM, NOT JUST BECAUSE HIS FRIEND WAS IN PRISON, BUT BECAUSE HE'D COME TO MANY OF THE SAME CONCLUSIONS.
WERE SUPERHEROES JUST AGENTS OF THE STATUS QUO? FOOT SOLDIERS FOR THE WEALTHY TO PROTECT THEM FROM THE MASSES?
WAS IT REALLY POSSIBLE TO BE AS PRIVILEGED AS WE WERE AND STILL BE CONSIDERED GOOD?
HE WAS ALSO TROUBLED BY JOHN ROCKEFELLER'S OFFER TO DONATE HALF HIS FORTUNE TO THE CHARITY OF HIS CHOICE IF HE GAVE HIM A SON WITH HIS SUPER-POWERED SPERM.
ON THE ONE HAND, THE MONEY WOULD GO A LONG WAY, BUT WASN'T THIS JUST CONSOLIDATING THE ELITE?
HIS ENEMIES WERE A CONSTANT CONCERN, LIKE THE BRILLIANT JACK HOBBS AND HIS EFFORTS TO DESTROY HIM.
SHELDON WANTED TO HARNESS THAT GENIUS AND INVESTED LONG EVENINGS IN AN EFFORT TO REHABILITATE HIM.

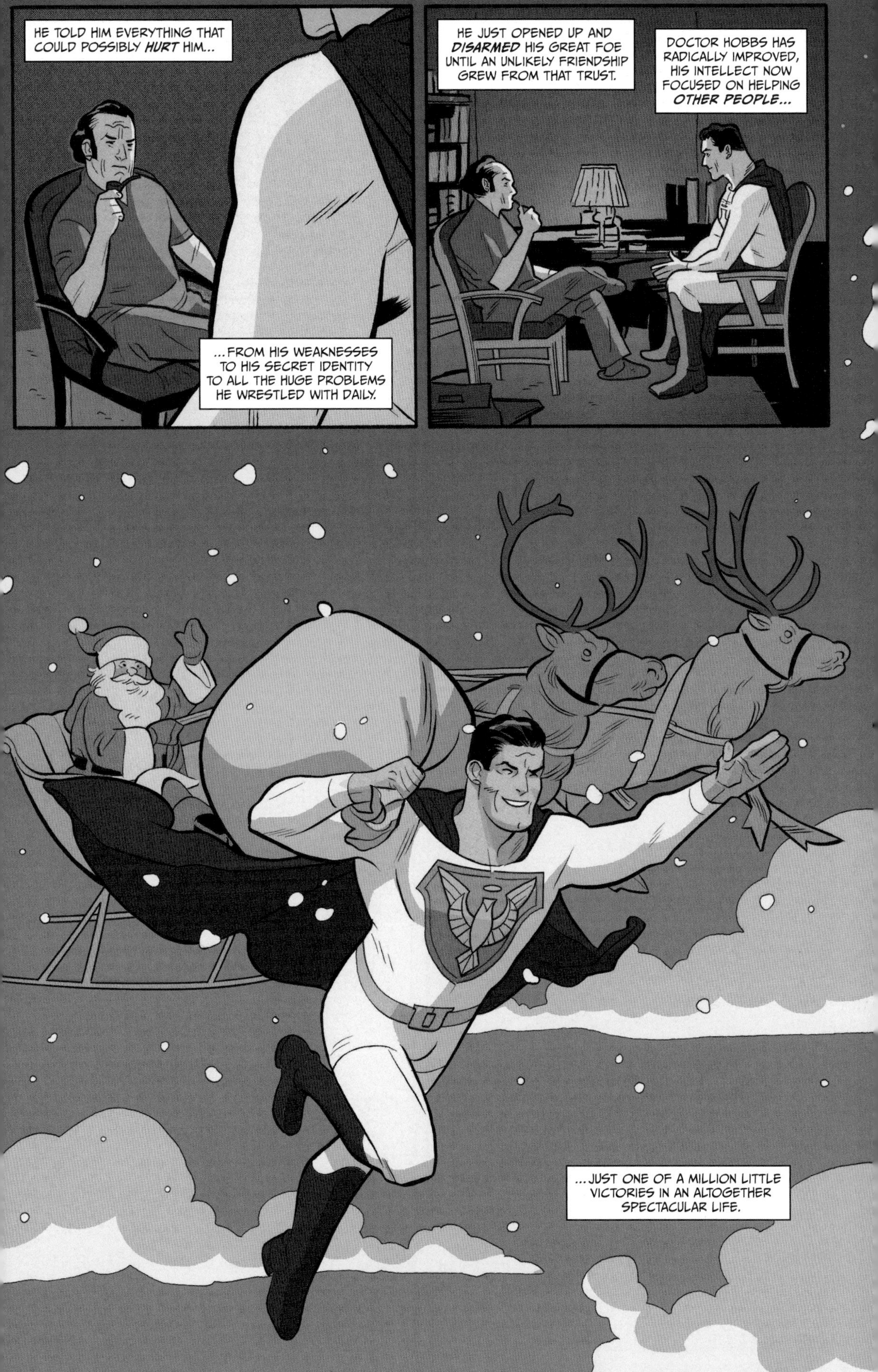
HE TOLD HIM EVERYTHING THAT COULD POSSIBLY *HURT* HIM...
...FROM HIS WEAKNESSES TO HIS SECRET IDENTITY TO ALL THE HUGE PROBLEMS HE WRESTLED WITH DAILY.
HE JUST OPENED UP AND ***DISARMED*** HIS GREAT FOE UNTIL AN UNLIKELY FRIENDSHIP GREW FROM THAT TRUST.
DOCTOR HOBBS HAS RADICALLY IMPROVED, HIS INTELLECT NOW FOCUSED ON HELPING ***OTHER PEOPLE...***
...JUST ONE OF A MILLION LITTLE VICTORIES IN AN ALTOGETHER SPECTACULAR LIFE.

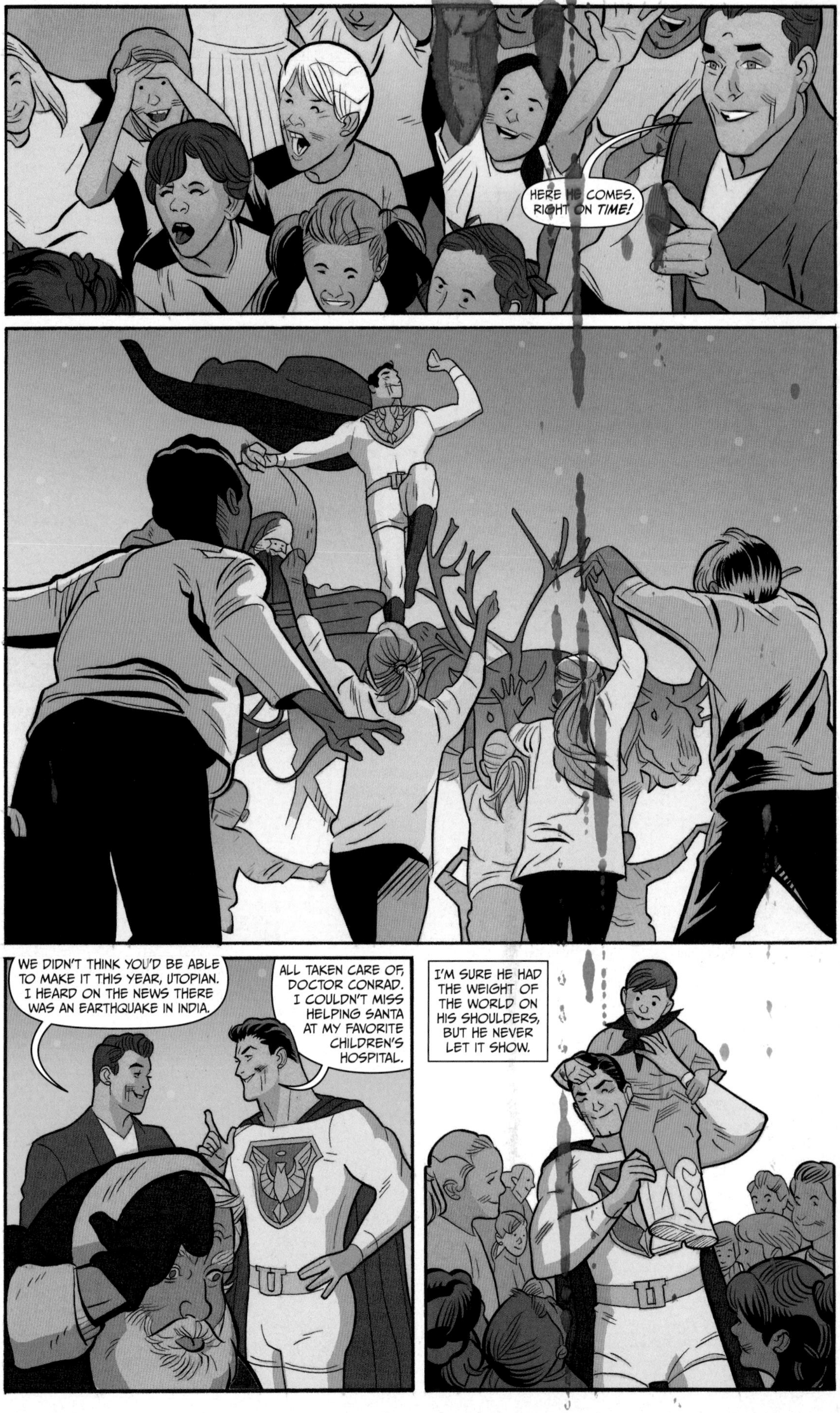
HERE HE COMES. RIGHT ON *TIME!*
WE DIDN'T THINK YOU'D BE ABLE TO MAKE IT THIS YEAR, UTOPIAN. I HEARD ON THE NEWS THERE WAS AN EARTHQUAKE IN INDIA.
ALL TAKEN CARE OF, DOCTOR CONRAD. I COULDN'T MISS HELPING SANTA AT MY FAVORITE CHILDREN'S HOSPITAL.
I'M SURE HE HAD THE WEIGHT OF THE WORLD ON HIS SHOULDERS, BUT HE NEVER LET IT SHOW.

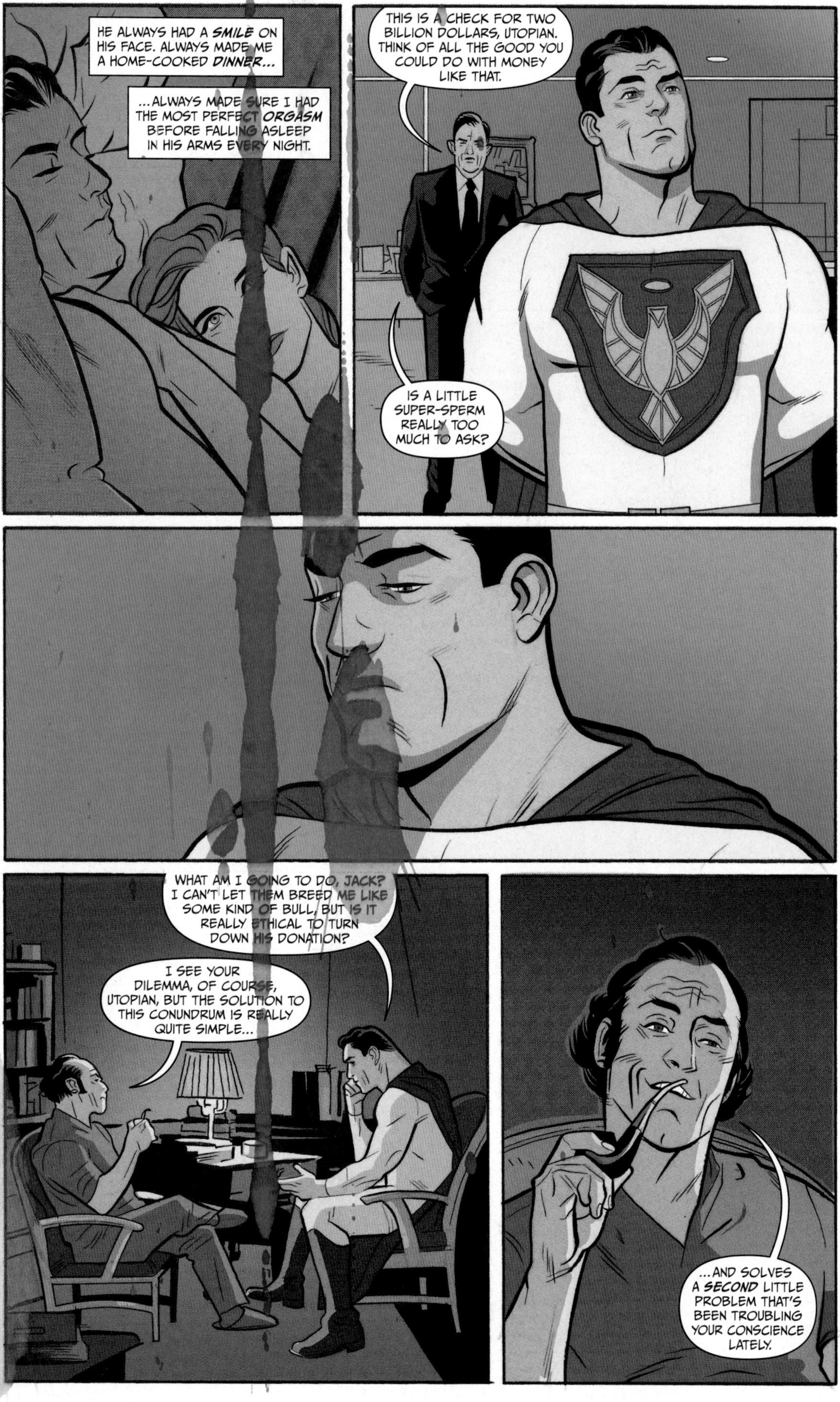
HE ALWAYS HAD A SMILE ON HIS FACE. ALWAYS MADE ME A HOME-COOKED DINNER...
...ALWAYS MADE SURE I HAD THE MOST PERFECT ORGASM BEFORE FALLING ASLEEP IN HIS ARMS EVERY NIGHT.
THIS IS A CHECK FOR TWO BILLION DOLLARS, UTOPIAN. THINK OF ALL THE GOOD YOU COULD DO WITH MONEY LIKE THAT.
IS A LITTLE SUPER-SPERM REALLY TOO MUCH TO ASK?
WHAT AM I GOING TO DO, JACK? I CAN'T LET THEM BREED ME LIKE SOME KIND OF BULL, BUT IS IT REALLY ETHICAL TO TURN DOWN HIS DONATION?
I SEE YOUR DILEMMA, OF COURSE, UTOPIAN, BUT THE SOLUTION TO THIS CONUNDRUM IS REALLY QUITE SIMPLE...
...AND SOLVES A SECOND LITTLE PROBLEM THAT'S BEEN TROUBLING YOUR CONSCIENCE LATELY.

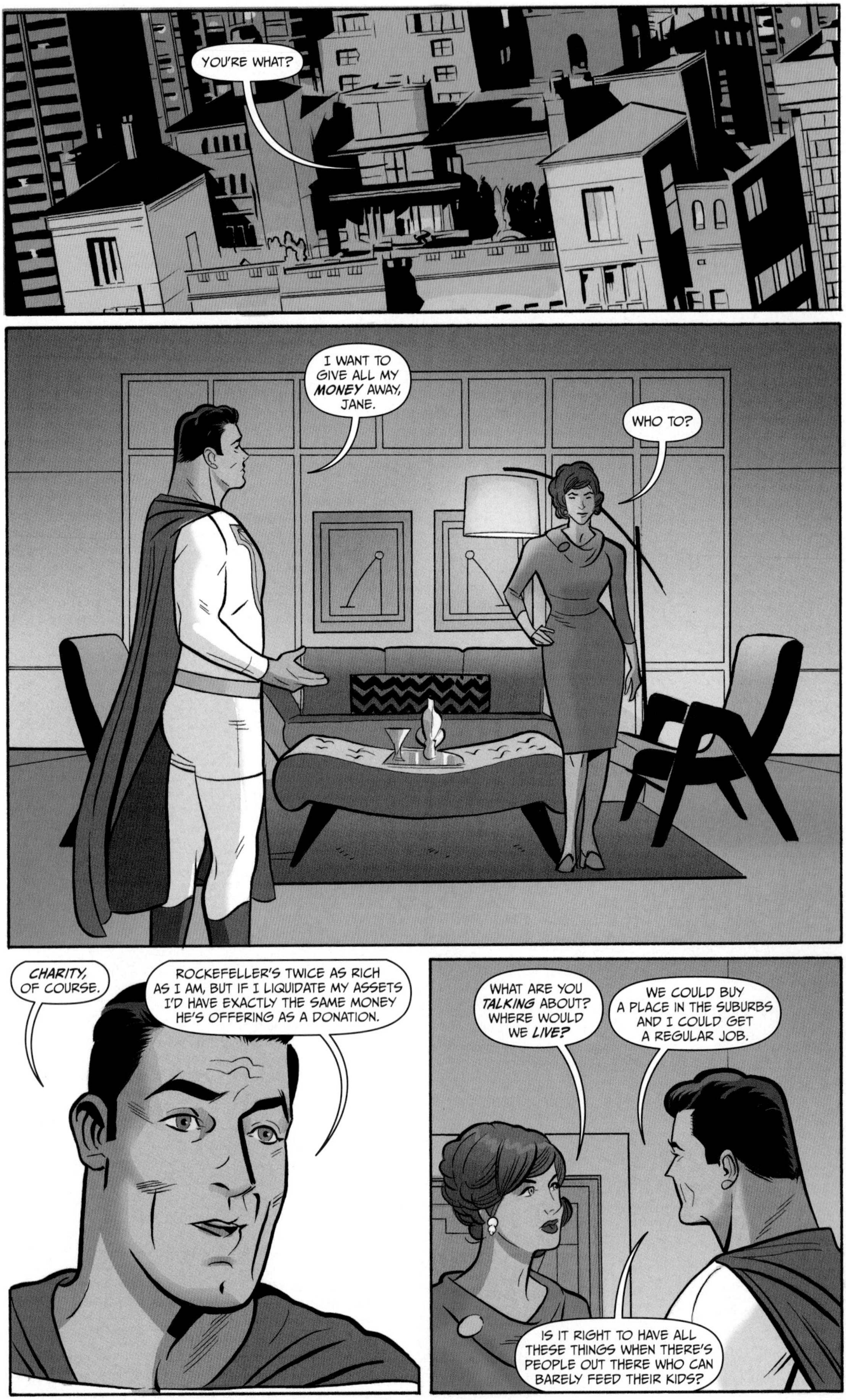
YOU'RE WHAT?
I WANT TO GIVE ALL MY *MONEY* AWAY, JANE.
WHO TO?
CHARITY, OF COURSE.
ROCKEFELLER'S TWICE AS RICH AS I AM, BUT IF I LIQUIDATE MY ASSETS I'D HAVE EXACTLY THE SAME MONEY HE'S OFFERING AS A DONATION.
WHAT ARE YOU *TALKING* ABOUT? WHERE WOULD WE *LIVE?*
WE COULD BUY A PLACE IN THE SUBURBS AND I COULD GET A REGULAR JOB.
IS IT RIGHT TO HAVE ALL THESE THINGS WHEN THERE'S PEOPLE OUT THERE WHO CAN BARELY FEED THEIR KIDS?

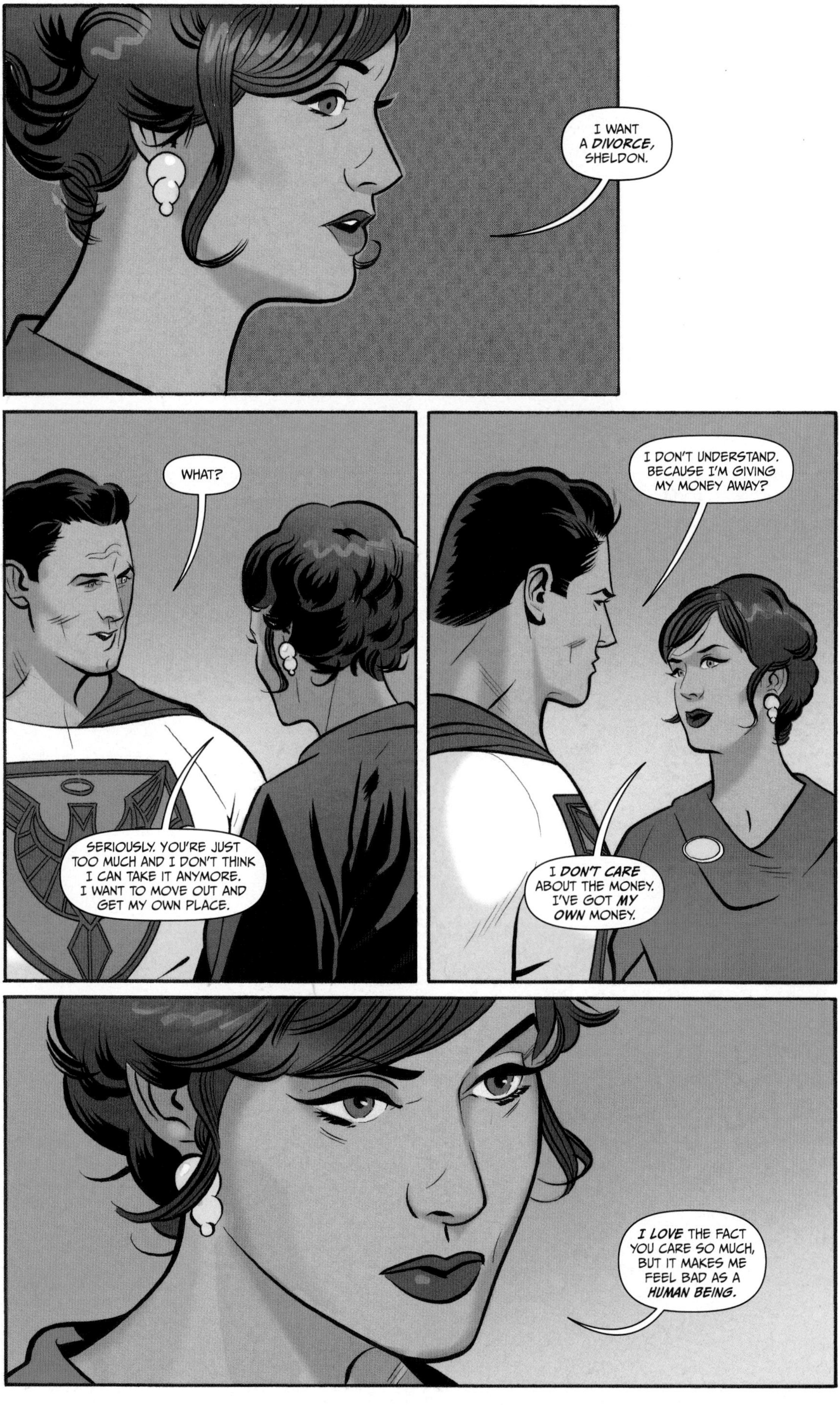
I WANT A DIVORCE, SHELDON.
WHAT?
SERIOUSLY. YOU'RE JUST TOO MUCH AND I DON'T THINK I CAN TAKE IT ANYMORE. I WANT TO MOVE OUT AND GET MY OWN PLACE.
I DON'T UNDERSTAND. BECAUSE I'M GIVING MY MONEY AWAY?
I DON'T CARE ABOUT THE MONEY. I'VE GOT MY OWN MONEY.
I LOVE THE FACT YOU CARE SO MUCH, BUT IT MAKES ME FEEL BAD AS A HUMAN BEING.

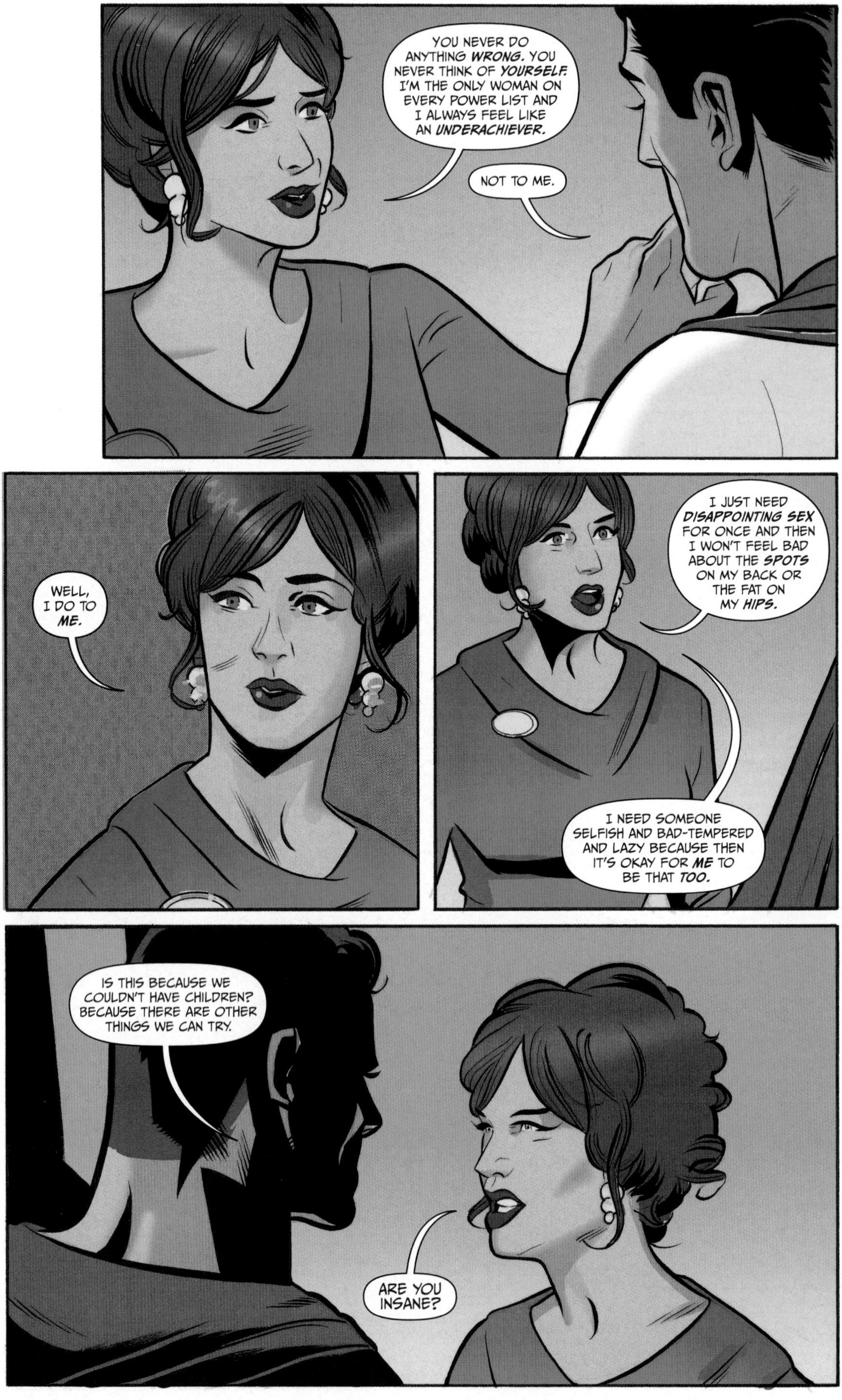
YOU NEVER DO ANYTHING WRONG. YOU NEVER THINK OF YOURSELF. I'M THE ONLY WOMAN ON EVERY POWER LIST AND I ALWAYS FEEL LIKE AN UNDERACHIEVER.
NOT TO ME.
WELL, I DO TO ME.
I JUST NEED DISAPPOINTING SEX FOR ONCE AND THEN I WON'T FEEL BAD ABOUT THE SPOTS ON MY BACK OR THE FAT ON MY HIPS.
I NEED SOMEONE SELFISH AND BAD-TEMPERED AND LAZY BECAUSE THEN IT'S OKAY FOR ME TO BE THAT TOO.
IS THIS BECAUSE WE COULDN'T HAVE CHILDREN? BECAUSE THERE ARE OTHER THINGS WE CAN TRY.
ARE YOU INSANE?

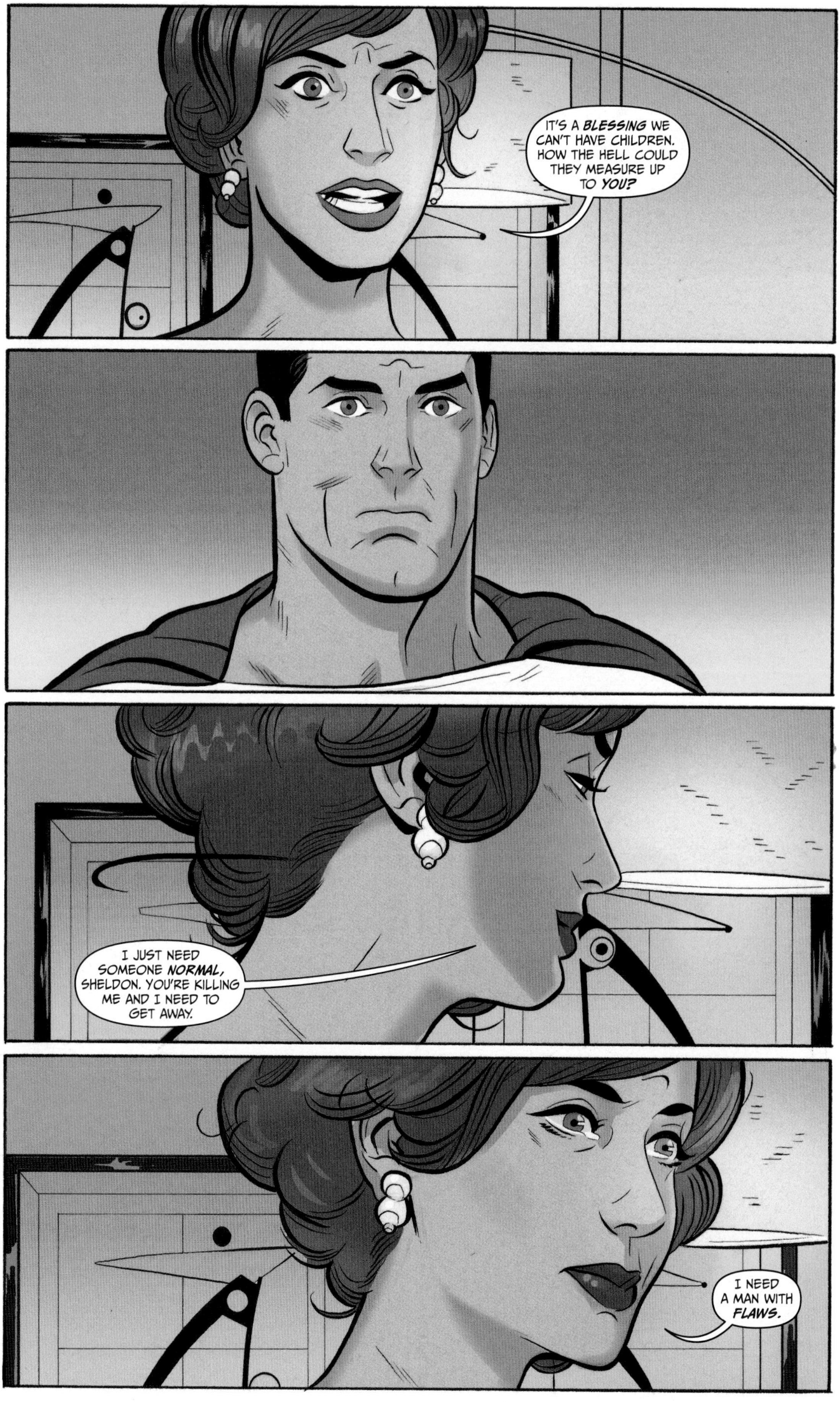
IT'S A BLESSING WE CAN'T HAVE CHILDREN. HOW THE HELL COULD THEY MEASURE UP TO YOU?
I JUST NEED SOMEONE NORMAL, SHELDON. YOU'RE KILLING ME AND I NEED TO GET AWAY.
I NEED A MAN WITH FLAWS.

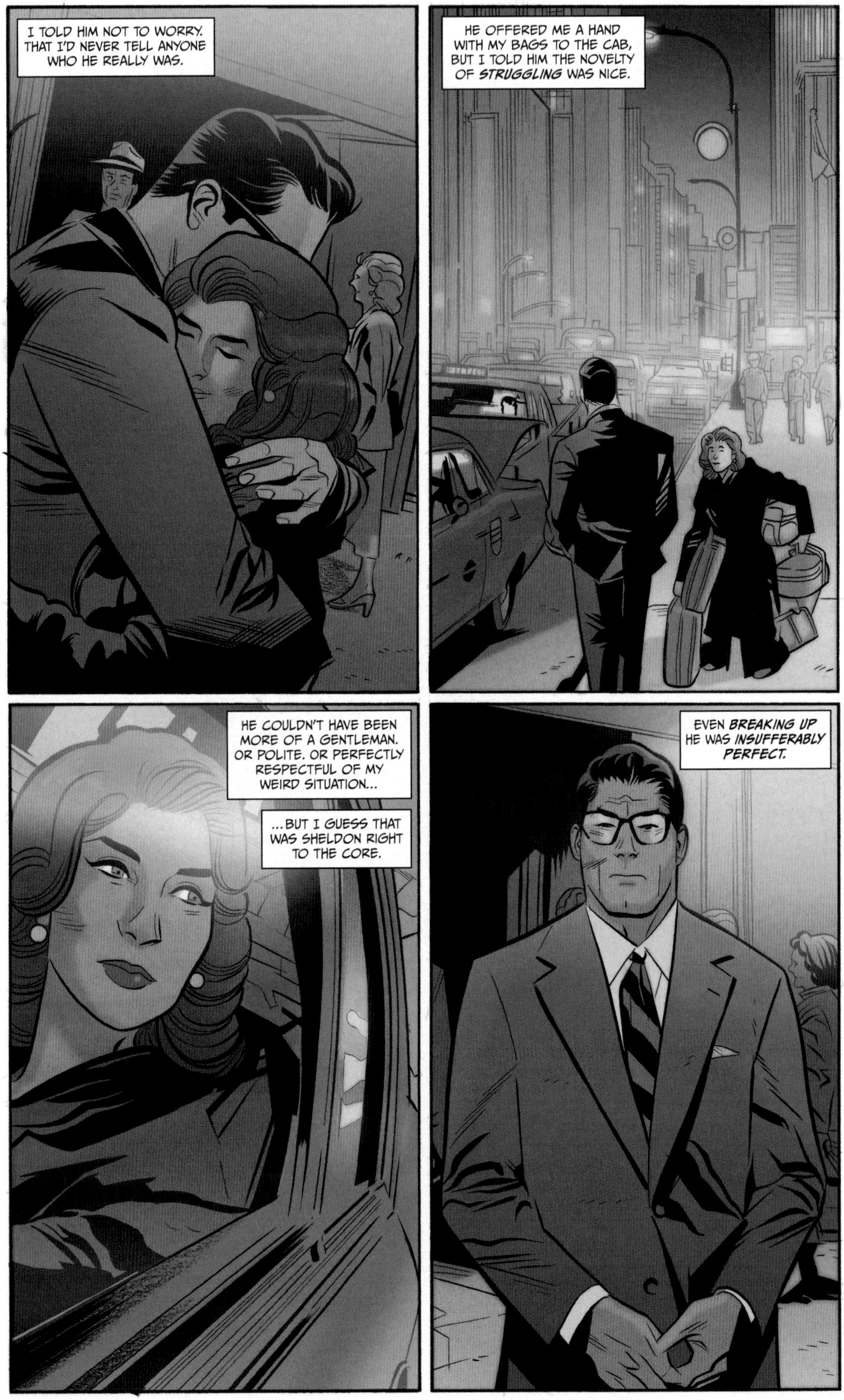
I TOLD HIM NOT TO WORRY. THAT I'D NEVER TELL ANYONE WHO HE REALLY WAS.
HE OFFERED ME A HAND WITH MY BAGS TO THE CAB, BUT I TOLD HIM THE NOVELTY OF *STRUGGLING* WAS NICE.
HE COULDN'T HAVE BEEN MORE OF A GENTLEMAN. OR POLITE. OR PERFECTLY RESPECTFUL OF MY WEIRD SITUATION...
...BUT I GUESS THAT WAS SHELDON RIGHT TO THE CORE.
EVEN *BREAKING UP* HE WAS *INSUFFERABLY PERFECT.*

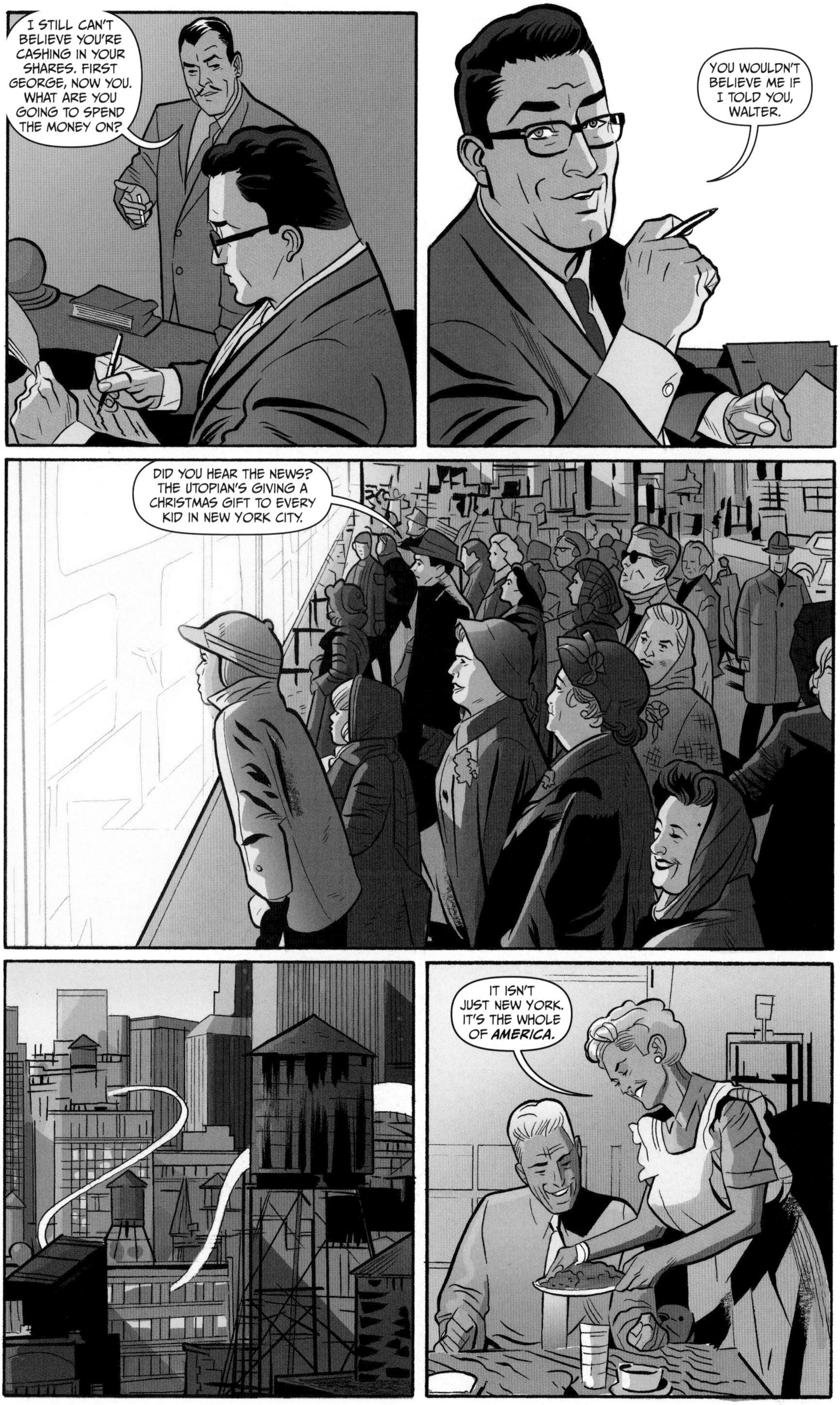
I STILL CAN'T BELIEVE YOU'RE CASHING IN YOUR SHARES. FIRST GEORGE, NOW YOU. WHAT ARE YOU GOING TO SPEND THE MONEY ON?
YOU WOULDN'T BELIEVE ME IF I TOLD YOU, WALTER.
DID YOU HEAR THE NEWS? THE UTOPIAN'S GIVING A CHRISTMAS GIFT TO EVERY KID IN NEW YORK CITY.
IT ISN'T JUST NEW YORK. IT'S THE WHOLE OF AMERICA.

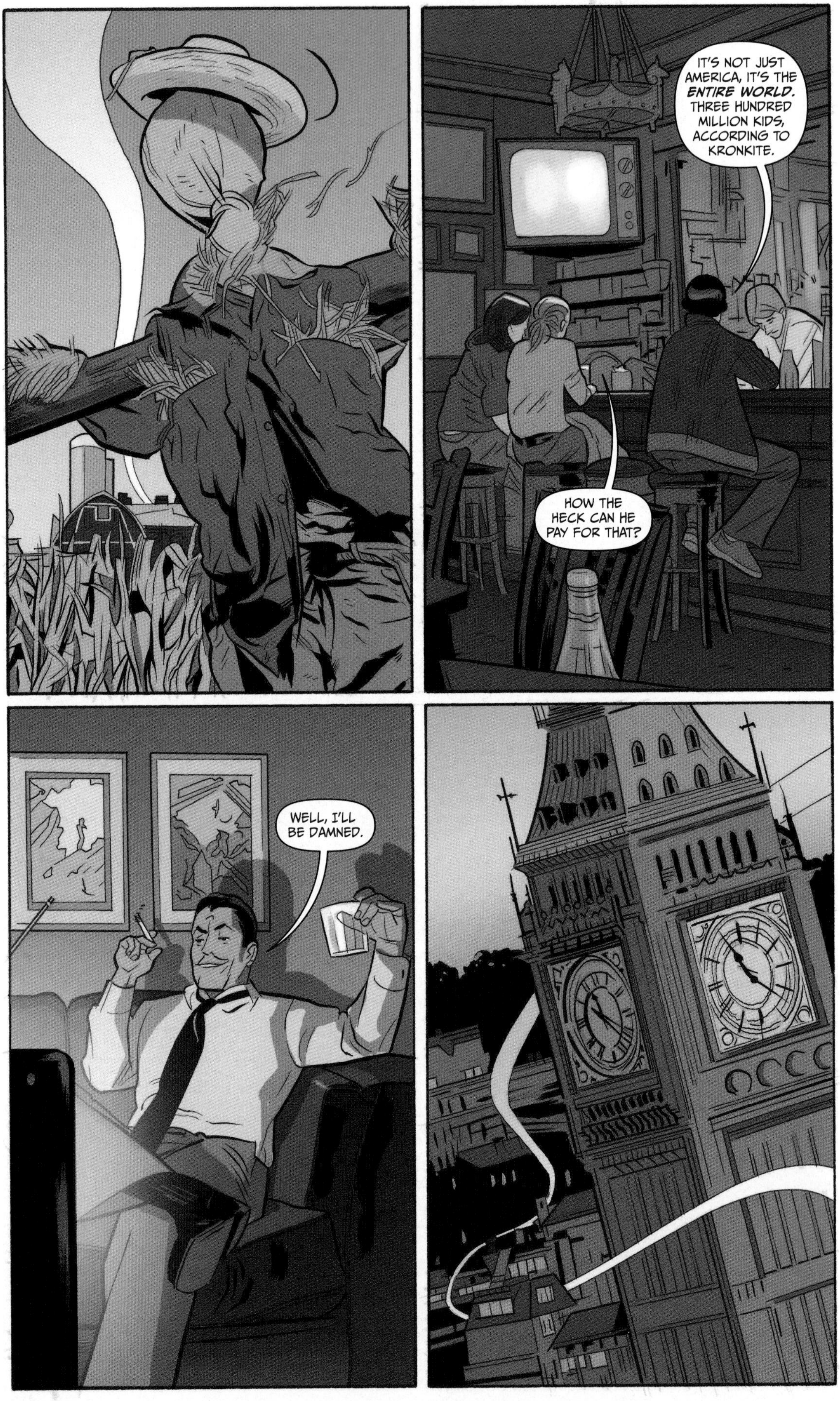
IT'S NOT JUST AMERICA, IT'S THE ENTIRE WORLD. THREE HUNDRED MILLION KIDS, ACCORDING TO KRONKITE.
HOW THE HECK CAN HE PAY FOR THAT?
WELL, I'LL BE DAMNED.

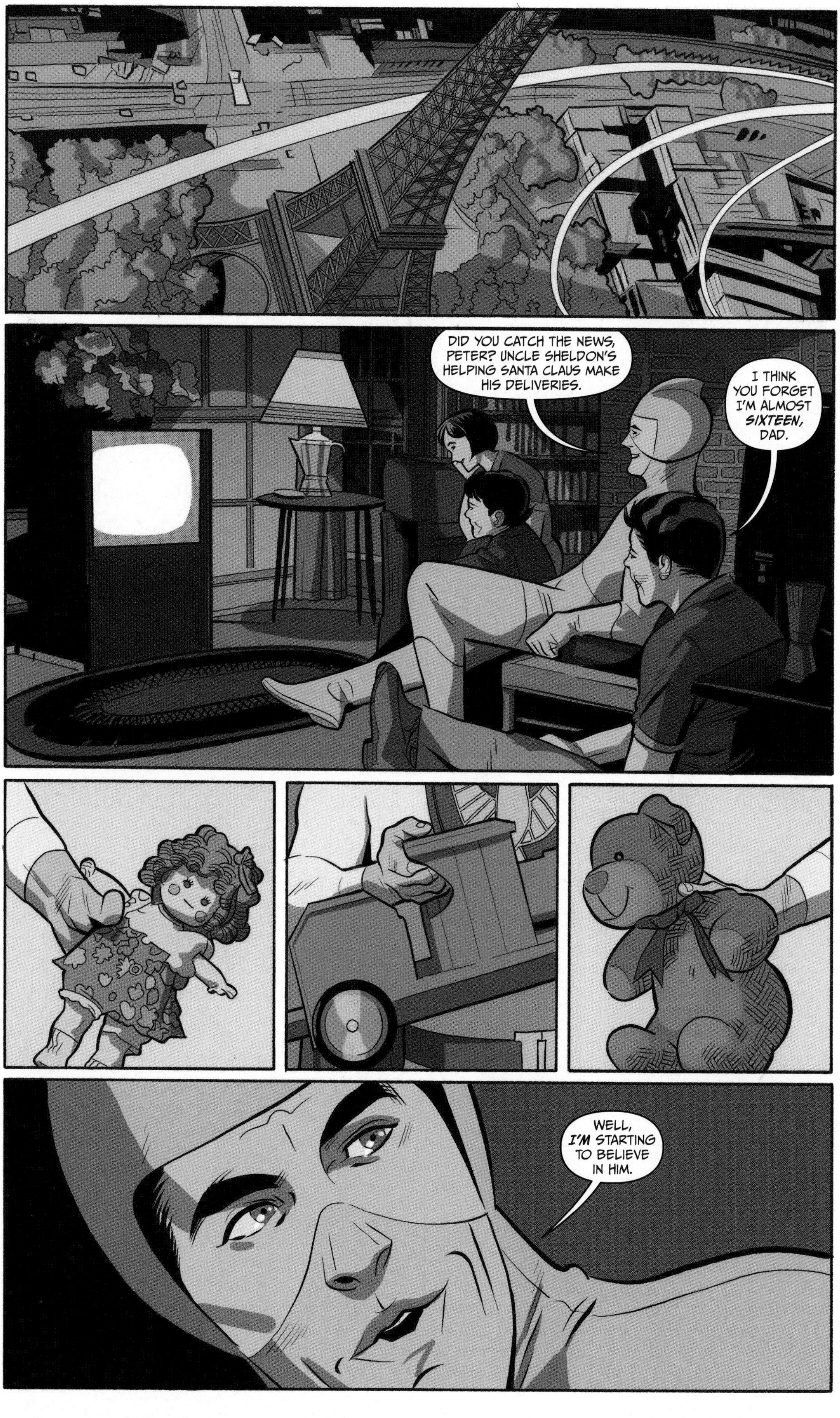
DID YOU CATCH THE NEWS, PETER? UNCLE SHELDON'S HELPING SANTA CLAUS MAKE HIS DELIVERIES.
I THINK YOU FORGET I'M ALMOST SIXTEEN, DAD.
WELL, I'M STARTING TO BELIEVE IN HIM.

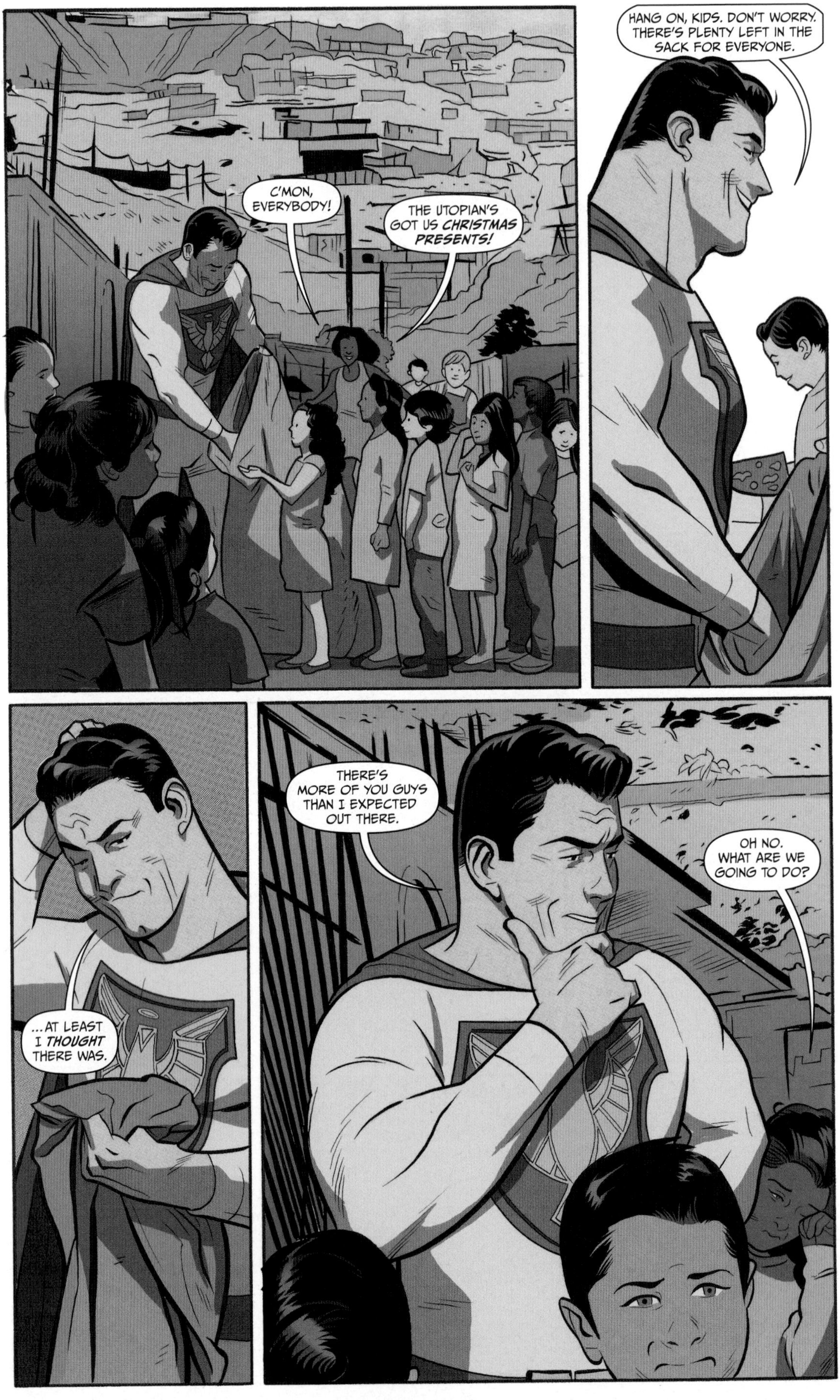
C'MON, EVERYBODY!
THE UTOPIAN'S GOT US CHRISTMAS PRESENTS!
HANG ON, KIDS. DON'T WORRY. THERE'S PLENTY LEFT IN THE SACK FOR EVERYONE.
...AT LEAST I THOUGHT THERE WAS.
THERE'S MORE OF YOU GUYS THAN I EXPECTED OUT THERE.
OH NO. WHAT ARE WE GOING TO DO?

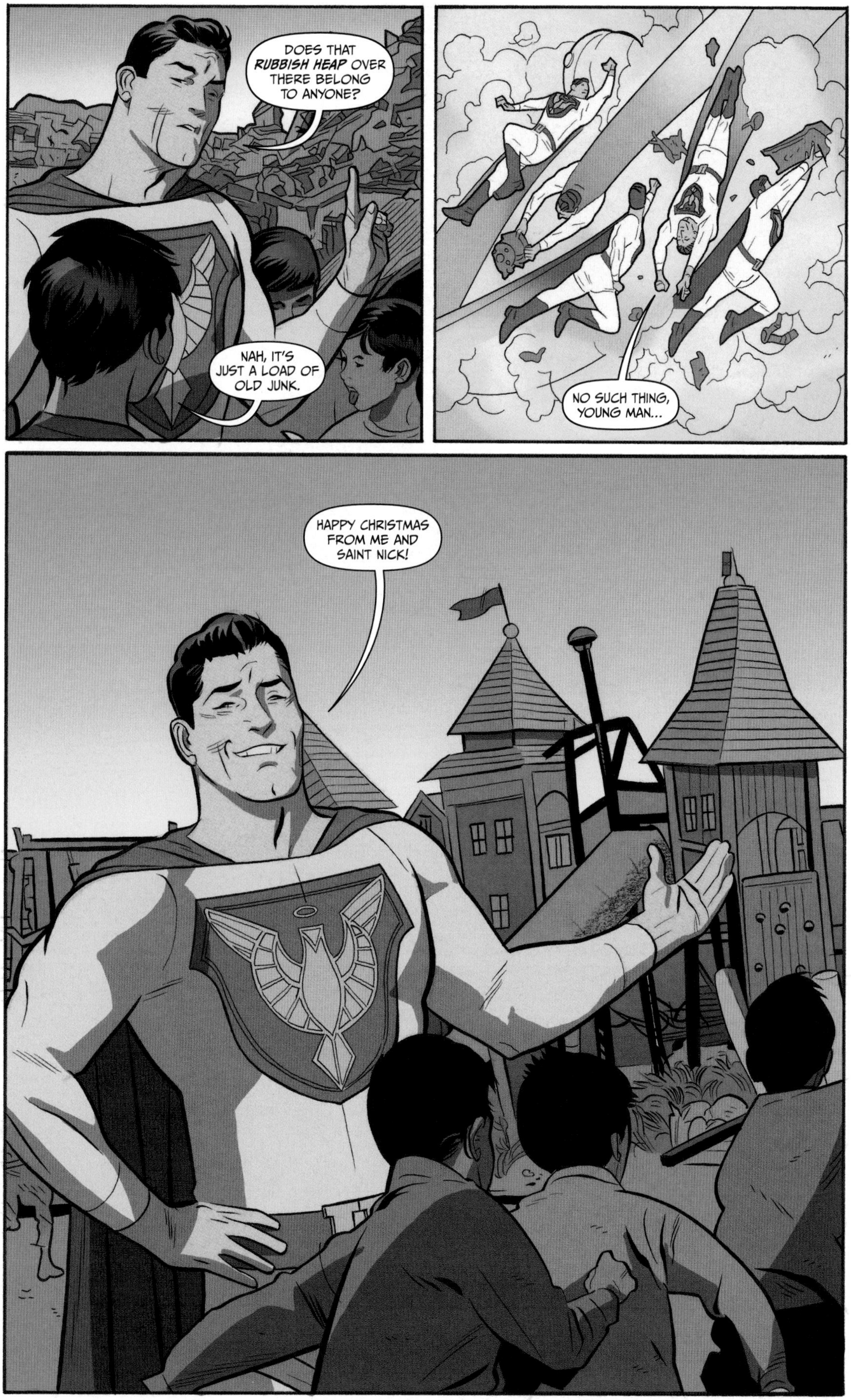
DOES THAT *RUBBISH HEAP* OVER THERE BELONG TO ANYONE?
NAH, IT'S JUST A LOAD OF OLD JUNK.
NO SUCH THING, YOUNG MAN...
HAPPY CHRISTMAS FROM ME AND SAINT NICK!

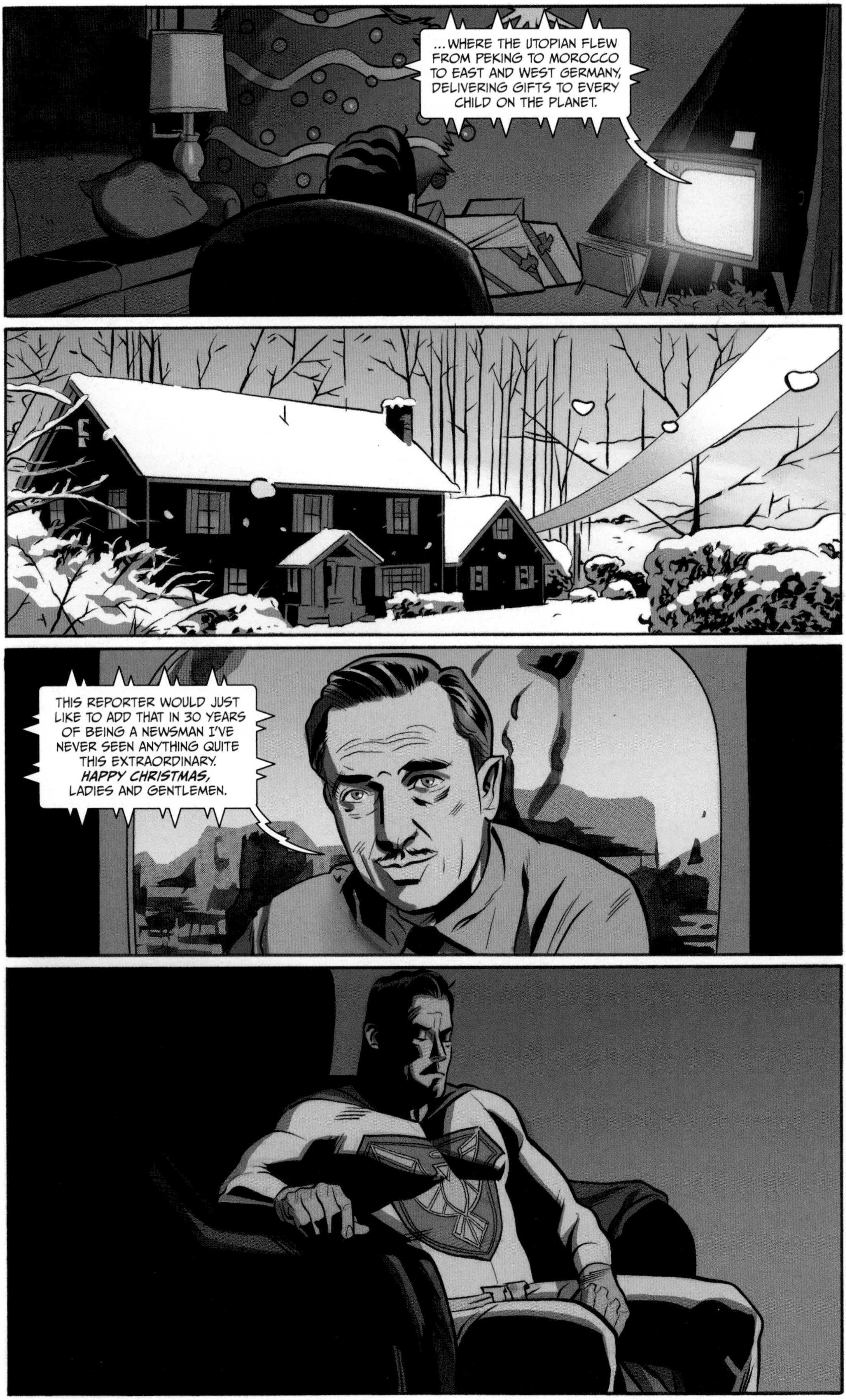
...WHERE THE UTOPIAN FLEW FROM PEKING TO MOROCCO TO EAST AND WEST GERMANY, DELIVERING GIFTS TO EVERY CHILD ON THE PLANET.
THIS REPORTER WOULD JUST LIKE TO ADD THAT IN 30 YEARS OF BEING A NEWSMAN I'VE NEVER SEEN ANYTHING QUITE THIS EXTRAORDINARY. HAPPY CHRISTMAS, LADIES AND GENTLEMEN.

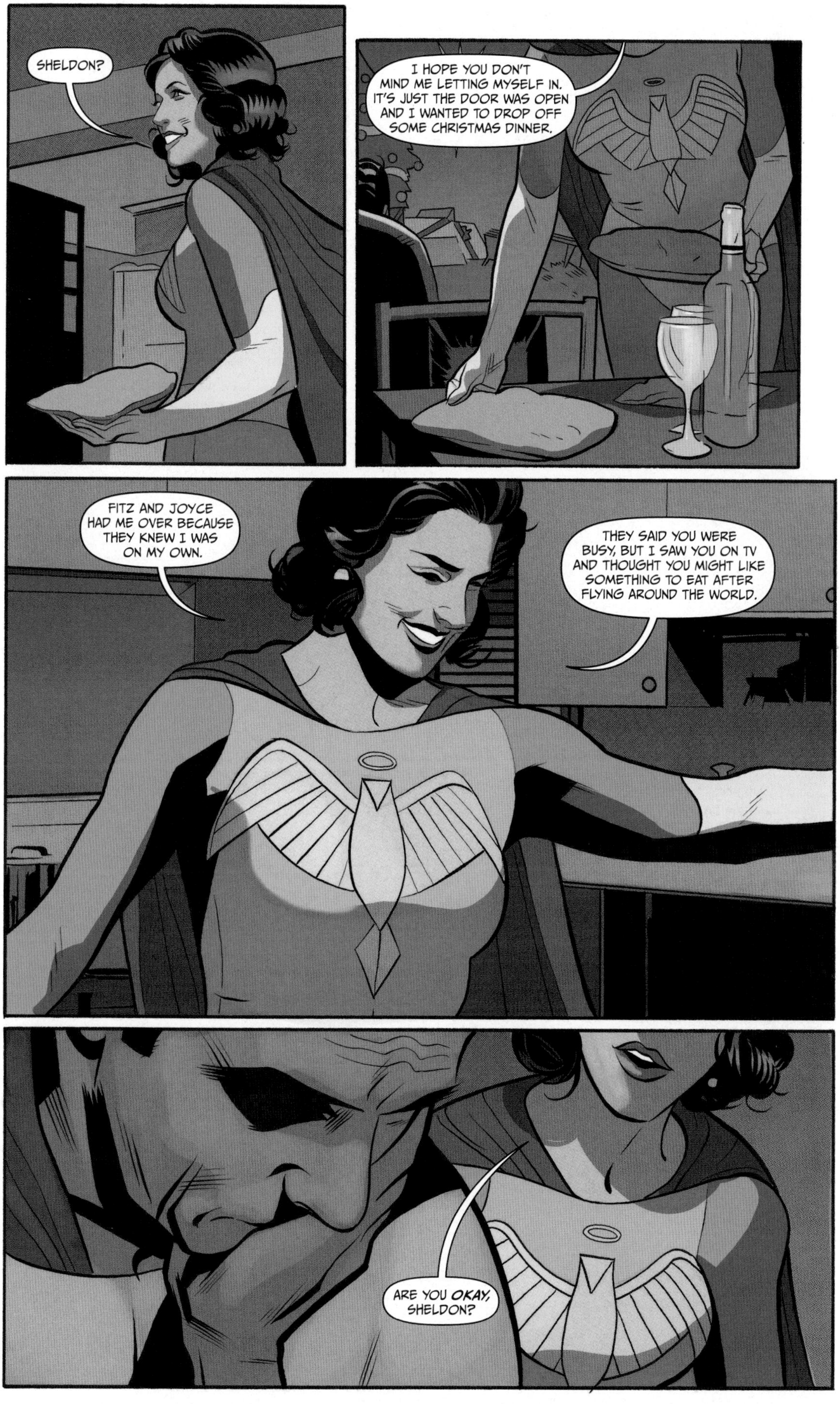
SHELDON?
I HOPE YOU DON'T MIND ME LETTING MYSELF IN. IT'S JUST THE DOOR WAS OPEN AND I WANTED TO DROP OFF SOME CHRISTMAS DINNER.
FITZ AND JOYCE HAD ME OVER BECAUSE THEY KNEW I WAS ON MY OWN.
THEY SAID YOU WERE BUSY, BUT I SAW YOU ON TV AND THOUGHT YOU MIGHT LIKE SOMETHING TO EAT AFTER FLYING AROUND THE WORLD.
ARE YOU **OKAY,** SHELDON?

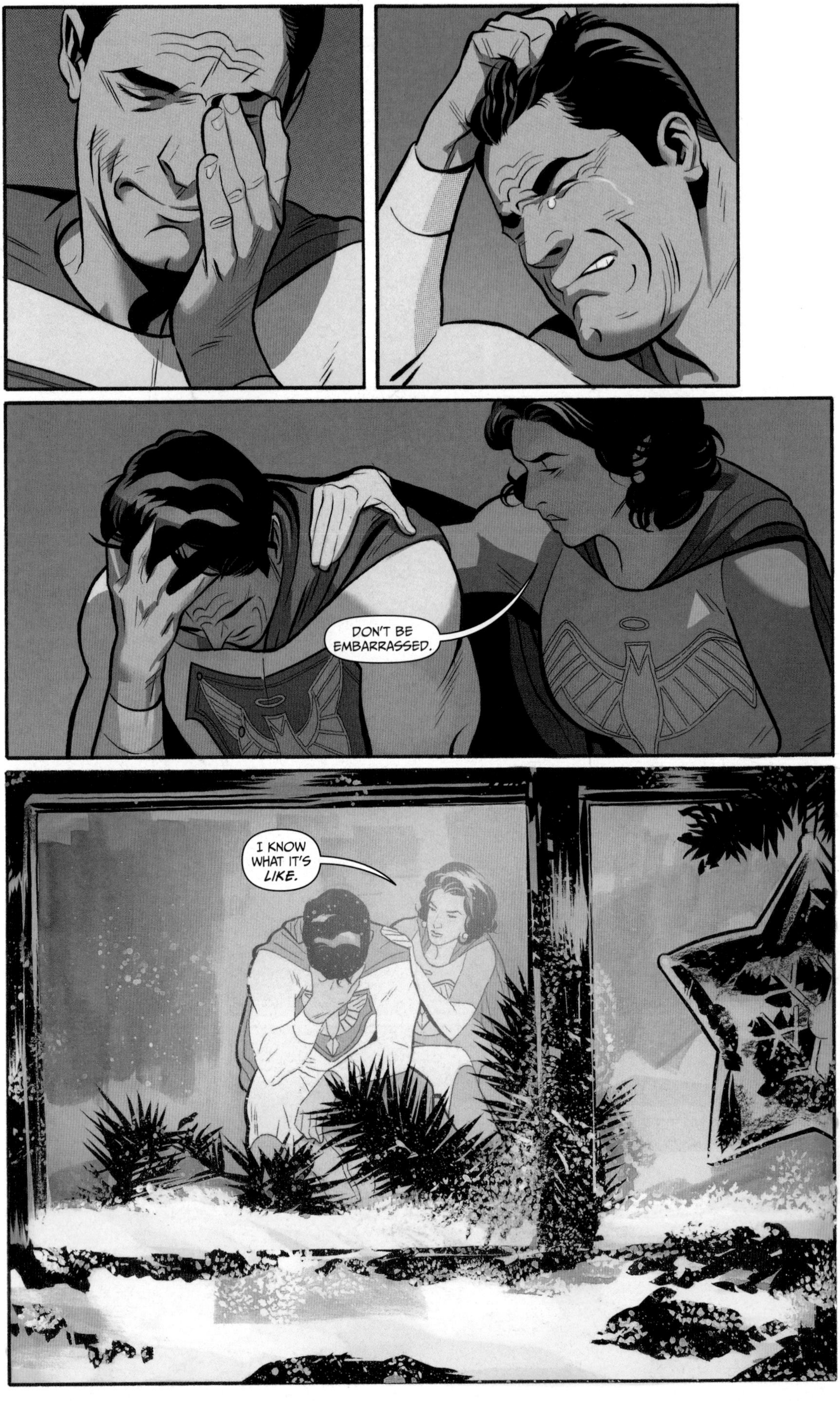
DON'T BE EMBARRASSED.
I KNOW WHAT IT'S *LIKE.*

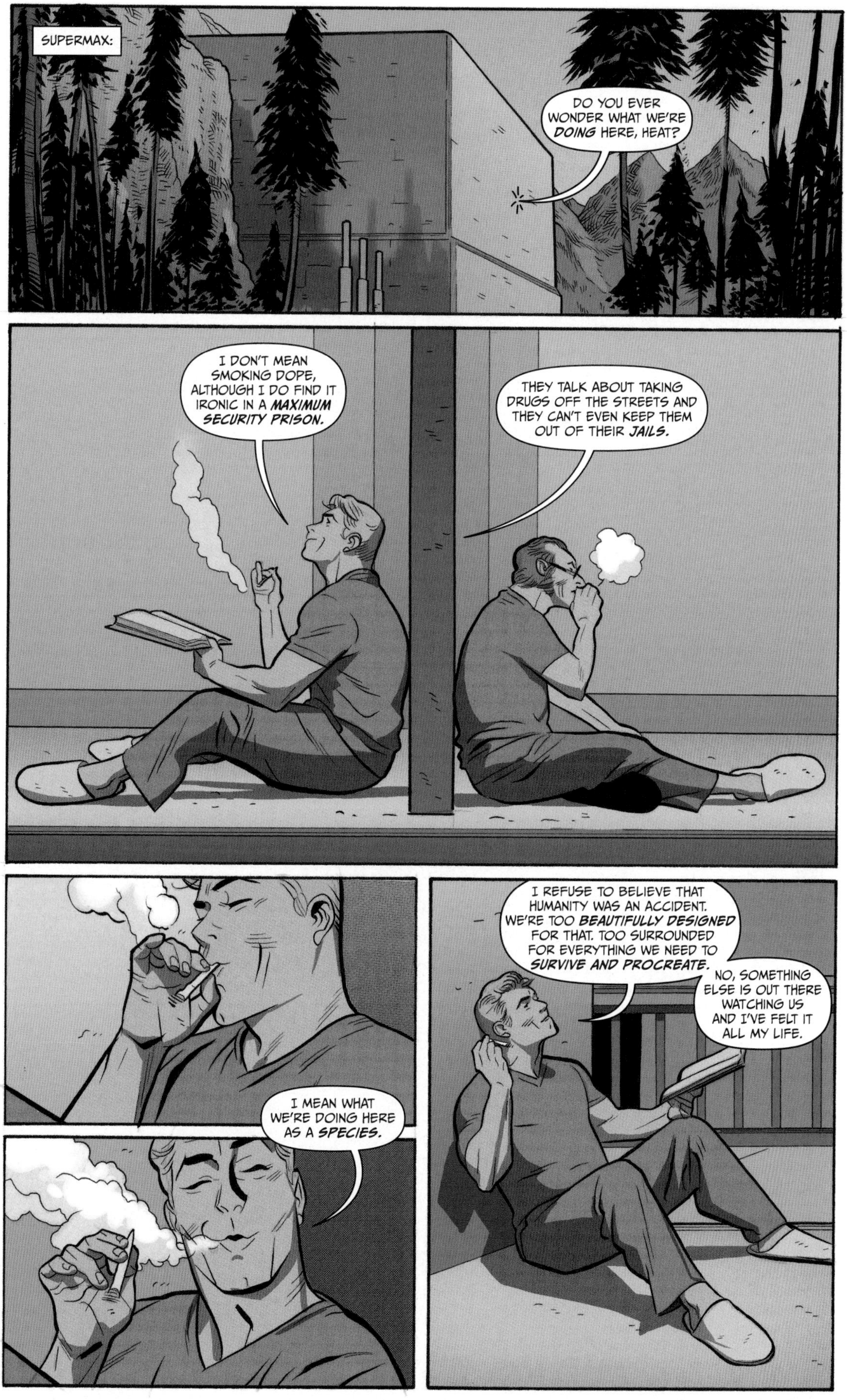
SUPERMAX:
DO YOU EVER WONDER WHAT WE'RE DOING HERE, HEAT?
I DON'T MEAN SMOKING DOPE, ALTHOUGH I DO FIND IT IRONIC IN A MAXIMUM SECURITY PRISON.
THEY TALK ABOUT TAKING DRUGS OFF THE STREETS AND THEY CAN'T EVEN KEEP THEM OUT OF THEIR JAILS.
I MEAN WHAT WE'RE DOING HERE AS A SPECIES.
I REFUSE TO BELIEVE THAT HUMANITY WAS AN ACCIDENT. WE'RE TOO BEAUTIFULLY DESIGNED FOR THAT. TOO SURROUNDED FOR EVERYTHING WE NEED TO SURVIVE AND PROCREATE.
NO, SOMETHING ELSE IS OUT THERE WATCHING US AND I'VE FELT IT ALL MY LIFE.

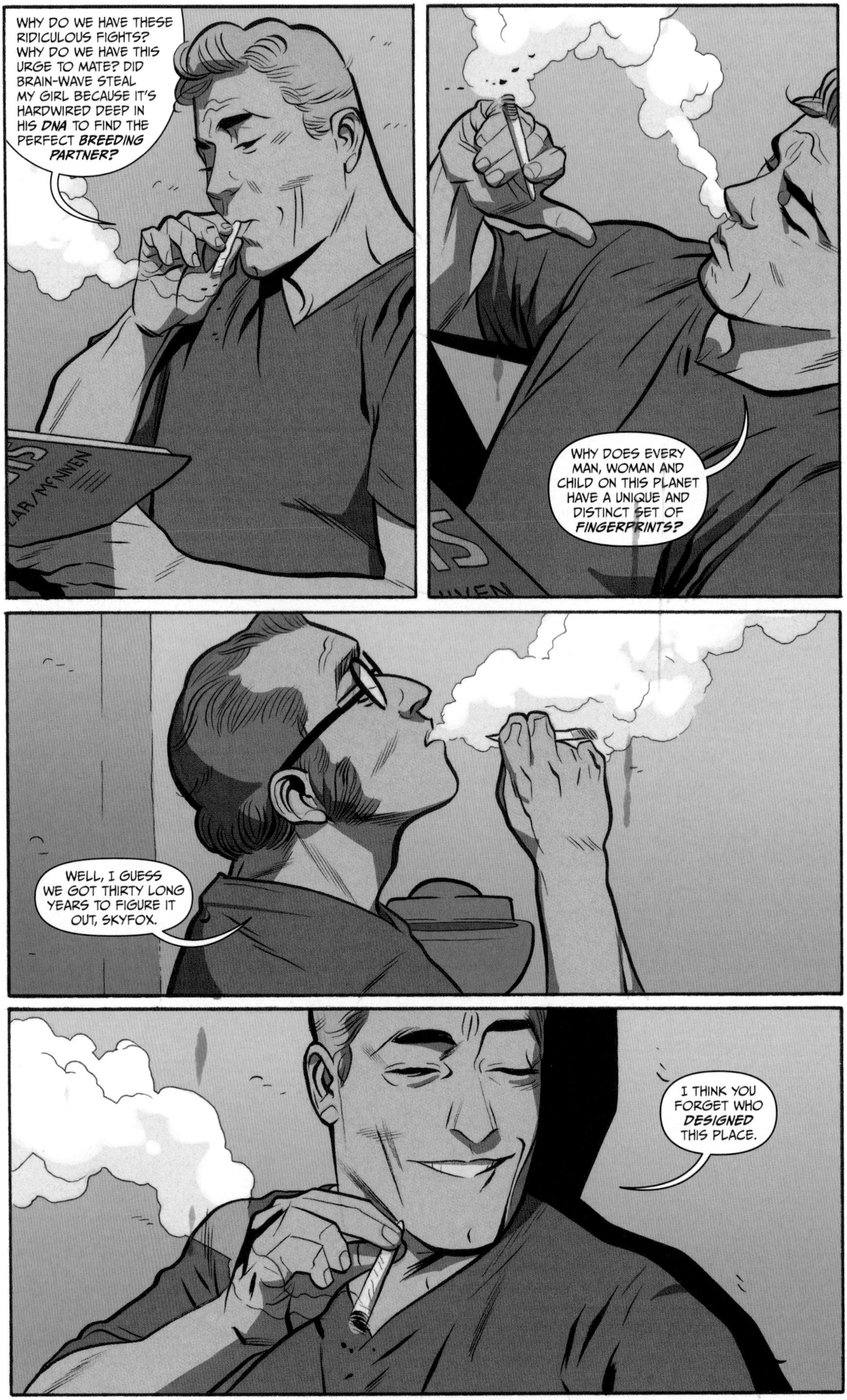
WHY DO WE HAVE THESE RIDICULOUS FIGHTS? WHY DO WE HAVE THIS URGE TO MATE? DID BRAIN-WAVE STEAL MY GIRL BECAUSE IT'S HARDWIRED DEEP IN HIS DNA TO FIND THE PERFECT BREEDING PARTNER?
WHY DOES EVERY MAN, WOMAN AND CHILD ON THIS PLANET HAVE A UNIQUE AND DISTINCT SET OF FINGERPRINTS?
WELL, I GUESS WE GOT THIRTY LONG YEARS TO FIGURE IT OUT, SKYFOX.
I THINK YOU FORGET WHO DESIGNED THIS PLACE.

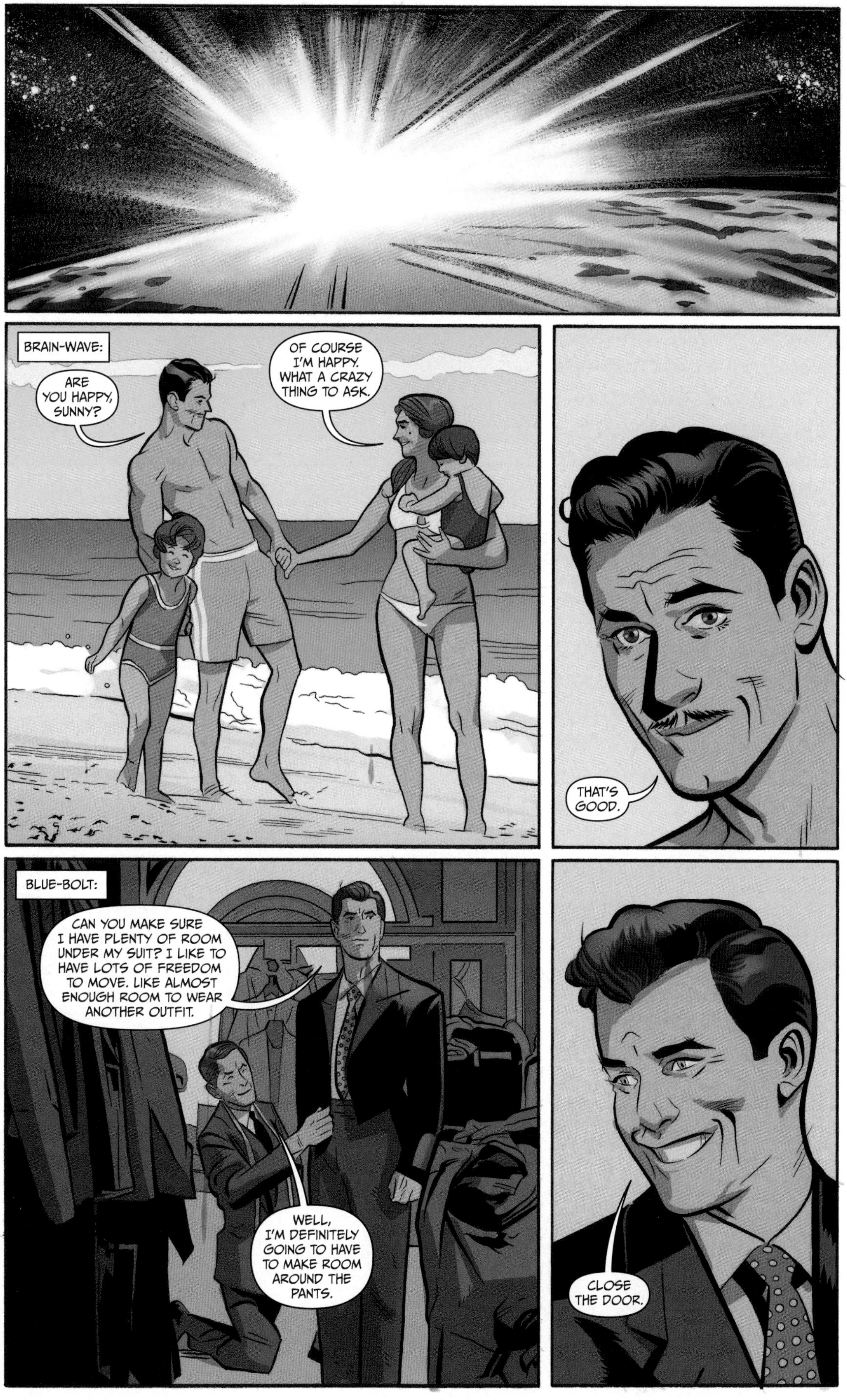
BRAIN-WAVE:
ARE YOU HAPPY, SUNNY?
OF COURSE I'M HAPPY. WHAT A CRAZY THING TO ASK.
THAT'S GOOD.
BLUE-BOLT:
CAN YOU MAKE SURE I HAVE PLENTY OF ROOM UNDER MY SUIT? I LIKE TO HAVE LOTS OF FREEDOM TO MOVE. LIKE ALMOST ENOUGH ROOM TO WEAR ANOTHER OUTFIT.
WELL, I'M DEFINITELY GOING TO HAVE TO MAKE ROOM AROUND THE PANTS.
CLOSE THE DOOR.

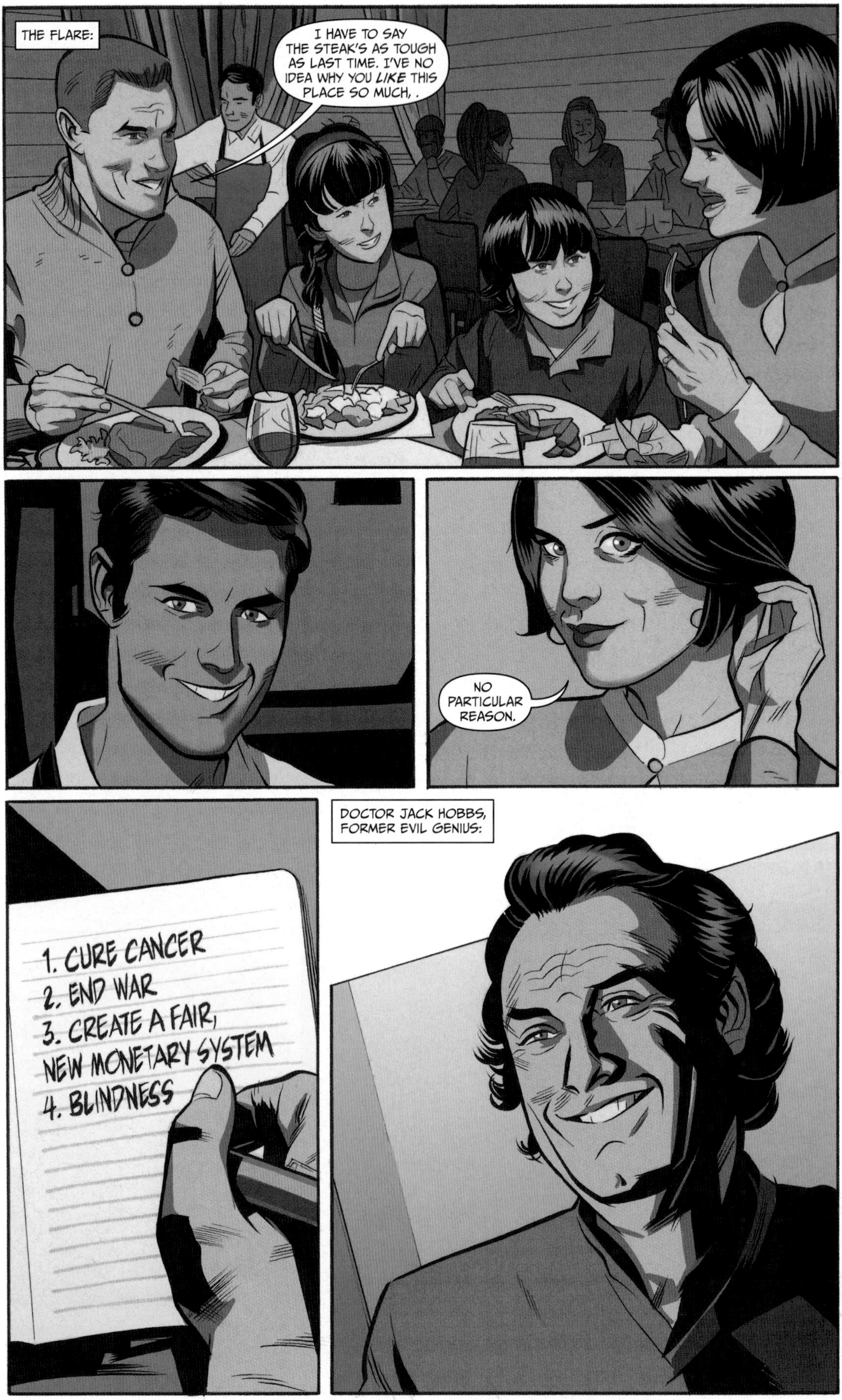
THE FLARE:
I HAVE TO SAY THE STEAK'S AS TOUGH AS LAST TIME. I'VE NO IDEA WHY YOU *LIKE* THIS PLACE SO MUCH, .
NO PARTICULAR REASON.
DOCTOR JACK HOBBS, FORMER EVIL GENIUS:
1. CURE CANCER
2. END WAR
3. CREATE A FAIR, NEW MONETARY SYSTEM
4. BLINDNESS

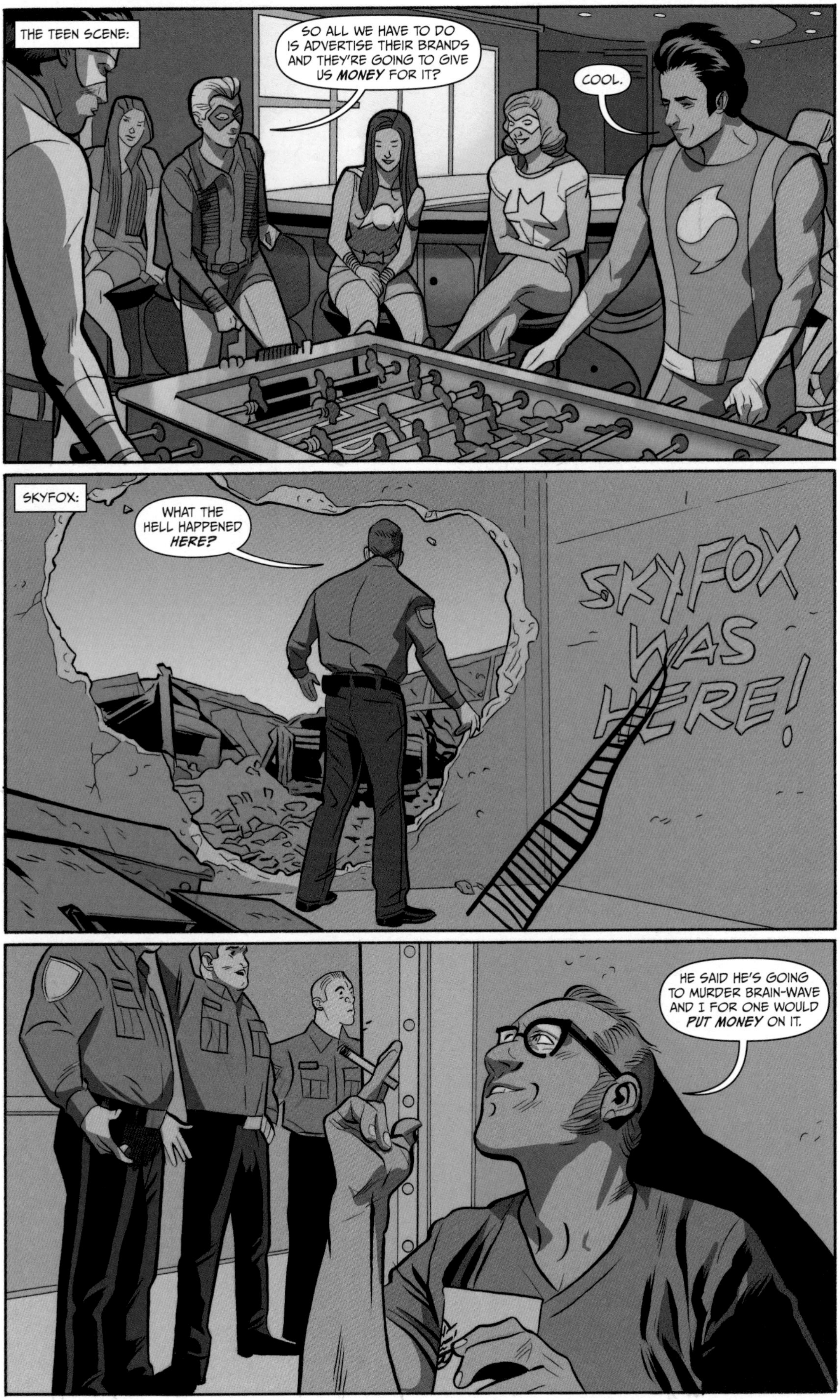
THE TEEN SCENE:
SO ALL WE HAVE TO DO IS ADVERTISE THEIR BRANDS AND THEY'RE GOING TO GIVE US MONEY FOR IT?
COOL.
SKYFOX:
WHAT THE HELL HAPPENED HERE?
SKYFOX WAS HERE!
HE SAID HE'S GOING TO MURDER BRAIN-WAVE AND I FOR ONE WOULD PUT MONEY ON IT.

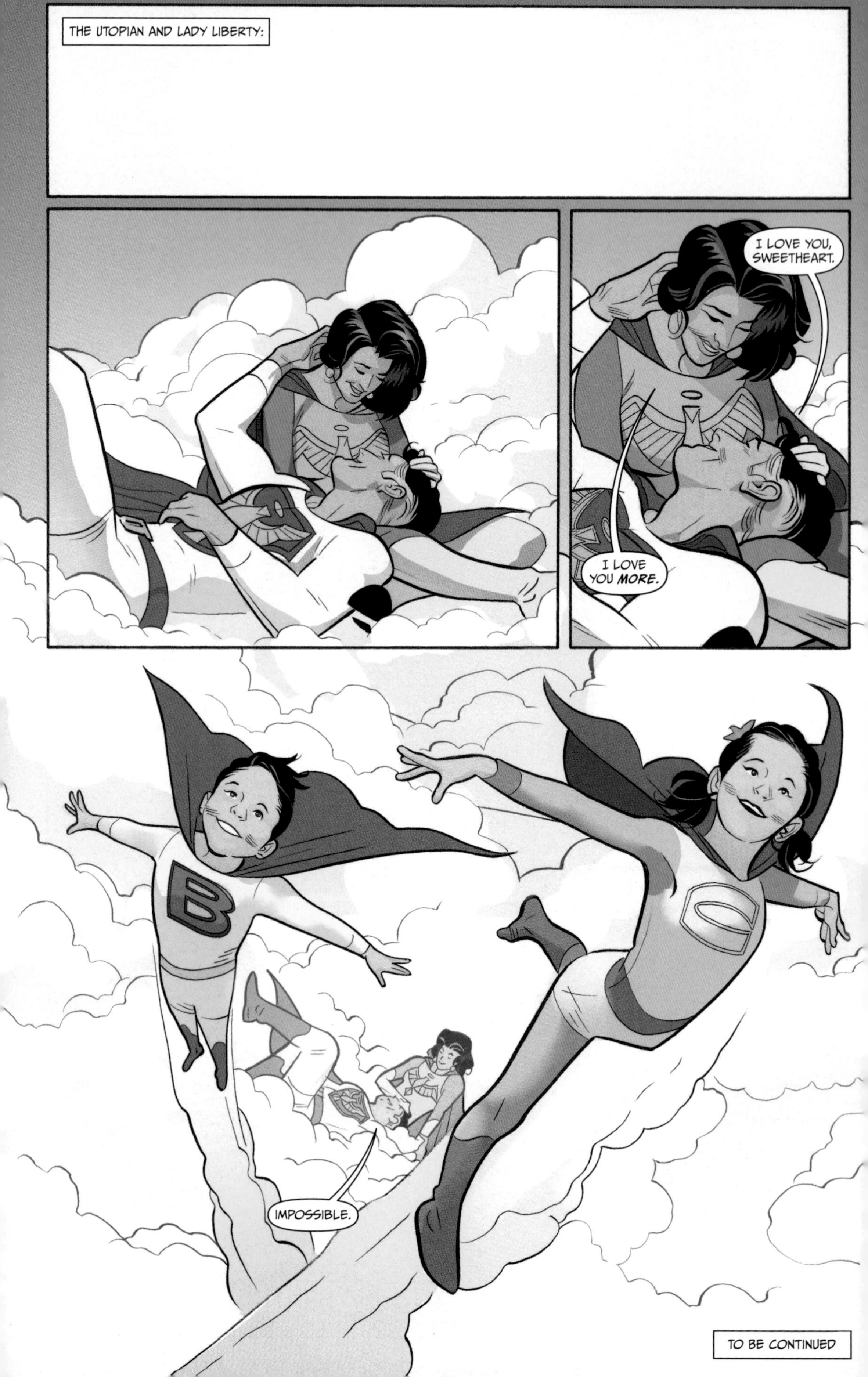
THE UTOPIAN AND LADY LIBERTY:
I LOVE YOU, SWEETHEART.
I LOVE YOU MORE.
IMPOSSIBLE.
TO BE CONTINUED

FIND OUT WHAT HAPPENS NEXT

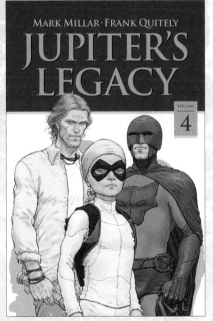

NETFLIX

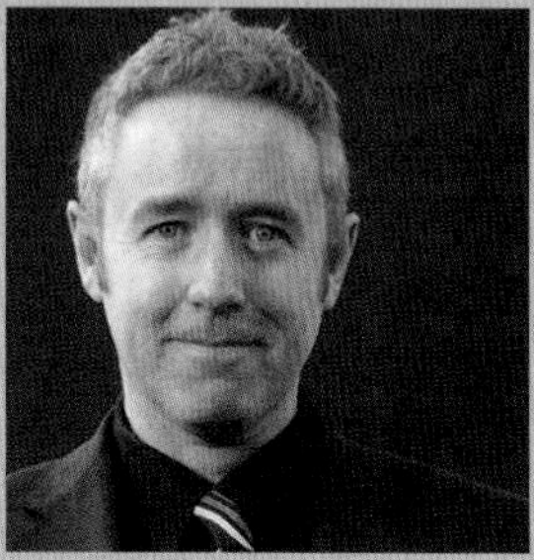

MARK MILLAR

MARK MILLAR is the *New York Times* bestselling author of *Kick-Ass*, *Wanted*, and *Kingsman: The Secret Service*, all of which have been adapted into Hollywood franchises.

His DC Comics work includes the seminal *Superman: Red Son*. At Marvel Comics he created *The Ultimates*, which was selected by *Time* magazine as the comic book of the decade, and was described by screenwriter Zak Penn as his major inspiration for *The Avengers* movie. Millar also created *Wolverine: Old Man Logan* and *Civil War*, Marvel's two biggest-selling graphic novels ever. *Civil War* was the basis of the *Captain America: Civil War* movie, and *Old Man Logan* was the inspiration for Fox's *Logan* movie in 2017.

Mark has been an executive producer on all his movies, and for four years worked as a creative consultant to Fox Studios on their Marvel slate of movies. In 2017, Netflix bought Millarworld in the company's first ever acquisition, and employed Mark as President of a new division to create comics, TV shows, and movies. His much-anticipated autobiography, *I'm Not Insulting You, I'm DESCRIBING You*, will be published next year.

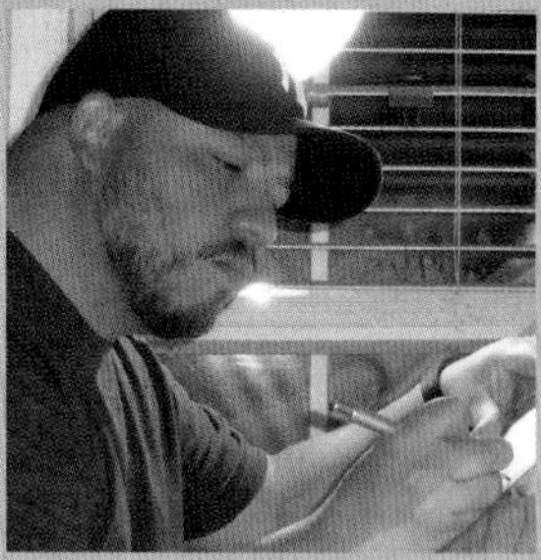

WILFREDO TORRES

WILFREDO TORRES is a self-taught American comic book artist and illustrator. He has been working as a professional freelancer since 2007. Before his work with Mark Millar on *Jupiter's Circle*, Wilfredo was best known for his work on *The Shadow: Year One* (Dynamite Entertainment), *Batman '66* (DC Comics), *Lobster Johnson: Prayer of Neferu* (Dark Horse Comics), and *Quantum & Woody* (Valiant Entertainment). Wilfredo redesigned and provided covers for *The Shield* (Archie Comics/Dark Circle).

Wilfredo is a process junkie who enjoys sleeping, pictures of puppies, home improvement shows, beer, long walks, and drawing people who wear their underwear over their clothes.

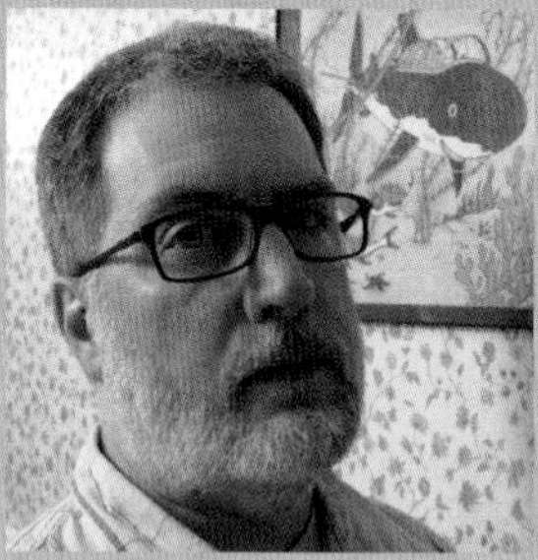

CHRIS SPROUSE

CHRIS SPROUSE has drawn comics for Marvel, DC, Dark Horse, Image, and other publishers over a two decade career, working on stories and series featuring Batman, Superman, Wonder Woman, the X-Men, Luke Skywalker, and Darth Vader. Sprouse also illustrated writer Warren Ellis' science fiction graphic novel *Ocean* in 2004, but he may be best known for his work on *Tom Strong*, a series he designed and drew for Alan Moore's *America's Best Comics* line.

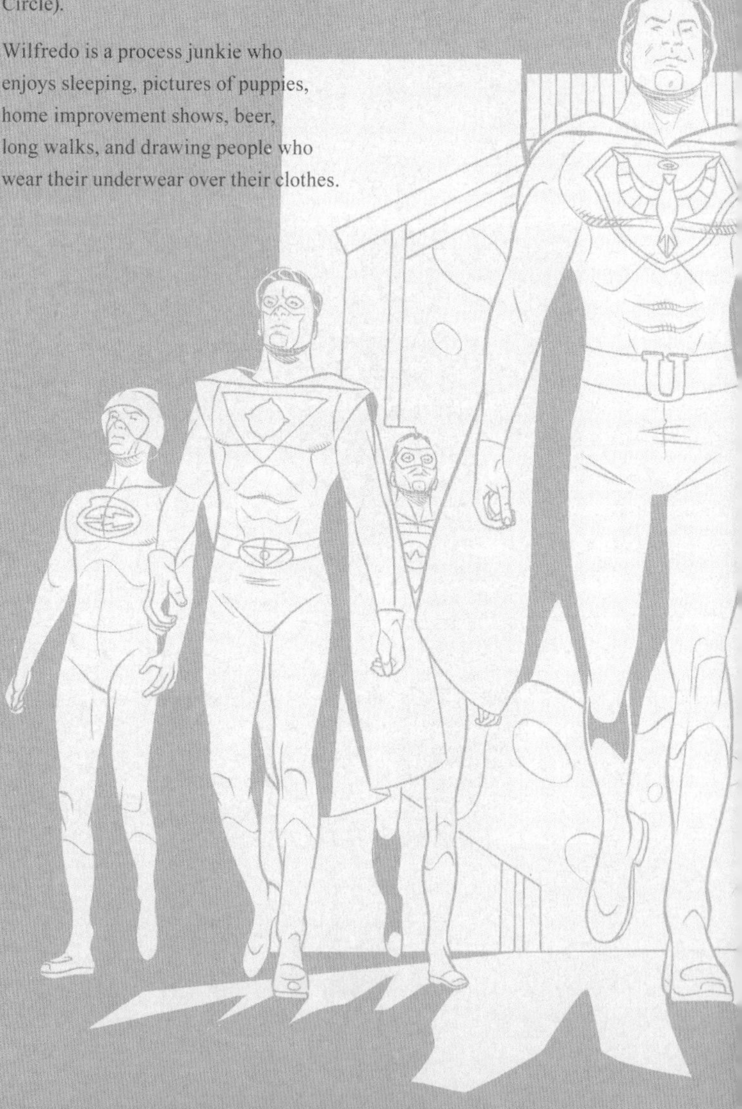

WALDEN WONG

WALDEN WONG is a well-respected veteran inker with a wide range of experience in the industry. Walden has worked with all of the major studios, including many high-profile projects. Located in the San Francisco Bay Area, Walden has worked for practically every publisher out there, including DC, Marvel, Image, Dark Horse, and even VIZ media. You can see his name on a variety of titles every year. He can currently be found working around the clock at his studio inking.

IVE SVORCINA

IVE SVORCINA was born in 1986 on a small island in the Adriatic Sea, Croatia. Being self-taught, he somehow managed to start his professional career in 2006, and since then he has worked for such publishers as Marvel, Delcourt, Image Comics, and smaller publishers in Croatia.

Notable achievements include getting kicked out of the computer science college and getting nominated for an Eisner Award for his work on *Thor*.

Currently he resides in Zagreb, thinking about moving somewhere warmer and sunnier.

PETER DOHERTY

Peter has worked in comics since 1990. His first job was painting artwork for the John Wagner-written *Young Death*, published in the first year of the *Judge Dredd Megazine*. For the next few years he painted art for a number of Judge Dredd stories.

He's worked for most of the major comics publishers, and also branched out into illustration, TV, and movies.

Over the last decade he's worked on projects in various different roles, including Geof Darrow on his *Shaolin Cowboy* project, and several Millarworld projects, notably *Jupiter's Legacy* with Frank Quitely and *MPH* with Duncan Fegredo.

Peter lives locally in the Yorkshire countryside.

RICK BURCHETT

RICK BURCHETT is a 35-year veteran of the comic industry, and has had the great fortune to work on a variety of projects for a variety of publishers. Among his better known works are *Batman, Huntress, Superman, Justice League, The Black Hood, Blackhawk, She-Hulk,* and *Archie.* He is a three-time Eisner winner and is currently working on a new series for Image, *Prima,* with co-creator Jen Van Meter.

DAVIDE GIANFELICE

DAVIDE GIANFELICE was born in Milan, Italy in 1977. Before his collaboration on *Jupiter's Circle,* he worked for Vertigo on the acclaimed first runs of *Northlanders* and *Greek Street.* His work can also be seen in Marvel's *Daredevil: Reborn, Wolverine: Weapon X,* and *Six Guns.* With Dark Horse he collaborated on a run of *Conan the Barbarian,* and with Skybound on *Ghosted.* In his spare time he enjoys cooking Italian food and has a passion for photography.

KARL STORY

KARL STORY is an American comic book artist specializing in inking. Over a career of more than two decades, he has worked on books such as *Nightwing, Batman, Star Trek: Debt of Honor, Aliens vs Predator, X-Men, Tom Strong, Ocean, Midnighter, Thors,* and *Serenity,* as well as many others.

TY TEMPLETON

TY TEMPELTON has written or drawn practically every major comic book property at some point, including Superman, Batman, Spider-Man, the Avengers, The Justice League, *Mad Magazine,* The Simpsons, *Star Trek,* Howard the Duck, *The Evil Dead,* and too many more to list. He's won a couple of Eisner Awards for his work on *Batman Adventures,* and was inducted into the Canadian Comic Book Hall of Fame (Joe Shuster Awards) in 2015. He's got a wife, four kids, three cats and a deadline looming at all times.

MIROSLAV MRVA

MIROSLAV MRVA was born in 1979 and raised in a small village in Croatia that's not even on Google Maps. After elementary school, Miroslav moved to Zagreb and finished aircraft mechanic school, then school of design. After a 10-year career as a graphic designer and freelance illustrator, he started coloring comics for Aces Weekly (*Santa vs. Nazis*), Image Comics (*Ghosted*), and Marvel Comics (*Master of Kung Fu, Secret Wars, Red Wolf*). When not working, he's playing vintage synthesizers.

FRANK QUITELY

FRANK QUITELY began his career creating work for the Scottish humor anthology *Electric Soup* and UK anthology *Judge Dredd Megazine.* Later, he worked extensively with DC on limited and ongoing series including *Batman, All-Star Superman,* and *The Authority;* with Marvel on *New X-Men;* and on creator-owned series including *We3.* He's currently finishing *Jupiter's Legacy* with Millarworld, and has several smaller creator-owned projects in the pipeline.

BILL SIENKIEWICZ

BILL SIENKIEWICZ is an Eisner-winning, Emmy-nominated artist, whose comics credits include *Elektra: Assassin* (Marvel); his own acclaimed graphic novel *Stray Toasters,* and the Eisner Award-winning *The Sandman: Endless Nights* (DC/Vertigo). A classically-trained painter, Sienkiewicz's renderings incorporate abstract and expressionist influences and a combination of media and techniques.

NICOLE BOOSE

NICOLE BOOSE began her editing career at Harris Comics' *Vampirella,* before joining the staff at Marvel Comics. There, she edited titles including *Cable & Deadpool, Iron Man,* and Stephen King's adapted novels. She also oversaw Marvel's line of custom comics, developing projects for corporate and nonprofit clients. Since 2008, Nicole has been a freelance editor in the comics industry, and served on the staff of the educational company Comics Experience.

RACHAEL FULTON

RACHAEL FULTON joins the *Jupiter's Circle 2* team as Associate Editor. She is an award-winning features writer, specializing in magazines and online journalism. Rachael was formerly a television producer, presenter, and reporter for Scottish Television, but now finds herself happily embedded in the Millarverse of superheroes, space operas, and explosive plot lines. Rachael is based in Glasgow and can be found on the Millarworld forum or on Twitter @Rachael_Fulton.